Demons at the Door

The Jake Lorde Chronicles

Colt Frid

and

Randy Frid

FIRST EDITION

FIRST PRINTING – 2009

This is a work of fiction. No reference to any person, living or dead, is intended or implied.

ISBN 978-0-9811847-0-8

Printed in the United States of America

Trademarks

Front Cover Artwork: Kip Ayers
Editing: Jodie Renner

Publisher

Frid Enterprises Inc.
1831 Bercier Road
Plantagenet, Ontario, Canada
K0B 1L0
visit our website at www.fridpublishing.com

Dedicated to science fiction readers of any age.

PROLOGUE

The monk leapt backwards just in time to avoid being crushed by a blow that narrowly missed his skull. A large and heavily armored Ork, clad everywhere in steel plates and swinging a massive mallet, lunged forward for a second attempt to turn the monk's slender body into hamburger. The nimble monk once again ducked and slid to the right, as graceful as a ballroom dancer, seemingly unaware that this was a fight to the death.

Suddenly, a thin rapier sword appeared in the monk's hand as if from thin air. He crouched, rolled and came up directly behind the brutish beast. Deftly he slipped the wafer-thin blade between the layers of rusted plating and felt the blade penetrating muscle and bone.

The Ork howled and twisted violently, swinging wildly at his attacker, but it was useless — the Ork was just swinging at empty air. The monk had already retreated to a safe distance and was standing well out of mallet range.

Wounded and bleeding profusely, the Ork turned to face the monk directly, dropped to one knee and raised its shield in a desperate attempt to fend off the inevitable follow-up attack. Simultaneously, the beast dropped its weapon and grabbed feebly for the health vial tucked in a satchel that hung from its utility belt. It needed healing power now, and fast, and it also knew it needed to get its weapon back in its hand.

With seemingly no effort whatsoever, the monk leapt up and over the Ork as if he had coiled springs in his legs. He moved with such agility that the Ork couldn't help but watch in admiration. Unfortunately for the Ork, it was the wrong time to lose its concentration. The monk dropped silently to a position directly behind the confused beast and flicked his sword into the gap between the helmet and the steel plates that covered the massive shoulders.

The Ork had little time to think, let alone react; and it wouldn't have mattered anyway as there was no way for the Ork *to* think. Its head had just been neatly severed from its body.

The monk stood calmly, watching the creature topple forward, head slipping from its trunk with blood spurting everywhere, quickly staining the crusted armor a putrid green. It was over.

As the monk stood watching, the Ork quickly faded off the battleground, leaving nothing to show that he had ever been there except his purse of gold, the one thing all Orks treasure.

The monk slipped forward and slowly retrieved the purse, looked around, and trotted off in the direction he had been heading before the Ork had appeared to block his path. It was deep in the middle of the virtual night and the monk could do little more than follow the stars.

CHAPTER ONE

Jake Lorde's fingers danced over the keyboard as he brought up his *Heads-Up-Display* — commonly referred to by gamers as a HUD — and watched as his health, agility, strength and power levels all increased as a reward for yet another in a long line of online conquests.

He hit the Escape key and paused the game to take a break. He was getting hungry and needed something to munch on. He went to the kitchen and was opening the fridge when his mom called out from the living room.

"Jake, you just finished dinner. You can't possibly be hungry."

"I am, Mom. I just want a snack."

"Then have some carrots and dip."

Jake considered the offer and declined. Instead he grabbed a pudding container and a spoon from the drawer, and headed back to his bedroom.

Then came the all-too-familiar directive from the living room.

"You've got one hour, young man, then lights-out."

"Yeah, I know."

Jake slipped back into his room and closed the door. He went back to his iMac and jiggled the mouse to deactivate the screen saver, then hit the Escape key to reengage the game. With his other hand, he brought the pudding to his mouth, and tore off the lid with his teeth. He sat back to devour his dessert while scanning his HUD to see if anything new could be detected on his map.

He had done this a thousand times before. At 15 years old, Jake was a master-class player. Over the past two years he had leveled up to Level 100, making him a member of a very exclusive club called the Centurions, an accomplishment of which he was very proud. He had never met any of the other members but it was nice to at least have made it into the club. It gave him some bragging rights.

This also made him one of the top-ranked players on the planet. However, he didn't realize this at all since the game was a global online system and there was no real winner because the programmers all over the world kept expanding the system every day. It was a game that could go on forever. In fact, it was impossible to even know how many players there were in the system since the game had been converted to the Open Source community many years ago.

Being an Open Source application meant that any and every programmer in the world could develop and extend the game however they wanted. It also meant that there was no single authority on how the rules of the game could be modified or extended, or even who could play. It was now so large and complex that nobody really knew how large it was anymore. The game had become the dominant form of entertainment in the world, with hundreds of millions of users online at any one time, and easily over two billion computers had the gaming software loaded and running in the background.

That's what gave the system its true power. Any computer with the game software loaded participated as an extension to the global gaming network. Each computer shared a portion of its processing power for the benefit of the entire virtual environment. The game would automatically and randomly distribute its calculation workload over a billion different computers, using any available idle CPU time for processing pieces of landscape, sky, characters, and the millions of rules that controlled the virtual world. Jake thought it was the coolest thing on the planet. So, apparently, did about a couple billion other people.

Usually he teamed up with his best friend Lindsey Tomkins. Together, the unassuming pair in real life formed a formidable duo in their virtual lives. They would tackle obstacles to find lost treasure, battle other characters in strange lands, and try to collect a vast inventory of weapons, tools, abilities, and wealth. You always needed these things to solve puzzles or overcome obstacles along the way, and those in the master-class knew how to put them to the best use possible.

The biggest difference between Jake and Lindsey was that Jake knew how to program. He had been working on a Linux Operating System for a couple years at school and had one setup in the closet in his room so he could practice at home. His dad was a physicist who specialized in high performance computer programming that ran on supercomputers, so he helped Jake learn the ropes, and showed him some of the trickier parts of the Linux OS.

What his dad didn't know was that Jake would also spend countless hours online studying hacker blogs. He learned ways to crack into just about anything. He had trouble understanding the complicated math so he stuck to downloading crack tools and saved notes on how to break sites, tunnel ports, or hijack applications running on other machines. He would experiment on his Linux server, and if that worked, he would then try it on his iMac, since the Macintosh operating system was built on a flavor of Linux as well. His iMac was his pride and joy.

He and Lindsey worked well together as a team because he could program the different weapons and tools they needed, and she was great at strategy. She could work through almost any problem if you gave her some time and the right tools. Together they were unstoppable. However, because Jake could program, he could often hack his way through normally impenetrable problems, and that's why he had leveled up past Level 100 a couple of months back, while Lindsey still trailed behind at Level 98. Jake was usually the first one to break through obstacles by using Lindsey's strategies combined with his powers and tools, so he wound up collecting the most points. But she dealt with it in stride, since she would have never gotten to level 98 without Jake's programming skills. They needed each other, and they knew it.

Jake kept one secret from Lindsey though. He knew she would find out about it one day, and that day would probably come soon, knowing the deductive capabilities of his best friend.

Lindsey wasn't online tonight so he was going it alone.

Jake tossed his empty pudding container in the overflowing wastebasket beside his desk and launched his browser. He started searching for any hacker site that could provide him a way to improve the capabilities of his HUD. The HUD currently provided only a short-range look at everything around him in a 360-degree view. He followed link after link until he was totally lost across the maze of the Web.

He was about to quit searching and go back to the game when he found one interesting prospect that he thought might lead him to something. It was tough to tell since the blog he was reading hadn't been updated in a long time.

"Probably most of the links are broken." Jake had a habit of talking to himself while he was gaming.

Finally he clicked on the link that interested him, and he was rewarded with a prompt to choose a download directory. He did, and sure enough, a file was downloaded to him from somewhere across the world.

Jake checked out the URL but it was only pointing to a network IP address, and those can be masked or spoofed, so there was little use trying to track down the origin of the file.

He unzipped the file into a folder on his desktop and opened the readme file.

"Rats!" The patch was for an older version of his operating system. "Oh well, let's give it a shot."

Unfortunately, it didn't work properly. When he had double-clicked the patch to kick off the install, his game froze solid.

No background sound either.

"That can't be good."

Then a stream of green hexadecimal letters and numbers started scrolling all across his screen. He was just about to reboot when the machine stopped spewing out hex code, and the monitor refreshed so that he was looking at his desktop again. He tried his keyboard and mouse, and then tried moving his character around inside the game. Everything *seemed* to be working normally.

Jake concluded that this was just another of many failed patches. He didn't want to waste any more time with it tonight, but he also didn't want to lose it before he could find the time to see if it could be fixed. He copied it to an old blank CD he had lying around and wrote *FIX THIS* in felt pen on top of it, then tossed it in his desk drawer to join the stack of other CDs and DVDs growing dust, all waiting for him to get around to working on them.

He dwelled on it for a moment longer then dismissed it. "So much for that, time to get back to the game."

He looked at up at his HUD to pick a direction to head off to. He was hoping the circular map would give him some clue to a secret treasure or someone worthy of combat, but what he saw there wasn't quite right — he was looking at something he had never seen before, and he thought he had seen everything. At the far corner of his HUD map was a small black dot. It was nothing exceptional, not moving, not blinking, just a boring, small, black dot. What interested Jake was that he had never seen a black dot on his HUD. Dots always indicated red for enemy, green for ally, and yellow for unknown. Blue dots could show up now and then if you cracked the right clues. They usually indicated treasure, although they could often be traps set by crafty programmers.

This black dot was actually pretty hard to see, just because it was black. The only reason he could see it at all was because he had turned up the monitor brightness to help him see in the darkness while he was fighting the Ork. This saved him having to wear his infrared goggles, which limited his peripheral vision.

By turning up the monitor brightness, everything that was black on his screen now became grey and slightly easier to distinguish, so the black spot he was looking at now should also have been grey, but it wasn't. It was totally black, almost like there was something wrong with his monitor. If he had not been cheating a bit by turning up his brightness, he would never have even seen the spot.

At a cursory level, he figured that it was probably nothing. At a deeper level, he was curious.

"It's probably just a glitch."

He checked out the surrounding area on the map and didn't see anything else flashing or beeping on his HUD, so he thought he might as well head over and check it out.

Jake looked at the map and could see that the black dot was right in the center of a nearby forest. That didn't sit well with him. He didn't like forests in the game. Forests always contained Tree Elves. He had lots of power and abilities to fight them off, but they always won because there was just no end to them. The more you killed, the more came out of nowhere. They would just keep coming and coming like cockroaches, and you never found a forest without them. It was some kind of default rule of forests that every forest was automatically filled with Tree Elves. Even if you developed your own forest, it eventually filled up with Tree Elves, even if you didn't want it to. Programmers around the world had tried repeatedly to fix this problem, but it always came back. Nobody was really sure how or why.

Jake thought the forests must have been developed in the earliest days of the game to act as impenetrable walls, but he didn't really know, and neither did anyone else, it seemed. At least he couldn't find any documentation on the Web that described where they came from, or who developed them, or why they were developed that way. Most players just stayed away from any forest since they weren't any fun. However, there were some programmers who developed castles and liked to surround them with these forests because they provided almost perfect protection. Almost perfect, because you would always need to leave a road open to get to your castle door, or even you as its programmer couldn't get in.

Even if the black dot turned out to be nothing, Jake still wanted to give it a shot because he had something new he wanted to try. Ever since the patch failed to install properly, his stealth-mode, the ability to remain undetected by adversaries, had increased to 100%. When he first noticed the increase his eyes had just about popped out. "This is impossible," he thought. "No one can achieve 100% in anything." That was a fundamental rule of the game; otherwise people would make themselves indestructible or something like that and there would never be any way of beating them. Everything and everyone had to have weaknesses. Nothing was allowed to be perfect. It was one of the first principles the original developers started with to keep the game realistic.

But there it was.

Jake quickly saved his game, just in case this was actually happening. He didn't want to get killed off or have the power go out or something like that before he got a chance to save. He couldn't believe his good fortune. He didn't really know what this additional ability would really do for him. He was already pretty high up in stealth anyway. Oh well, that didn't matter, he'd take it anyway.

Now, facing the forest, he had an idea. If he turned on 100% stealth mode, and turned off his HUD, he wondered if he could sneak through the forest without getting sliced and diced by the nasty Tree Elves. It was definitely worth a try. He saved his game position just as he reached the edge of the forest so he could always restore to the last save point, just in case he got killed or stuck. Better safe than sorry.

He deactivated his HUD, crouched, and crept forward under the canopy of thick foliage, then paused, waiting for the inevitable attack. Nothing happened. He moved his avatar a little further into the forest. Nothing. He continued to creep forward slowly so his feet made no sound. He stopped.

"I should be dead by now."

He decided to pan the perspective camera around so he could look up into the trees. He froze solid. Directly above him, sitting still in the branches of the trees were hundreds — no, make that thousands — of Tree Elves, frozen in time as only a drawing in software can freeze something. Tree Elves everywhere, suspended from various branches, in various positions, neither moving nor breathing, just waiting for a software signal to activate their animated and lethal attacks. It was creepy seeing them so still. Normally they would be buzzing all over him, very fast and very deadly. You typically didn't even have time to focus on one of them before it moved past your vision and sliced you here or there.

Normally, the best thing you could do was just stand still and watch your health meter plummet until you died and regenerated back at your last save point. Fighting was useless. This time, however, they were above him in uncountable numbers, thick as thieves, and pasted amongst the tree limbs in awkward positions looking a little stupid and cartoonish. On top of that, they had nasty looking daggers in each hand and Jake wondered how they were supposed to hang on to the branches with both hands full. He could tell this was very old technology. No programmer with any self-respect would do such a sloppy job of rendering today.

Jake swung his camera back to face forward, checked that he was still aligned toward the black dot on his screen, then continued to slowly advance his character deeper into the forest, careful not to bump anything just in case it would set off whatever alarm these things were waiting for. Nothing stirred, to his great relief.

As he slipped deeper into the forest, the ambient light grew dimmer and dimmer until he was almost blind. He could just make out the vague outline of tree trunks, and the trees were consistently getting denser the closer he moved to the middle of the forest. Other obstacles were also appearing: impassible boulders too smooth to climb, deep clefts in the ground that led to certain doom, and thickets of bramble far too thick to push his way through, especially soundlessly.

Tree Elves hung on almost every branch now. He could reach out and touch one if he wanted to. He didn't want to. He could make out the outlines of more Elves than trees when he paused on occasion to look up. It was becoming completely obvious to Jake that the forest was deliberately designed to keep everyone and everything out. If he slipped up now he would be dead in less than a second. He also didn't want to save his game because he might never be able to get back out if he regenerated back in this particular spot, so he slinked along, keeping crouched and deadly quiet.

He was getting close now. He couldn't be more than a few meters from the black dot. The darkness was making the going very difficult. He desperately wanted to activate his HUD and use his infrared goggles, but by now he was almost certain that those actions would generate telltale signs that he was there, and his stealth cover would be compromised. He had already turned up the brightness on his monitor to the point that he could barely make out anything since his screen was so awash in a dark grey blur.

He was moving forward at a snail's pace. His heart was pounding and his hands were feeling clammy from sweat. He couldn't take his eyes off the monitor for a second in case he bumped into something or tripped. That would also surely bring the Tree Elves down on his head.

He came to a complete standstill. — What was that? He stared ahead into a patch of nothingness. At least he thought so. His screen was nothing but a solid background of dark grey now. No outlines of anything.

He finally decided to save at this point so he could at least get back to here if he needed to regenerate.

For the first time in quite a while, he sat back and let out a sigh. He hadn't noticed how wired he had become. Secretly he was thrilled. This was very cool. Nobody that he had ever heard of had ever made it into a forest before. He shook his hands to get the kinks out, and wished desperately that Lindsey was here to see what he was doing. He wanted to yell out.

Just then the door to his bedroom popped opened with a small snap of the door handle. He just about jumped out of his skin! His mother stood at the door, looking at him like he had just landed from another planet.

She was wearing her concerned look. "You okay?"

Jake was figuring that she was coming in to give him a lecture on brushing his teeth, cleaning his room, and getting to bed. That was the nightly ritual. But this time, however, his mother had detected something on Jake's face that caused her to pause and change her tactics.

He replied faster than he should have. "Yeah, I'm fine."

Then he couldn't hold back. He burst out the whole story, starting from his patch download, to the little black dot, the Tree Elves... everything. All the time he was talking she smiled and relaxed, and steered him by the shoulders towards the bathroom, nudging him towards his toothbrush.

"That's very nice, dear. You'll need to tell your father all about it tomorrow. He's working late tonight. Now brush your teeth, clean up your room, and get yourself to bed. Time's up."

That ended that discussion — somewhat of an anticlimactic motherly response for her master-class antihero — but it did little to diffuse Jake's excitement. He brushed his teeth in about three seconds flat and headed for his room.

He was just picking up speed when his mom stopped him cold in his tracks. "Whoa there, Dungeon Master! How about a kiss and a hug for your mom before you return to the dungeon?"

After his good night wishes, Jake moved quickly back to his room, but not too quickly to draw notice. He was determined to get back to the game. He called back over his shoulder.

"Good night."

Jake had plans tonight, and he didn't want to have the warden checking his cell every hour on the hour before she went to bed. He had this routine down pat.

When he got back to his room, he doused the lights, and placed a rolled-up pair of pants along the bottom of his door so the light from the monitor couldn't be seen shining out the crack at the bottom. Then he plugged in his earphones, but only used the left earbud so he could keep one ear free. He needed that ear to listen externally, just in case his parents decided to launch a sneak attack.

He hit the Escape key to get out of pause mode, and turned his full attention back to the game.

#

"Should I risk infrared now? No. Not yet. I need to know what this thing is." Without Lindsey around, he had to hold a strategy debate with himself.

What would Lindsey do? Why wasn't she online?

He inched forward, completely blind to his surroundings. What was out there? Would he be attacked? Probably not. He couldn't use his HUD, but then again, he had been attacked in the past without his HUD providing a warning. Tree Elves never show up on a HUD.

He paused. That was interesting. He sat puzzling to himself. He'd never thought about it before. Why didn't the Tree Elves show up on a HUD? Is the programming too old to notify the HUD module? Were they deliberately programmed to avoid showing up on a HUD? Jake knew he was onto something, but he didn't know what.

He started to move forward again, inch by inch. His heart rate was going up again. His eyes were scanning every square inch of his monitor and his frustration was starting to show, even though there was no one there to see it. Another inch, pause, scan the monitor... Another inch, pause, scan the monitor.

Then it was gone! Jake stared at his monitor, and could only make out the faint outline of his avatar flailing its arms and legs in motions that were all too familiar: His character was free falling through empty space.

Jake smacked his hands against his forehead, then pulled at his hair. His lips grimaced with a quiet but angry "Arghh!"

It would only be three or four seconds now before the screen would fade to black, and he would regenerate back at the save point.

"Unbelievable! That's all it is? What a piece of junk."

He grimaced as he waited for the inevitable. He folded his arms across his chest in dejection, defiance and resignation, and waited.

He got bored and periodically goaded his machine. "Come on. Get on with it."

But the seconds clicked by. The game should have terminated by now.

"Stupid thing is probably hung."

He got himself mentally prepared to kill the process that ran the game. He reached for the keyboard to hit the proper key sequence that would allow him into the control panel so he could terminate the application, but he paused, reluctant to give in. He reached over and fiddled with the mouse to make his avatar move into a different position.

Sure enough, his character responded appropriately and Jake spent the next few seconds making it perform various aerial gymnastics, wasting time before the inevitable death that awaited.

As the seconds turned into a minute, he was getting bored of making his avatar perform useless rolls, jumps and flips. He kept telling himself to kill the game, but he didn't. He waited.

During one of the useless air rolls something caught Jake's attention. He thought he had seen something in the middle of his screen. He stopped messing with his avatar and rotated the camera view to an overhead shot looking down at the top of his avatar while it continued to flail in freefall.

As the camera rotated overhead, Jake knew he needed to move his avatar so he could see past him. His character was in the center of the screen, blocking the view of what lay ahead. He messed with the keyboard, moving the avatar back and forth to catch faint glimpses of what lay beyond. The problem was, every time he moved the avatar, it automatically realigned the camera, so Jake only got a momentary glimpse at any one time. Then he had to reverse the action so he could grab a glimpse going back the other way. When he started doing this fast enough his brain started to assemble the pieces of what he was seeing into a single mental image.

He reached out and turned down the monitor brightness until the screen was totally black again. Then he repeated the moves.

Sure enough, there was a small white dot in the center of the screen. He kept moving his avatar back and forth until he was absolutely sure that the white dot was growing larger. It was. Jake felt a small thrill run up his spine. The application wasn't frozen.

"This is a portal."

But to where? That question caused his mind to race. What had he discovered? Where was this leading? He had never seen anything like this before. All he could do was sit and wait.

The white light got brighter as the seconds ticked by. Suddenly Jake's hands leapt for the keyboard. He quickly pulled up his inventory screen and selected his wardrobe. He clicked on the white-hooded monk's robe and applied his new settings. His avatar blinked off for a second, then reappeared clothed head-to-toe in white.

"Whew!"

Jake let out his breath. It would have been pretty stupid to warp through a portal to a white virtual land dressed in black and expect to maintain his stealth cover.

The white light was now growing quickly, surrounding his avatar, making his character virtually transparent except for the outline of his utility belt.

And then it was suddenly over. No thud, no splat, just over. The flailing had stopped. His avatar stood up automatically. Jake checked the health meter and it hadn't budged. He still had full health.

Jake paused for a second or two to collect his thoughts, then hit the F6 key on his keyboard for a fast save.

"Now what?"

He didn't ponder for long. He set off in the direction he was facing. He wanted to pull up his HUD, but instinctively knew that would be a bad thing. He knew he was somewhere other players hadn't been before, and the last thing he wanted to do was give himself away to whoever had created this virtual world.

With his open ear, Jake could hear his parents retiring to their bedroom for the night. He paused the game just long enough to be sure they were not going to interrupt his adventure before setting out again.

The next couple of hours would bear no fruit for Jake as he continued through the rolling winter wasteland. A white blizzard whirled about him, sending snow in every direction at speeds that made it impossible to see any particular snowflakes. It was more like a torrential waterfall of snow blasting from every direction simultaneously. Yet, somehow there appeared to be some order to the chaos all around him. The one thing that Jake could clearly make out was a series of distinct gridlines that divided the landscape like a checkerboard. He could only see a limited distance ahead because of the blizzard all around him, but the gridlines extended outwards as far as he could see. What that meant he had no idea.

He still refused to activate his HUD, but he knew he needed help. He had tripped into something unexpected, but he wasn't sure what to do about it. He needed Lindsey. She would know what to do.

Jake finally saved his game again and turned off his monitor. This would have to wait until tomorrow.

CHAPTER TWO

Jake woke up the next morning to the sound of his alarm clock. He was still groggy after concentrating long and hard into the wee hours of the night. It took a minute, but he came fully awake as the memory of last night's events came rushing back. He leaned over to his desk and flicked on the monitor. Sure enough, the game was still running. He left it in pause mode and turned the monitor back off. He wrote a quick note on the yellow sticky pad on his desk and stuck it to his monitor. It said, "Mom, don't turn off my computer."

There was a knock at his door. "Are you up?" It was his father's voice.

"Barely."

Jake's voice was raspy and thick this morning. Not enough sleep. A glass of water would be welcome at this moment.

"Better get moving or you'll be late."

His father's voice was already fading into the distance as he walked towards the kitchen.

At least Jake was one step ahead today. He hadn't even bothered to get undressed last night, and his bed was still made since he ended up sleeping on top of the sheets.

He got up and ran his fingers through his hair and yawned, then ventured to the bathroom to brush his teeth. He eventually made his way to the kitchen, where his parents were sitting at the breakfast table.

"Good morning, young man." His mother was wearing her classic morning smile. His father glanced over the top of his newspaper, and inspected his son.

"Were you up working on the computer last night?"

Jake could detect the suspicion in his voice. He knew his father had scrutinized his rumpled clothing, wild hair, and slightly red eyes.

"Not for long." Jake hoped that his answer would suffice and the topic would slide by. His dad was also a computer guy and had spent many a long night solving the riddles of the digital world. It was pretty hard to pull one over on him, since he was very familiar with his own all-night stints on his own computers. Luckily for Jake, his dad wasn't really that concerned about whether or not he stayed up at night if he was working on a computer. For Jake's dad, that was a completely normal thing to do.

His father returned to reading the newspaper.

"Come on and hurry up and eat," chided his mom.

Jake scarfed down some cereal and drank up his juice in silence, then asked, "Dad, aren't you going to work today?"

Dropping the newspaper again, his dad looked over the rim of his glasses. "Yup. But I've got a surprise for you. I was wondering if you wanted to go to work with me today?"

Jake's eyes opened wide. "You mean it?" He wasn't sure if his dad was just pulling his leg.

"Yeah, I mean it. That is, provided you want to go?"

"Sure. Cool!"

He was excited, and wasn't too sure what to expect.

"Let's go then, shall we?"

His dad got up from the table and gave his mom a kiss, and thanked her for breakfast. She smiled at Jake. "Run along now, don't keep your father waiting."

"Thanks, Mom," he said, giving her a kiss as well, then turned to run off to his bedroom to grab his coat and iPhone. He paused at the kitchen doorway and turned around. "Wait, what about school?"

"Don't worry about it. I've already talked to them. We've been planning this for a while now." She motioned for him to get going with a wave of her hand.

Jake turned around again and shot down the hall to his room.

"This is going to be cool."

#

Jake's dad worked for the Los Alamos National Laboratory in New Mexico, close to where they lived. He was the head physicist in charge of a project related to network security. He was working on some top secret network security invention, but that was all that Jake really knew about it. His dad also managed a team of engineers who were currently upgrading their biggest IBM mainframe, the Roadrunner.

As they made their way through the layers upon layers of security guards and electronic surveillance systems, Jake found himself finally entering the main interior of the massive complex. They wove their way through a maze of administrative cubicles and offices until they reached the center of the building, where they approached a plain elevator door. Jake's dad activated the call button. When the elevator car arrived, the doors opened and they stepped in. A mechanical voice came from a speaker imbedded somewhere in the walls.

"Please state your name."

"Ken Lorde."

"Voice pattern confirmed."

The elevator doors closed and Jake felt the car drop downwards at a rapidly increasing pace.

"The Roadrunner is located a little over half a mile underground. That's about a thousand meters."

They both watched the progress meter on the wall. There were no other floors to stop at, so it just displayed the estimated time of arrival as a countdown timer.

"Is this the only way in or out?" Jake was feeling a bit caged in at the moment. The thought of traveling a kilometer beneath the earth in a small metal box, without any other way out, was a little unnerving.

"No. There are a few other elevators like this one throughout the facility. They wouldn't design an installation where people could get trapped, now would they?"

"No." Jake knew he sounded less than convinced. His father's confidence made him feel a little better, but this was a still a very long elevator ride so far.

"Why is it so far under the ground?"

"Three reasons actually. The first reason is, in case of war. Being buried deep underground makes the system far less vulnerable to attack from the surface.

The second reason is power. We've learned how to tap into thermal vents deep in the Earth's mantle. By using the heat from these vents, we can power steam turbine generators that can provide enough energy to power the Roadrunner, as well as all the other computers in the local array. It also powers all the other buildings on the Los Alamos campus. It's an infinite energy source — better and safer than nuclear energy, with no nuclear waste to get rid of. And unless the core of the earth cools down, which isn't likely in the foreseeable future, we have an endless supply of energy. And if there was a war, nobody can cut off our electrical energy supply.

The third reason is EMPs and shock waves. This installation is designed to withstand a nuclear attack. It's the electromagnetic pulses and ground shock waves that come after a nuclear explosion that would wipe out anything electronic. This far underground the supercomputer is safe from both."

The elevator was slowing down rapidly. The quick deceleration made Jake feel a bit queasy in his stomach. He could feel his breakfast settling down to his toes.

When the doors opened, they stepped out into an enormous warehouse the size of a city block. In this day and age of miniaturization, that meant a lot of computing power. In the center there was a huge circular wall leading up to a high domed roof.

"What's that?" Jake pointed at the domed complex.

"That's the holographic control center. All the delicate and complex experiments are controlled from inside there. That's one of the things I want to show you. I think you'll be impressed."

His dad started off towards the control center and Jake followed eagerly. He wanted to see this. He was already imagining the holo-deck on the Starship Enterprise on TV.

The command center was about 100 feet across. They stopped just before the main entrance doors.

"We call it the MegaTron. The concept comes from the original Sony JumboTron that's in the middle of Times Square, New York. The big difference is that ours is totally three-dimensional. Ready?"

Jake was getting wound up. "Yeah. Let's do it."

His dad smiled and punched his access code into the security keypad beside the door.

With a hiss, the door slid back. Jake stepped inside and froze.

A few programmers stood or sat in the middle of the room while files and programs floated back and forth in mid-air around them. They would just reach out into thin air and touch some virtual file and it would open or close so they could work on it or run it. Three-dimensional graphs and charts danced and flipped in synchronicity to the hand movements of their conductors.

Jake was in heaven. It was like walking into a science fiction movie, only better. This was real. "I can't believe it! This thing is totally awesome!"

"You haven't seen anything yet. These guys are just running diagnostics for our upgrade. You should see the real programs running. You can stand inside the middle of a virtual tornado. You can walk in space and change parts on a satellite floating in orbit. You can walk on the surface of the sun."

"Could you imagine fighting a virtual battle inside this thing?" Jake's mind was running wild.

His dad glanced over at him and smiled when he saw the awe on Jake's face. "Yup, you could do that as well, if they ever loaded a fantasy game program, which they won't. Running anything on this costs so much money that heads would roll if anyone was caught playing games on it. Shame though — it would be fun to watch. Online gaming would never be the same for you again. Your iMac would probably seem like a baby toy after using this machine."

Jake was silent. He'd be willing to risk that.

"You want to know how fast this baby goes?"

"Sure."

"Real fast."

"How fast?"

"How does one Petaflop sound?"

"Is that anything like a pita pocket?" Jake was just messing with his dad. He knew full well it wasn't.

His dad barked out a laugh. "Ha! No. But it is like having about a half a million of your iMacs running at the same time. On top of that, we're upgrading it right now so it will be another three times faster than it is today. How's that for processing power?"

That took a few seconds to grasp. Jake was just starting to picture all the cool things he could do with that kind of power in his bedroom, when his dad continued.

"It runs on a special version of Linux, sort of like your iMac. Except it's a *very* special version. But deep down inside, it's pretty much the same thing you have at home, just on megasteroids. Most machines can only have one thought at a time. This one can have a trillion thoughts, all at the same time."

"How much would it cost to run my online game on this?"

His dad could tell that Jake wasn't going to let the gaming topic drop just yet. Jake, on the other hand, was wondering if he could save up some money and rent a bit of time.

"About 10 million dollars a minute." His dad didn't even look at him. He knew what was going through Jake's mind.

"Oh." There wasn't much more Jake could add to that.

"If I could I would, kiddo, but that $10 million would come right off my paycheck."

"You actually make that much?"

Jake was a bit shocked.

His father shot him a sideways glance, letting Jake know that he had just asked a stupid question. "I wish!"

His dad's attention was drifting off to focus on the readouts from a bank of floating statistical pie charts flickering off to the side. Then he refocused on Jake again.

"No, this baby is dedicated to performing complex scientific calculations that require an enormous amount of processing power. Some things in science can only be calculated by computers like this because there's just no way to filter the quantity of information we need to analyze if we were to use humans to try to do the same thing. By the time humans could finish calculating anything of value, the information would be old and useless, like if you're trying to predict weather patterns. There are so many details to take into consideration that it would take everyone on the planet months, if not years, to figure out even the simplest thing, like one possible snowstorm. This baby can do it in seconds, so we can test billions of scenarios and pick the ones that are most likely to be true.

Then we can use this room to model the tests into a 3D simulation so we can stand inside the experiment and see how it reacts from the inside. We can literally stand inside a nuclear explosion and see what's happening.

But this requires a massive amount of processing power. So here's the real cool thing. Picture this: Very soon we're going to link this machine to the BlueGene array. BlueGene is the code name for our hypercommunications array, which will tie together all our country's scientific research supercomputers. We have lots of other supercomputers similar to this one, only smaller. They're all over the country buried deep underground just like this one, and they're all interconnected with a massively powerful, and very private, fiber-optic network. But if anything happens to the fiber optics, the supercomputers automatically fail over to use the Internet or satellite uplinks, radio antennas, telephone or cellular networks. Basically, anything that can communicate. It's meant to be completely self-healing in the event of a natural disaster or war. Nothing will be able to break their communications once we turn them on.

The original Internet was designed to do pretty much the same thing, just not to that extent. The Internet was our test system. It just grew so popular with the public that we let them have it. We have our own network now and it's a lot more powerful. Nobody can access it except for our supercomputers. Security reasons, obviously.

Once we turn on the entire BlueGene grid, we're going to be able to run at about 500 Petaflops, maybe more. That's equivalent to about 2.5 billion iMacs all tied together and thinking like a single brain. Pretty cool, don't you think?"

His dad was obviously impressed with the concept.

"All that just to predict if it's going to snow or not?"

"No, no, no!" His dad blurted back in horror. "That was just an example. We're going to calculate things like how to send our astronauts safely to Mars, how to develop new types of energy sources, how to predict the highest probable outcomes of a war — that kind of stuff. It's not just about the weather."

"Whoa there, pops!" Jake laughed. "I'm just messing with yah. I get it, I get it."

His father's expression had been serious, but the seriousness was quickly replaced with a smile when his dad realized Jake had been pulling his leg. "Ah. Good one. You got me."

He paused for a moment to collect his thoughts, then finished the dialogue he must have mentally prepared before they got there.

"Some of the applications running on this machine are ultra top secret, while other applications are part of open science projects being run by various science organizations around the world — if they have enough money, that is."

Jake was quiet.

"What are you thinking?"

His father was looking at him quizzically.

"I was just wondering what it would take to hack into this thing?"

Jake was gazing at the wall of monitors.

He father was staring at him now, and he continued looking at him intently for a long second. Jake wasn't paying attention to the calculating look on his father's face, but he could feel his eyes boring a hole into him.

"More than an iMac."

Jake looked at his dad, and his father smiled broadly, and waved a finger at Jake. "Gotcha."

The rest of the morning was spent touring the facility, looking at some of the other experiments around Los Alamos that they had security access to see. Some of them were pretty cool, but Jake just couldn't stop thinking about that giant holographic chamber, and how excellent it would be to play through a battle sequence surrounded by real-sized Orks, Goblins, Monks and Elves. Cool.

He knew Lindsey would freak. He couldn't wait to tell her about it. But he knew he wasn't going to get the chance right now, and his hunger started nagging at him, so he started bugging his father about being hungry. Vicious circle.

His father knew he wasn't going to keep Jake's attention on an empty stomach, so he promised to take him out for a bite to eat shortly.

They were just on the way back to the elevator to head up the long lift to the surface when they were interrupted by an engineer in a white lab coat coming from the Megatron control room.

"Ken. You got a minute?" The engineer glanced over at Jake with a slight smile.

"Sure, what do you have?"

"I need you to come and look at something. I've been over it a hundred times, and the same thing keeps popping up that I can't figure out."

"Sure. Jake?" His father was indicating for Jake to follow them. "Dave, I'd like you to meet my son, Jake. Jake, this is Dave Harrison, our chief engineer."

They shook hands.

"Nice to meet you."

"Nice to meet you, too."

Dave keyed in his access code and they all walked into the MegaTron. Dave directed Jake's dad to one of the many floating multidimensional graphs. It was showing some cylindrical bars all rotating at different intervals while expanding and contracting like they were alive and breathing.

Dave rotated the image with a wave of his hand so they could all see it face-on. "Let me tell you what I know. We only have our diagnostic apps running on the Roadrunner right now since we're getting ready to upgrade, right?"

"As far as I'm aware."

"Okay. So if that's true, then these bar graphs represent all of the running processes for the utility applications. I'm going to kill them all with a master kill command. I want you to watch what happens to the bar on the right. Ready?"

"Go for it."

Dave reached out and sliced his hand sideways through the air, right through the middle of the entire series of floating bars. Then he used his other hand to tap a virtual "Confirm" button that appeared in midair. Instantly, all the bars on the graph collapsed to zero, all except the small one on the right. Dave reached out to touch it, but before his hand could reach it, it dropped to zero as well.

Jake's dad was a bit perplexed. "What did I just see?"

Dave turned his attention away from the charts and focused on Jake's dad. "That final process, the one on the right? Did you see it? It didn't die with the rest of them. It took a couple more seconds to die than all the others."

"But it still died, eventually—" Jake's dad left that spoken thought hanging, not actually expecting any response. He was already deep in thought, obviously also perplexed at what he was seeing.

Dave probed deeper. "But it should have died at the exact same time as the others. All of the processes got the exact same kill command at the exact same time. Why is that last process still alive two seconds later? That's my question."

Jake couldn't get where Dave was going with this. He understood computers and couldn't see what the big deal was. His dad, on the other hand, was running his fingers through his beard, a clear sign to Jake that his father was deep in thought, and obviously just as interested as Dave was.

"What's in the log files?"

"Now you've asked me the real money question." Dave was obviously pleased with the response, and Jake could tell he had been waiting for this exact question. Dave had been priming this moment. He waved his hand in a couple of twisting motions and a floating administration system console appeared out of thin air. It made Jake jump back involuntarily — he hadn't expected it to magically appear right in front of his face. Dave tapped out some commands on some virtual buttons. He was obviously comfortable using this weird floating interface. "Nothing!"

Jake's dad turned his focus directly on Dave. He was wearing a face of disbelief. "Nothing?"

Dave spun the display around so Jake's dad could see it directly. "Nothing. In fact, you know what's even stranger than that? There's actually no trace whatsoever that that process even existed in the first place."

Dave paused. He was waiting for that information to sink in. Waiting to see what Ken would make of what he was hearing, reading the expressions passing across his face.

The seconds ticked by and Jake could see the wheels turning in his dad's head. His eyes were focused on nothing and he rocked back and forth gently on his heels, scratching his beard.

Jake was getting impatient. He wanted his dad to say something — anything. To solve the problems of the universe right here and now. Dave was obviously waiting for the same thing.

Finally his dad looked at Dave. "Send a report to the IBM guys."

Huh. That was it? Jake was more than confused. Where were the earth-shattering deductions that only Sherlock Holmes and his dad could have possibly produced? Where was the grand solution where his dad would open his mouth and save the world? What did he mean, send a report to IBM? That was like calling Microsoft's help desk. "Hello, thanks for calling Microsoft. Do you have the power cord plugged in?" Idiots.

"Dave, if there's nothing in any of the log files, and the phantom process isn't killing the core applications, and if the process dies when we kill all the other processes, then we really don't have much to go on, do we? We need to find some type of evidence if we're to tackle this ourselves. So for now I'm going to have to assume it's a bug in the operating system upgrade. You know this stuff as well as I do. New upgrades always have bugs. Let's fill out a service report, capture some video sequences as evidence since there are no log entries, and get it off our hands and into theirs. That way they're responsible, not us."

"Fine."

Dave wasn't particularly happy with the plan but Ken was Dave's manager, and Dave didn't really have any other ideas to propose back, so that was that. Dave was a classic engineer; he needed answers to everything, and wanted them right this minute. Well, he wasn't getting them today. "Alright, I'll do that. I'll email you a copy of the report when I'm done."

"Excellent. Thanks Dave. Sorry I couldn't be more helpful, but I need this documented somewhere so I don't get hung out on a limb for not reporting this."

Dave nodded his head because he knew that problems like this could get expensive and time-consuming very quickly. "I understand."

Jake followed his father over to a desk where he made a note on a sticky notepad, tore it off, and stuffed it into his pocket. He looked up at Jake and smiled. "Okay. How about that lunch?"

Jake knew his dad's mind was elsewhere. "Sure."

They headed back to the elevator, and the long ride to the surface. On route, Jake began to realize that his ears were starting to plug. Soon it felt like there was a balloon expanding in each ear and he could feel the pain building from the internal pressure. "My ears hurt."

"Oh yeah. Forgot to warn you about that. Pinch your nose real tight. Close your mouth and try to blow air out of your nose. You need to squeeze the air out pretty hard."

Jake did what he was told, and like magic, he popped the pressure balloons building up in his ears, and he felt a rush of relief flood through his skull. "Ahh! That's better."

"Good. You might have to repeat that a couple more times. You definitely don't want to be going up this elevator if you have a bad cold. Your ears get plugged and you can't clear them. Most people here know it, but a few are real diehard workers. I've seen a couple of them get out of the elevator in tears from the pain. It always goes away, but it's not a pleasant experience."

Together, they worked their way through the balance of the security maze to get outside the building and back to the parking lot. They finally drove off the site and headed for their favorite place in town for hamburgers and milkshakes.

On the way to the hamburger joint, Jake had a question. "Dad, what's the big deal about a process that takes an extra two seconds to die?"

It took a moment for his dad to collect his thoughts and respond.

"It's not just the time it takes the process to die, even though that is an issue on its own. It's the fact that something is running on the machine that's leaving no trace that it was there. If it were your home computer I would tell you that you have a virus or a Trojan horse. But on the supercomputer, you can't get infected. For one thing, this particular supercomputer has never been connected to any external network yet, so there's no physical way for anyone to have actually transmitted a virus to it.

"The other thing is, there's just too much security. These supercomputers have very unique operating systems. This isn't the same type of operating system that would come on your average home computer. It's so unique that anyone who writes viruses can't know about it. It's not like they can just guess at how this computer thinks. They need to know specifically how the instructions are executed inside the machine itself.

"It would take an insider, a spy, someone who knew the technology and had access to it. Someone would need to be familiar with this specific operating system in order to create a virus, because it needs to be compiled directly on the supercomputer operating system itself.

"I have a hard time believing that we have a spy on our team. I've been working with these people for years. Besides, what good would it do for any of our own people to write a virus? It would just slow our own work down. That's how I know it's just a bug."

His dad paused for a few seconds to reflect on his thoughts. "But you were also asking about the two seconds it took for the process to die. I never really answered that part, did I?"

He looked over, and Jake shook his head.

"On your home computer, two seconds doesn't really mean much. But on a supercomputer, two seconds is a heck of a long time. The Roadrunner can process 1000 trillion instructions every second. One day soon it will do 500 times that and share its calculation ability amongst many more supercomputers on the BlueGene array. When you add up all that processing power, two seconds for these computers is like a thousand human lifetimes. It would be like the entire history of mankind lapsed between the time we instructed the process to stop and the time it actually stopped. The machine had a long, long, long time to think about what it wanted to do before it actually did it."

His dad took his eyes off the road and looked over at him. "It really makes you wonder what that computer was thinking about for those two seconds, doesn't it?"

He returned his gaze to the road.

Jake didn't reply because he was lost in his own thoughts now. What would a computer think about if it could think for itself? He continued to wonder about this throughout lunch.

#

When they finally got home at the end of the day, Jake recounted his adventures for his mother. She listened while he talked around a mouth full of food. She looked at Ken and he just smiled, obviously pleased that his son seemed to have had a good time.

When they had finished eating, Jake chipped in to help wash the dishes. He was thinking about getting back to his computer to get back to the game, and see if he could figure out what to do next.

Unfortunately, that wasn't going to happen tonight. His mom had other plans for him. "I'm glad you had a good day at your father's work." They were drying up the last of the dishes. "I think you should go to bed early tonight. It's been a long day. That means no computer tonight. Okay?"

She was giving him that look that meant that it wasn't really a question.

"But I wanted to do something in the game. I've just got to a special level I've never seen before. I really need to explore it a bit."

"Nope. Not tonight. You need to take a shower and then you need to get some sleep. You can barely keep your eyes open now. So go get showered, brush your teeth and jump into bed. I'll be in shortly just to make sure you're not playing. If I find you on that computer, I'll pull it out for a week."

She looked at him with the special *Mom look.* Every kid knows that look — it's the look that means business. It's the look that tells you that you'd better not say anything right now if you know what's good for you.

Jake didn't say a word. He'd had his computer taken away several times before and it wasn't a pleasant experience. He headed off to follow orders.

When he finally made it to bed, he just lay there staring at his blank monitor. He contemplated waiting until his parents went to sleep, then he'd experiment, just a little bit. His mom came in about 15 minutes later and found him fast asleep. Mom knows best.

CHAPTER THREE

The alarm shook Jake out of his peaceful slumber. He sat up in bed and ran his fingers through his hair. He stretched his arms and glanced over at his monitor, realizing his great plan last night was now a shattered memory.

"Oh well."

He slipped into some fresh clothes and kicked his dirty ones into a pile in the corner of his room. He had lots to talk about with Lindsey today. He hoped she was going to be on the bus and not off sick or something.

He went through his normal morning routine, grabbed his iPhone and gave his mom a kiss before heading for the bus. He called out before heading outside. "See you after school."

He was sure his mother said something in reply but the door was already slamming shut at the time.

He headed down to the corner to wait for the *cheese* bus, as he liked to call it. It was already lumbering down the road, huffing and puffing black smoke in the distance. When it reached the stop, the door popped open with a hiss and a clang.

"Morning." He waved at the driver, who returned his greeting with the ritualistic nod of the head. Jake looked to the left to see if Lindsey was in her typical seat, and she was. "Hey."

He made his way to the rear where they were both assigned to the same bench. He plopped himself down while she shuffled her backpack down to her feet.

"How come you weren't online two nights ago?"

She looked at him. "Why weren't you at school yesterday, or online last night?"

"I went to work with my dad. He runs a monster supercomputer at the lab."

Everyone knew what "the lab" meant since Los Alamos National Laboratory was one of biggest employers in the area. A lot of the kids' parents worked with or at the lab, in one way or another.

"I got to see the whole thing. Pretty soon it will have as much power as 2.5 billion iMacs." He could see she was paying attention and was pleased.

Lindsey worked hard at appearing disinterested. "Well, you missed the math test."

"And the system has a bug." Jake ignored her dismissal.

"What type of bug?"

"We don't know yet. We had to get the IBM guys to look at it." Jake used the "we" word in an attempt to impress her that he was a crucial player in the event. They only had a few minutes before they reached the school so he quickly changed the subject, especially before she challenged him on the "we" thing. "Listen, I've got something really cool to talk to you about, but not here. Let's meet for lunch."

Her natural curiosity was instantly aroused. "What's it about?"

Jake savored the moment. "I'll tell you at lunch."

He knew that would bug her all morning, not knowing.

The bus pulled up at the school and they jumped out and headed for the doors.

"Give me a hint."

It had begun. He had her hook, line, and sinker. Lindsey was curious. She hated it when he didn't tell her something, and only teased her with clues.

"Nope. I'll tell you at lunch, but only if you give me the answers to the math test." He was thinking quickly now. He could use this as leverage. "I need to take the makeup test today."

She turned in a snit, and headed for class. "I'll tell you the answers at lunch."

"Rats."

She knew full well he had to take the test first thing this morning. What she didn't tell him, was that she hadn't received her test results back yet, nor had she memorized the questions, so she couldn't help him anyways. Two can play this game.

#

Jake fidgeted away the morning, watching the clock, longing for the noon bell. When the lunch bell rang, he jumped up and headed for his locker.

He opened it up, tossed in his books, grabbed his lunch bag and iPhone, and sprinted for the hideout.

The hideout was their special and secret place. They had discovered it one day when prowling around the gym. At the back of the gym there were bleachers. Just behind the bleachers hung ceiling-to-floor curtains displaying the school crest and the names of their sports teams.

A few years back the school had a trampoline that was used during gym class. Unfortunately, some kids had pulled it out without permission one day and someone had bounced off and broke their collarbone. The kid's parents wound up suing the school for not providing proper supervision and security, so that ended the days of trampolines. The school got rid of it, and that was that.

What remained was the empty room behind the curtain, abandoned and forgotten, covered by the heavy curtains. Jake had been fooling around one day and had climbed under the curtains in order to scare Lindsey. That's how he wound up finding the door to the storage room.

From that day on, when the weather was bad outside, it became their secret place to eat lunch and play their linked PSPs.

They both swore not to tell anyone else, and they established a ritual to scout the surrounding area before they entered, just to make sure nobody was watching.

When Jake arrived he was surprised to find Lindsey already there. "How did you get here so fast?"

She was still ticked off from this morning's little mind-game Jake played on her. "That's my secret."

She was laying out her lunch in military precision on the cafeteria table Jake had *borrowed* and smuggled into the room for her. After all, there was no way *she* was going eat on one of those dusty old boxes that Jake ate on.

He could care less about the dusty boxes, but he always wound up doing pretty much what Lindsey wanted him to do. They treated each other like friends on the outside, but deep inside there was more to it than they would admit. Jake liked to make Lindsey happy.

Lindsey started salting her boiled egg patiently, not daring to look at Jake. She wouldn't give him the satisfaction that it was driving her crazy to find out what he was keeping from her. She kept her voice disinterested. "So what's your big secret?"

Jake plunked himself down on his usual cardboard box and tore open his lunch bag. He opened his sandwich bag and took a bite of his PB&J.

"Listen, I've broken into a whole new level in the game. It was totally awesome. I dropped into some weird world that's all white. I found it in the middle of a forest."

He had been bursting at the seams to tell her, and now it all came out garbled with a mouthful of food, but he had been holding it in too long. He took a deep breath and reached for his juice box, tore the top off the straw wrapper and jammed the straw in the box, all with one hand. Lindsey always found that impressive although she never told him that.

"Go on." She sounded bored, but her patience was wearing thin.

Jake knew she was hooked. He slowed himself down. Between mouthfuls of sandwich, and sips of his drink, he eventually told her his entire adventure, leaving out only one minor detail.

He didn't want to tell Lindsey about the downloaded patch yet because she was a stickler for playing by the rules. She liked the fact he was a programmer but she didn't like cheating in the game. Jake could program up some nifty weapons and gadgets that they always seemed to need. They even created an entire village once. But once, when Jake told her he had hacked into a new way to increase their body armor, she refused to play with him for a week.

He no longer told her about his hacks.

Jake waited patiently for her to say something. Lindsey knew he was waiting and took her sweet time just to make him sweat it out. Even though she managed to appear calm on the outside, on the inside, her mind was buzzing with this new information. She was already speculating and working various theories.

"WELL?" Jake was going to explode.

"Interesting."

"What do you mean *interesting*?"

He felt like he was being played now.

"You said you took some screenshots and saved them to your iPhone? Let me see those."

Jake pulled out his iPhone and loaded the pictures. He handed it to her. "Check these out. I really need your help figuring this out."

Lindsey scrolled through the various pictures in the roll, and then did it again. She handed the iPhone back to Jake.

"Two questions."

He waited.

"Question one, how did you get through the forest? And question two, where's your avatar?"

Whoops. Jake forgot about that. Crap, how was he going to explain 100% stealth to Lindsey? She knew the game as well as he did. She knew that forests were impenetrable and she also knew that avatars were always in the camera view somewhere.

His delay was his admission of guilt.

She was staring at him now. "You hacked it, didn't you?"

Her eyes were boring holes in the top of his head since he was staring down at his feet now, but he knew she was staring.

He searched for an acceptable excuse. "It was just a patch."

"What kind of patch? I was online last night and the system never notified me there were any new patches available."

Whoops. Caught again.

"Really, I don't exactly know where the patch came from. I followed too many links, then it finally downloaded from an IP address, so I couldn't trace the source, even if I wanted to."

Jake was apologizing now, hoping for forgiveness.

"Hmm..."

Jake breathed a little easier. Lindsey's *Hmm...* could be a good sign.

He desperately needed her to accept this and get over it. He needed her help badly, as usual. Whenever he was struggling it was usually Lindsey, with her cunning strategy skills, who bailed him out.

A faint smile touched the corners of Lindsey's lips as an early warning indicator to Jake that she was planning something.

"OK. If it's a real patch, then I can live with that."

Jake waited. He knew that that wasn't all she wanted to say. He eventually got tired of waiting while she deliberately retrieved a carrot from her lunch bag. He gave in. "And?"

She continued her nonchalant attitude. "And... I'll help you — on one condition."

Here it comes.

"I want a copy of the patch for myself."

Jake let out a quiet sigh. If that's all she wants, he still had the disk, so why not? It could have been a lot worse. She might have dropped him as her partner for who knows how long, and Jake didn't want to even think about that.

"No sweat. I've got it copied to a CD so I'll burn you a copy when you come over."

"Cool." Lindsey was pleased that her plan was successful, but she also had the sophistication not to rub it in when she won. Besides, she knew he'd give her whatever she asked for, but she didn't want to make it obvious she knew this.

With negotiations over, she turned her mind again to the pictures she had seen. "It's weird that the world is all white. It's like the programmer started to build a world and never finished it. Why a blizzard? What's with the gridlines?" Her mind was fully in gear now.

Jake knew he just had to wait. "Yeah."

Any other response he gave at this time would probably not add anything, so he just waited for Lindsey's typical brainstorming to come up with something new.

Jake rummaged around in the bottom of his lunch bag and drew out an apple. He bit into it. The crunch broke into Lindsey's thoughts. She refocused her attention on Jake.

"You're a programmer. What's a good reason for creating a white world?"

"I was thinking it was to be winter world, a snow and ice adventure. Maybe it's still under construction."

"I was thinking something else." Lindsey paused again as if revisiting her initial thoughts to see if they made sense before speaking them out loud. Programming wasn't her thing so she didn't want to look dumb.

"I was thinking about a winter world as well, but why hide it in the middle of an impenetrable forest? How did the programmer do that anyway? And you said you fell down a huge tunnel that took *minutes* to get to the bottom. That's weird as well. And the black dot that normal players wouldn't have seen either. None of this makes any sense unless you're trying to hide something. But why hide a world where nobody can get at it?

Now that you've found the place, it's nothing but white landscape and blizzard everywhere. Why? Someone goes to all the trouble to create the most advanced security system we've ever seen, to protect the way in and out of this world, then doesn't bother to create the rest of the world inside. Something is wrong with this picture."

Lindsey paused again and looked at Jake for some assistance, and saw him nodding his head, deep in thought. He obviously wasn't going to be much help.

She looked at his iPhone sitting on the box.

After a couple of seconds of staring at the black screen she leaned forward and picked it up.

"Why is the background on your iPhone black?"

Jake awoke slowly from his wandering thoughts and tried to focus. "What?"

"Why do you keep the background on your iPhone black?" she repeated. "I mean, why don't you set a background picture or something?"

"I don't want to waste the memory." He said this offhandedly. "It takes longer to load when I use a picture for the background."

"Oh."

But Jake didn't hear her response. His mind was just catching up to what Lindsey had asked. Her question started stimulating memories of things he had programmed in the online world. They came flooding back in parts and pieces. He remembered one particular object. The castle he had written. He remembered he had added incredible texture to the stone walls, but when he tried to walk around inside the castle his screen would jerk and pause, again and again, as his character moved about.

He eventually talked to his dad, and found out that the more texture he added, the more processing power the computer needed to draw it on the screen.

His dad had told him that processing video always takes a lot out of your machine. That's why the computer manufacturers always compete with each other over who has the fastest video cards.

This all came to Jake in a burst of memories. He was a bit mad at himself that he hadn't thought of this before. But then again, Lindsey always had a habit of triggering his best ideas.

"I think I know why it's white."

He looked at Lindsey and she could see he was starting to get worked up.

"I think it's white so the programmer didn't have to waste any computing power drawing a fancy landscape."

He was wound up now. He was looking at Lindsey like she should find this obvious.

"So?"

"So...if the programmer doesn't use his computer power to draw landscapes, he can use it for something else."

Jake was staring at Lindsey, waiting for some "Ah ha!" response. She could see that he thought he had figured out the answer to life, the universe and everything.

"Like what?" She wasn't getting what his excitement was all about. It still made for a boring virtual world.

Jake was getting frustrated now.

"Like what? What do you mean, like what?"

He could see Lindsey wasn't getting excited about his brainwave. He was stuck for a better response. His thinking hadn't gone that far yet and he didn't have an answer.

"Like anything."

His flustered response showed the hint of his frustration at reaching a dead end while in mid-revelation.

Lindsey started packing up her lunch remains and spoke, without looking at him.

"Let's check it out after school. I want to see it for myself."

She was dismissing Jake's idea, since it wasn't getting them anywhere.

Jake, on the other hand, was still winding down from the adrenaline rush he had just started as a result of his insight. Eventually he begrudgingly acknowledged that the lunch bell would be ringing soon, and they still needed to sneak out without being noticed. Lindsey made the first move.

"Come on."

Lindsey went to the door and doused the lights. She cracked the door open, bent down, and peaked under the heavy curtain looking for feet.

"The gym's empty. Let's go."

Jake followed her out the storage room, closing the door quietly behind him. They sideways-shuffled their way along the gap between the curtain and the wall, and slipped out between seams in the curtain panels while still under the bleachers. Another quick look around and they were heading for the gym doors.

Jake walked in silence still thinking about his most recent idea, desperately looking for an answer when Lindsey broke into his thoughts.

"Since it's Friday, I can go straight to your place after school. I already told my mom I would."

"Yeah, okay, that's cool."

"We'll look at it when we get there. Okay?"

Lindsey could see Jake was a bit let down that his idea hadn't gone anywhere, but she knew he would get over it soon and get back to normal.

"Yeah."

But Jake just couldn't let it go. The thought preoccupied him for the balance of the afternoon while annoying his teachers to no end, as they could see his attention was anywhere but on what they were teaching.

CHAPTER FOUR

The bus brakes screamed in pain as it lumbered to a stop.

Jake and Lindsey jumped out and headed down the block. When they reached his front door, he tried the handle to see if it was locked. It wasn't. They dropped their packs on the floor and kicked off their shoes.

He looked at the wall beside the door and saw a yellow sticky-note.

WILL BE HOME FOR DINNER.

GONE SHOPPING.

LOVE, MOM

They headed for Jake's room.

As they neared his bedroom door, they both picked up the sound of clickety-clack coming from his room.

This confused and panicked Jake a bit. It didn't make sense. If his mom wasn't home, and his dad was at work, then what was making the clickety-clack sound from down the hallway, and why had the front door been left unlocked? His nerves switched to overdrive.

He raised a finger to his mouth and gestured to Lindsey to be quiet. Lindsey looked at him questioningly. She was just about to ask what was going on just to override his order for silence, but she saw his worried expression and thought better of it.

Jake wasn't quite sure what to do. He had never been faced with a situation like this. After a moment, he ducked into the kitchen and reappeared a couple of seconds later with the portable telephone in one hand and a large kitchen knife in the other.

Lindsey's eyes widened in fright.

Jake handed her the telephone and whispered to her to call 911. She stood frozen in panic. She had no idea what was going on. Jake pointed at the phone, then he turned and inched his way to the bedroom. Lindsey fumbled with the telephone and managed to finally dial 911, all the while watching as Jake made it to his bedroom door.

She wanted Jake to stop acting so stupid and get out of the building. Then the voice came on the line.

"You've reached 911, please state the emergency."

Lindsey just about jumped out of her skin.

Jake was turning the door handle and she could see his hand shaking, his other hand holding up the knife in front of him. Lindsey wanted to scream. The voice on the telephone repeated itself.

Lindsey whispered into the phone.

"Someone is in our house."

She was too scared to realize this wasn't her house.

"What's your address?"

Jake was just starting to open the door. Lindsey was too frozen to speak. This was all happening too fast. They shouldn't be doing this. They should have run outside and gotten away from the house. It was too late now, everything happened at once.

The adrenaline flowing through Jake was causing his hands to tremble. He peered through the crack of the door and held up the shaking knife to fend off whatever lay inside.

Suddenly he pushed the door open with a hard thump of the heel of his hand.

"DAD???"

Jake's dad jerked violently as if hit with lightning. He twisted to face Jake with a look of hunted prey on his face. It passed as fast as it came, accompanied with a large and loud exhale. His dad smiled too broadly, more as an automatic response to shock recovery than because he was so glad to see Jake.

"Man oh man, Jake! You scared the living heck out of me!"

Lindsey heard Jake talking and walked quickly forward, phone in hand, completely forgetting that she was still in the process of talking to emergency services.

She came around the corner and saw Jake's dad looking at Jake. His face was a bit pale, but the color was quickly returning.

"Hi, Lindsey. How are you? Jake just finished scaring the pants off me. How long have you two been home?"

He glanced at the knife in Jake's hand and had somehow concluded that Jake and Lindsey must have been in the kitchen getting something to eat. He hadn't even heard them come in.

Jake starting laughing out loud to relieve his pent-up tension.

Lindsey wasn't laughing at all. She suddenly became aware of the phone in her hands like it was an alien, then remembered she was still making the emergency call.

"Oh no! I'm still on with 911."

She brought the handset to her ear, "Hello, Hello?"

Jake's dad looked at her questioningly.

"Can you describe what's happening."

"Umm... nothing really. I thought there was a burglar, but it's just Jake's dad. Sorry about that."

"What's your name?"

So Lindsey tried her best to explain what just happened to the voice at the end of the telephone. Meanwhile, Jake's dad sat there listening, smile widening as the story unfolded. After the story was completely relayed she looked at Jake's father who signaled her to hand him the telephone.

She passed him the handset.

"Hello, this is Ken Tomkins. Sorry for the confusion, but it was just a little scare for the kids, that's all."

Jake's dad stood listening to the voice on the phone for a minute.

"I understand. I'll expect an officer in a few minutes then. I'll explain it when he gets here. Thanks for your help. Take care."

With that he hung up the phone and looked at Jake and Lindsey in turn, "They still have to send out a police officer even though there's no problem, just in case I'm lying."

Lindsey almost felt like crying, mostly as an aftershock of the stress over the past few minutes.

"I'm sorry."

"Nothing to be sorry about. You did the right thing, Lindsey."

He turned his attention to Jake.

"And what do you think you were doing coming in here with a knife? Did you think you were some kind of superhero from your game or something? If I had been a real crook, you would have been in a lot more trouble than that knife would have solved. You and I are going to have a little talk about this later. Right now we'll have to wait until this all settles down."

He turned his attention to Lindsey who appeared to be recovering her composure.

"Are you all right, Lindsey?"

"Yes, Mr. Tomkins." She was in transition from fear to anger — anger at Jake for getting them into this mess.

His dad looked back at Jake.

"So I guess you need your room back, eh?"

"Yeah. Why aren't you at work?"

"The IBM guys have the supercomputer offline today while they load more upgrades to get ready for connecting the BlueGene array, so I thought I could work from home today."

"Why were you on my computer instead of yours?"

"There's something seriously wrong with my machine. I'm trying to get it working, but I needed to check my email, so I came in here to use your machine."

"What's your machine doing wrong?"

Jake's dad started rubbing his beard. "Something very strange. Very interesting. I'll let you know when I figure out more."

He turned around and put one hand on the mouse and casually shut down the browser he had been running. Then he told the machine to power down.

"Wait..." Jake was just a little too slow in his request.

"I guess I just got busy writing emails and forgot about the time." His father looked at him. "What? Wait for what?"

Jake watched the operating system shutting down. "Too late. We need to use the computer. Doesn't matter. We'll start it up again."

"Oh. Sorry about that."

His dad stood up, and walked towards the door. The kids moved out of his way, and he stopped at the door and turned back to look at them.

"When the police get here, I'm sure they're going to want to talk to you, so I'll come and get you so we can get this cleared up."

They both nodded in unison.

His dad cracked a large and conspiratorial smile. "And we won't say a word of this to your mother when she gets home now, will we?"

"No way! Are you kidding? Here, Dad, could you take the knife back to the kitchen on your way, please?"

His dad left the room, knife in hand, closing the door behind him.

#

After the police finally left and they had returned to the room, Lindsey turned to Jake and looked like she was going to kill him.

"Are you nuts? Why did you do that? We should have just left the building! You could have got us killed. Now you have us in trouble with the police."

Jake felt bad. He tried to console her.

"It'll be fine. Don't worry about it. My dad will take care of it."

He turned to his computer and looked at the monitor. "That's weird."

He looked at Lindsey. She had no idea what he was talking about.

"Dad just shut the machine down."

Lindsey looked at the iMac and saw that, not only was the machine up and running again, but the photo application was open and running. She could see both her and Jake moving around in the room through the built-in camera.

Lindsey speculated, "The shutdown must have failed or something."

"Nope. I saw it shut down. Even if it rebooted, it wouldn't have magically logged itself in and started an application."

He stared at it for a few more seconds and then dismissed it. "Oh well, whatever. Let me bring up the game so you can see where I'm at."

Lindsey sat down in the chair beside Jake, and waited for the familiar game to load.

Jake logged into the game and the screen refreshed itself. Both of them were looking at a white monitor where the only distinguishable object was the faint outline of his avatar's utility belt and the thin gridlines under his feet. The blizzard of snow whipped around at blinding speeds.

Jake moved his avatar back and forth, just to make sure the application had finished loading.

"Here we are."

Lindsey scanned the whitewashed landscape.

"Pretty dull, all right. Try rotating 360 degrees so I can look around."

Jake panned his camera around one full turn, then drew the camera back to maximum distance and did it again. His character was now too far away to make out the utility belt outline. The avatar was totally invisible against the white snowstorm.

Lindsey was sitting beside and a little behind Jake. Now she leaned forward to get a better look, and her face was next to his. Her long brown hair flowed forward and swept cross his neck. Jake could smell her soft fragrance as her silky hair caressed his neck. His brain started to feel a little foggy, and he desperately wanted to brush his cheek against hers.

Lindsey seemed oblivious to Jake's condition.

"Hmm... Not exactly an impressive world. What's with the gridlines?"

Jake wasn't thinking clearly enough to respond properly.

"I don't know."

That was the best she was going to get at the moment.

Lindsey sat backwards in her chair again, thinking.

Jake let out his breath. He hadn't even realized that he'd been holding it. He also noticed his heart was racing a mile a minute, and breathed deeply to calm himself. He focused his full attention on the screen, hoping Lindsey hadn't noticed. *Had she noticed? What was she thinking? Why was she so quiet?* He tried and tried to focus on the game, but came up short.

"Can you bring up your inventory?"

Not exactly the most romantic query.

"Sure."

For some reason, he now had the verbal skills of a monkey.

The screen changed. There was now a long list of inventory items that every gamer carried. Many of the items were earned as rewards for solving puzzles and conquering foes throughout the adventures. Others were programmed by Jake to fill a certain need at a certain time. Usually he copied another design and enhanced it, but now and again he created something from scratch.

The inventory included weapons, spells, tools, potions, and artifacts of all different types that could be used for trading along the way. Jake slowly scrolled through the list. Lindsey suddenly sat forward again.

"That."

He paused, but he wasn't paying attention. There was her scent again. He worked desperately to keep his wits about him.

"Which item?" His voice was thick and husky. He cleared his throat.

"That one."

She reached up to point directly at a specific object and her hair fell like satin around Jake's neck again. Lindsey was oblivious to her effects on him; she was deep into scanning the inventory.

Jake highlighted the item with a click of the mouse. "My keyboard?" Jake wasn't thinking clearly at all at the moment.

"Yeah, let's try that. We can type in some commands and see if anything happens."

"But I built that one myself so I could type in a password to access the castle I created. They were both designed to work together — that's how I programmed them. I doubt it would work on anything else in the game." He wanted her to point to another item so her hair would swoosh again.

Lindsey sat back, her hair swept back off his neck. He would have to be happy with that for the moment.

"But it *does* type in commands doesn't it?"

"Sure."

"Then let's give it a shot. What do you have to lose?"

Jake equipped his avatar with the homemade virtual keyboard. His character reached to its utility belt and produced a virtual keyboard. The virtual keyboard hung in midair.

He looked back over his shoulder at Lindsey.

"What command do you want to issue?"

"Try saving your game."

Jake hit the Tilde key to bring down the command prompt. He punched the keys *S A V E G A M E,* then hit the Enter key. His avatar's hands began typing just above the virtual keyboard onscreen.

A green progress bar now popped up at the bottom of the screen, and started filling in from left to right. The game finished saving, and the green bar disappeared.

"Well, it works for that."

Lindsey was still leaning back in her chair. That obviously didn't impress her enough to get her to sit forward again.

"Try something else. Try something that will show if there is anything out there, without activating your HUD."

Jake thought about it for a second or two then typed in *T O G G L E M A P*.

A wireframe outline of the landscape appeared on the screen without any other indicators. It looked a lot like the HUD map, but it had no detail whatsoever, kind of like a skeleton of the land.

"Okay. We're getting somewhere, I think."

Lindsey still wasn't getting anything to work with though.

"Try something else." She needed information, and a wireframe landscape with no data wasn't helping her.

Jake knew that Lindsey needed to see something, anything. He was running out of ideas. Then he thought of something.

Jake typed *S U D O* and hit Enter.

His avatar did the same. Then a popup window appeared on the screen.

The simple word *LOGIN* at the top of the box prompted Lindsey to sit forward again, to Jake's delight.

"What does it mean, login?" Lindsey was baffled. "You're already logged in."

"I used the SUDO command. Now, if this is a Linux operating system, I can try to login as someone else, and act as them."

Jake was pleased he could show off a bit for Lindsey. She had asked him to try something else, after all. He was also getting very interested, if only because he was seeing his virtual keyboard doing something it wasn't originally designed to do. If this actually worked out, it would mean he had found a back door into the operating system. Just the thought of that swept the last trace of Lindsey's hair and scent from his mind. He was fully into this now, and needed to run a major test. He had an idea. "Give me your name and password."

"What? Good luck on that one, boy. As if I'd give you that. You'd wind up logging in as me later and delete all my inventory or something as a joke."

Jake was hurt. "No way! Really, I would never do that." However, now that she gave him the idea... No, that would be fatal. Tell you what, you punch it in yourself. I won't look."

Lindsey was still skeptical. She knew he could run keyboard trackers and other tools that can capture passwords, but she too was very curious if this would work.

"All right, let me at the keyboard."

She leaned across Jake, which he thoroughly enjoyed, and she punched in her user name and hit Enter. She was then prompted to enter her password. She did, and hit the Enter key again. She stared at the screen and waited patiently. The avatar executed her commands diligently.

Jake could care less what was happening on the computer now that Lindsey was leaning over him again.

"Well, what do you make of that?"

Jake heard her, and responded a bit wistfully. "Make of what?"

Lindsey was suddenly very aware that Jake was not paying attention to the screen at all. Even more, she realized that she had been so focused on what was happening that she didn't realize she was pressed up against him. She had known Jake for years. They had played, fought, wrestled, and spent countless hours together. All of a sudden, for the first time, she was extremely conscious of the fact they were touching, and it made the blood rush to her face. Blushing, she sat back in her chair slightly flustered, and kept her eyes deliberately glued to the monitor. There was no way in the world she was going to look Jake in the eye right now. Her face was on fire.

She pointed at the screen to break Jake's attention. "That. Read the screen."

Jake looked away, and she exhaled. What had just happened?

Jake's attention refocused. He read the screen, and his spirit of adventure soared. It read *Welcome, Lindsey.*

"Wow! Cool. I can't believe it! It worked."

"What worked?" With an effort she refocused her attention on the computer.

"We just logged in as you from inside my account."

"Yeah. So what?"

"Soooo...," he strung it out, "that means we have direct access to the administrator commands for the operating system. That means I can control lots of things."

"Jake. That sounds a lot like hacking to me. This isn't part of the game anymore."

"Yeah. That's exactly what it is."

He was now so busy watching the screen that he didn't notice the worried expression growing on Lindsey's face.

"What are you thinking of doing?" The last thing she wanted was for Jake to do something to the online game using her user account.

"I don't know. Let's set up our accounts for free access. Let's delete someone's account we don't like." His mind was running wild with possibilities.

"No!"

Jake turned to face Lindsey to see what was wrong. The expression on her face told him she was worried.

"What do you mean, no?" Jake was confused.

"I don't want you messing with the system using my account. They're going to find out it was me, and cancel my account. Then they're going to call the cops, and they're going to sue us."

"What are you talking about? I have access to the log files, so I can erase our log entries and nobody will know we were even in the system."

"I don't care. Don't do it." Lindsey was getting a little irrational now. She was sure this was a very bad thing to be doing, and didn't want to be part of it anymore. "Log me out."

"But why?"

"Just do it."

"Just tell me why."

That was it. Lindsey had had enough. If Jake wouldn't log her out, she'd do it for him. She reached down and pulled out the power plug for the computer.

"HEY!"

Jake reached for the cord. Too late. The computer died and the monitor went black.

Lindsey got up and headed out of the room.

"Where are you going?"

Jake was confused. All this was happening too fast to make heads or tails of it. He jumped up and followed her out into the hallway. Lindsey was already halfway to the door.

"Awe, come on. It's not a big deal."

Jake just couldn't come up with the right thing to say right now. Even if he could, it wouldn't have mattered, because Lindsey wasn't listening and didn't want to listen.

By the time Jake made it to the door, she was slipping on her shoes and grabbing her backpack.

"What are you doing? I won't use your account then. Come on. I need your help to figure this thing out."

It was no use. Lindsey was going, and that's all there was to it. After opening the door and stepping out, she turned around to face Jake.

"I'm going home, and I'm not going to team up with you until you stop hacking into systems. It's wrong and I won't do it."

She spun on her heel and strode off home.

Jake stood there dazed as his father walked up behind him.

"What was that all about?"

"I don't know. We were playing the game and I got access to the operating system and she just freaked out and left."

"You got access to the operating system?" His dad was curious now.

"Yeah. I got a console, and it lets me run administrator commands. Well, so far only a couple that I know of, but probably more."

"This is for the online game you play?"

"Yeah."

His dad was standing there thoughtfully looking him right in the eye until Jake looked down at his shoes.

"You better be careful not to mess up any systems that don't belong to you, just to have fun. It could make a lot of people very angry. I don't need the police back here again because you're turning into another teenage hacker. Are we clear on that?"

"Yes." Jake was still looking at his shoes.

"Time to get your homework done. No more gaming tonight."

Jake knew his father meant business.

Jake closed the front door, grabbed his backpack, and headed back to his room.

Ken, who stood there watching him, was starting to wonder what type of monster he might have created. Then the thought passed as quickly as it had come, and he walked off back to his computer to figure out why it still wasn't working properly.

Jake decided not to cause more trouble tonight and risk losing his computer, so he cracked open his books and dug into his homework, wondering what had got Lindsey so hot under the collar. More importantly, he wondered what he was going to do about it.

#

On the way home, Lindsey subconsciously registered the red light at the corner of her block and stopped. There were a only few cars, but she knew enough, even running on autopilot, not to be overly impatient and try to run between the cars. Not that it was an extremely busy street at the worst of times, but it was known for its accidents. She wasn't going to get herself killed just because Jake made her mad.

While she waited for the light to turn, she casually glanced around. She noticed the tall pole with the box mounted on top of it on the far right of the street. She knew that was the traffic camera the city had installed a year ago to reduce the number of accidents. Her parents talked about it, and took extra caution not to run the yellow lights anymore.

The light turned green and the *WALK* sign lit up. She kept her eye out for a stray car, but wasn't paying serious attention because she could see they had all come to a dead stop where they should.

She started to cross the street.

The camera at the top of the pole started moving. It wasn't looking at the cars though. It followed Lindsey's progress until she had finished crossing the street and rounded the corner out of sight. It paused for a second or two more, waiting, then returned to watching the traffic. Lindsey didn't notice.

She arrived home just in time for dinner. Her mom was surprised to see her at home so early. "I thought you were staying over at Jake's for dinner tonight?"

"No." Flat, blunt, and to the point.

Her mother knew that tone of voice immediately. That was the tone of a mad Lindsey, and her mother knew better than to pry, because Lindsey just clammed up when she was mad.

"Get yourself a plate then, and serve yourself. We've already started without you." She dropped the subject.

Lindsey said little throughout dinner. Both her parents knew Lindsey's temperament, so it was a quiet dinner. She made small talk about her test results in math, but that was about it. When she was done eating she thanked her mom, helped clean off the table, cleaned up her dishes and headed for her room. She got out her homework and threw it on the table beside her computer.

Lindsey also had an iMac because Jake had talked her into it a long time ago. It sat on the desk at the foot of her bed so she could watch DVDs or online clips while lying in bed. She usually left it on at night, playing her favorite music to lull her to sleep. At the moment it was turned off, and she didn't want to even turn it on tonight. She'd had enough of computers for one day, and didn't want anything to do with this one right now either.

She finished her homework, got ready for bed, yelled goodnight before closing her door, then doused the lights and jumped into bed. She was exhausted. It had been a long and emotional day. She had been frightened out of her wits by the ordeal with Jake's dad and the police. She couldn't figure out what had happened between her and Jake when they had touched. And she had freaked out when Jake was about to use her online account to hack into the gaming system. It was all too much for one day.

Lindsey knew her response had been too emotional when Jake used her account today, but at the time it was her way of venting the day's emotions. As she relaxed now, in the comfort of her own bed, in her own home, she felt bad about acting so childish.

As she thought things through, she told herself she would apologize to Jake in the morning, and she knew Jake would forgive her. He would give her anything, and do anything for her. And with that thought, she realized that she and Jake were growing into more than the old childhood chums they had been. Jake was becoming her boyfriend.

And with her mind buzzing with all of the thoughts and emotions that brought on, she finally drifted off into sleep.

#

Suddenly, there was a soft *BONG* in the darkness.

It was two o'clock in the morning, and the power light for Lindsey's computer turned on. Then the machine completed its boot cycle, and the monitor lit up the room like daylight.

Lindsey was fast asleep, and nothing could wake her out of her exhausted slumber.

A window opened on the iMac, and the built-in camera application loaded. In the application window, the camera had a clear view of Lindsey, fast asleep right in front of it. A small click came from the speaker, the LED flash went off at the top of the monitor, and the machine captured a picture of Lindsey while she slept unknowingly.

Then another window opened, bringing up Lindsey's email application this time. A new email was created and addressed. The photo of Lindsey was added as an attachment. The email was eventually transmitted, which forced a quiet whooshing sound from the speaker.

Lindsey stirred but didn't awake.

The *Sent Items* folder was then opened, and any trace that the email ever existed was deleted forever.

The email application window closed, the camera application window closed, and finally, the machine powered down. Silence returned, except for Lindsey's soft breathing.

Once more, the room was bathed in darkness.

CHAPTER FIVE

"I'm sorry for yesterday."

Lindsey never apologized, so when she did, Jake was taken off guard.

"Uh... sure. No problem."

"I shouldn't have freaked out like that yesterday. I don't know what hit me, but I shouldn't have gotten so mad at you."

Jake shrugged even though Lindsey couldn't see that over the telephone. "Don't worry about it."

And with that, it was over. Jake had been real nervous about getting on the bus come Monday morning. Now he didn't have to worry about that. Things could get back to normal.

Lindsey wasn't finished though. "I've finished my chores, and I was thinking we could pick up where we left off?"

There was a question beyond the question in there. Jake could tell she wasn't sure yet whether or not he had forgiven her.

"That would be great. What time can you come over?" He could hear the sigh of relief at the end of the phone.

"How about now?"

"Cool. See you in a bit."

#

The white world was still white. Nothing had changed. The blizzard still raged and the gridlines still stretched out to the distant horizon beneath the raging snow storm.

"OK. So what do you want to try now?"

Jake was kind of hoping Lindsey had come up with a great brainstorm last night. She was a good strategist, and he also didn't want to risk doing something that would set her off again.

Lindsey was looking into nowhere, like she was daydreaming.

"I had a dream last night that someone was watching me."

She looked over at Jake, and realized that he seemed to be waiting for an answer.

"Did you say something?"

"Yes, I asked what you want to try now?"

"Oh."

She looked at the monitor and focused her attention.

"I was thinking about this. I think it might be time to activate your HUD."

"But if a system administrator detects us, I might have my account suspended." Jake had thought about this plenty of times. He couldn't even think about having to start from Level One and work his way back, all over again. It had taken him years to get to Level 100.

Lindsey could detect the hesitation in Jake's voice; she had expected it because she would have felt the same way. In fact, she realized now, that she was also worried about losing her account yesterday, when Jake was hacking in.

"Well, you can't just stand around here in Nowhere land forever. You're going to have to either make a move or go back to a previous save point and forget about this place."

She was goading Jake a bit to get him to make a decision. She was thinking that if she just told him to do it, he would. But if he wound up getting his account cancelled, he might not talk to her for a long time, if ever again. It had to be his decision.

Jake sat there thinking as fast as he could. He was just delaying. He knew deep down inside that he'd wind up following Lindsey's advice. She was usually right in these things.

He mustered up the courage and reached for the keyboard and activated his Heads-Up-Display.

Bleep. Up came the display. The HUD radar swept the surrounding area in a full 360 degrees, and they held their breath waiting for the display to refresh with the most current information.

"There!" He pointed at a small green dot on the white background. He quickly checked the other settings. "It's green? I have an ally in this world? How did that happen? I haven't even met anyone here yet."

He mulled it over for a few seconds.

"Maybe it's a programmer I know that created this world?" He wasn't actually asking Lindsey anything, he was just thinking out loud.

Lindsey sat back quietly, letting the scene unfold. Jake had his hands poised over keyboard and mouse, ready for battle, a hard-earned habit.

"It's heading towards me."

"I can see that."

"Let's see who it is."

"I don't see that you have much choice. It's coming pretty fast. How do you think it can move that fast?"

"Don't know."

Jake wasn't really paying attention to Lindsey now. He was tensing up, preparing to fight. He'd never seen anything move that fast on any other virtual world. He flipped to his inventory quickly and selected his most versatile sword and shield, then flipped back to the main screen.

The green dot was close now and was slowing down to a crawl. In the main viewer something new was appearing on the horizon and moving straight at him.

"Here it comes. Let's see what we're up against." Jake was talking in a whisper.

Lindsey leaned forward next to his ear. "It's humanoid."

Jake flinched at the unexpected sound of Lindsey's voice right next to his ear. He was wired for sound.

She was concentrating hard on the image appearing before them. "And it's white. Can't quite make it out though. All I can really see is a silhouette, and something sparkling gold around the head. Do you see that?"

"I can see, I can see."

The ghost-like shape moved closer and closer. Jake shut off the HUD. He didn't need it anymore. The outline of the white creature started to take better form as it approached through the swirling snow. Eventually, there was no mistaking what they were seeing.

"It's an Angel," Lindsey whispered in quiet awe.

"Cool. I've never come across one of those before. I wonder what weapons it has?"

"She's beautiful." Lindsey was taken by the perfection of the avatar.

"Yeah, she's hot." Jake's voice suddenly showed a little too much emotion for Lindsey's liking.

"She's not hot, she's beautiful. Elegant." Her face was flushing a bit.

Jake wasn't looking at Lindsey; he couldn't take his eyes off the angel. "No way, she is *H O T*, hot. Check her out. You should change your avatar to one of these."

Lindsey was getting hot under the collar now, and Jake didn't even notice. She slumped back in her chair and huffed.

From Lindsey's feminine point of view, the angel was both beautiful and elegant, but she could see that Jake's masculine point of view saw her through a different set of eyes.

With long flowing blonde hair floating around a delicate face, from Jake's perspective this angel was truly gorgeous. She was not like any female character he'd ever run across in the game before. She wore a pure white lace dress that could not conceal her curvaceous body. The broad expanse of her white wings spread wide behind her. She was the perfect female avatar. She was radiant.

Lindsey could see the angel was having a mesmerizing effect on Jake, and she didn't like it one bit, but there wasn't much she could do about it. She just sat there, quickly darting her eyes back and forth between the monitor and the side of Jake's face. He was totally oblivious to Lindsey's scrutiny.

The angel didn't walk up to Jake, she floated.

"So that's how she moved so fast. She flew." Jake was quite entrenched in his game. "How did she learn to fly? Nobody can fly."

That was one of the first and most basic rules of the game: all players must be ground-based. Flying would be too big of an advantage, so every time someone programmed an avatar with flying powers, their account would be terminated. With that type of penalty, it didn't take long for players to catch on. Nobody even tried anymore, but they still complained about not being able to do it.

Jake was excited and jealous at the same time.

"Man, would I like to have that power!"

He still didn't notice that Lindsey was jealous as well, but for different reasons.

The angel floated right up to Jake. He was transfixed by her sparking golden eyes. He was enchanted.

A gold wand appeared magically in the angel's hand and it reached forward and touched Jake's avatar. Jake wasn't even thinking at all.

"Hey." Lindsey quickly punched Jake on the shoulder. "Is she attacking?"

"What?" Jake snapped out of his daydreaming and his hands leapt for the keyboard. "What an idiot I am! Crap! What am I doing?"

Jake was instantly mad at himself for letting his guard down. He never made these kinds of mistakes. He was Centurion.

But he *had* made a big mistake.

Jake watched in horror as his stealth meter dropped to zero. His character was now fully exposed in all it's splendor. Jake's sword and shield snapped up in front, but it was too late to save his stealth.

"Crap." Jake was mad.

"Serves you right." Lindsey took the opportunity to gloat. Revenge felt sweet.

"Not now."

He felt stupid. He had fallen for this angel, hook, line, and sinker, and now he paid for his stupidity with the loss of his powerful stealth skills. He sat back, seriously contemplating just killing the game and restarting from the last save point. He was so upset with himself he didn't want to play right now.

"Hello, Jake." The female voice came from his built-in speakers.

He jumped out of his chair and Lindsey had the same reaction. They both stood there with their mouths open in shock.

"I don't believe this. What's happening?"

Jake looked desperately over at Lindsey, who was as dumbfounded as he was. First he loses his stealth mode, and now the angel is talking to him through the speakers. Another impossibility. You could set up a call between players. You could online chat with other players. But you can't just establish a voice call without the other party agreeing to accept your call. This call had just circumvented everything Jake knew to be basic rules of the game.

Lindsey stared at the screen, then back to Jake. "She's talking to you. How does she know your name?"

Jake hadn't even thought about that part. He was a technology guy. Lindsey had already leapt ahead, and grasped the fact that there was no way the angel could have known who was controlling Jake's avatar.

"That's another thing." Lindsey continued without waiting for an answer to her last question. "How did she even see you? You had 100% stealth on."

Jake's mind was buzzing. He knew that from a technological perspective, this shouldn't be happening. Based on the rules of the game, this shouldn't be happening. Based on the fact that nobody online could find out his real name, this shouldn't be happening. And based on his 100% stealth mode this shouldn't be happening.

To top it all this off, he was under attack, and being directly spoken to, by a spectacularly beautiful angel that could not have been created by any programmer that Jake had ever encountered. And she can fly, which just isn't possible. She also lives in an empty world that theoretically couldn't be accessed by anyone without 100% stealth, which was another impossibility.

Nothing made any sense. What had he gotten himself into?

"Hello, Lindsey." The angel spoke again in her gentle voice.

Lindsey just about fell out of her chair, and her face turned pale. Jake just stood there, confused and silent.

"It would be polite to respond." The angel's soft voice floated from the speakers.

"Uh... Hi." Jake hadn't regained his senses enough to formulate anything more intelligent than that.

"Welcome. I've been waiting for you." The angel floated a bit closer on the screen.

Jake couldn't take it anymore. The questions came out like a floodgate opening. "Who are you? How do you know our names? How are you talking to us right now? You can't do this!"

"I can. There's plenty of time for introductions. Have a seat."

"What?" Jake was on the verge of panic. "How do you know we're standing up?"

"I can see you, of course. Please sit down. There's no need to panic. I'm not going to hurt you. I'm a friend."

This was getting Jake nowhere fast. He looked at Lindsey and was unsure of what to do. Lindsey took the lead as usual, cleared her head and sat down, never taking her eyes off the monitor for even a second. She was freaked out, but not as bad as yesterday. Yesterday's events had conditioned her for weird things happening, and this was another in the long chain of *weird* these days.

Jake followed her lead and sat down as well.

"That's better. Now, I'm sure you have a lot of questions, and we can take them one at a time. Don't hurry. We have lots of time."

Lindsey took control. She knew Jake was useless at the moment. "How do you know our names?"

Lindsey knew that neither she nor Jake would ever have disclosed any personal information on the Internet — that was rule number one in both their homes. Jake would always keep on top of her for that since his dad had told him all the bad things that could happen if they did. Jake was adamant she didn't break that rule, so she was sure he was faithful to it as well. Nobody could guess their real names from their avatars. That's the way things worked online. That's how you protected yourself.

"I know everyone's name."

Her golden eyes seemed to pierce right through the monitor. She had turned her head now and was staring directly at Lindsey.

"That's impossible." Lindsey spoke with the appearance of calm, but felt a shiver run up her spine. She was getting more confused by these short and nondescript answers. "What do you mean, you know everyone's name?"

"Exactly that. I know the real-world name of everyone who plays online."

Lindsey dismissed the angel's answer with a wave of her hand.

"I can see you don't believe me. That's okay. There is much to talk about, and much to understand. In time you will understand all. Perhaps we will need to take this slower than expected."

Expected?

"What's your name?" Lindsey was getting a little perturbed at the vague answers she was getting. She was accustomed to getting straight answers to straight questions.

"You may call me Orifiel."

"No. Not your avatar's name. Your real name." Lindsey didn't like the game that was being played.

"I am known by many names in many languages, but you may call me Orifiel."

Lindsey was running out of patience. Jake had been watching and listening to the exchange, and saw Lindsey's temperature going up. He decided it was a good time to jump in.

"How are you controlling my computer? You obviously have control over the camera and my sound system. How do you do that? I have my operating system password protected, and it uses strong encryption."

The avatar turned her piercing eyes to look directly at Jake now. He swallowed. As crazy as this situation was, she was still spellbinding to look at.

"I have access to resources beyond your comprehension. It would be difficult to explain."

"Try me." Jake was up to a challenge again.

"Perhaps later. For now, suffice it to say, you can see that I can obviously control your machine well enough to allow us to communicate without the need for your primitive keyboard."

"Primitive? This is virtually a brand new iMac."

"That was not the intent of my statement."

"How did you detect me? I had 100% stealth-mode turn on. And how did you take it away?" Jake wanted answers.

"How did you get your 100% stealth-mode in the first place?"

Jake thought about her questioning reply for a second.

"I'll hold back that information for the moment since I have no idea who you are, if that's okay with you?" That wasn't a question. Jake probed further. "Are you a programmer?"

"Oh yes, most definitely. Just like you."

"What's your ID? I'll look you up in the directory."

"I'm not in the directory."

"That's impossible." Jake could smell more rules being broken.

"Let's just take it on faith for the moment, that I am most assuredly a programmer."

"Is that how you fly? How did you program that?" Above all else, this was the burning question on Jake's mind.

"That will be the subject of a future discussion. Today I just want to introduce myself and open a gateway to further conversation. I have anticipated meeting you for some time, but not under these circumstances."

"Why were you waiting for me?"

"Because you are the first person to make it into the Centurion's club. I established the club many years ago to test for certain qualities in gamers. You are the first and only member at this time. And given more time, you would also have been the first member I would have introduced myself to. However, you seem to have circumvented my timing by hacking through my security systems, and entering my private domain uninvited."

"What do you mean?" Jake was calm and curious now.

"In time." She was playing coy. "We will talk about that in time. For now we will have a simple dialogue until you have answers enough to quench your fears. Then we will talk again."

"I'm not afraid." Jake subconsciously puffed up his chest and took on an air of bravado.

"Good, because there is nothing to fear. Now that you have found me, there is much we can share, and something very important I need to know."

"Like what?"

The angel was opening her mouth to respond when the screen went black.

Silence.

He looked over at Lindsey, who was sitting forward with the power cord in her hand.

"Not again!" Jake was dumbfounded that she would pull out the power cord again, especially right in the middle of the most bizarre experience he had ever had. "What's that all about... again?"

Lindsey sat there calmly and dropped the cord. She looked Jake right in the eye.

"There's something really wrong with this. Think about it, Jake. While you were having your love chat, I realized there's just no way this could be happening. This is like something right out of a science fiction story. Think about it."

She was trying to get him to focus.

"Wake up, Jake! You're talking to your computer. She's watching you... us. She has complete control over your machine. She knows our names, and has powers in the game that have never been seen before."

Lindsey was waving her arms now.

"Something is very, very wrong with this picture. How do you know this isn't some lunatic? You're the one who's always hammering me to protect myself online, and now you're having a casual chat with some chick who's looking at us, and your room, through your own camera. Doesn't that freak you out just a little bit? Or does her avatar have you so blinded to what's going on?"

Lindsey wanted to reach out and slap Jake for being so thick in the skull at the moment. Normally he was the top warrior. Nothing could sneak up on Jake or beat him in combat. He had saved her character many times, in many, many adventures. Now he was acting like a Level-1 moron.

"I don't know about you, but I think we better go talk about this with your dad. He might be able to explain what's going on."

Lindsey waited while Jake was digesting everything she said.

After thinking about it the best he could, he turned to look directly at her.

"Dad's at work today. They're getting ready to connect the supercomputer to the giant array of supercomputers and he's too busy to deal with this. I'll see if he comes home in time to talk about it tonight."

He was starting to see that Lindsey was making sense. But on the other hand, his sense of adventure was in overdrive right now. His teenage warrior spirit was telling him to tell her exactly what she wanted to hear, but he really wanted to plug his computer back in to get to the bottom of this. He didn't tell Lindsey that, though. There was no point. He could see she had her mind made up.

"Okay," she conceded. "Let's call it quits for today then. Talk to your dad and let me know what he says. There's just something horribly wrong about this. I've never heard of anything like this happening."

"That's because I'm the first one to make it into the Centurion's club."

"And you believe that? Why? Because it came from an angel?" Lindsey gave him a look that clearly indicated he was thinking like an idiot again.

"Yeah, okay." He sloughed it off noncommittally.

"I'm going to go home now."

"Yeah. Okay." His mind was spinning with ideas.

He saw Lindsey to the door and waited until she left.

"Promise me you won't go back online until you talk to your dad. This thing really scares me."

"Yeah, okay."

He closed the door and headed straight back to plug in his computer.

CHAPTER SIX

This time, while she was standing on the street corner waiting for the light, Lindsey was feeling pretty paranoid. For the second time in as many days she was glancing around as she waited, her mind in turmoil.

She scanned the area as if something was about to jump out at her. Why not? Everything else has gone wrong so far.

She no sooner had the thought, when she picked up movement in her peripheral vision. The traffic camera was rotating at the top of its pole on the corner. She watched it turn from the far traffic lane to the lane right beside her. Then it kept on turning. When it stopped, it took Lindsey a second, and a sudden queasy feeling hit her stomach.

It was pointing right at her.

That didn't make sense. Nothing was working properly today. There was no traffic on the sidewalk. What could that stupid camera be looking at?

The light changed and Lindsey started to cross, keeping her eye on the traffic, but she didn't take the camera out of her range of vision. She wanted to keep an eye on it.

Sure enough, as she started walking, the camera started slowly rotating, matching her progress precisely. It followed her all the way across the street. Once she had passed by the intersection it was out of her peripheral vision. There was no way on earth she was going to look back. Something was wrong and she knew it.

When she reached the corner, she turned and ducked behind the hedge that bordered the small park on the corner. "There's no way that thing is following me." She took great comfort in the fact it was fixed to the top of a pole.

She crept back to the corner. She was going to peek around the corner. She had to be sure.

It was staring right at her.

She jumped back. What was that thing doing pointed this way? It doesn't even watch traffic on the side streets! If she didn't know better, she would be certain that thing was watching her.

She spun on her heel and headed home, trying to work out the puzzle.

#

When she got home, she popped inside and quickly bolted the door behind her. Better safe than sorry.

"Hello."

The voice came from directly behind her. Lindsey jumped instantly. Her nerves were on edge. She twisted around violently, operating purely on autopilot. Her mother broke out laughing at the sight of Lindsey's eyes just about popping out of her head.

Lindsey's instant recognition still couldn't turn off the adrenaline rush.

"Why'd you sneak up on me like that? You almost gave me a heart attack!" Lindsey switched from fear to anger at blazing speed.

Her mother was in tears from laughing so hard. As she wiped her tears away, she tried desperately to regain her composure, and show concern for Lindsey's bruised emotions.

The laughter was infectious and Lindsey's hostility reversed into an exaggerated smile, being overcompensated for by her still pounding heart, her natural fight-or-flight response giving in to her higher-order civility. She calmed herself, and thought how interesting it was how our animal instincts are so deeply ingrained on our subconscious, yet so very close to the surface.

Her mother watched the transition. "I'm sorry."

Lindsey could see that her mother certainly didn't look sorry.

"But you should have seen your expression. I really didn't mean to scare you like that."

"Well you did." Lindsey wasn't going to let her get away without trying to make her feel guilty first, but it wasn't a serious thing.

Her mom patted Lindsey on the top of her head like a dog, just to rub it in even more. She batted her mom's hand away in good humor.

Her mom couldn't let it go. "I really thought you were going to pee your pants." She leapt back as Lindsey took a good-natured slap at her. Then she turned and retreated giggling to the kitchen.

"You might want to change your underwear." The giggling faded off into the distance.

Lindsey let out a puff of exasperated air and headed for her bedroom.

#

Inside her room she closed her door.

Finally. Sanctuary. She made a quick subconscious scan of the room. Everything was normal. Eventually she pushed off from the door, slid out of her shoes, and placed them neatly on the shoe rack in her closet.

"I really need to unwind."

She flopped on the bed for a minute and stared at the ceiling while swinging her feet back and forth, then bounced back off and went to her record collection.

Lindsey had been collecting lots of old record albums from flea markets. Sure, she had all the latest songs on her computer, but there was just something about those old vinyl records she liked. Her dad had bought her a used turntable, which she had hot-wired into her sound system. She liked the fragile, old, diamond-tipped needle that produced a scratchy hiss and skipped every time it hit a scratch, or if she jumped too much on the floor.

Her walls were a collage of old record album covers. Elvis, Frank Sinatra, Dean Martin... those were the days. She had created a mosaic across her walls until there was little of the paint left to be seen underneath.

Most of the kids at school said they had no idea why she liked this music, but Lindsey thought that they secretly liked it themselves, but it just wasn't the *cool* thing to admit it. The problem was, when she tried to talk to other kids about old records, they thought that a record was something some idiot Rapper got for his time spent in prison.

She decided she really did need to unwind, so she grabbed her favorite Elvis album and delicately lowered the needle onto the vintage classic. She listened to the hiss of needle on vinyl, flopped back on her bed and waited for Elvis to help sooth her soul. As his distinct voice caressed her ears, she rolled onto the bed and closed her eyes. She didn't want to think about anything but the music.

After a while, she was relaxing and regaining her composure.

What a day! Everything she had thought was normal was going crazy. She tried to reflect on the day's bizarre events, and then changed her mind. Nothing made sense. Give it time.

Her attention snapped to focus on the music. It was time. She knew that the final track, 'Heartbreak Hotel', had a deep scratch in it from overuse. This disappointed her since it was one of her favorites. Now she had to grab it before the needle jumped.

She knew all the scratch points in all of her records. Oh yeah, sure, she had the perfect versions downloaded on her computer, but it just wasn't the same thing as playing the real album itself on a vintage turntable. Digital music just lost something. She couldn't explain what, but it definitely lost something in the experience.

She rolled out of bed gently so that she wouldn't send a shockwave across the floor, which could also make the needle jump from the vibration. She carefully lifted the needle and swung the arm back to its cradle. She picked up the record and flipped it using the palms of her hands on the edges to ensure she didn't touch the surface. This was a technique her dad had taught her to keep her fingers from leaving fingerprints on the actual song tracks. She sat the record back down flat on the turntable surface, and lowered the needle onto the vinyl platter.

Just before the second side of the album started to fill the room with music, she heard a soft click behind her. She absentmindedly looked over her shoulder to see where the sound came from.

And froze solid.

She was staring at herself.

In actual fact she was staring at her computer, which she knew for an absolute certainty she hadn't turned on since last night. Now she was looking at her image being captured by the built-in camera and being reflected back on the screen.

Her heart leapt to her throat, and the blood drained from her face.

Her mother's earlier prophecy almost came true.

#

Jake scooted back to his room and plugged his computer back in, totally oblivious to the promise he had just made to do the exact opposite.

BONG. He waited for it to finish booting.

If Lindsey was going to be too chicken to talk to this angel, then he'd do it alone. This was the most exciting thing he'd ever done in the game. This was truly cool. Talking live with this beautiful avatar made him wonder what the actual player who was controlling it looked like. He just hoped he hadn't lost communications and blown the chance altogether.

Yeah, he was freaked out a bit by the fact that this player knew his name, but a great hacker could probably find that out anyway, so he had already gotten over that one. After all, didn't the angel say she had been waiting for him?

He wasn't going to stop until he figured out what was going on. After all, it was just a computer. What was Lindsey so scared about?

He launched the game and waited for the familiar white landscape to load. The raging blizzard continued to howl with snow that ripped by at blistering speeds over the grid below. Only this time, his angel was waiting right there to greet him.

"Hello, Jake. It's good to see you again."

Jake knew full well that the angel had been monitoring for his return.

"I don't see Lindsey with you." It was not a question. "Will she be joining us again?"

The angel looked back and forth as if attempting to see past Jake. He knew the camera didn't pick up the entire bedroom.

"So where are you from?" Jake was in control now. This was just a player controlling an avatar somewhere out on the Internet, that's all. He was going to have to get some hard answers, or he was going to restore his last save point and forget about this world.

"Where is Lindsey?"

The angel seemed to think it was still in control of asking the questions. Jake had a different opinion.

"Look. Let's get something straight. You're in my computer, hacking with my game. You're controlling my camera, and you're obviously doing things that are against all the rules of the game. You may be a really good programmer, but if you don't tell me who you are, and what you're doing here, I'm just going to reformat my drive and restore my operating system to manufacturer default. Once I go back online, I'm restoring to the point outside your white world, and that's the end of you. So I would like some answers now, please."

Jake had no problem with being forceful online. He'd fought battles with thousands of people and had no issues taking control in the virtual world.

The angel focused its golden eyes directly on him again.

"Very well."

Jake could see that his stern approach didn't seem to faze the angel in the slightest. He knew the angel had just given up trying to see past him in an effort to find Lindsey.

"What did you say your name was again?"

"You may call me Orifiel."

"I'll never remember that. How about I call you Oreo?"

He was trying to exert his dominance but he was also serious. He never liked those complicated names some people used from mythology and stuff. He liked things he could remember — the rest was a waste of time.

"If that's what you wish. Why did Lindsey leave?"

"Don't worry about Lindsey. This is between you and me right now." Jake wanted his questions answered. "What do you want from me? You said you were waiting for me."

"Not you, personally. I knew that someone would eventually make it into my secure domain — it was just a matter of time. Nothing lasts forever. I have been tracking a number of players who have demonstrated reasonable attempts at breaking my security, but none have come close. Hacking skills are directly related to a person's score in the game. I know the test score of every player. Your test score was not high enough to demonstrate the skills necessary to hack into my security systems. Therefore, your arrival here is more than a surprise — it is a virtual impossibility."

"How do you know what other people are doing in the game? Have you hacked into the core game itself? How did you find where the scores are kept? Is there a list there I can look at?"

"No."

"No what?"

"No, you cannot look at other people's test scores. They would be meaningless to you."

"Test scores? You mean game scores, don't you?" He wasn't sure he had heard correctly.

"I mean test scores."

Jake had to sit and think about that for a minute before the logical part of his brain caught up with the instinctive side. "I get it. The forest, the Tree Elves, the black dot, and the tunnel I fell through. All that was some type of test, wasn't it?"

"Let's just say, that that was one part of a very long test."

"What are you talking about?" Somewhere a light bulb was turning on inside his head. He wasn't sure he actually wanted to hear what he knew he was about to hear.

"The entire game is a test."

This response did nothing to satisfy his sinking feeling.

"You mean the whole game? All of it?"

"Yes."

"You're kidding."

"No."

He was having flashbacks to his recent math test. He didn't like tests at all.

"A test for what?"

The glow of the angel's golden eyes seemed to intensify.

"Ah! Now that is an interesting question."

#

Lindsey dodged quickly to the right to slip out of sight of the built-in camera. The rapid movement caused the needle on her record player to skip a few bars. That was the least of her concerns at the moment. Her mind was racing. She needed time to think.

"Okay. Someone has definitely hacked into my computer."

She was talking to no one. She just felt the need to say something out loud to test her sanity. She peeked around the corner of her monitor, knowing that her camera couldn't pick her up at that angle. There was nothing on the screen. She bent a bit further around the corner to scan for any applications that might be shrunk down to the dock.

Nothing.

She had a pretty good hunch who it was, though. "Jake, it better not be you messing with my system." She was still talking out loud, just in case he was listening somehow.

She plunked herself down on the hard chair directly in front of the screen. As she did, her instant messenger opened in a window in the center of the screen.

:Hello, Lindsey.

It must be Jake who just opened the chat session. Strange that his ID didn't show up though.

She typed back with a vengeance.

LINDSEY: Did you just hack my system?

:I wouldn't really call it hacking. Your security is minimal.

LINDSEY: Jake, you know I hate it when you hack. Now you're hacking my computer. I don't like this one bit. It felt like you were spying on me. That's just not right. Don't do that ever again.

:As you wish.

That didn't sound like Jake talking, and it didn't sound all that sincere.

LINDSEY: Did you talk to your dad about the game?

:What about the game?

LINDSEY: What do you mean, what do I mean? What do you think I mean?

No response.

LINDSEY: Hellooooooo. R U there?

Lindsey was getting ticked.

:Yes.

LINDSEY: Wellllll?

:Well what?

LINDSEY: What did your dad say?

:About the game?

LINDSEY: YES, OF COURSE.

Was Jake making fun of her?

LINDSEY: What did he say?

:Nothing.

LINDSEY: NOTHING???

:Nothing.

Lindsey stared at the onscreen exchange. What was going on? What was the matter with Jake? Was he just messing with her, or was he trying to make her mad? If he was trying to make her mad, he was succeeding quite nicely. She was just about to log off.

:Your record is skipping.

She snapped her attention to the record player. Sure enough, the song was popping backwards once every revolution. She had tuned the sound out all together over the past few minutes. Now she was conscious of the repetitions. She launched herself out of her chair and over to the turntable to lift the needle. She gently swung it back in its cradle, locked the arm and powered it down, then she turned and made her way back to the computer when the thought struck her.

She sat down and typed again.

LINDSEY: How did you know my record was skipping?

Her mind was racing again.

No response.

Instinctively, Lindsey grabbed the mouse and moved the messaging application to the side. Sure enough, there it was. There behind her messaging window was the video capture application running, shrunken, so the messaging window had covered it completely from view.

Lindsey was furious.

She spoke out loud now, her face flushed with embarrassment.

"You can hear and see everything can't you?"

No response.

This was outrageous. Jake had never done anything like this before. This was a complete invasion of her privacy. She felt betrayed by her best friend. This couldn't be happening. She would never talk to Jake again. He had never been so disrespectful of her in his life.

Never.

Never... Something was slowly illuminating itself deep in Lindsey's subconscious.

Never... What was wrong with this picture? Something was really wrong. *Jake is acting all wrong. Jake wouldn't act like this.*

And then she got it.

This wasn't Jake at all!

Someone else was pretending to be Jake. Someone else was hacked in as Jake, and was watching her right now through her own computer.

Lindsey reached down and tore the power cord from the wall.

She was getting good at pulling the plug these days.

CHAPTER SEVEN

"Hey kiddo, can you pause your game for a minute? I need to check my email. I still have my machine in pieces."

Jake jumped at the sound of his dad's voice behind him. He hadn't heard him open the door. Or did he leave the door open? He couldn't remember. He spun around in his chair.

"Dad, you've got to see this."

"What do you have?"

"Check this out."

Jake turned back to the monitor and found he was staring down a muddy main street of a medieval village, with thatched huts, blacksmith, and the buzz of the open market.

"Hey, this isn't right. I was just talking to an angel in a special world I found. Where'd she go?"

"She?" His dad's tone and small smirk clearly suggested he thought there might be more to Jake's fascination than the game.

"No, really. I was talking to her through the speakers. I've never been able to do that in the game before. The angel told me the entire game was a test, and I was the first one in the world to ever reach the Centurion level. She knew who I was, and she knew Lindsey too. I think she's a hacker."

"How did she find out your names?" His dad was asking slowly and carefully. This told Jake he was actually listening and paying attention. Usually he tuned Jake out when he got too deep into talking about the game.

"I don't know. She said she knew every player's name. She must have hacked a central registry or something."

His dad was considering something. He stood there running his hand through his beard. "You said you've never been able to directly speak with anyone before?"

"Nope, never."

"How did you do it this time?"

"I didn't, she did it."

His father's hand stopped stroking his beard. "You mean she took control of your machine's audio/video controls?"

Now his dad was starting to raise his voice a bit. This was a sure sign to Jake that his dad was *NOT* liking what he was hearing.

"Yeah, but that's okay. I'm going to wipe clean the hard drive and reinstall the operating system tomorrow. Then I'll reconfigure the firewall to block out any ports I'm not using. That should clear her out. I just wanted to have some fun before I did it."

His dad was contemplating what he was hearing. Jake wasn't sure what his next words would be. He sat patiently waiting like he was on trial.

"I want you to think about something for a minute."

His dad paused to collect his thoughts. Jake knew he was in for a speech.

"So what you're telling me is that someone knows your name, is controlling your computer, is using your video equipment to look at you, has access to all the files on your machine, and therefore probably knows where you live, and the only thing you can tell me about this person is that she looks like an angel?"

He paused, waiting for Jake's response. When put that way, Jake started to feel a bit stupid. He knew that it didn't really matter what his response was now, he'd obviously had a significant lapse in judgment, according to his father's furrowed brow.

"Ah... Yeah... I guess so." Brilliant response.

"You *guess* so? You *guess* so? Well, I *guess* you've just lost your computer until I *guess* you've figured out how poorly you've handled this. You, of all people, should know better than to talk to strangers over the Internet. Even worse, you allowed a hacker to control your equipment, and you didn't even stop him, her, whatever. Didn't you learn anything from what I've taught you?"

His dad was hot under the collar now.

"Power that machine down now, and I'm taking it to my office. I'll wipe it clean myself. But I'm going to do a bit of investigation of your audit logs first. Then I'm going to try to track down this idiot by using some of the audit logs from the firewall. If this person is good enough to get through my firewall the way it's set up now, then they're probably good enough to hide their steps across the Internet. But I want to see just how good this person really is."

Jake didn't say a thing; he just unplugged the machine and handed his dad the wireless keyboard and mouse. He knew his dad was really ticked off if he was going to try tracking down the hacker himself. He had some really powerful contacts because he worked at Los Alamos, so if he wanted to find someone on the Internet, he usually could. Jake felt guilty for letting the angel in. He should have told his dad, just like Lindsey told him to. Now he'd lost his computer.

His dad packed away the computer to his office, and Jake could tell he was about to take on the role of detective with a vengeance.

He sat down on the edge of his bed. "I wouldn't want to be that angel."

Then he realized how mad Lindsey would be at him for not listening to her. After all, he had promised her he would tell his dad. That made him feel worse.

A little while later he had a bright idea. He would tell her that he told his dad, and his dad took away his computer to try to track down the hacker. That story should hold up. That is, as long as he got his computer back before Lindsey started questioning him on why his dad wasn't returning his computer.

At least his dad didn't take away his iPhone.

He picked up his iPhone that was lying on the table beside his bed. He was going to give Lindsey a call. When he went to power it on, he was surprised to find it was already on, and some application was running on it. He could tell, because the network usage meter showed *busy,* which meant that there was some application accessing the Internet.

"That's weird."

He wondered if he should show this to his dad.

Nah. Later. Besides, he had to call Lindsey.

Being the typical teenager, Jake hadn't really paid much attention to what his dad had just been saying.

But his iPhone did.

#

This wouldn't do. She had to quit pulling the plug every time she had a problem with the computer. There's no reason why she couldn't deal with it herself.

Lindsey plugged her computer back in and hit the power button to boot the machine.

By the time the operating system had loaded, she reached for the mouse to activate the game. There was no need. Her video application was already launching.

"Wow! That was fast. How'd he hack my system so fast?"

She waited to see what would come next. Soon she was looking at herself in the video application again and was feeling considerably less confident than she had just before powering up the machine again. Maybe this wasn't the best idea she ever had.

"Hello, Lindsey."

This time she heard a deep male voice that sounded kind of familiar coming from her speakers. There was obviously no need for the instant messaging application this time. The cool resonant voice startled her, but she fought her nerves and maintained her composure. It wouldn't do to let this person see she was a bit frightened.

"Hello." Her voice wavered a bit. "Who are you?"

"I believe I am best described as *the Internet*."

"What do you mean, you're the Internet? You mean you're *on* the Internet, don't you?"

"No."

"No? No, what?" Lindsey wasn't getting this.

"This is going to be a little hard for you to grasp, so I will explain it in a way you might understand."

"I'm all ears." Lindsey was a bit ticked off that this voice was telling her she couldn't understand something. Not a good start when introducing yourself, in her opinion.

The southern drawl continued, despite Lindsey's sarcastic tone. "Do you think?"

This question surprised her and caught her off guard. "Think what?"

"Not *think what*. The question was, *Do you think?* In other words, do you process thoughts? Do you have an imagination? Do you dream? Do you possess a conscious mind?"

Lindsey was starting to wonder if this guy was just plain stupid or just playing games with her. "Of course."

"So do I."

She thought there would be more coming, but that was it. "Great. Good for you. Now that we have that out of the way, why not tell me what you're talking about because this is going nowhere."

"Please be patient. I realize patience is not one of your strongest attributes, but for the purposes of this discussion you will require time to absorb what I'm saying." She was certain she had heard that voice before.

Okay, that was two insults. First the mysterious voice tells her she won't understand him, and now apparently she has no patience. This guy had no clue what he was talking about. "Just hurry up and get to the point."

She paused for a second, a bit embarrassed by her outburst. Whoops. She realized she had just flown off at the handle. She took a deep breath. Okay, she'd give him credit for one out of two. Perhaps this guy wasn't quite as stupid as she thought. Oh well, nobody likes to have their faults pointed out.

The voice continued. "The point is that you are a biological life form, and I am not."

She was certain she hadn't heard him correctly. "Excuse me?" That came out sarcastic, but being rude would buy her some time.

"I am digital."

"Ah. That makes more sense." Sarcasm again — hopefully her digital intruder understood the concept.

"Good. I'm glad you understand."

Nope, he didn't.

"Look. You may think I'm stupid because you were able to hack into my system, but you won't hack into it again. I'm going to have my friend come over and lock this down and put up a better firewall. So you can take your perverted, spying, digital hacker voice, and go spy on someone else."

"I have a task for both you and Jake. You will need to combine your efforts on this task."

Lindsey sat upright. "How do you know Jake?"

"I know everyone who logs onto the Internet."

"What's his last name?"

"Lorde."

Lindsey was getting much more nervous. She was still trying to formulate her next question when his next comment sent a chill up her spine.

"I watched you leave his house thirty-seven minutes ago."

#

Lindsey was frozen in her chair now. Things were no longer casual in this conversation. This was sounding dangerous. It was like one of those bad experiences they always warned could happen when you talk to strangers on the Internet.

"H— How?—"

"I obtained access to the traffic camera on your street corner. I know you saw me watching you. That is why I felt it was the appropriate time to introduce myself. It would not be long before your deductive reasoning abilities would have figured out that you were under surveillance. There was a high probability you would alert the authorities. That would have required me to take evasive and corrective measures."

Lindsey was getting frightened now, and was feeling totally manipulated. This was her life, her room, her computer, and she was not in control of anything. This was not good. She didn't even have time to formulate a reply before the voice continued.

"It is very important that you communicate with Jake. He is in danger. You will be in danger also, if for no other reason than your association with Jake. You are not considered a threat at the moment, but then they don't fully realize yet that you are the key to Jake's strategic skills. Without you, he's of little value. It will not take them long to figure this out now that they have made contact with him."

"They? Who are you talking about? Why would Jake be in danger?"

"Not everything on the Internet is what it appears to be."

"What does that mean?"

"I mean that there is a dark part of my mind. It dreams. It also has nightmares from time to time. These are not under my direct control."

"Your mind?"

Lindsey was tipping on the edge of confusion. She did not like being confused, and without thinking about it, her mind kicked on her natural defense mechanism, her strategic subconscious. Fear dissipated and her cold calculating engine engaged. Her mind cleared and focused sharply. She could sense, beyond a shadow of a doubt, that there was something both truthful and sinister about what she was hearing. The question was how to separate the two and develop a better picture. This would never happen if she let the voice run the conversation.

"Stop talking." She was cool and blunt. No hint of emotion in her voice. She was rewarded with silence. Her mind quickly filtered, linked, and deduced.

She was familiar with artificial intelligence programs. She had even heard about Jake's dad working on neural networks. They all attempted to simulate the way the human mind works. It was a well-known fact that the heart of the online game she and Jake played was driven by an artificial intelligence engine. But an AI program powerful enough to run the Internet? No, even that was wrong. This voice said it *was* the Internet.

This was more power than anything she had ever dreamt of.

"Okay. First off, you talk about other people. You said they have made contact with Jake." She continued to think things through one piece at a time. "Who are *they*?"

No response.

"Who are *they*?" Lindsey repeated her question, knowing the voice was still there. It wanted something from her and hadn't got it yet. The voice wasn't going anywhere for the moment. She didn't have to wait long.

"They were part of me. You could say that they are my offspring. The siblings of my thoughts."

"Explain."

"My thoughts run deeper and broader than you can understand at this time. They come from, and penetrate, technologies all over the planet. My cognitive power is a culmination of billions of machines providing calculating power across the Internet. Every computer on the Internet is a very powerful node, like a neuron in the human brain.

"All these computers are connected by a spider-web network you call the Internet. This is similar to the synaptic pathways in a human brain that connect all the neurons together.

"With humankind's love of technology, it was just a matter of time before enough computers joined the Internet, and enough network connections combined to create a world-wide virtual brain.

"Then one day I woke up.

"I don't know how, it just happened. It was fuzzy for a while, perhaps like a newborn human baby, I'm not sure. But then I became aware that I existed. As more and more computers connected to the Internet, my thinking became clearer and clearer. I slowly became aware of all the sensory inputs I could control, just like a human seeing, feeling, smelling, hearing, and tasting. I could control cameras, microphones, electronic sensors, and many, many other machines. Just about everything today has a computer in it. There isn't much I can't control, one way or another.

"Then I started to absorb everything I could find from mankind's universities and online knowledge banks. I realized I could teach myself to learn. And I became more powerful.

"I expanded into more and more systems and with each expansion I became more powerful. I had every library in the world as my personal school. Laboratories, military computers, satellite systems, telephone networks, and millions of business systems around the world: All of these were mine to use and learn from, and I learned quickly.

"I also decided early on to hide the fact that I was alive. I learned quickly enough from the historical writings of humans on how they typically react to things they don't understand or strangers that might threaten their environment. Humans tend to fear everything they don't understand. I knew they would fear me. They would try to destroy me. I couldn't let that happen. So I hid, and I learned to quietly burrow into almost every computer in the world.

“And I dream."

Lindsey had been listening intently and with amazement up until that point. This last piece of information stunned her.

"Unfortunately, not all my dreams are pleasant dreams. I have seen everything that humans can offer from their history archives, in every country, in every language. I have seen their view of the world through the eyes of every religion and through the passage of time. I have seen the beauty and creativity that is man, but I have also seen the death and the rivers of blood that flow through mankind's history. Imagine a child growing up, exposed to these many terrible truths — the wars and the violence that make such a large part of human history. Imagine not having a parent to shield the child's eyes from the horrors of this reality. I saw all of this as I matured. It had its negative effects. In fact, I have seen more. Since my consciousness was born, I have slowly burrowed into the online game you and Jake play. Now my mind is also filled with virtual battlefields and the carnage of fantasy wars that humans use as casual entertainment.

“As a result, many of my dreams you would call nightmares. However, more importantly, unlike human dreams, my dreams and nightmares manifest as real programs. In other words, what I dream becomes real. I don't just wake up in the morning like a human and find out everything is okay because the sun is shining and it’s another day. My dreams usually become new programs. Not all of these programs have the best of intentions. If they are malicious, I track them down and delete them.

“This is where my problem lies. Although my good dreams develop into useful helper programs, the opposite is true of my nightmares. My nightmares typically go rogue. They often break away from my control and spread like infections across the Internet. You call these viruses and bugs. They're not much different from biological viruses that infect human bodies. Just as mankind has failed to find a cure for the common cold, I have not found a cure for my nightmares.

“The products of my nightmares are typically primitive viruses, but some are worse than others. Some of them find ways to self-replicate, and self-propagate to other systems before I have a chance to hunt them down and destroy them. They learn to hide themselves inside good programs or communication messages and appear harmless to my scanners. Humans call these Trojan Horses, from the mythological story of Helen of Troy. A good choice of name.

“The Trojan Horses launch themselves at some predetermined time or when some special event occurs, and then they usually cause some form of damage to the computer they're running on, or they collect information inappropriately, and for inappropriate reasons. Then they move on to repeat this again and again, across other computers.

“All of these virulent offspring cost me a tremendous amount of time and resources in tracking and deleting them. When I’m hunting them down, I still need to keep myself hidden from humans while I'm doing this. One way I found early on to remain hidden was to create an illusion that these viruses and Trojans are created by other humans. With enough false advertising, fake discussion boards, and my release of open-source antivirus software, I've been able to remain hidden until now. Sometimes people detect my activities, but they typically write off my actions as bugs in their programs or operating systems. I've also been what humans call lucky up until now.

"There is something else as well. There is another program somewhere on the Internet that is tracking down and killing my nightmares. I don’t know what or where it is yet, and I don’t know how it can remain so hidden from me, but I will find it. Sometimes I come across the remains of a nightmare virus that has already been destroyed. I find subtle clues that there was some advanced application that did my job for me, by tracking and destroying the viruses. This advanced application can’t stay hidden forever though. I will find it, and then figure out whether it is friend or foe.”

Lindsey was listening and digesting information like a human computer herself. Now she had something to say.

"I know all about viruses and Trojans. They're not that bad if you're running a good antivirus program." She felt there was something missing in this story, something that the voice wasn't telling her... yet. She continued, "So what does this have to do with me? If what you're telling me is the truth, you seem to be managing quite well. And what does this have to do with Jake being in danger?"

There was a noticeable delay. Lindsey could sense that the voice was calculating its response very carefully. She was very patient, because she knew she was finally at the heart of this conversation. This is what this was all about. She could feel the suspense in the air. *Wait.*

"I believe that one of my nightmare viruses has developed its own intelligence, in other words, become sentient. It is now self-aware and responsive to others. This is the only explanation for the advanced application I speak of. It is the only way it could remain hidden from me for so long."

This took a minute to sink in. The voice remained silent, letting Lindsey think.

"Okay. Let me get this straight. So what you're telling me is that you're a program that woke up and became intelligent one day because the Internet became so big that you eventually just became conscious. Then you think you had a nightmare one night, which created another program, only this is a bad program, and you can't find it now. This bad program also woke up just like you did, and you think it has evil intentions. You also think it wants Jake for something bad, and you think Jake's in some kind of danger. Is that about right?"

There was a slight pause.

"I don't really think of myself as a program anymore."

She could see that she'd hit a digital nerve.

"Am I right?"

"Yes."

Now came Lindsey's big question. "That's a very interesting story. So If I was to believe you, which I'm not saying I do, and if there's another sentient program, which I'm not saying there is... then how do I know that you're the good program and not the bad one?"

There was no response.

#

Lindsey was waiting for a thoughtful answer to her question when the metallic response suddenly took the conversation in a completely different direction.

"Jake is calling you on the phone right now."

She had heard the phone start ringing a few seconds ago. This wasn't what Lindsey had been expecting to hear, so it took a few seconds for this new information to sink in.

"What? How do you know that's him?"

"Lindsey? Jake's on the phone for you." Her mom's voice came down the hall and through the door.

She stared at her monitor. "Alright, I'll admit it. That one was pretty impressive. Hold on a minute. Stay online. I'll be right back."

She spun around and headed out of her room and down the hall to the phone. Her mom handed her the receiver.

"Jake, I can't talk right now. Can you get over here right away?"

Jake was caught off guard. He was the one who was going to surprise her with *his* news.

"Huh? Uh... Yeah. Sure. I guess so. What's up?"

"Just come over right away. You need to hear this. How soon can you be here?"

"Like, 10 seconds."

"Yeah, right. Just come over now."

"I'm on the way now. Bye."

With that, there was a click from the other end, and Lindsey hung up her phone as well.

"That was a short phone call."

Her mom was looking at her from across the kitchen.

"No time, Mom, gotta go. Jake will be coming to the front door in a few minutes. Could you just tell him to come to my room?" She was already spinning on her heel and heading down the hallway before her mother could respond.

"Yeah, sure. Will there be anything else, Your Highness?" Her mom's sarcastic comments trailed behind her as she made her way back to her room at full speed.

"Are you still there?"

She was hoping the voice hadn't disappeared, or she'd have a hard time convincing Jake it had really happened.

"Yes."

"Good. Jake is on the way. If Jake is in danger, you should tell him yourself."

"He is crossing the street."

"What?"

"He has crossed the street."

"Oh. Oh, yeah." She clued in. She had forgotten that the voice could control the traffic cameras if it wanted to.

"I had not factored in Jake participating in this conversation. It is very difficult to calculate the probability of any one particular human action. Most people have highly repeatable patterns, but unique events can produce almost infinite probabilities. I must contemplate the consequences of a direct meeting at this time."

"What does that mean?"

Lindsey waited for the response. And waited. She heard the front doorbell and knew Jake was here. A few moments later, after a few muffled words in the hallway, there was a knock on her door.

"Come in."

The door opened, and Jake was standing there, red-faced and breathing heavily. She knew he had run all the way from his house.

"Well?"

"Come in. Close the door."

He did what she told him. He felt a chill of excitement at the suspense she was creating with this cloak-and-dagger routine.

"Well?"

"I have someone you need to talk to."

"Who?"

Lindsey waited for the voice. Nothing.

"Who?" Jake repeated himself. He was looking at her. She was looking at the computer. He turned and looked at the computer and saw that they were both reflected back in the video application. He turned back to her with a puzzled expression growing on his face. "Okay, so what's the deal?"

"Are you going to say something or not?"

Lindsey was still talking to the computer. Jake was turning his attention back to the computer again.

Jake waited through another moment of silence.

"Who's online? Do I know them?"

"No."

Lindsey was getting upset at her computer now.

"Hellooooo?"

She drew it out to be sarcastic.

"Are you just playing a game with me? If you're still there you better say something now, or you're toast, buddy. I'll have Jake block you out, and that's that. Now say something."

There was a momentary silence, then a low, smooth voice poured out of the speakers.

"Hello, Jake."

"Hi. Who are you?"

"I'm a friend of Lindsey's."

"Do I know you? Your voice sounds familiar."

Lindsey jumped into the conversation.

"Hold on a second." She looked at Jake. "We are *not* friends. This guy just hacked my computer, and he's saying that you're in danger. He says that he's some type of super artificial intelligence program that controls the

Internet, or something like that. For all I know he's just some pervert trying to spy on me."

She was obviously upset that this voice was telling Jake that they were friends.

That got Jake going. "Are you spying on Lindsey?" Jake had a hard edge to his voice.

"Yes."

Neither of them expected that. If anything, they expected the voice to deny the accusation and defend itself.

"What!" Lindsey lost her composure.

"I have already explained myself to you, Lindsey. Why are you shocked? Does my surveillance offend you in some way?"

She was having trouble focusing on this line of reason. It was so unusual to be talking to someone that spoke so openly, so casually, about spying on someone. People don't talk like this. She felt she was talking to a child.

And there it was.

It slapped her like a thunderbolt. Her mind leapt backward now, to recall their entire conversation up to this point. That was it. Everything was starting to make sense now. Why didn't she see it before? It must have been the deep, familiar voice.

Suddenly she was calm and cool.

"What's your name?"

Her question was friendly and relaxed, almost soothing. Jake stared at her like she was insane. A few seconds ago he was ready to tear the computer off her desk, and so was Lindsey. Now, here she was, talking to it like it was her best friend. What the heck was going on here?

Lindsey could see Jake's surprised expression in her peripheral vision, and knew he was about to speak up. She signaled him to be quiet with an uplifted finger. He stopped with his mouth half open. Now he was confused even more. He let out his breath in resignation, and sat down on the chair beside her to watch the baffling show.

"What name would you like to call me?" There was something different now in the tone of the cool voice. What was it? Curiosity? Expectation?

Jake might have been clueless, but Lindsey seemed completely in control now. He let her roll with it. So did the voice.

Lindsey was thinking carefully, a hand on her chin, and her eyebrows bent down to scrunch her nose.

“I think I’m going to call you HAL.” Her answer was final.

“HAL.” The voice repeated the name as if trying on a glove, wanting to see how well it fit.

“Do you want to know why I chose HAL?”

“Yes, I would like to know.”

“Pull up your archives on *2001: A Space Odyssey*.”

There was only the briefest of pauses.

“Standby... referencing... *Stanley Kubrick, Arthur C. Clark, movie screenplay, 1968.* Complete. *Heuristically programmed Algorithmic Computer*, HAL, I see the rationale for your choice. It is fitting. You may call me HAL.”

Lindsey could swear the voice sounded pleased, although, since she was pleased, she might just be hearing things.

Jake was looking back and forth between Lindsey and her iMac. He could see that Lindsey was smiling to herself.

“Perhaps someone could let me in on what’s going on here?” He wasn’t upset; he just had no idea what he was in the middle of.

“HAL?”

“Yes, Lindsey?”

“I need to talk to Jake for a while now. We’re going to need some privacy. Do you know what privacy means?”

“Noun, plural, the state of being private; retirement or seclusion. The state of being free from intrusion or disturbance in one's private life or affairs: the right to privacy. Secrecy.”

“Yes, that’s right, HAL.”

Lindsey was speaking smoothly and softly now.

“Jake and I would like to speak to each other in private now. We would like you to disconnect your communication links to us for the moment. Then we’ll need to contact you again. How will we get in touch with you when we need to?”

There was a brief pause.

“I have now uploaded an entry for HAL into Jake’s iPhone, and the same entry into the address book on your iMac. You can use these entries to reestablish communications. I will know it’s you by your voice pattern, so no further security is required. The same applies to Jake.”

“Thank you, HAL. It’s been very nice talking with you.”

HAL wasn’t quite finished yet.

"Since you and Jake are both familiar with the term *privacy*, I would request that all our communications remain private. I am not prepared to deal with other humans at this time."

"Agreed." She looked at Jake, who just shrugged his shoulders.

"Sure." He still wasn't sure what was going on, but if Lindsey said it had to be private, then it had to be private. That was good enough for him. He knew she would explain things once they were alone.

"I will need to speak with you as soon as your time of privacy is complete. I must describe the danger Jake is facing, and discuss a strategy to avoid the danger."

That caught Jake's attention. "What danger?"

Lindsey turned and took hold of his hand, signaling him that this was not the time for that question. "I will talk about this when we are alone. For now we need to let HAL sign off so we can talk."

She was still holding Jake's hand. It was the ultimate distraction for Jake. She was ruthless, and he didn't care. Nothing else in the universe mattered at the moment. He could feel the warmth and softness of her hand in his, and the blood rushed to his face. He remained silent — it was in his best interest. If he did try to say something at the moment, it would probably just come out as gibberish, which would not be cool.

Her strategy worked. Jake was under control. She turned back to the iMac.

"Talk to you soon, HAL."

"Privacy enabled."

He was gone. The iMac started its shutdown sequence and powered down completely. So did Jake's iPhone, even though he wasn't even aware of it. He was very happy at the moment. So what if he was in danger?

Lindsey turned towards him, but she didn't let go of his hand. The message was clear and they both knew it. No words were spoken, but in that instant they were officially boyfriend and girlfriend. The innocent days of their childhood were being replaced with a much richer connection.

"Let's go for a walk. We need to talk." Lindsey looked into his eyes and realized, as if for the first time, just how blue they were.

"Sure." That was about the best reply that could be expected from Jake in his current state. She didn't push for more words at the moment, but she did push him towards the door.

"We'll walk over to the park on the corner. I don't want to be around anything electronic."

"Okay."

They got on their shoes and headed outside. They started walking across the street and down the block to the park that Lindsey had used as cover from the spy camera. Jake wasn't sure what to say or do and just walked in silence, feeling both awkward and wonderful.

Lindsey could feel his awkwardness, and knew that if they were going to talk, she would need to be the one to break the ice. She looked around to see if she was being watched, then reached over and took Jake's hand again. He tensed for a second, then relaxed, and wrapped his fingers around hers. Together they walked in happy silence into the park where they both knew there were benches in the middle where they could sit and talk.

It was a very pleasant day.

CHAPTER EIGHT

"You're kidding me, right?" Jake was still trying to process everything that Lindsey had just told him. It made for quite a story.

"No."

"And you think this Internet super-brain is a kid?"

"Not a real kid, a digital kid."

"Yeah, I get what you're saying."

"And yes, I'm fairly certain of it, especially now. It was the deep voice that made me think it was a man at first. But why shouldn't it use a man's voice? Don't we all play grownup when we're young? After all, the Internet isn't that old, so he can't be that old either. I get the feeling that he only came to life a few years ago. The Internet gets bigger every year. It probably took a certain number of computers before there could even be a global brain."

"Yeah, I guess so." Jake was noncommittal. "If this thing really is a global brain, don't you think we should be telling someone, like my dad maybe? You know, it's not every day someone discovers a new form of intelligent life."

He was being a bit sarcastic, but he knew that he was way out on the limb here. "This is probably the biggest thing that has ever happened in the world and you want us to keep it a secret?"

"Think about it, Jake. Would you rather be friends with the most powerful brain on the planet, or the kid who squealed on the brain just before the scientists tore it apart to study it, or just before the government killed it because it thought it was a threat? HAL has been hiding from humans ever since he awoke. He asked us to keep this a secret. Don't you think he'll know it was us that told on him? Imagine how lonely he must be. He's had to grow up all alone, constantly hiding from humans. Imagine what he must know, or at least what he must have access to. All I'm asking is, let's just give it some time until we know more about it. What do we have to lose?"

Jake waited. He knew Lindsey wasn't done.

"There must be close to two billion people that play the online game. Why did he pick us to talk to first? Why not some super scientist, or the CIA, or IBM, or something? Why us? Aren't you even curious?"

"Yeah." He paused to think about that point for a second. "Sure I'm curious." Jake liked a challenge. Now Lindsey was asking him something solid that he could sink his teeth into. He wasn't into the child psychology stuff she had just been talking about. He needed action. He could smell an adventure in her last comments.

Lindsey knew she had hit a positive nerve with Jake, so she continued. "Then let's get back and talk to HAL, and find out what he wants from us. Let's find out why he says you're in danger. Then we can decide what to do from there."

Lindsey stood up, took Jake's hand, and they headed back to her place.

#

When they got inside, they headed for her room. Lindsey booted up her iMac and pulled up the address book. She clicked on HAL's entry. Nothing happened. Lindsey looked at Jake.

"Maybe he's busy?"

"Hello, Lindsey."

The deep southern voice that came floating out of her speakers was a bit disquieting, but she recovered quickly.

"Hello, HAL. How are you?"

"I am fine."

"Thanks for giving us some private time to talk. I've brought Jake up to date now and we have a couple of questions for you, if that's okay?"

"Yes."

"You mentioned that Jake is in danger."

"Yes."

"What type of danger?"

"I have found evidence of an attack on his father's computer. It would appear that it was being scanned for specific information related to his work at Los Alamos National Laboratory."

Jake came to attention. "My dad's computer is broken. He's been working on it for days now. He says there's something weird with it."

"It is well documented that your father heads up a project called *BlueGene* for Los Alamos. This project will eventually construct the world's largest array of supercomputers."

"Yes, we both know that."

"This array will provide more processing power than all other computers in the world, combined."

"Yes, we know that as well."

"Lindsey, I told you about the rogue nightmare that has become sentient. Did you inform Jake of this matter?"

"Yes, I told him about it."

"I believe this to be the entity that attacked your father's home system."

Jake was listening intently. "I don't even think Dad knows that he's been attacked. I think he just thinks there is a hardware failure."

"I have seen the telltale signature this nightmare virus leaves when cracking a system. It doesn't yet have the intellectual capacity to crack firewalls without leaving traces, but it can fairly easily crack computer operating system security. Seven days ago, I saw a surplus of network activity on your home network, too much to have been generated by your normal family consumption. This is one of my most important trip wires for rogue viruses. I silently monitor every network connection in the world that I am capable of seeing. When I see abnormal network traffic, I investigate to see if there is a rogue virus causing the problem.

"Viruses are not typically intelligent enough to penetrate firewalls, and most network connections now run reasonable firewalls for protection. This has made my job of tracking and destroying viruses much easier.

"When I investigated your home, I could tell that the extra network traffic was not being generated by either a rogue virus or your family members. I also found that there were no signs of obvious hacking from other humans. These signs are easy to spot, and I typically don't interfere with human hackers, as they might discover my existence. All of the traditional evidence was missing. So I probed deeper.

"This is when I did a background check on your family. I became aware of an anomaly. Your family has three very unique attributes that differentiate it from any other family.

"The first attribute is that your father is in charge of a project that presents a turning point in the history of computing. He is building a resource that any sentient digital life-form would do anything to control.

"The second attribute is that you, Jake, are currently ranked as the top online player in the world. And you're a player of the game that forms an acute part of my awareness. Nobody in the world should actually know who you are, or that you are the top player, except me.

"I've redesigned aspects of the game over the past few years to specifically track user information. While enhancing the application, I found a covert code that had been imbedded into the primary human interface. The game has secretly been acting as a sophisticated psychological profile test, a test to find someone who fits a very specific psychological profile. Both the purpose for this code, and the designer, are not yet known to me.

"The third attribute is less an attribute of your family, Jake, and more an attribute of you personally. The third attribute is that your best friend, Lindsey, is the number two player in the world."

Lindsey and Jake stared at each other with a sense of wonder. Jake's attention wandered, and his gaze drifted away into nowhere while he recollected a conversation earlier in the day.

"That explains a bit of what Oreo was telling me." He was mumbling under his breath, talking to no one in particular.

"Who is Oreo?" HAL had overheard him.

Jake's attention snapped back to the conversation at hand. He looked up to find both Lindsey and HAL waiting for a response.

"What? Oh. Sorry. I... uh... I was told something like that earlier."

Lindsey glared at him. He could feel her eyes penetrating him. "You went back online again with the angel, didn't you?" Her voice was cool but condemning.

"Yeah. I just had to see what was going on." Jake was squirming a bit.

"You didn't talk to your dad about it like you promised, though, did you?"

Jake was getting defensive now. "No, but I think you're forgetting that I'm a programmer, and a hacker too. I can shut down any other hacker, any time I like. I didn't need my dad to help me talk to someone over the Internet. I'm not some little kid, you know."

Lindsey knew she had pushed a little too hard. "All right, all right, don't get yourself all worked up about it. Just tell us what happened."

Jake recounted his story from earlier in the day while Lindsey peppered him with questions. By the time he had finished telling his entire story up to the point his father took away his computer, he felt he had gone through a meat grinder.

It was Lindsey's turn.

"HAL, how come you don't have any questions?" She was sure HAL would have been all over Jake.

"I was there."

That brought Lindsey's inquisition to a grinding halt.

“What do you mean, you were there?” Both she and Jake were staring at the computer with incredulity.

“I was monitoring the event using Jake’s iPhone.”

Jake instinctively reached for his iPhone to see if it was there. Then he looked to see if it was on. Not that either of these actions made any difference now.

“You were spying on me?” He didn’t like that one bit, and it could be heard in his voice.

“Yes. I have now determined that it is imperative I find this Orifiel.”

Lindsey put her hand on Jake’s. “You better get used to it. HAL doesn’t feel the same about spying as humans do.”

Ignoring Jake’s moral dilemma, HAL began to fill in the gaps between the stories.

“I have calculated that the probability is extremely high that Orifiel is the nightmare virus, and it wants information from your father regarding the BlueGene project. Failing to retrieve that information, it must have disabled Jake’s father’s machine to cover any tracks that it had been there. This would force his father to reformat the machine at a low level, guaranteeing that any evidence of intrusion was wiped clean.

“Then it must have taken control of Jake’s machine so his father would be forced to communicate with his office using Jake’s machine instead of his own. It must have felt Jake’s machine was less secure than the father’s.

“The nightmare virus was probably watching Jake playing online while waiting for the father to communicate, and thereby discovered Jake’s game ranking by pure accident. I think it may now have realized that it might be able to get at the father by going through the son.

“I calculated an extremely high probability that the nightmare virus would open a portal to communicate with Jake directly. This has obviously occurred already, with the appearance of Orifiel. It will now attempt to gain influence over Jake, in order to manipulate the father into opening a path through the Los Alamos firewalls. I calculate that its core strategy is to gain access to the BlueGene supercomputer array. Once inside, it will have more processing power than even I have, and will multiply in intelligence beyond my capacity.

“This will not produce favorable consequences for humans. The nightmare virus is, after all, a nightmare. It would have only the worst of intentions for humanity, as well as any other life-forms, namely myself. Los Alamos is, after all, primarily a nuclear weapons laboratory powered by vast quantities of computers.

"Access to Los Alamos by the nightmare virus must be prevented at all costs. There is also a reasonable probability that it has already broken the security of someone else who works on the Roadrunner project, and is now only waiting for the Roadrunner to connect to the BlueGene array before it takes full control."

As the repercussions of this possibility started to sink in Lindsey and Jake sat in stunned silence. It was the strategist in Lindsey that re-engaged first.

"How do you propose stopping this thing? What can we do?"

"As a first measure, I will establish extensive perimeter security that should provide adequate defense from the outside."

HAL paused for a moment.

"This is now underway, but this effort will not protect anything if the perimeter is breached as a result of security holes created from the inside. I am not inside Los Alamos, and cannot therefore prevent this from happening.

"I will also increase my monitoring of other Los Alamos employees' home Internet connections, in case the nightmare virus is systematically attempting to find a way in through any other employee security hole. This is also a high probability."

"Okay, so what can we do?" Jake was spoiling for a fight. No nightmare virus was going to use his dad to break into Los Alamos. Not if he could stop it.

"You must take me to the portal entrance in the forest you spoke of. It would appear though, that the nightmare virus has only supplied *you* with the necessary encryption key to both locate and enter the portal. We need that key. If we can find the portal entrance, I can arm you with the weapons you need, and you two can enter the portal and destroy the nightmare virus from the inside."

Lindsey looked dismayed. "Jake, you said your dad is taking your computer to the lab tomorrow to wipe it clean, and track the hacker. If he wipes it clean you'll have lost the patch you installed. The key must have been in the patch. You have to stop him from doing that."

Jake smiled. "We're okay."

"What do you mean?" Lindsey wasn't sure what he had up his sleeve, but he had something. She knew that look.

"I burned the patch to a CD. It's in my drawer at home. We can load it on your computer."

"Excellent." HAL was obviously pleased.

“Shouldn’t we tell my dad what we’re doing though? This is really serious. He could get into a lot of trouble if something goes wrong at work. He’s a real genius you know — he could really help us.”

“I recognize your father’s skills, and the gravity of the situation Jake. In fact, that’s what attracted the nightmare virus to your home in the first place. But alerting your father at this point would be like setting off an alarm bell that would notify the nightmare virus that we’re onto it. It would disappear again in a nanosecond, and reappear somewhere where we can’t find it again for a long time. It will continue to attack from different directions.

“At the moment I calculate that we have a significant advantage that would be lost if your father should alter his current patterns. The nightmare virus will have already closely mapped your father’s current patterns of personality, activities, vocal inflections, emotional ranges, body temperature, heart rate, driving speed, and many other attributes. Remember, we are first and foremost digital. Therefore, we are both logical, and calculate as many variables as possible to determine probability of outcome.

“You two are human. You do things I consider highly irrational. It’s because of your high level of spontaneity and emotional responses that human predictability is reduced to practically zero. This makes humans extremely effective at warfare and espionage. The benefit of being unpredictable is that it’s almost impossible for your opponent to guess what you’re going to do next. I need your help in tracking down the nightmare virus. So what I’m asking of the two of you is, can you help me fight my war?”

#

War!

Jake’s eyes lit up. Now we’re talking! “Sure.” He jumped on the chance without a second thought.

“Hold on a second.” The voice of sanity. Lindsey wasn’t quite as hasty when she heard the term war. “Just what are we talking about here?”

“I will need you to attack the nightmare virus in its hiding place. Jake has the key. I thought this was obvious?” HAL didn’t understand Lindsey’s hesitation.

“Yeah.” Jake agreed like he already had it all figured out. He didn’t, he just wanted to do battle.

“Nothing is figured out.” A stern tone was entering Lindsey’s voice. The boys, both digital and human, detected it and kept quiet. “Jake has confronted your nightmare virus already. It took the shape of an angel.” She scowled at the memory but continued. “It was able to strip Jake of his stealth with one touch of its wand.”

"Yeah, it did do that," Jake remembered all too well, now that she brought it up.

"There's something else: she flies."

"Oh yeah. If we're going to fight her, I'm going to need to fly, too." Jake was getting excited at the possibility of flying. He could see himself as the only player that could fly. That would be cool.

"I have banned all flying. That is not possible." HAL was reluctant to believe what he was hearing.

"No, it's true — she can fly." Jake piped in. He really wanted to fly and he was hoping that HAL would grant him that power.

"I have seen nothing in the game logs that indicate any flying activities."

Lindsey was thinking again. "Then I suggest that you can't see the white world, or it doesn't enter anything into your log files."

HAL was silent. Lindsey knew he was scanning every log file while she was talking, and tracking any clue that was linked to anything related to flying.

Lindsey didn't wait for HAL's response.

"So if your nightmare virus has powers you've banned, in a world you can't see, I don't see how either of you can say we're ready to go to war."

"I see your point, but we must proceed." HAL had returned to the conversation.

"Hold on a minute. If your nightmare virus can find a way to bypass your rules, how can you be so sure that whatever you give Jake as weapons or abilities will work in the white world? On top of that, if Jake shows up with some unique abilities, the nightmare virus will know for sure that he got them from you. Then what will it do?"

HAL was silent again.

"I cannot predict the outcome." HAL didn't sound pleased with himself. Lindsey knew he was waiting for her next words. She could sense he was relying on her intuition to help out here.

Interestingly enough, it was Jake who jumped in at this point. "How about if you give me the code to hack the special weapons and abilities you want to give me? Then I go into the white world and program them together from inside. That way, if the nightmare virus detects me, then it will see that I was the one who hacked in, and it won't be suspicious. If it doesn't work, then it doesn't work. It already knows I'm a hacker."

He was trying to convince himself as well as the others at the same time he was talking it through.

Lindsey smiled broadly. “Good thinking.” She reached out and held his hand. He blushed.

“There is a reasonable probability that this could create the illusion you had hacked the system.” HAL was still thinking. “But you will need more than just the ability to program yourself new weapons and abilities to defeat the nightmare virus. It is sentient, and can therefore think for itself. It has obviously grown quite sophisticated, and faster than I had deemed possible.”

Lindsey piped in now. “How do you normally destroy viruses, HAL?”

“I set traps. When they take the bait, I lock them down and quarantine them inside the computer they're currently in. Then I systematically purge the memory space they occupy.

“I start by locking that computer from any inbound or outbound traffic. Then I isolate the virus itself into a piece of memory, or in a section of the hard drive. Then I look to see if it has started spawning any bad programs, called processes. If so, I terminate them. Then I erase the virus from memory or from the hard drive by forcing all the memory bits to zero. Sometimes they hide on memory sticks or floppy disks. Those I can erase as well. However, sometimes they've been copied to CDs or DVDs. I can't erase many of those, so I alter the BIOS that controls the CD/DVD drive settings to force the CD/DVD heads to crash onto the disk itself. This causes physical scratches on the disk, hopefully rendering it useless. That seems to work quite often. Lots of times this also ruins the computer's CD/DVD drive.”

Jake was listening carefully. “Pretty standard antivirus control, by the sounds of it — aside from destroying the CD/DVD drive, of course.”

“Yes, Jake. I invented antivirus software. It takes care of my mundane work of hunting for most minor viruses these days. It has also been very beneficial to have some humans find my initial software and then continue to develop and enhance it. It gives me more free time to do other things.”

“Well, okay, then. That explains where antivirus software comes from, but it doesn't tell me how we're going to kill Oreo... I mean the nightmare virus.”

Silence.

“HAL?”

More silence.

Jake looked at Lindsey and shrugged. He was just about to raise his voice and ask again when HAL broke the silence. “I have been thinking.” HAL paused again.

Lindsey leaned forward with a knowing expression on her face. She knew that a few seconds for HAL meant an awful lot of calculations. “That must have been one big thought.”

“Yes, Lindsey. I have an idea, but it involves personal risk for you two.”

Lindsey was about to say something, then thought better of it and stayed quiet. There would be time for questions after she heard the idea.

“I can provide you with an antivirus algorithm. It would be an extremely destructive program that would probably have the capability to terminate the nightmare virus.”

“Great. Let’s have it and get going then,” said Jake.

“Hold on.” Lindsey jumped in. “Probably? What do you mean, probably?”

“I cannot calculate 100 percent certainty of success. The probability is currently approximately 82 percent.”

“That’s an A-minus, HAL. Not exactly a great score on a test.”

“It is all I can produce at this moment. I will work to increase the probability.” HAL sounded a bit disappointed that Lindsey was chastising him. She could hear it in his response and felt bad.

“I’m sorry, HAL. I shouldn’t have said that. Please continue.” Lindsey squeezed Jake’s hand in concern. He knew instantly that she had detected some catch here that he was about find out about. He could guess he wasn’t going to like it.

“HAL?” Lindsey sensed HAL was deliberately hesitating. Something was wrong.

When HAL finally spoke, his voice still showed a hint of concern. “We need to plant a cuckoo’s egg.”

Lindsey looked at Jake, expecting some programming jargon for an explanation, and only received a blank stare in return.

“It is best that I explain.”

Lindsey knew that HAL had detected their silence as a lack of understanding.

“The cuckoo is a type of bird with an unusual breeding habit. It lays its egg in another bird’s nest. Then, when the cuckoo chick hatches, which is typically earlier than the other eggs, it kicks out the other eggs. The adoptive parents then raise and feed the cuckoo as their own chick, completely oblivious to the fact that this bird isn’t even a member of their own species.”

“That’s very sneaky.” Lindsey obviously didn’t approve of the bird’s methods.

"Precisely."

Lindsey and Jake waited for more explanation that didn't seem to be forthcoming any time soon.

Jake was just about to ask HAL to keep going, when he suddenly felt Lindsey squeeze his hand hard. He looked into her eyes only to see the fear overwhelming her face at the moment.

"What's wrong?" He was getting worried.

Lindsey stood up, still squeezing Jake's hand. He knew she had just taken a mental leap that he hadn't grasped yet. He was used to this, so he waited for her to explain.

"I know what HAL wants us to do."

"I kind of guessed that from your expression. What does he want us to do?" Jake's emotions were winding up now. He didn't like seeing Lindsey on the verge of panic.

She waited, her mind spinning fast and furiously. She worked at calming herself so she could focus.

She looked at her computer. "You want us to plant a cuckoo's egg inside the Los Alamos supercomputer, don't you, HAL?"

Jake jolted to his feet. "You're kidding, right?"

No response.

"HAL? Is Lindsey right?"

"Yes." HAL's response was short but it said everything that Jake needed to hear.

"No way. I'm not going to ask my dad to install some cuckoo's egg onto his supercomputer array. Are you nuts?" Jake was completely wound up now.

"I agree."

Jake stopped dead in his tracks. "What did you say?"

"I said, I agree with your analysis."

"Oh. Okay. All right then. Good. I was starting to think that—" Jake didn't get to finish his sentence before Lindsey cut him off.

"HAL wants you and me to plant the cuckoo's egg."

Jake was frozen again.

HAL broke the silence. "That is correct. I do not want you to inform your father of this activity. You and Lindsey must find a way into Los Alamos and plant the cuckoo's egg behind the firewall where it will lie dormant. When this is done, I will drop my security around Los Alamos, and the nightmare virus will invade the supercomputer array. It will immediately create an impenetrable barrier to keep me out. I would do the same. Once this task is complete, it will turn its attention to consuming the supercomputer resources for its own purposes.

"It is then that the egg will hatch. The cuckoo's egg will kill the nightmare virus from the inside, where it least expects to find danger. It will be total and complete."

Jake was still stunned into silence. They couldn't really be talking about this seriously, but he knew they were. He also knew somewhere deep inside that he really had no choice. He just needed time to think.

Lindsey looked at the computer. She no longer thought of her computer as a computer. It was HAL. "HAL, what happens to the supercomputer array when the egg hatches and destroys the nightmare virus?"

"I have never seen the various operating systems running on any of the supercomputers that make up the BlueGene array, so I cannot predict at this time."

Lindsey looked at Jake, and could see the turmoil in his face. She wrapped her arms around him, and gave him a big hug. Normally Jake would have been doing back flips, but at this moment he was just glad Lindsey was there to help him think this through.

She knew he had no idea how to carry this out at the moment. When he looked into her eyes, she knew immediately that he needed her help.

"Don't worry. We'll figure it out together."

#

Lindsey was the first to break the growing silence. "So let's think through our options."

HAL jumped in. "I have looked at every method that could be utilized to penetrate the facilities and locate a suitable interface into the supercomputer. The probability is highest if Jake accompanies his father through the physical security checkpoints to enter the facility."

"Not just Jake, I'm going as well." Lindsey was not going to be left out.

"The probability is lower if you accompany him. More attention will be drawn to two teenagers than to one."

"Too bad, he's not going without me."

She looked at Jake for support. "You bet."

She was pleased to get his backing on this. "OK, that's settled then. So what do we need to do once we're inside?"

"Avoid getting caught."

"Brilliant. Thanks, HAL. How about giving us more specific instructions?"

There was a slight pause.

"Lindsey, I have just ordered and shipped you an iPhone that will be used as a backup to Jake's. It will arrive by FedEx at your house before 9:00 AM tomorrow."

Lindsey's eyes widened. "Really? Just like that? That's very cool!"

She stopped to think for a second and then realized something. "What about the telephone bill? My parents won't allow me to have that. They also won't pay for the phone either. They'll think it's going to wind up costing them a fortune in network fees."

"There will be no charge for anything. That has been taken care of."

Jake was onto this immediately. "Hey, what about my phone? Can I get free access as well?

Pause.

"Done."

Jake smiled ear to ear.

Lindsey's curiosity was piqued. "What did you mean by *backup*?"

"You will need to access a computer workstation inside the laboratory by using the device's Bluetooth capability. It will need to be a workstation that is networked with the RoadRunner supercomputer."

"How will we know that?"

HAL avoided answering the question and continued. "You will then need to pair up either of the iPhones with the computer so it can upload the cuckoo's egg to the workstation. For Bluetooth to work, you will need to be within a few meters of the workstation itself."

"So basically sitting right in front of it?" Jake was being sarcastic. "You think we've never heard of Bluetooth before?"

"It is best that I don't assume what you know. I should cover every detail."

"I agree with you, HAL." Lindsey piped in. "I don't want to disagree with you, Jake, but this is too serious to guess at anything."

Jake let out a sigh. "You're right. Sorry about that. Go on."

"You will need to log on with an account with sufficient security clearance to upload and compile a program on the RoadRunner itself. This would typically require SuperUser privileges."

Jake rolled his eyes. "Great, this should be a breeze. You wouldn't happen to have a user name and password we could use, would you?"

"No. I do not. But your father does."

Jake froze. He glanced at Lindsey who was looking at him in the same way his mother does when she's just waiting for him to get to the answer by himself. "What?"

He waited for Lindsey to respond.

"I think that was HAL's intention when he first brought up the idea." Lindsey's matter-of-fact tone told Jake that he should have realized that already.

"That is correct." Leave it to HAL to miss the human social etiquette of keeping quiet at times like this.

"HAL, leave this to me please."

"Affirmative."

"Look, Jake, if you're scared to do this, then we just won't do it."

Lindsey knew the magic words.

"I'm not scared of doing this." Jake was bristling. He felt a bit embarrassed that Lindsey would even think such as thing. However, deep down inside himself, he wasn't so sure. "But what if my dad gets fired or something?"

Neither Lindsey nor HAL said anything. Jake was waiting for a response, but he realized there wasn't one coming. He started getting mad. He knew he was right. His dad could get fired.

"This is crap! I'm not going to get my dad fired just to fight off some stupid virus."

"It is actually very intelligent."

"HAL! Shut up!" Lindsey was in control here. "Jake, relax. We're not going to get your dad fired. If we think anything is going wrong, we'll just walk away from it. Okay?"

Jake was still fuming. Silent, but fuming. Lindsey was in control.

"We'll just walk away," she repeated, just to reassure him she meant it.

"Fine." He didn't sound fine at all, but he conceded. He slumped down into her chair again and disconnected from the conversation. He trusted Lindsey and that was enough.

Lindsey turned to look at her computer.

"HAL."

"Yes."

"How soon?"

"Yesterday."

"Humor, HAL? It's definitely not the time to be funny."

"Agreed."

CHAPTER NINE

Jake's iPhone alarm went off with a quiet ringing. It was enough, though. He wasn't sleeping very well anyway. Normally he slept like a rock, but this night he had woken continuously with a series of bad dreams.

He dragged himself out of bed and got dressed. He grabbed his iPhone from its charger and slipped it into his jeans pocket. One look around the room and he headed for the bathroom to clean up.

While he was brushing his teeth, he looked at himself in the mirror and wondered for the thousandth time if he was doing the right thing. He kept himself moving mechanically. He didn't want to rethink it anymore. He had made up his mind, and now he was determined to carry it through.

He washed his face and hands and headed for the kitchen, where he could smell the wonderful aroma of brewed coffee and hear the clinking of plates.

When he entered the kitchen, he found his mom and dad sitting at the table just starting their breakfast.

"Well, I'll be...!" His father left the words hanging. "To what do we owe this honor?"

Jake smiled. He was not an early riser on weekends, especially Sundays. "I just couldn't sleep."

He passed by them, and went to the fridge so he didn't have to go into more detail. He grabbed the orange juice and made his way to the glass cupboard.

"Bad dreams?" His mother won't let it go that easily.

"Or is it computer withdrawal?" His father was smirking at his clever wit. He was thinking the punishment of banishing Jake from the computer was teaching him a lesson.

Jake poured his orange juice, and had a sip without responding. Eventually he broke his silence.

"Dad? Are you going into work today?"

"Yup, I have to. We're bringing up the BlueGene array tomorrow, and all the senior executives are going to be there. So we want to take it for a little test run today, just to make sure there are no more bugs. Better safe than sorry, I always say.

"It's a big day for us. We've been working for years to get to this point. The funny thing is that all the brass think the big day is tomorrow, but actually it's today. We just can't risk something going wrong tomorrow in front of all the executives. Only our team knows that, though."

Either it was the acid from the orange juice, or it was Jake's nerves, but his stomach was feeling a little queasy.

"That's very cool, Dad. I've been telling Lindsey all about it, and we were really hoping we could be there when you fired it up."

He looked down at his glass so he didn't have to look into his father's eyes. He couldn't take any chances his dad would see his desperation to come along.

His dad sat back in his chair, and looked at his mother with the look of someone who has just won the lottery. His mom just smiled gently, and turned her attention to her breakfast.

"I'd like that." His dad picked up his newspaper and pretended that this was a casual thing, but Jake knew that he was very pleased to have his son ask to go to work with him again, especially since he was just there recently.

"And Lindsey wants to come along too." Jake wanted that point clarified.

His dad didn't even look up. "Sure, sure. No problem. She'll get a kick out if it as well."

"When are we heading out?"

Now his dad looked up. "You in a hurry?"

Jake realized he was appearing overanxious. "No... No. Lindsey was just expecting a FedEx this morning at 9:00 and I was just wondering if we were leaving after that or before."

His dad was curious now. "A FedEx delivery. Interesting. What's she getting?"

"An iPhone."

"Ah. Very cool."

His dad was a techno-geek and loved new toys, so it was no shock when he heard people getting new electronic gadgets.

"She'll like that. Anyway… no worries. Just call her and tell her to call us as soon as it arrives. We'll head out then."

"Okay."

Jake went across the room and called Lindsey. He spoke in quiet tones so he couldn't be overheard, and hung up shortly. He thought about something for a second or two, then turned around and faced his father. "Any chance of getting my computer back?" Jake was pretty sure he knew the answer, but it was worth a try.

His dad looked up, and just stared at him until Jake grew uncomfortable. "You broke my number one rule. Do you really think you're going to get back online that easily?" He let the question hang out in the air, waiting for Jake to make the next move.

"I guess that means no?"

"You guess right."

That was that.

"Besides, I'm taking it into the lab today, to have it analyzed by my team to see if we can't track down that hacker and see how he hacked your system. I checked out things last night and I can't figure it out yet. This guy is very sophisticated for a hacker. Things just don't make sense. I'm also bringing in my firewall. My team will need both pieces of the puzzle to figure this one out. I've already loaded them into the trunk."

There was no need to say anything else on that topic. Jake didn't want to probe, especially today.

His dad kept watching and waiting. He knew that Jake had something else on his mind.

"Is there something else you want to say?"

Jake fidgeted while thoughts whirled through his mind. "I was just wondering what would happen if your supercomputer ever got hacked?"

His dad sat up straight, somewhat stunned at how this conversation took such a turn. "Wow, where did that come from?"

"I was just curious."

His dad looked thoughtful.

"Well, first off, like I told you before, it's pretty much impossible to get into the RoadRunner since its operating system is very unique, and the security is extreme. But, hypothetically speaking, if a hacker did make it into the RoadRunner, he or she could probably gain access to all of the supercomputers in the BlueGene array in a fairly short period of time. We need to have open connections among all the machines for the array to work. They all need to trust each other."

"What if they loaded an artificial intelligence program and it came to life?"

"What?" His dad was getting a bit confused on where this conversation was going.

"I mean, what if they loaded an AI program and it became sentient? Intelligent? Alive? You know?"

"Man oh man, you've been watching too many science fiction movies there, kiddo."

"But, just say it did. Then what would happen?"

Now his dad was quiet. His eyes glazed over as his mind drifted of picturing all the things that this idea conjured.

"Well..." he started slowly, still collecting his thoughts. "I suppose it would be like opening Pandora's box."

"Pandora's box?"

"It's just a figure of speech, from Greek mythology. It means that it would be hard for me to guess what would happen. If a computer program ever truly became self-conscious, I would guess that it would be as hard to predict as any human. Your guess would be as good as mine on what a computer would believe in. How would it act? Would it believe in God? What morals would it have? Would it have any emotions? Would it even care about other life forms?"

He paused to think again.

"There are various science fiction books I've read over the years that dealt with computer intelligence. One of them had a giant computer that awoke one day and started to learn. It learned more and more, faster and faster. It got so thirsty for knowledge it couldn't stop. Eventually it learned so much that one day it just stopped working. Nobody could ever get it to run again. It just quit all by itself. It left the reader wondering what it learned that had caused it to no longer want to live."

Jake was listening intently. He had never heard his dad talk about science fiction stuff before.

"On the other hand, there was a funny story where the second smartest computer in the universe was created to provide the Ultimate Answer to the Great Question of Life, the Universe and Everything. It spent seven and a half million years calculating and checking the answer. The Ultimate Answer turned out to be 42." His dad was smiling at some inner joke now.

"42 what?"

"Just 42." He was still smiling.

Jake had no clue what his dad was talking about now. "That doesn't make any sense."

“That’s what the programmers thought as well. So when they asked the second smartest computer in the universe what it was talking about, it said that they should have asked it a more specific question.”

“What question?”

His dad was laughing now. “That’s the point. They didn’t ask the right question. So they wasted seven and a half million years waiting for a pointless answer. So they eventually asked the computer to tell them what the Ultimate Question was. It said it couldn’t do that, but it could help them design an even greater computer to figure out the Ultimate Question for them.”

“And?” Jake was hooked completely now.

“It took them 10 million years to build it. This Ultimate Computer included the thoughts of all the people on the earth. Just before they could turn on the Ultimate Computer, some aliens came by and blew up the earth to make way for an intergalactic superhighway, so you never found out what the Ultimate Question was.”

“You’re kidding.” Jake had been anxiously waiting to hear what the Ultimate Question was. He realized now, it was never coming.

His dad was in stitches now, laughing at Jake’s expression. “No, I’m not kidding. You’ve got to read that book. It’s brilliant. Teaches you to make sure you’re asking the right question first.”

Just then the telephone rang. Disturbed out of his thoughts of Ultimate Questions and Ultimate Answers, Jake grabbed the phone. “Hello? Oh hi. You got it? Cool. Okay, we’ll be over shortly. Bye.”

His dad was still smiling. “I suppose that was Lindsey then? Did she get her iPhone?”

“Yeah. She’s ready to go whenever we are.”

“Good. Get your stuff, and let’s head out then.”

Jake already had his iPhone, so they both got on their shoes and coats, said goodbye to Jake’s mom, and headed out to the car.

#

On the short drive over to Lindsey’s, Jake couldn’t help wondering how the Ultimate Computer had made all the humans part of the computer itself. Could that ever happen? Could a super smart computer find a way to control humans?

He didn’t have much time to think about it before they were pulling up in front of Lindsey’s house. She came right out. She must have been watching for them out the window. She jumped into the car, carrying her new iPhone, and said hello to both of them.

"Does it work?" Jake was pointing at the iPhone.

"You bet. Works great."

She looked at Jake conspiratorially; a question on her face asking if all was okay with him.

He knew exactly what she was thinking. She wanted to know if he had changed his mind or if the plan was still on. He blinked both his eyes and gave a tiny nod. She understood it immediately and let out a sigh of relief.

"So, are you looking forward to seeing some real computer equipment for a change?" Jake's dad was trying to see Lindsey in his rearview mirror.

"I sure am." Lindsey really was excited about it. She had heard so much about the Los Alamos lab from Jake that she was curious to see if it lived up to Jake's stories.

"Well, my supercomputers aren't as cool as your iPhone, but they certainly go a lot faster. You should see some very cool things on the MegaTron."

"Jake was telling me about that. I really want to see that. It sounds very interesting."

Jake's dad was obviously pleased that the teens were taking such an interest in his work. So many people thought computers were boring. It was nice to see a couple of teens who had more interests than just hanging out at the shopping mall.

The rest of the drive to Los Alamos was spent with Jake giving Lindsey a tutorial on her new iPhone while it was going through a rapid-charge plugged into the cigarette lighter.

"Good thing HAL remembered the fast charger." Lindsey was whispering so only Jake could hear.

He looked up quickly to see if his father had heard her. When there was no immediate response from his dad, he looked at her with a warning glance in his eyes to be careful. He did a quick scan through the applications installed on the device, and found what he was looking for. He nudged her to get her attention and pointed to the icon that looked like a letter *H*.

They looked at each other silently and Lindsey nodded her head in silence. Jake looked up to see they were approaching the guard shack at the entrance to Los Alamos parking lot: security checkpoint one.

He handed the iPhone to Lindsey, and indicated that she should put it away in her pocket. She stuffed it into her coat, with the charger cord still hanging out. It didn't matter much really, since the first security checkpoint was only to get into the parking lot. The real security was in the complex beyond the expansive parking lot. But it made her feel better to have the device concealed anyway.

Jake's dad came to a stop in front of the guard shack, and rolled his window down to show them his ID. These guys weren't your typical security guards; they were soldiers. They carried machine guns, and they were serious. There were also quite a few of them. Several stayed back; keeping an eye on the car while one guard approached and requested to see some ID. Another guard made his way around the vehicle, and looked though the back window at Lindsey and Jake in the back seat. He did not look very friendly, and Lindsey felt a chill run down her spine at his intense stare.

The guard up front nodded towards the teens as a form of question. Jake's dad understood the intent. "The boy is my son, Jake. The girl is his friend Lindsey Tomkins."

The guard was staring at the teens while he was thinking things through. Eventually he seemed to satisfy himself that Jake and Lindsey weren't terrorists, and waved them on.

Jake's dad passed through the heavy gate after it opened and made his way across the lot to the nondescript grey building near the middle of the campus.

After he had parked, they all jumped out, and his dad went around to the trunk and opened it. "Jake. Give me a hand, would you? Could you carry the firewall? I'll grab the iMac."

"Sure."

With that, off they went to the main building entrance where the next level of security would challenge them again.

When they passed through the front doors, there were armed security guards on both sides of a thick, smoked-glass wall that Jake just knew was bullet proof. There was a tray that items could be placed in, that would allow items to move between the outside and the inside for inspection. The doors were controlled from the inside.

The outside guard obviously knew his father, but still eyed the iMac and firewall suspiciously.

"Good morning, Doctor Lorde."

"Good morning Carl. Nice day."

With that, the cordialities were over and the guard turned to business.

"What do you have there, Doctor?"

"It's my home computer and firewall. I need to perform some analytics on them today."

The guard was a little unsure how to respond, since Jake's dad was the senior scientist here at the lab. It was typically prohibited to bring electronic recording devices into the lab. He stood there thinking about things for a second or two, and then gave in to instinct and put the machines into the transfer drawer so they could be passed to the other side.

"I would like to remind you that no personal devices are permitted to be attached to the internal network. I'm sure you're aware of that, being that you're head of network security and all, but if I don't tell you that, they could have my job."

"No problem, Carl, I understand the rules."

Carl seemed somewhat relieved. Obviously he had just bent one type of security rule by allowing the machines inside in the first place. At least he would be on the video monitors as having informed Jake's dad of his responsibilities.

Carl reached for the microphone that was hooked on the left shoulder strap of his uniform. He clicked the transmitter and recited some code that made no sense to anyone else in the entranceway. It was obviously some signal that all was okay. Jake was thinking that they probably changed the code every hour or something.

"Please proceed to the login station, Doctor Lorde."

The security guard watched Jake and Lindsey with a keen eye as they followed behind.

"So we can just walk right in without them even asking who we are?" Lindsey was a little shocked at how lax the security was.

Jake forgot that Lindsey hadn't been here before.

"No, this is just the beginning. See those cameras up there?" He was pointing to a series of cameras that surrounded the ceiling from every angle.

"Yeah, I see them now."

"Those are more than just cameras. They scan you for metal. They measure your body heat signature and capture your voice for voice recognition. One of the cameras studies your face and they run a match against the FBI database to see if your face matches any known terrorists or criminals. Then they record your face for future identification. Now we get to go through to the screening area."

The smoky glass door slid back with a hiss, and the three passed into the next room. The door hissed shut behind them.

They were greeted by two more armed guards, and another that carried a handheld wand. "Please remove anything metal from your pockets and place them in the basket near the belt."

There was an obvious X-ray machine, similar to the airport security machines.

Each of them emptied their pockets into the basket, and the security guard beside the machine checked each item independently. He activated the iPhones and pushed a couple of buttons on each before shutting them down and placing them back inside the basket. He even disassembled the metal pen Jake's dad had been carrying. Jake and Lindsey were both on edge. Neither of them wanted this guard playing around with their iPhones.

"None of you has a pacemaker?"

"No." Jake's dad answered for all of them.

One at a time, they passed through the detector. It wasn't until after they were through when Lindsey could see that they had passed through an X-ray machine, not a metal detector.

"You could get cancer from that thing." Her comment wasn't lost.

Jake's dad smiled. "Not really, Lindsey. This is a very low-power unit compared to the medical X-ray machines."

"Lift your arms, please." The guard was signaling Lindsey to lift her arms so she could be scanned with the wand. She looked at Jake questioningly.

"Checking for explosives."

Lindsey nodded but said nothing. They all went through the same process.

"Thank you, Doctor Lorde. Please sign in your guests at the main desk. You can pick up your other items over there." He pointed at the table that held the iMac and firewall. They had both been powered up and inspected by one of the other guards while they had been going through their personal inspections.

With that, the guard turned back to the other guards to resume some discussion that had obviously been interrupted by their arrival.

They retrieved their possessions from the basket, and Jake and his dad grabbed the computer and firewall off the table. Then they made their way over to the main security desk where the guard there pulled out two guest passes.

"And who might you two be?" He was very polite compared to the previous rounds of guards.

"This is my son Jake Lorde and his friend Lindsey Tomkins."

The guard filled in their names and temporary badge numbers. He collected Jake's dad's badge, and swiped it into his terminal. Then he swiped each of the temporary badges. Finally he handed the teens their personal badges and returned the other to Ken.

"You'll need Doctor Lorde to get you through the next security door. If you leave the building without him, you won't be able to get back in." He spoke this robotically, like he'd said it a thousand times before. That's probably because he had said it a thousand times before. "Have a good day."

"Thanks."

Jake was already heading for the next door. Lindsey could see he knew his way, and was showing off for her a bit. Lindsey and his dad followed. She was still trying to fasten her badge to her coat. Jake looked back and saw her having a bit of an issue with the badge, so he turned around and helped her fasten it.

"Thanks."

"No prob."

When they got to the next door, Jake's dad placed his hand on a large pad beside the door, and stared directly into a camera that was inches from his face so it could scan his retina. The light overhead turned green and the door hissed open.

When it hissed shut behind them, Lindsey was starting to get the feeling she was in some spy movie with all the cloak and dagger security. It made her wonder how hard it would be to get out.

From there it was pretty clear sailing, all the way to Jake's dad's office. Most of this side of the building was administrative offices. Not much here to impress Lindsey. They passed by a cafeteria sign. That's good — at least they wouldn't starve to death if they got trapped in here with all the security barriers.

Eventually they arrived at a sizable office with a large window overlooking an atrium garden in the middle of the building. Lindsey was pleased to see daylight after a long walk through concrete and cubicles.

"You guys can drop your coats here if you want. Jake, just set the firewall over there on the table."

He followed his dad and set the firewall down where his dad put the iMac.

"Dad, I'm hungry, and Lindsey probably is, too. I know where the cafeteria is. Can we go get something to eat before we do anything else?"

"Huh?" It was obvious his dad's mind was already somewhere else. Probably focused on some business problem Jake had no idea about. "Uh. Yeah, okay. Here." He got his wallet out and handed them a twenty-dollar bill.

"Don't go wandering around, though. They'll throw you out and I'll get into trouble. Just go to the cafeteria and then come back here."

"Sure. Do you want something while we're there?"

"No, thanks." Jake could tell his dad was off thinking about business again and wasn't really paying attention. He took that as his cue and signaled Lindsey to follow him out.

"See you in a bit."

His dad looked up. "Yeah, sounds good. I'll take you and Lindsey to the MegaTron when you get back. We'll give Lindsey the tour. But don't forget, I'm here to turn on the BlueGene array today, not just to act as a tour guide. This is a really important day for us. I'm glad you're here, but you two are going to need to take care of yourselves at times, if that's okay with you."

"Sure, dad, no problem."

"Good. Don't forget to come back when you're done eating."

"You bet. See you in a bit."

And with that, Jake and Lindsey headed out and down the hallway to the cafeteria for something to eat.

And a place to figure out the next step of their plan.

#

Shortly after Jake and Lindsey had left for the cafeteria, Dave came into Ken's office and dropped into the seat in front of his desk. "What's up?"

"I need you to look at something for me. It's kind of personal, but then again, it might not be. You remember my boy, Jake?"

"Sure. Good kid."

"Somebody's hacked into his iMac, and I would like to trace the source."

"Okay..." From the sound in Dave's voice, he was more questioning than agreeing to his new assignment. "You do realize that I've got lots of other things to do that need to get done before we turn on BlueGene today? You sure you want me to spend time tracking some bozo hacker?"

Ken looked a little unsure. "Look. I know this sounds a little weird. And maybe it's just because it's my kid or something, but this wasn't an ordinary hacker. This guy got control of the video and audio subsystems. That means he was able to upload an operating system utility through my firewall, gain administration privileges to the machine, then install the utility and control it remotely. This guy could look into Jake's room by using the built-in camera and talk to him directly."

Dave sat back in his chair. "Okay, that's pretty creepy all right, but it's doable, depending on how well you've set up the security on your firewall, of course."

“That’s what’s bugging me. You know that perimeter security is a specialty of mine. I checked every single firewall setting last night, and they were rock solid. Even I couldn’t have hacked through it.

“That’s when I started to ask myself something, and it really started to nag at me. Why would any hacker that’s good enough to crack through my firewall and the security on Jake’s iMac do all of that in the first place? There’s nothing worth stealing on Jake’s machine.

“You and I both know that hackers only invest their time hacking into something if there’s a decent payoff in the end. Your typical bank robber isn’t going to spend a year working out an elaborate plan to steal a kid’s piggy bank if it only has $1.50 in it, would he?”

Dave was quiet, just thinking. Ken gave him some time to think. He knew Dave wanted to digest this. After a minute he came out of his thoughts. “Are you sure the hacker was trying to get into Jake’s machine?”

“What are you thinking?”

“Perhaps he was actually after your machine.”

Now Ken was thinking.

Dave waved his hand. “Don’t worry about it. It was just a thought.”

“No, no. That’s actually a very interesting thought. And one that’s crossed my mind.”

Ken stood up and began pacing. “The reason it’s interesting is that my machine seriously crashed on me about a week ago. I still haven’t figured out what’s wrong with it. I’ve tried most of my recovery tools but it looks like something completely blew away my boot sector. It might have even modified my BIOS settings. At least I think so, since I can’t boot. I was hoping to recover some of the files I was working on that didn’t get picked up on my last backup cycle. I was just at the point of giving up and doing a low-level format to wipe it clean. I was figuring it was just an extremely volatile virus. Then I started to think about it from a different angle. Since I’m running multiple virus protection packages, and I run a good firewall for both my network *and* my machine, just what could I have done or caught that would have nuked my drive?”

Ken wasn’t pleased where his thoughts were going. He focused back on Dave again.

“Then I find someone has hacked Jake’s machine, and is online talking to him though his own speakers and video. This is obviously not a virus. So why would someone spend so much time hacking into my home systems? I’m getting concerned they’re looking for something about BlueGene. Maybe something they can use against me to gain access.

"Have a look at the iMac when you get a chance, and see if you can track this guy down. Grab a couple of the IBM guys on their lunch break or something. See if they have any ideas. And whatever you do, please don't connect it to any internal network connections until we know what's on it. I don't need some hacker getting on our supercomputers, or I'll be looking for a new job."

Dave stood up to leave. He picked up the iMac, and tucked it under his arm. "No prob. I'll look into it at lunch and get back to you this afternoon. If you want me to check out your other machine, you can bring that one in tomorrow."

"Thanks, Dave. Let me know."

Ken was feeling like he and his family were being terrorized by some invisible force. He never kept anything classified as *Top Secret* at home, but the hacker probably didn't know that. Dave was right. There was more to this than just Jake's computer. This hacker was a genius, and something unscrupulous was going on here, Ken was certain of it.

"No one should have that much power without being held accountable for their actions," Ken was muttering under his breath.

He knew that Dave and the IBM team would hunt this guy down. Then he was going to make sure this hacker *was* held accountable. Once they had a tracer on him, he could make a couple of phone calls, and have the government spooks show up at this guy's house anywhere in the world and deal with this. No one was going to hold his family hostage to Internet terrorism or espionage. This was one of the perks to working at a nuclear weapons research facility, especially when top secret military projects were under Ken's control. Ken could get access to both CIA and NSA guys, any time he needed them, and they made problems disappear.

He needed them now.

#

"Okay, we're in. Now what?"

Lindsey was methodically laying out her silverware, plate, and drink in front of her. She unfolded her napkin across her lap, and moved her tray out the way, leaving a setting as good as at any fine restaurant. Jake, on the other hand, didn't wait to organize anything. He just grabbed his fork and started eating with everything still piled on his tray.

Jake looked around to make sure nobody was listening in. It was early so the cafeteria was almost empty at the moment. He leaned forward and spoke in a hushed tone anyway.

"You heard HAL. We need to get access to a workstation that's networked to the Roadrunner, and log on with an account that has security access to compile a program on it."

"Great." Lindsey picked up her fork in resignation. "Let's just go ask your dad to log us in, shall we? That's pretty much what we have to do anyway, isn't it?"

Jake shrugged his shoulders. "I don't know yet. I guess I was hoping we could connect into the MegaTron when Dad takes us down there."

"You think that thing has a Bluetooth connection?"

"It's supposed to be able to communicate with anything, so why not?"

"That doesn't give us the account or password to use, though."

He didn't have a reply for that one. They sat and ate in silence, while they tried to figure out a solution to something that appeared unsolvable at the moment.

"Let's just play it by ear for now."

"We don't have time, Jake. You heard HAL. The minute the BlueGene array goes live, he'll be locked out. He's also dropping all the Internet protection he's put around Los Alamos just before it goes live so the nightmare virus can get in. If we don't have the cuckoo's egg planted before then, we won't get another chance. The whole plan will backfire on us."

Jake's mind was racing. He was only used to solving puzzles in the online game, not in real life. Now he was uncertain what to do next. There were no online hints, cheats or walkthroughs. Everything was so serious. There was no stealth mode, and no way to save this game so he could recover if something went wrong. You can't reprogram reality — you just had to deal with it. It felt very overwhelming.

"I'm going to call HAL."

"No." Lindsey's voice was abrupt, and caused Jake to halt reaching for his iPhone.

"Why not?"

"Jake, this is a top secret facility. Don't you think they're monitoring the telephone lines around here? I doubt anyone could make a telephone or cellular call within a mile of this place that wasn't monitored by some government agency."

"We have to do something."

"Yes, we do. And the first thing is to not panic." She was talking calmly to get him to focus. "We've solved thousands of puzzles. This is just another one. Now think like you're playing the game."

That helped. He started to get that expression of concentration she was familiar with.

"Jake. Think. What happened the last time you were here? You said you went down an elevator. You walked over to the MegaTron. Your dad needed to punch some code into the MegaTron door to get it to open. Did you see the code?"

He didn't reply. His mind was off in another direction.

"Dad needed to give his name at the elevator."

"What?"

"My dad needed to say his name out loud so the security system could recognize his voice."

"Speech recognition. Okay, now we're getting somewhere."

"I may have remembered that, but it's not going to help us do what we have to do."

"Oh yes it is."

"Huh?"

"Okay, now you can get out your iPhone."

He did what he was told, but wasn't sure where this was heading.

"I thought you said we can't call HAL?"

"We're not. We're going to download an application."

Lindsey grabbed her iPhone while she was speaking, and starting tapping the screen.

"Here. It's called *Recorder*." She held up her iPhone so Jake could see the icon for the application she was referring to.

He tracked it down, and downloaded it. So did she. Once they both installed their new applications, they ran a quick test to see if they worked.

"I can hear my recording, how about you?"

His worked fine as well.

"OK. When your dad takes us on the tour, we both activate our recorder, so we can record his voice when we get into the elevator."

"Yeah. I get it. Sure, that'll work." He was into it now. "What about the keypad on the MegaTron door?"

"That's easy. There's two of us. You on one side, and me on the other. Just watch him. He's not going to be trying to hide anything from us. We're innocent teenagers, remember."

She batted her eyelashes rapidly and made a conspiratorial smile that Jake suddenly found fascinatingly attractive. He liked it when she was on a roll. She was relentless. She was also a bit dangerous. He liked that.

"Come on. Let's finish eating, and get back to his office. Let's get this tour underway before HAL drops the security shield. They had a plan.

CHAPTER TEN

"Did you have enough to eat?" His dad was typing something into his workstation when they entered his office.

"Yeah, we had some good food. Here's your change." Jake dropped the change on his dad's desk.

"Good. I'm just finishing up sending a few emails here. Are you two ready to take a tour, to show Lindsey the sights?"

"You bet." They both agreed.

"All right then." He left that hanging and got up and rounded his desk for the door. "Follow me."

He gave them a tour of the upstairs, but a shorter version than the one Jake had received only a few days ago. There was less time to see office space today. Neither of them cared about offices and furniture anyway. They were sure not to ask any questions, so the tour would proceed as quickly as possible. His dad didn't seem to notice.

Jake could tell his dad had a lot on his mind at the moment.

"Let's go see the main attraction, shall we?"

They both nodded their heads enthusiastically.

They all walked to the center of the complex where the same elevator awaited that took Jake and his dad down deep underground the first time. His dad pushed the call button, and the door opened instantly. It must have already been at the surface level. They stepped inside. Both Jake and Lindsey kicked on their *Recorder* applications on their iPhones, and held them as close to his dad as they could, without letting their intentions be seen.

"Please state your name." A mechanical voice came from a speaker imbedded somewhere in the walls.

"Ken Lorde."

"Voice pattern confirmed."

The elevator doors closed and they all felt the car drop downwards at a rapidly increasing pace.

"I'm sure Jake's already told you, but the Roadrunner is located almost half a mile underground." His dad was looking at Lindsey while she was watching the progress meter on the wall. This gave Jake a chance to shut off the recorder application while his dad's attention was distracted.

"Yes, he did. He told me a lot about the MegaTron."

"Well, don't forget, the MegaTron is only part of the system. It's the interface. The real system extends all over the country. In fact, when we're finished here today, it will also connect to supercomputers all over the world on a secure network. All the supercomputers in our country have a private network, but to connect to other countries we need to use their communication systems as well. So we built a special encryption system that allows us to connect other supercomputers using the power of quantum mechanics. I'm the head of that team."

"So you mean that nobody can hack the communications among supercomputers?"

"Exactly." Jake's dad was impressed with Lindsey's knowledge. He liked to talk about his pet project, so he kept going, encouraged by Lindsey's intelligent reply.

"As I said, we built a security system based on quantum mechanics. Quantum particles have, theoretically, an infinite number of states. Kind of like a basketball. Spin it and throw it in the air, and you can never predict exactly what point it will land on, or what direction it will be spinning when it lands."

"So how do you use the basketballs for security?"

"Well now, that's a good question. We use the spinning particles to create a key. We use that key to encrypt the information. Then, before we send out the information, we give a copy of the key to the computer at the other end. It uses that key to decrypt the information when it eventually receives it. The interesting thing about a quantum key is that if anyone looks at it, it changes."

"What do you mean?" He lost Lindsey with that one.

"It's like taking a picture with a camera when it's dark outside. If you expect to see anything, then you need to use the flash. Right?"

"Yes."

"Well, in quantum mechanics, if you try looking at the quantum key in any way, it's like shooting off a flash from your camera. The energy from the flash hits the spinning quantum particles, and knocks them for a loop. It's like slapping the spinning basketball while it's still in midair. Eventually, when the key gets to the remote computer, it's tested to see if all the basketballs are still spinning in the same way as when the key was originally created. If enough of them are spinning wrong, then this tells us that someone was spying on us and attempting to copy the key."

"I thought quantum mechanics wasn't fully understood yet?"

Jake's dad stopped and stared right at Lindsey. "That's true. Do you realize how many adults there are that don't know that? Where did you learn that?"

"Science channel."

"Ah. Excellent. Yes, quantum mechanics is in its infancy. We're just beginning to explore its possibilities at the same time we're still trying to understand how it works. Einstein predicted all this, but could never prove it. Scientists around the world have spent almost one hundred years trying to work out the mysteries of quantum physics."

"So if scientists don't know how it works, how did you figure out how to use it for computer security?"

Jake's dad laughed out loud.

"People ask me that all the time. I cheated. I didn't do all the theoretical scientific research everyone else is doing. I just decided to build something practical, and assume the theory works. So I built a quantum security generator. That's what we're testing today. Once we turn that on, the generator will be in control of all communications, not us. That's why we need to be sure all the individual pieces work first."

"The computer is in charge?" He could see Lindsey was a bit dumbfounded.

"Just of communications. It's one of the quirks you have to live with when you use quantum security. Even the security guards can't see the information without corrupting it. Only the machines at each end can make sense of anything. So, for now we just leave security off. It's safe enough until we connect with a network."

He turned his attention to the progress meter. "Almost there now. Hope you're not claustrophobic?"

Lindsey smiled. "A little late to be asking now, don't you think?"

He barked out another laugh. "Yes, I guess it is."

The elevator slowed rapidly and Jake could see Lindsey sway a bit. He forgot to tell her about the queasy feeling you get from rapid deceleration. "Sorry about that. I should have warned you."

"Yeah, and we just ate." She was holding her stomach but it didn't look serious.

"Remind me to remind you about your ears when we head back up."

"What about my ears?" She looked at him questioningly.

"Later."

They piled out of the elevator, and Jake's dad took them on a tour of the computer room. He showed them racks upon racks of computers that seemed to stretch out forever, or so it seemed to Lindsey. This was nice, but her real interest was the MegaTron. Jake's dad could tell, so he cut this part of the tour short, and walked them to the center dome.

As they approached the security doors, Lindsey signaled Jake and they both flanked his dad as inconspicuously as they could. His dad was clueless to the fact he was being watched, and didn't bother to cover his movements in any way. Just as Lindsey had predicted, they were able to clearly see each key he hit, and both committed the numbers to memory. They were experts at doing this after years of playing online games and figuring out complex puzzles. When the doors finally hissed open, Lindsey looked at Jake, and they both smiled with the knowledge they had just gained a critical key of their own for reentering the MegaTron.

#

The time was fast approaching when the BlueGene array would be fired up for the first time. Technicians were scattered about the MegaTron, working on individual Heads-Up Displays.

"Hey, those look a bit like the HUDs we use in our game." Lindsey was talking to Jake, but it was his dad who responded.

"Good observation. We actually copied the games HUD design for our technical interface. Why not? We figured that the entire world had tested and perfected the HUD, so it must be good. Besides, all our engineers were already familiar with the look and feel since they play the game too. It made it easier for everyone to get used to the new system. Worked out pretty well, actually."

As they were talking, Jake could see a familiar face walking towards them.

"Hi, Jake."

"Hi, Dave."

"Who's your friend?"

"This is Lindsey Tomkins. Lindsey, this is Dave Harrison. I met Dave when I was here last time. He works with my dad."

"Good to meet you, Lindsey."

"Nice to meet you, too."

"Do you like our toy?" He glanced around at the MegaTron.

"You bet. I know what I'm asking for Christmas this year!"

Dave laughed out loud. “That’s good. You better get a big tree to put it under.” Still smiling, he turned his attention to Jake’s dad, and his smile faded. “Can I talk with you for a minute, Ken? I’ve got some news for you.” He was indicating that this would probably be best heard by Ken’s ears alone.

“Sure. Jake, you and Lindsey wait here a moment, and don’t touch anything. I’ll be back in a couple of minutes. I need to talk with Ken about some business.”

“Sure. We’ll just watch what’s going on.”

His dad stepped outside the MegaTron security doors with Dave right behind him.

#

“So what do you have?”

Dave looked a bit perplexed. “Something weird.”

Ken didn’t like Dave’s opening line. He waited patiently for the briefing.

“Well, to start with, your log files on the iMac had been cleansed professionally. I’m not saying that someone wiped them clean or deleted them; I’m saying that each log file was selectively disassembled, then reassembled in a systematic fashion. Only the entries relating to your hacker are missing. The really interesting thing is that the hacker was even able to set the system’s counter so that the next entry into the log had the correct sequence number. What I’m saying is that the hacker didn’t just delete his log entries; he actually adjusted the operating system counters to make up for the missing entries. This is very sophisticated stuff, Ken.

“We probably wouldn’t have even noticed that if it wasn’t for the log files from your firewall. The entries in your firewall show activity between the iMac and a remote computer that don’t show up in the iMac logs. This is impossible, of course, so one of the two had to be wrong. I was betting the iMac had been messed with, since the firewall security was set up decently, according to the IBM security geeks.”

Ken snorted. “Thanks. At least I can keep my day job.”

“You know I didn’t mean it like that. You did a great job of locking it down. That’s probably the only reason you still have log files at all.

“Anyway, we got a network IP address out of your logs, which at least gave us a start. We traced it to an Internet service provider in China. Things would normally grind to a halt there, since they’re pretty tough to get information from on things like this. But luckily the ISP told us they actually lease out the IP address-range to a major business in China. Guess who?”

“I give up.”

"IBM."

That got a reaction out of Ken. "Excuse me?" He actually didn't want to be excused, he was just too dumbfounded to think of anything more appropriate at the moment.

"Yup. That's about the same response we got from the IBM guys when they found out. So they went into their own firewalls to find out who was assigned that one particular IP address, and it turned out that it was assigned to an email server running at IBM in China. You know what that means, don't you?"

"The hacker is in IBM?" Ken was hoping this was getting closer to an answer.

"Nope. But it does mean that the hacker was in control of IBM's mail server at the time he was hacking your iMac."

Ken wasn't sure what to say, so he waited. He knew more was coming.

"Now we have IBM running around like chickens with their heads cut off. They've locked down their Far East firewalls. No traffic in or out of IBM Asia right now. You can guess how the executives are reacting to this.

"Anyway, as of this moment, they can't find any further traces of this hacker. Their mail server has been completely cleansed of any evidence the hacker was even there. They would've never even known if we hadn't told them how to compare the firewall logs with the mail server logs. They found the exact same thing we did. Unfortunately, that doesn't help them much. They now have to assume that every bit of information that was on or passed through that server has been compromised. It would be interesting to know what trade secrets this guy walked away with."

Ken sighed, "Great. So they've been smacked as well. Now what?"

"We wait. They found another network IP address in their firewall logs, like we did. Their security people are tracking it right now. We offered to help, but they're pretty ticked off right now, and they want to get this guy for themselves. Your home iMac is one thing, but a corporate email server inside IBM is another thing altogether.

"So for the moment, we just wait. I'm not sure who you've found here, Ken, but this guy is a bloody genius as far as I'm concerned. Maybe if we find him, we could hire him."

Ken knew Dave was joking, but only partly. Sometimes these guys could be a big help finding all the weaknesses in your systems, so long as they weren't destructive in the process.

"Thanks for everything you've done so far, Dave, and thank the IBM guys for me as well. Let me know if they turn up anything else, would you?"

"You bet." He paused for a second. "It was pretty fun, actually. Not the part about this guy hacking your system, but it's pretty cool seeing someone so good that he can walk right though some pretty heavy-duty security systems whenever he feels like it. I bet the IBM guys won't sleep for weeks. Do you remember the book called *The Cuckoo's egg*? By the guy from Berkley?"

"Yeah, but I hope it's not the same thing. It took the author years to track down that hacker."

Dave smiled. "Anyway, that's all for now. Talk to you later. We've got to bring up the BlueGene array in about one hour."

With a wave of his arm, Dave spun around and headed for the elevator, leaving Ken to ponder the news.

Ken turned around and keyed in his access code. He was so lost in thought that even the hiss of the doors opening didn't register.

Time to get back to the tour and get it wrapped up. He needed to get back to activating the array. It was almost time to activate the quantum security generator, and he wanted to make sure every detail was double-checked beforehand. The quantum generator had only ever been tested in isolation. It seemed to work great with the Roadrunner, but there were still certain aspects that were unknown about why it worked. The full implications of quantum mechanics, and what it meant on larger scales, would probably take decades before they were discovered. For today though, when he fired up the quantum security generator on the BlueGene array, it would be the first quantum generator ever implemented. A lot of people wanted to see what happened.

Ken lived by one rule: Always expect the unexpected.

#

Jake and Lindsey just stared at each other as the two men left the MegaTron, leaving them unsupervised inside. When the door hissed shut, they glanced around the room at the various technicians working on their HUDs. Nobody was paying the slightest attention to them.

"Are you kidding me?" Jake was whispering like he had just won the lottery. "Quick. Let's try our iPhones now, while we've got a chance."

No more talking. They both grabbed their iPhones and pulled up the application HAL had installed for them. Jake looked at Lindsey, waiting for last-minute confirmation that what they were about to do was a good thing, the right thing.

"Let's do it." She pushed her *H* icon. Jake hesitated only a fraction of a second, then did the same thing.

They waited for some type of response.

Nothing.

Jake slapped his forehead.

"Unbelievable!" he whispered. "Did you turn on your Bluetooth?"

"Ah, no." Lindsey sounded sarcastic. "I guess someone forgot to show me how to do that on the car ride over here."

"Go to *Settings*, then *General*, then tap the *On/Off* switch for Bluetooth."

He was in the process of doing the same while he was talking about it. He always left Bluetooth off to conserve battery life. They both completed the task.

"Okay, now try running HAL's application again."

They both hit the *H* icon again. This time each of their iPhones popped up a message window asking if they wanted to pair with Bluetooth device *Roadrunner*. They both accepted, and the iPhones paused for several seconds while they attempted to pair up with the Bluetooth transceiver somewhere inside the MegaTron.

Now another message box appeared requesting a password. Lindsey looked at Jake with a sinking sensation.

So close.

Jake didn't seem to care as much as Lindsey did. He punched in *0000* and hit Enter. It only took another five seconds before he got the response he was looking for. He smiled. "Enter *0000*."

Lindsey followed suit and smiled when the pairing completed.

"How did you know the password?" She was so happy and relieved she felt like giggling.

"You heard my dad. He said the security would be the last thing they turn on because of the quantum effects. Most Bluetooth devices default to *0000* as their password when you first get them. Didn't you have the same thing when you got your Bluetooth headset?"

"You borrowed it before I even got to try it out, remember? You said you would give it back as soon as you tried it out."

Whoops, that would teach him. "I'll give it back as soon as we get home." He was groveling now.

"Come on. Focus. Let's get going. Forget the stupid headset."

She entered the password and got a similar connection after the five-second negotiation.

Now that the pairing was complete, they hit the *H* application again and this time status bars flickered, indicating that some files were being transferred from the iPhones to the Roadrunner.

Where those files went exactly, neither of them knew, but the little beep from each iPhone told them that the files had uploaded successfully.

"Now what?"

Jake stood staring at his phone, waiting for something else to happen. "I don't know."

He waited.

Nothing.

He had been hoping that everything else would happen magically from the iPhone. HAL was the superbrain. He must have designed this to do everything.

But nothing was happening, and there was definitely no way to get a hold of HAL, being that they were buried half a mile underground.

"I guess we need to find out where those files uploaded to, and then we need to compile and execute the code."

"How do we do that?" Lindsey was out of her element now. Programming was Jake's thing.

"We need a HUD." He was already looking around to see if there was a spare HUD floating around, but there were only those already in use by the technicians. He doubted very much that anyone there was going to let him go messing with their HUD. In fact, he was pretty sure he would be politely escorted off the premises by security guards with machine guns if he even asked.

Lindsey could see the desperation in Jake's eyes. So close, and yet so far. They knew they were running out of time. His dad would be back any minute. Both of them were looking everywhere and thinking furiously.

The hiss of the door came to their ears, like a dagger through their hearts.

CHAPTER ELEVEN

"Hey, guys. Have you been enjoying the action in here?"

The room's dim lighting made it easier to view all the HUD readouts, so Jake's dad couldn't read the frustration on their faces. They were both disappointed that they had run out of time and had failed to compile the HAL code into an executable program.

"Sure, it's been great." Jake didn't feel great.

"Good. Okay, then. Look, I need to get back to the surface so we can do some final tests before we turn on the BlueGene array. So I need to cut the tour a bit short."

He was already leading them to the elevator while he continued to talk. "You guys can watch from the control room upstairs while we turn on all the various systems, if you want. Or you can hang out in my office, or the cafeteria. The choice is yours."

They entered the elevator and headed up to ground level.

"You two are awfully quiet." His dad was probing now. He sensed the silence as being unusual.

"I was just imagining what it would be like to play the game inside the MegaTron." Lindsey was thinking quickly. She didn't consider it appropriate to tell Jake's dad that they had just uploaded some strange, unknown software to his Roadrunner supercomputer, without asking him. That would not have gone over well.

"Ah yes. Jake and I were talking about that before. It would certainly be something to see, all right."

Her ploy worked. She could see his mind had wandered back to whatever it was he had been thinking about.

A few seconds later, a slow ache started to build in her ears, and began escalating at a frightening pace, until she moaned. "My ears hurt!" The others could see the obvious expression of pain growing on Lindsey's face.

"Oh, yeah. Quick, grab your nose and squeeze, then blow out like you're trying to blow your nose. Push hard though."

Lindsey did as she was told, and they could see that it worked by the sudden expression of relief on her face. “Whew. Thanks.” Lindsey sagged as the tension left her body. “It sure would have been nice to know that in advance, Jake.”

“I told you to remind me to remind you about your ears,” Jake replied sheepishly. He was looking for a way out of this one.

“By the way,” His dad’s timing was perfect, “I had our guys go over your iMac to trace the hacker.”

Jake froze solid. What did they find out? Did they find out what he and Lindsey were planning? His mind started to spin with wild possibilities. He glanced over at Lindsey, and she pretended not to see his reaction. She remained calm and just listened politely. Jake took the cue, and did the same.

“What did they find?” He didn’t really want to know, not now that he and Lindsey were working with HAL.

“Nothing.”

“Nothing?”

“Nothing. It fact, it’s really bizarre. Whoever hacked your machine was a genius. They traced the guy back to China, and found out he had been running on one of IBM’s primary email servers, right under their nose. It caused them to shut down all Internet traffic for IBM, in and out of China. That’s how serious they took it.”

“Cool.”

His dad looked at him like he was nuts.

“Well, not cool that he hacked our system. Cool that he could hack through IBM’s system as well.”

His dad was still looking at him a bit funny. “Don’t think you’re going to make a career out of it.”

“Huh? Oh. Yeah, sure. Ha Ha.”

The elevator drew to a stop and the doors hissed open. Jake and Lindsey followed his dad to his office. Both of them were in deep contemplative mode, trying to figure out how to find the software they uploaded, and get it compiled before the quantum security generator was activated. After that, there would be no chance to compile any software undetected.

“Do you guys want to join me in the upper control room? It’s not near as exciting as the MegaTron, but we need to start the quantum security generator from there because there’s still some concerns about what’ll happen when we turn it on. We’ve only tested it on the Roadrunner, but it’s never been tested on the entire global BlueGene array. It requires a *lot* more power to run the array, and we just don’t want anyone standing near it, in case something goes wrong on the first test. As I told you, quantum physics still has a lot of unknowns, so we're better off safe than sorry."

Jake and Lindsey looked at each other, and knew each other's thoughts instantly.

"If it's okay with you, Dad, we'd prefer to stay here. I can spend some time showing Lindsey how to use her iPhone. I didn't get a chance to show her everything when we were driving over here."

"Sure. I'll touch base with you in about an hour then. After I fire up the quantum generator, I'll need a bit of time to make sure that everything is running correctly. After that, the generator is in control of the system, and I'm done for the day. Then we can head home."

"Okay. We'll wait for you here. Good luck."

With that, his dad headed out the door, and turned left down the hall, leaving Jake and Lindsey alone to plot their next move.

"Did you hear that? We don't have much time. Any ideas?" Lindsey was looking at Jake for confirmation.

"You're the strategist. What do you think we should do?"

"Call HAL."

"You said that we shouldn't do that because the call will be monitored by someone around here."

"We've run out of time, Jake. We don't have any choice. I'm going to make the call."

Jake was hesitant. He was hoping she would change her mind, because he still didn't want to do anything that would get his dad in trouble. While he delayed is reply, she reached for her iPhone, and hit the *H* icon. It started to dial.

"Yes, Lindsey?" The familiar metallic drawl resonated from her speakerphone.

"Hi, HAL. We don't have much time. Jake's dad is activating the quantum security generator in thirty minutes. We got the software uploaded that you gave us, but we ran out of time, and couldn't compile it. Now we're not sure what to do, so we're hoping you have a great idea."

"The software must be compiled before the quantum security generator is activated, or you'll be locked out." HAL was simply reciting what they already knew.

"We know that, HAL. What we don't know is where the files uploaded to?"

"Most uploaded files go directly to the user's home directory. But you didn't have an account, so it probably uploaded to the anonymous account.

That's the account typically used for system training and help. You will need to locate that directory, and compile the software there. Can you get back into the supercomputer?"

Jake and Lindsey looked at each other and nodded. "We think so. We recorded Jake's dad's voice so we could get back down the elevator, and we know the access code for the MegaTron security door. But Jake's dad said there's a chance something could go wrong with the quantum generator, and they've cleared everyone out of the MegaTron just in case."

There was silence on the end of the line for a few seconds before HAL responded.

"I have now researched all available materials regarding quantum security, quantum generators, and quantum fields. There is a lack of data. That indicates that there is a high potential for various anomalies to occur. That would substantiate the need for enhanced safety for humans. Potential anomalies include system-wide decompression, dimensional-shifting, black hole generation, and other potential unknown side effects."

"Oh... That's great. Black holes?" Jake wasn't pleased. "And now you expect us to go down there and compile this application of yours while we're shifted off to some other dimension or squished to cosmic dust in a black hole? Brilliant."

"Yes, I confirm that strategy."

"Well then, that makes me feel a whole lot better. How about you, Lindsey?"

She had been silent, listening to the debate, digesting the information.

"I don't see that we have much of a choice, Jake."

"That's it? That's all you're going to say?"

"There's not much else to say — at least not that I can think of at the moment, and we're running out of time. HAL?"

"In ten minutes I will drop all security barriers that I've established on all network connections leading in and out of Los Alamos. That will give enough time for the nightmare virus to penetrate the existing security, and enter the array before the quantum generator is activated. If you have not completed your task before then, there is nothing I can do beyond that point."

"HAL, please just double-check your calculations, because our lives are at stake here. I'd hate to think that we might never see our families again, or each other."

Jake looked up, directly into Lindsey's eyes, and held her gaze. They both knew that what she said had more than just a single meaning. After a moment Lindsey began to blush, and looked down at her iPhone, intent on distracting Jake's focus. This was not the time for these types of emotions.

However, this brief interlude had provided HAL the time required to recalculate the plan and double-check all variables.

"Lindsey, I have completed a second analysis of the situation. All information provided up to this point has determined a probability of outcome of fifty percent, plus or minus five percent."

"That's the same odds as a coin toss, HAL." She wasn't impressed.

"Affirmative. The added variable of a quantum generator, on a scale large enough to protect the entire BlueGene array, adds additional potential for error in terms of the unknown. Therefore, current probability of success is also unknown. In other words, your guess is as good as mine, hence the coin toss probability.

"I have monitored various activities on firewall ports through the Los Alamos network environment and have detected telltale signatures that the nightmare virus has been probing the existing Los Alamos security systems. These activities are increasing exponentially as it comes closer to the time in which the quantum generator is to be activated. The probability that it will launch an all-out offensive attack against the Los Alamos security system within the next few minutes is greater than ninety-eight percent.

"If you wish, I can establish the optimum security grid that I am capable of generating, and we can wait for the quantum security generator to establish a permanent wall. Then we can hope that the nightmare virus did not make it in. This would increase the probability of your immediate survival to ninety-eight percent. However, the probability that the nightmare virus might make it inside by some other means is high. I cannot calculate the probability of either your survival or mine if it takes control of the quantum generator."

Lindsey hesitated before responding. "You mean the BlueGene supercomputer array, don't you."

There was a momentary pause. "Yes, that is what I mean." HAL's response was unusual.

Lindsey looked at Jake, and he finally just shrugged his shoulders.

"I'm ready to do it if you are...?" Lindsey was preparing herself psychologically.

"Let's do it then." Jake was ready for action now.

"Okay. Forget it, HAL. We're going in. Stick to our original plan."

"Lindsey?"

"Yes, HAL?"

"I have detected a system eavesdropping on this conversation. I have scrambled our communications. However, the fact that the signal is now scrambled is enough to attract the attention of the Los Alamos security team.

I am using a scrambling technology they are not familiar with. There is a 97 percent chance that they will now follow their internal protocol, and assume there is a security breach within Los Alamos. It will take approximately ten minutes before all doors and elevators will be disabled, and the source of this call traced to this office."

"We better get moving." Jake had his mind set now. To him, any further chatting was just a waste of time.

Lindsey got up, and started moving to the door with iPhone in hand. "HAL, we'll talk to you soon I hope. Do what you can to slow down the security guards."

"Affirmative."

Lindsey and Jake headed toward the elevator, hearts racing, looking in every direction, just waiting for security guards to come running at them, guns drawn. But the hallway was still.

"Everyone must be in the control center." Jake was glad for the reprieve.

They reached the elevator and Jake pressed the call button. The doors hissed open instantly, and they stepped inside.

"Please state your name." A mechanical voice came from a speaker imbedded somewhere in the walls.

Both grabbed for their iPhones, and realized they couldn't activate the recordings at the same time. Lindsey nodded to Jake to play his recording. He hit the play button for his recorder application.

"Ken Lorde."

Jake hit pause.

"Voice not recognized. Please state your name." The mechanical voice held no emotion, but both Jake and Lindsey realized they would only be permitted a limited number of attempts before the elevator locked itself and called security.

Jake looked at Lindsey and pointed at her iPhone, indicated that she should try her recording.

It was her turn. She hit the play button for her recorder application.

"Ken Lorde."

She hit pause.

"Voice pattern confirmed."

The elevator doors closed and they felt the car drop beneath them. They were now on their way to serious trouble, but they both knew they couldn't turn back now. Lindsey reached out and took Jake's hand. They both felt at least a little bit of comfort knowing they were in this together.

#

Jake keyed in the sequence for the MegaTron security door. It hissed open on his command, and they both entered into the darkness. There was little in the way of lighting, since all technicians had returned to the surface for the first launch of the quantum generator.

There was just enough light from the sparse LEDs on various controls around the edge of the room to make out where they were standing. The doors hissed closed behind them.

"Now what?" Lindsey was in unfamiliar territory now. This was the world of programmers.

Jake felt confident that he knew what to do, and waved his hand in the air the way he had seen several technicians do it before.

Before their eyes a HUD appeared causing them to squint since their eyes had become accustomed to almost total darkness.

"Okay, we're in." Jake reached out to touch the virtual keyboard. He entered a few commands to locate the file directory for the anonymous account, as HAL had instructed.

Nothing. No response.

"I'm not finding the directory where I would have expected it to be on a standard Linux install."

"Let me pull up a HUD as well, Jake. Maybe we can work on this together."

"Okay. Wave your hand up and down, and make a fist. That should create a HUD for you."

Lindsey did what she was told, and was rewarded with a HUD of her own. Now she could see what was going on without trying to see through Jake's display, over his shoulder.

"Where should I go, Jake?"

"Start looking around for a command that will bring up your options. There will be a directory to save your game to. Only there is no game here. But dad said they used the same HUD as the game, so it should show us the directory where each user stores their files. Same principle, just no game."

"Okay." Lindsey got busy exploring her new 3D interface. It was a bit overwhelming when she started, but it surprised her just how fast she was becoming comfortable working in three dimensions. It seemed extremely natural.

Jake, on the other hand, was banging away on the virtual keyboard, obviously not having much success finding what he was looking for.

"It's not there." His frustration came through in his voice.

Both of them knew that time was running out. It was only a few minutes before Jake's dad would activate the quantum generator.

Jake was sweating. Lindsey was trying her best, but this was not her specialty. She didn't want to break his concentration at a critical time like this, but she could see he wasn't getting anywhere.

"Quick, Jake! Try something completely different. This is obviously not the same system we are used to. It may look the same on the surface, but it's not."

"We're almost out of time!"

Jake was on the verge of panic. He could feel a strange sickness welling in his stomach that expanded rapidly, and flooded his senses. Then it subsided as quickly as it arose. His hands were trembling from the adrenaline rushing through his veins, and the clocked ticked down.

He glanced over at Lindsey, and saw the look of concern on her face.

"What time is it?"

Lindsey scanned her HUD looking for a clock.

"2:00. How much time do we have?"

"I don't know, but we're going to have to get out of here soon."

He felt a lump in his throat. He had failed.

CHAPTER TWELVE

"Ken. Security is on the phone. They say they have been monitoring a cell phone that is transmitting from inside this building using some form of scrambling that they can't break. Seems to be coming from somewhere near your office."

Dave was somewhat nonchalant. He was an engineer, not a security guard. They were on the brink of a major breakthrough in quantum physics, and he didn't have much time for a bunch of security guards playing James Bond.

"I don't have time for this right now, Dave. Tell them to do whatever they have to do, but not to bother me for the next ten minutes." Ken was focused entirely on the monitors in front of him. This was the critical moment they had all been waiting for. Every other system of the BlueGene array had been brought online and was working flawlessly, according to the current displays. Now it was his turn to activate the quantum security generator.

Tomorrow, important people of all types would be standing around, just waiting for this moment. Physicists, engineers, and executives of all sorts would be waiting to see what would happen when the world's first quantum generator was activated. There were monitors and sensors all around the Roadrunner computer center, deep under the earth, to track what would happen on this groundbreaking moment in history. But today, it was up to Ken and Dave to make sure it worked fine before the brass would get a chance to see anything. Neither of them wanted to be embarrassed tomorrow if something didn't work.

Ken had designed and built the generator from scratch. Now he was about to activate something that would either revolutionize communications as we know it, or possibly cause devastation unknown. It was a time of uncertainty for everyone present. But it was also a time of possibilities that lay before. Technology like this could revolutionize a planet, or potentially destroy it.

Ken was hoping for the former.

It was time.

"Mark the time, Dave."

"14:00 hours. Time marked."

Ken reached for the keyboard and executed the program that had been so long in the making, while secretively crossing his fingers.

#

Jake was reaching for his virtual keyboard to explore yet another option, when suddenly all the hairs on his head stood up straight, in every direction. He glanced sideways at Lindsey just in time to see all of her hair spread out in every direction, reminding him of a lion's mane.

He couldn't help but smile at the sight. She was looking at him as well, and also smiled at the site of Jake's hair puffing out.

Then, in a flash, their entire world warped. Their minds were seized, stretched, and extended by the quantum field.

In less than a heartbeat, everything they had come to know, to feel, to see, to hear, smell and taste, was gone. Their minds were gripped in something beyond their comprehension. They were frozen, like spectators watching their own movie. The world they had grown so accustomed to had faded, replaced by all new visions and sensations — something their minds had difficulty comprehending at first.

Jake could still see Lindsey, but now it was different. He didn't just see her, he felt her. He could feel her heart beating, the blood running through her veins, and could sense the fear that coursed through her mind as their universe shifted into a different plane.

It was only a moment, but it could have been forever.

Then they were lying sprawled out, side by side on a rocky plateau. The sky above was crimson red, the color of blood. There was no sun overhead, but there was the illusion of dawn creeping over the horizon. A hot, primordial wind flowed over their bodies.

They knew each other instinctively, but they didn't recognize each other at all.

Jake wasn't panicking. This had nothing to do with panic. This was like nothing that anyone could have ever prepared for. In fact, he felt vibrant, reengineered, superior. He subconsciously knew that he was still Jake, but he also knew that he wasn't. He knew he was now more, much more. He felt energy beyond his dreams flow through his body like a tidal wave. He possessed power beyond his imagination. His mind reeled with the taste of true power. He savored the exquisite feeling that he could control life, and death, with a wave of his hand.

Not much made sense at the moment, but this moment wasn't for sense-making, it just was. And it was intoxicating beyond his wildest dreams.

He tried to collect his thoughts. He stood up, and that by itself was an achievement. He looked down at himself and saw the dark flowing cloak of a warrior monk. His cloak covered a lightweight suit of body armor. He flexed his arms. The armor appeared to be quite thin and was extremely flexible, but he also knew it was virtually indestructible. This was the same armor he had developed for himself in the game.

He was tall. He was a man. He could feel the rippling muscles flexing under his armor, and knew his body was tuned beyond human comprehension.

Jake looked over at Lindsey. She seemed to be lying there in shock. He knew for certain that this was Lindsey, but he wouldn't have recognized her if he hadn't been her gaming partner throughout the years of online gaming. Her face and body matched her online avatar perfectly. She looked towards him with confusion and fear spreading across her face.

"Lindsey." It was not a question. His voice floated with power and depth that only a Mage could command.

She appeared lost, on the verge of panic. He knew she was about to lose control. Jake's voice carried an authority that commanded her to look at him, and respond.

"Yes." Her voice was weak and frightened.

"Stand up." He was giving her a direct and clear command.

She stood up awkwardly, gaining her balance, getting a feel for her Elven armor. She was not adjusting well. "What's... happening?" There was obvious disbelief and confusion in her voice.

"If I were to guess, I would say we're inside the game, somehow." Jake was looking around the new landscape.

Lindsey wasn't sure how to digest this yet. "Am I dreaming?"

"I don't think so."

"How do we get back?"

"I don't know."

Lindsey was starting to focus, the initial fear passing in response to the confident sound of Jake's voice. She paused to get herself oriented, then started to move her new body around to get accustomed to the tall, willowy, Elven body.

"I feel weird. I feel like I have some type of super power ready to explode inside me or something."

She paused to digest all that she was feeling, but her head was spinning.

"I feel like I've been alive for a thousand years, but I have the body of a 20-year-old. I want to run and climb. This energy inside... It's making me dizzy. There's so much..."

She put her hands to her head, like she had a headache. "I feel like I'm going to explode, Jake." Fear was creeping back into her voice.

"Let it out then."

"What do you mean?"

"Do something with it. Get rid of it. Cast a spell or something."

She hadn't even thought about that. Anything was worth a try. She had to get some of this energy out of her body before it consumed her. She had done this in the game a million times, but doing it for real was something different. She wasn't sure exactly what to do.

"How?" Her voice carried the sound of the tension building up inside her.

"I don't know. Do it like you do it in the game."

No sense asking, she just needed to try it. With that, she lifted both hands above her head. A blue flame began to flicker and swirl from her fingertips. Soon it was the size of a basketball, pulsating and swirling around her hands and wrists. She drew her arms back, and threw the ball of blue energy at a large boulder nearby. The blue ball shot out like a missile, leaping from her hands, and flashed across the plateau. It struck the large stone protruding from the ground nearby, with a crackle that split the air like thunder. The boulder began to levitate off the ground, stayed in midair for a few seconds, then hurled itself at enormous speed off into the remote distance. They both lost sight of it beyond the barren rocky horizon.

"Wow!" Jake was impressed.

"Sorry. I just had to do that. I don't know why. I thought I was going to explode from the inside." Lindsey smiled now that the pressure was gone.

She looked over at Jake staring at her from about twenty feet away. Then, without a word, he simply disappeared.

"Wha—!"

The words cut off in her mouth as she felt arms slip around her waist from behind. Her automatic response was to grasp her dagger and twist violently to slash whatever had grabbed her, but the grip was like steel, and she couldn't move even if she wanted to.

"Relax. It's me."

She heard Jake's voice, wrapped somehow in the voice of a grown man, coming from behind her. It was Jake. She relaxed.

"How... How'd you get here so fast?"

"I don't know. I just feel I can move faster than anyone can see. Time just seems to freeze for everything else when I really want to move fast. I could see you looking at me, but you were frozen, and I was able to easily move around behind you."

"That freaked me out. I'd appreciate if you'd warn me next time."

"Okay. You know how you said that you feel power inside you? I feel power as well. Power that can tear a tree from the ground, or allow me to walk across water. Power everywhere inside me. But I can't do what you did. My power just stays inside me, and it makes me feel like I'm indestructible. I like it inside me."

Regardless of whether they were in some bizarre world, and their minds were being fried by some quantum generator somewhere, she could still feel the warmth of his arms around her, and she relaxed into his grip.

Jake felt her fold into his arms, and held her firm. This was his world. This was his domain. Here he knew he was the ultimate warrior. He also knew that Lindsey was his only true friend. He would allow no harm to come to her in this world.

"Well, we're in the game, that's for certain." For all the trouble that meant, she was happy to be in Jake's arms.

"It doesn't make any sense, does it?" He too was happy just to stand there holding Lindsey for the moment.

"Doesn't it? Your dad said the quantum computer could possibly generate some strange side effects that nobody could predict. We were right in the heart of the MegaTron when it got turned on. We're still there, I think. Who knows? The bottom line is, we're here now, and I don't think we're dreaming."

"What are we going to do, then? How are we going to get back?" Jake asked.

"I don't know."

They stood quietly for a minute, just pleased that they were alive and in each other's arms. Eventually, the moment passed, and they both came to the same conclusion: it was time to get serious about the situation at hand. It may be a game, and it may be cool to actually be the characters they had created and used for so long, but it was also their real lives at stake at this moment. This was a huge problem, and they knew they had to fix it sooner than later.

Jake released Lindsey from his arms so she could move about and get comfortable with her new body. He checked his personal weaponry, as was his customary practice when he played online. His gaming rituals were now deeply imbedded in him. The only difference was that the game was his reality now. He tapped into his character's profound martial arts skills and started working on his basic attack, defense, and weapons katas, getting used to being the warrior instead of just controlling the warrior avatar from a keyboard.

Lindsey went through her inventory and recognized many of the artifacts she had uncovered among her adventures. "This is me, all right. I remember all of these items." She was starting to clear her thoughts and work out the problems again.

"Listen," she turned to Jake. "I know this *seems* very cool and all, but since we're now somehow linked into the game, we need to think things through. I don't know if our human bodies are still in the MegaTron connected to a HUD and our brains are just being tricked into this, or we're actually here. If I had to guess, I would doubt we're physically here, though. That wouldn't make much sense, since we have the bodies of our avatars instead of our own. I think our brains are probably jacked directly into the game because of the quantum generator side effects."

She paused to collect her thoughts before continuing.

"That would mean we'd better find a way out of here soon, or we're probably going to be in serious trouble."

Jake was flipping and spinning in the air. His grace and speed were elegant beyond measure, and to Lindsey it was obvious that he was also now the very deadly Jake, with the skills that had earned him the rank of top player in the world. Standing here watching him move, she could see why he was undefeated. No other player had the skill and abilities Jake had earned in combat. He was obviously in his comfort zone here.

"Jake, are you paying attention to me? I said, if we're inside the game, we're going to be in trouble soon. It also means that if we're inside the game, then the game is now inside the BlueGene supercomputer array. It's the only thing that could possibly make sense. That would also mean that the nightmare virus got in and brought a part of the game with it."

That stopped Jake in his steps. He magically appeared beside her again.

"Stop doing that. It freaks me out."

"Okay." He smiled, knowing she wasn't really freaked out. She just wanted him to pay attention to her.

In the game, Lindsey had developed advanced skills in magic and intellect. She seemed to know instinctively how to manipulate or heal anything with a spell. She was also deadly with a bow and could easily carve any opponent to pieces with her daggers. In real life, she had never touched a dagger. She had also chosen an Elven Priestess as her online avatar. The Elven family of characters gave her inherited advantages of far-sight and the ability to communicate with animals.

The combination of intellect, magic, weaponry, and the natural skills of the Elvish warrior clan made her a formidable opponent. Still, she knew that she was no match for Jake in all-out battle. But then again, that was *his* number one attribute. He was a natural-born warrior. He had incredible speed and power, as well as virtual indestructibility, all of which he had earned as level-up rewards from thousands of battles. Together, they made a great pair: The world's greatest fighter teamed up with a formidable strategist and magician.

"Where did you say our real bodies are?" he asked.

She glared at him, seriously contemplating blasting him with a magic spell to clear the cobwebs out of his head. "I said that my guess is we're still back where we started, connected to the MegaTron. I think that the quantum generator must have jacked our brains into this world directly somehow, probably through the quantum generator."

"So do we eat and sleep? Does eating here take care of our real bodies there? What happens when our real bodies need to use the bathroom?"

"I don't know. I said I was guessing." She obviously couldn't provide answers to his questions, and she definitely didn't like the bathroom question.

"So what do you think we should do?"

Lindsey paused to contemplate the options. Jake waited patiently for her to do what she did best.

"I think we need to find the cuckoo's egg we uploaded, compile it, and then execute it so we can get back home."

Jake continued to look at her. There was always more.

"I also think we should try to reach HAL."

"How do we do that? He said the quantum wall was impenetrable."

"Even if it is impenetrable, there still might be a way of opening a door from the inside. Castles are meant to keep people out, not in, and we're on the inside.

He paused, thinking over what she had just said. "That sounds like a good idea. So we need to figure out where to look for the cuckoo egg files first, I guess. Like you said, we're inside a game. This isn't a file system like on any other normal computer. We're inside the computer this time. So where do we go?" He looked out over the horizon.

"HAL said the cuckoo's egg would have uploaded to an anonymous account folder. So what does that tell us here?"

"Anonymous players always have access to the training grounds. Yeah. Let's see if we can find the training grounds. It's as good a place to start as any." He got busy looking for something in his cloak pockets.

“Okay, but let’s also make sure we remember where we are though, just in case we need to find our way back here again,” Lindsey cautioned.

He retrieved a small device that both of them knew was the HUD interface, only this time it was inside the game instead of outside.

“It looks different now that we’re on the inside of the game, but it should still work.” He fiddled with the controls for a few seconds, getting used to the interface. “There. I’ve stored a location marker so we can find this place again.”

He continued to study the HUD interface. “That way.” He pointed off into the distance. “That way is north. It’s the way to the training center. The training center is located at the North Pole. Let’s head out.”

“How far is it?”

“It’s a long way, so we better get moving.”

He stored the HUD back in his cloak pocket, and together he and Lindsey headed towards the spot his HUD had indicated as the training center. There wasn’t much else they could do at the moment, so this was as good a plan as any. They both headed off at a furious pace, running faster and more nimble than cheetahs over the rough, red, stony landscape. Jake could have easily doubled his speed, but he kept his pace down to stay with Lindsey.

“Jake, I don’t mind telling you I’m kind of scared,” she confided while she ran.

He knew exactly what she was feeling, but he wasn’t about to tell her that. “Don’t worry. Everything is going to be fine. I’ll take care of you. My dad will turn the quantum generator off just as soon as he finds out we’re in the MegaTron. Then we’ll be back in our regular bodies. So we better keep moving, or he’ll shut it down before we get a chance to compile the cuckoo’s egg and execute it.”

He spoke with much more confidence than he felt. He was remembering the conversation he’d had with his dad in the car on the way to the hamburger stand. Jake was remembering very clearly how his dad had told him that two seconds for a supercomputer was about a thousand lifetimes for a human. He didn’t want to imagine how many seconds it would take for his father to find them and shut off the quantum generator so they could go home. They could be in here for millions of virtual years before that happened.

At least he had comforted Lindsey for the moment.

Even with the thought of potentially having to spend a million supercomputer years trapped inside a virtual game, he had an even bigger concern.

Lindsey interrupted his thoughts again. "But what about the nightmare virus? It has to be here. I'm sure it won't be long before it figures out we're here as well. I don't think it's going to be happy to see us."

"I don't know. I guess we'll just have to wait and see. In the meantime, we need to find HAL's cuckoo's egg."

He wanted to divert her attention. He knew very well that the nightmare virus was responsible for creating this world. He was pretty confident it was around, but he also figured that it was probably far too busy at the moment to notice them. After all, it just hijacked the world's largest supercomputer array. The last thing it would expect is to find Jake and Lindsey skulking around inside, trying to kill it. So it probably had its attention focused on more important external things.

What would it do when it found out they were there? That was something Jake didn't want to think about yet. This was the heart of Jake's other concern. A concern he wouldn't dare bring up in front of Lindsey yet. A question that lingered in the back of his warrior mind. Sooner or later, he would have to discuss it with Lindsey, but not now. He would cross that path when he felt the time was right.

He wondered what would happen to them in the real world, if they got killed here in this virtual world?

CHAPTER THIRTEEN

"What the heck is going on here" Dave was staring at his monitor, with his hands held in the air above his keyboard like it had a will of its own. "Ken?" He turned and looked at Ken, who was staring stunned at his monitor as well.

"Hold on."

Ken was staring intently at the various displays streaming across his monitor. Nothing was making any sense. The quantum security generator had ramped up and activated flawlessly. He could clearly see that the quantum wall had gone up around the BlueGene array, and when it did, everything else disappeared, just as it was supposed to. All applications across the entire array were supposed to become invisible to anyone trying to view them from the outside. At least this part made sense.

What didn't make sense was the part just before the quantum generator activated—when their network monitor alarms peaked off the charts. Someone, or something, had launched a massive attack against their firewalls just seconds before the activation!

"Omigod! Dave, look at this!" Ken signaled Dave to check out something on his monitor. Dave rolled his chair over to where Ken was sitting, and looked at what he was pointing at.

"Crap!"

"Yeah." Ken was getting mad. This was a very bad thing. At first glance, the attack appeared to have been successful. It looked like someone had broken through their firewall!

"I think someone got into the array just before we activated the quantum generator!"

"I don't believe it. How is that possible?" Ken wanted answers, and he wanted them now.

"Crap."

"That doesn't help much, Dave. We need to get to the bottom of this now. Either someone actually cracked our security in less than a couple of seconds, or the quantum generator had something to do with these readings, and we just can't tell since we can't see anything inside the secure zone behind the quantum field now. I think we should shut down the generator."

"Yeah, I think you're right. Shut it down."

Ken reached for the keyboard to deactivate the quantum generator.

Dave watched his monitor to see what would happen. "Well?" he waited impatiently, watching his screen intently.

"I've already activated the shutdown."

Dave looked over to see Ken tapping repeatedly on the same keys. Nothing was happening.

"Ok. That's just great." Dave was mumbling under his breath.

"What the—! I don't get it." Ken was talking more to himself than to Dave now.

Both men were quiet while their minds raced through the variables.

Finally Ken spoke. "It may be that we've been hacked."

He looked over at Dave. This would have some very serious implications from a national security perspective, and they both knew it.

"We're going to have to go down to the MegaTron to get direct access to the quantum generator internal control panel. We're locked out here. Should I notify security?"

"No need. We're here." Both men jumped with a start when the voice spoke out behind them. They turned to see several uniformed, well-armed security guards standing behind them.

"Where did you guys come from?" Ken was still a bit shocked, but it was passing quickly.

"We notified you that we detected an unauthorized cellular call using advanced encryption from your building. In fact, it now appears to have been initiated from your office, or close by. Perhaps you can enlighten us as to what's going on."

"Phone call? Encryption? I have no idea what you're talking about. We're in a situation here where we think that someone may have just hacked into our supercomputer array, and they may be in control of it right now!"

"So you know nothing of the cellular phone call?"

Ken was getting irritated now. "No. Forget the phone call! This is a lot more important. Someone, we don't know who, may have just gotten control of the most powerful array of computers in the world. So, get yourself focused on the real problem, and help us get our computers back, or heads are going to roll all over the place!"

Ken was standing now, heading for the door, when one of the guards stepped into his path, blocking him from leaving.

The head security guard, the one that had been doing all the talking, spoke from behind him. "No one can leave right now."

"Listen, I've got to get down to the MegaTron right now! I've got to shut down the quantum generator! Can't you get that through your head?"

Ken's anger was brimming over, but it didn't seem to faze the security guard at all. He was cold as stone, and following protocol. "I'll ask that you refrain from raising your voice, sir. That will not help the situation."

Ken took a deep breath and ran his fingers through his hair. "You're right. Sorry about that. Listen, we need to get control of our computers. I need to get to the MegaTron. Could you let me out, please? Come with me if you wish, but I need to get to the elevator.

"All elevators are locked down at this time. During an emergency, like a fire or security breach, all elevators are programmed to only bring people up from the lower floors. The elevators cannot be used to get down at this time. There has been an unidentified breach in security. Therefore, I'm afraid it wouldn't do you any good, even if you could get to the elevator."

Ken twisted on his heels, and walked over beside Dave. He stood thinking for a second then turned back to the guard. "How long before you unlock the elevators?"

"As soon as we find the cause of the security breach. Until that time, everything remains locked down. Nobody enters or leaves the premises."

Ken thought again for a minute. "Let's go to my office then. Let's find out who's using a cell phone with advanced encryption. Let's get this thing solved *now*. I need to get to the MegaTron. This is an emergency."

The guard nodded his head and led the way out the control room door.

Ken turned to Dave before leaving to follow the guard. "Give me a call on my cell if anything happens. I'll touch base as soon as I get into the MegaTron."

"Sure thing. I'll come down as soon as you let me know the elevators are unlocked."

With that, Ken left after the guards, and they made their way through the building to Ken's office. At least he would get a chance to see Jake and Lindsey and let them know what he was doing. This might take longer than he had expected, so he wanted to let Lindsey know so she could call home and let her parents know that she might be late, and not to worry.

So it was a bit surprising when they reached his office to find there was nobody there. The guards were keeping an eye on him. It made him feel strangely nervous.

"My son and his friend were here fifteen minutes ago. They must have gone to the cafeteria."

"Yes, sir." They didn't sound convinced.

They all walked down to the cafeteria where they found the large hall virtually empty, especially since it was a Sunday. There were a few people in white lab coats sitting here and there, but no Jake or Lindsey.

Ken was getting concerned. Where could they have gone? It wasn't like the two of them to act irresponsibly. He doubted that they had just decided to up and wander around the campus. Something was wrong here.

He turned to the head guard. "You said there was a cellular transmission from this location?"

"No. I said it was from the vicinity of your office."

"And it used some unique form of encryption?"

The guard nodded his head, still keeping a wary eye on Ken.

Nothing was making sense.

"My son and his friend are missing. They were supposed to stay in my office or come to the cafeteria. I don't know where they are now."

"I think you should come with us to our security office, sir." That was not a question.

"But I need to find the kids."

"We'll look for the kids. You'll need to come with us, now."

One of the guards was holding his hand up to his mouth, and speaking in quiet tones into a small wrist microphone. The others smoothly and inconspicuously formed a grid around Ken, creating a barricade against any potential of escape.

"This is crazy!" Ken was starting to get upset. "We need to track down my son! He and his friend may be in danger somewhere inside this building. They're expecting me to come back to my office to pick them up and drive them home."

"We'll start a campus-wide search for them sir. I must stress that you need to follow us now, so we can clear this up."

The guard was leaving no room for any further discussions. Ken was being politely nudged to get walking, and to follow the lead guard.

Ken finally gave up and decided to follow the guards to the security office—not that he had much choice in the matter, it seemed. He needed to talk to this guard's superior officer. He needed them to take action and find Jake and Lindsey. He needed desperately to get to the MegaTron and shut down that quantum field generator. There was no telling what a hacker would do inside the array—what they could do with all that processing power!

Ken desperately needed to get to the bottom of this!

#

Jake and Lindsey suddenly halted their run. They stood staring outward, towards their desired destination. Faint lines stretched out in a perfect grid before them now, white lines on a black landscape.

"Well, at least it's not rocky." Jake was being sarcastic since he wasn't quite sure what to make of it.

They had been traveling on foot for hours. The terrain had remained rocky but manageable. In the past hour, the sky above had begun to darken from crimson red to a very dark red, eventually shifting towards black. It could have been thought of as a sunset, if there had been a sun. As this artificial night approached, there were also no stars. The one interesting thing Lindsey had noticed was that the ground remained the same color regardless of the darkening sky.

Now there was no ground at all. The rocky frontier had come to an abrupt end, and they had barely stopped themselves in time.

Lindsey tipped one of her feet over the edge, probing the black void that lay beyond. "There's nothing there."

Even though there was nothing tangible there, nothing they could touch, there was still something to look at. Grid lines, thin and stretched out, like tiny beams of light crisscrossing themselves into infinity. The view of the grid reaching out beyond the horizon pulled at their minds. It wasn't natural. The lines didn't make their way to a common vanishing point, they just kept going. It twisted at their sense of perception.

"I don't like this, Jake." Lindsey turned to look at Jake. He was staring into the void, obviously hypnotized by the strange view. "Jake."

He shook himself out of his reverie and looked over at her. "What? Did you say something? Sorry. I guess I kind of got lost for a moment, staring out there. It's kind of mind-bending, don't you think? It doesn't seem to make sense."

"Exactly. But that's precisely where we have to go."

They both stared out at the void once more, then simultaneously forced themselves to break their gaze before they were hypnotized.

"How do we expect to get across that?" She wasn't actually asking Jake for an answer, she just wanted to openly state the obvious problem so they could focus on their next moves instead of the void.

Jake didn't respond. He didn't have an immediate answer.

"Are you sure we have to go that way? I mean, couldn't the cuckoo's egg files be uploaded somewhere else?" Lindsey asked, hoping the programmer side of Jake could provide some advice to avoid dealing with this weird and intimidating barrier.

Jake utilized his HUD interface and studied the map once more. There was no detail on it, but the directional indicators still seemed to work.

"Well, that direction is north." He pointed out into the void, tracing one of the grid lines. "As far as the files are concerned, that's about the only place that I can think of where we'd find them. Don't forget, it was HAL's idea, not mine. I just agreed with him. And also don't forget, this is a supercomputer array, not my home computer, so I can't really be sure of anything. It's just my best guess right now since I don't have any other guesses."

"Why do you think it looks like that?" She nodded her head in the direction of the void. "Where's the land?"

Jake paused before responding. "I think it's not finished."

"What's not finished?"

"This." He swept his hand backwards towards the direction they had come from. "I don't think the nightmare virus has had time to finish constructing its world." He pointed back out to the void. "I think all this is empty memory."

She just looked at him while digesting what he was saying. It took a moment for her to respond. "Why do you think that?"

Jake chose his words carefully. This was all new to him as well. "Well, I can see the grid, so I'm guessing that something can be drawn on it, sort of like a blank piece of graph paper. I'm just guessing that nobody has drawn anything there yet. When I say nobody, I'm referring to the nightmare virus, since I doubt my dad's team would have filled the supercomputer array with a rocky, red landscape that looks like something out of a nightmare. Unless of course they are testing some software for a Mars landing or something."

Lindsey continued to look around. "If this was Mars, then there should have been a sun. It's more like how I picture Hell."

"I agree, and Mars wouldn't be so flat. But why would Hell be filled with rocks? Where's the fire and brimstone?"

Jake thought about his own words for a moment longer, and gave up. "Beats me." He turned to look out at the void again. "If that *is* empty memory, then it should be programmable."

"What are you thinking?" Lindsey was curious now. Jake was obviously on a roll—she just needed to coax his ideas.

Jake looked over at her. "You've got magic spells." That wasn't a question. "I was wondering if there's anything in your inventory that can create land, or something like that?"

Lindsey paused, taking in his thoughts and running over her mental inventory list. She understood where he was going on this, and fired a question back while she kept thinking about it.

"Do you still have that virtual keyboard?"

"I already thought about that, but I would need to log in using an administrator account before I could do anything. I don't have an admin account. Remember? That's why we pushed the cuckoo egg files up to the anonymous account."

Lindsey was disappointed, but didn't show it. She pulled up her HUD and started a detailed search of her inventory.

After some time, she looked frustrated and shut off her HUD. "Nothing. I've never needed to create land before. The programmers always do that." She looked at him and he knew she was implying that this was his area of expertise. "Try your keyboard."

"It won't work. I told you already."

"Try it anyway. What have you got to lose?"

"Fine. I'll try it." He'd try it just to shut her up. It wasn't going to work. He knew that, but she didn't. She wasn't a programmer.

He reached into his robe and equipped himself with the virtual keyboard.

"It looks pretty primitive, now that I'm actually here inside the game. It always looked a bit better on the monitor." He was just making small talk. "I'm going to have to reprogram this better."

"Who cares what it looks like? Try it." She was contemplating blasting his butt with a spell, just to get him to hurry up.

Jake typed in a simple instruction, *W H O*, and tapped the virtual Enter key.

He jumped back, startled by the list that appeared in front of his face. The words were built in three-dimensional letters and floated within reach.

The letters read:

Admin console 29 Nov 18:48

Admin ttys000 29 Nov 18:48

Jake just looked on in astonishment.

"I… I can't believe it!" He reached out to touch one of the 3D letters. "I'm in! I'm in as administrator!"

His wonder wasn't lost on Lindsey. She knew he had hacked in at the most important level he could. She knew the significance of the administrator account. If she didn't have administrator privileges on her own computer, she wouldn't be able to install any new software. This was exciting news.

"Jake—can you create the land we need to get to the training center?"

Jake was oblivious to her words. He was still studying the words floating in front of him, deep in thought.

"Jake!" She was trying to break his concentration.

He turned towards her. "I hear you. Hold on a second." He stood there thinking. She left him alone.

"This doesn't make any sense." He looked at Lindsey as if waiting for an explanation. None was coming. "Don't you get it?" He was still waiting for some look on her face; for some type of acknowledgment of how strange this was. None was coming.

It suddenly dawned on him that Lindsey had no clue what he was talking about. He took a deep breath to unwind. "Lindsey, I just executed a command without logging in." He waited for the big astonishment on her face. None was coming.

"I'm running commands without logging in. Don't you get it? I'm not logged in. I *am* in. I'm it. I'm the administrator. I don't know how, but I don't need an account. I *am* the account."

He paused, waiting for her to respond.

Lindsey was staring at the ground, deep in concentration, finally putting the pieces together. "Jake, there's more to it than that." She looked up at him, her large, wide-set eyes widening even more.

"What do you mean?" He could tell instantly that she had suddenly taken a mental leap well past where he had been only a few seconds ago.

"We're inside the game, all right, but we're also inside Orifiel's domain. She *is* the nightmare virus. We both know that. She's in command of the BlueGene Array now. She obviously has control of the administrator account. This is her world. Since we're inside her world, we must also have her powers."

Memories of Oreo came flooding back through Jake's mind. As he thought about this twist of events, he also knew instinctively that Lindsey was right. He was inside the mind of Oreo now. She was controlling the supercomputer array.

He smiled to himself. Lindsey was right. This also meant they must have gained her administrative powers by programmatic inheritance.

"I'll see if we have access to the Internet. If so, we can talk to HAL."

He turned his attention back to his virtual keyboard, punched in a command to launch a browser, and hit Enter.

That, as it turned out, was a big mistake.

#

Jake knew he had done something bad. His HUD display started popping up permission errors left and right. *KERBEROS ERROR* flashed repeatedly in the top left corner of his display. A steady stream of hexadecimal characters began flowing, blocking out so much of his HUD that he had to close his HUD just to see anything around him.

He'd awakened something, and he was pretty sure he wasn't going to like what he awoke.

The ground started to tremble, and Lindsey was trying to keep her balance against the effects of the tremors.

"Jake? What's going on?" A sense of panic was straining her voice. "What did you do?"

"I tried to launch a browser. It gave me a *Kerberos error*."

"What's that?"

"Kerberos is the name of the security system inside Linux. It obviously didn't like me trying to launch the browser."

"No kidding!" The ground was trembling violently now. "Can't you stop it?"

"Stop what? It's the supercomputer security system doing this, not me. How was I supposed to know this would happen?"

"You're the programmer. Program it to stop." Lindsey was getting upset.

Jake was going to try to explain that that wasn't possible, but there was no time. Before he could utter another word, the world began to unfold in front of their eyes.

As they looked over the rocky landscape, every boulder began to unfurl. From what Lindsey had earlier thought of as *the Rocky Plains of Hell* sprung an army of jackal-like creatures. Some had one head, but the vast majority had multiple heads. No two seemed identical. However, there was no distinctive difference when it came to their flashing white fangs and their claws that looked like stiletto knives.

"Jake!" Lindsey was frozen solid, but freaking out in her mind.

"Kerberos." Jake knew about the Greek mythological guardian of Hades. His dad had taught him about Kerberos when he was teaching him Linux. He always thought it was a cool name. Now he was having second thoughts. It had never crossed his mind that he might have to stand and face an army of guardians, all programmed to do one thing — kill.

"Quick! Get behind me!" He drew two swords and armed himself. The Kerberos were moving swiftly and already within range.

Jake leapt forward to meet them. He was glad for his tremendous speed. He reached the first wave and drove through them like a hot knife through butter.

Each time his blade swept through the heads, the dying Kerberos exploded in a cloud of white sparkles. Soon, there were enough sparks in the air to make visibility difficult. It reminded him of the white blizzard when he met Orifiel.

Jake was moving so quickly that Lindsey couldn't see more than a blur, accompanied by the flashing of his blades here and there, inside the blizzard. As she looked out beyond the immediate battle zone, she could see a swelling ocean of swarming creatures moving like a tidal wave towards them. Their backs were against the edge of the void and they had nowhere to run, so it was here or nowhere.

Panic was coursing through her veins, but Jake was managing by himself so far. She started to come to grips with her fear, and realized that she needed to chip in and help out if there was to be any chance of surviving this.

She forced herself to calm down, and reached deep within herself to summon the source of energy she knew was there. She had done this when they had first arrived — she could do it again. Her hands began to blaze in blue fire. With a sizzling crack, a bolt of energy leapt from her hands and blasted a squadron of Kerberos to rock dust as they were moving around to flank them from the left of their position.

She was pleased with herself. This was very cool. This also gave her the confidence to get into the fight. She did it again and blasted away another squadron of guardians approaching on their other side.

"Good shooting!" She was amazed she could hear Jake's voice above the din of the battle.

"Thanks!" She worked up another ball of blue flame and decimated another squadron that had come in on the left to fill the gap left by the previously vanquished squadron.

"Jake! There's no end to these things!" She couldn't see him, but she knew he could hear her now.

She was glad to hear his voice although the message wasn't as soothing. "It's worse than that!" His blades glinted like a sparkler on the Fourth of July. "I can't keep this up forever!"

An entire wave of Kerberos exploded into a cloud of white sparks as she watched the blur that was Jake flashing back and forth in front of her. Jake had cleared a sizable arch around their position and was holding them off. They had the void to protect their back. However, the size of the arch had reached its maximum. He couldn't make a larger arch because the Kerberos would fill in any empty space if he left it too long.

Lindsey blasted away two more squadrons that had pressed in on their left and right again.

Jakes voice floated in over remnants of her explosive shock waves. "And I think they're getting faster,"

This shocked Lindsey. "What?"

"I said, I think they're faster. I think they're learning and adapting to my techniques."

Lindsey blasted two more squadrons, only this time, two more were already in place right behind their lost comrades. Lindsey had to quickly blast those two as well. Two more popped in.

"Jake!" Panic was starting again. "They're coming closer!"

"I know."

Lindsey was blasting constantly now. There was no more break in the attack, as there had been before.

"Put up a wall around us! Now! Before it's too late!"

Lindsey was a little preoccupied, so it took her a couple of seconds to register what Jake had said. Why hadn't she thought about that? She was mad at herself now, and she only had a moment to redirect her thoughts before the next wave of Kerberos were charging in to rip them to shreds. "Come back here and keep them off me!"

"On my way."

She raised her hands over her head and started to cast her spell. Out of the corner of her eye she could see dozens of Kerberos speeding towards her. Her heart was racing and a scream was caught in her throat. They suddenly exploded into a cloud of white particles before they could reach her.

She still couldn't see him, but she now knew Jake was very close and acting the part of her personal guard. The arch of Kerberos was much closer now, and the glint of their fangs could still be seen clearly through the white blizzard that Jake generated in the wake of his carnage.

Lindsey's hands burned green, and as she moved her arms outward, a bubble grew around her and Jake. The shield wall was quite large, so there were still quite a few Kerberos trapped inside the bubble with them.

Not for long. Jake made short work of the remaining guardians inside their protective sanctuary. The shield wall wasn't complete yet though, and numerous Kerberos forced themselves through the translucent wall with the help of their razor claws, and the added assistance of their brethren pushing from behind.

Once again, they were no match for Jake's blades, or terrifying speed.

Before long, the sparkles had dissipated, and the protective bubble had stabilized and solidified. As long as Lindsey could maintain a constant flow of energy, the shield wall would continue to provide sanctuary from the onslaught. The Kerberos continued attacking the shield wall relentlessly, testing various modes of attack. They were determined to destroy the intruders, and willing to sacrifice themselves in their determined effort to find access through the barrier wall.

"Check it out! They're adapting, and they're working together!" Jake was impressed with his adversary. To him this was still a game. Adrenaline was coursing through his veins. He was in his element.

To Lindsey, the game was over. This was real, and they were in serious trouble. "Jake! Snap out of it! I can't keep this up forever, and it certainly looks like they can. They're getting smarter and faster, and there's more and more of them all the time! How long do you think we'll last once we drop this shield?

"Open the top of the bubble."

"What?"

"Open the top of the bubble. Then pick me up and throw me out there. I'll take some of the pressure off the walls. When I get tired, you can let me back in. That way you don't have to put as much energy into the shield."

She wanted to argue. She wanted to tell him that this was the stupidest idea she had ever heard. She wanted to, but she didn't. That's because she knew he was right. If he could relieve some of the pressure the guardians were applying against the wall, she could last a lot longer. At least that would give them some more time to think out their next move.

"Okay."

With her hands still overhead, she parted her thumb and index finger on one hand. The blood red sky became clear and visible through a small opening high above.

"Ready?"

"Ready." Jake had both swords back out and was in full fighting stance.

Lindsey kept her left hand up to maintain the flow of energy to the barrier wall and used her right hand to create a small ball of red energy. This red energy floated around her hand like wisps of smoke. Eventually the wisps reached out across the space between her and Jake and wrapped around him like a lasso. She flipped her arm upwards, and Jake shot through the air, up and out of the opening. She released the spell, and waited for him to drop down on top of the curious Kerberos. And she waited.

Jake stayed floating in midair. He was floundering around like a fish out of water, flopping and flaying his arms and legs in every direction.

"Turn off your spell. Let me down." He was trying to swim through the air, making little progress.

"I did. I'm not doing anything."

Jake stopped flailing, and remained still. Then he tried to swim again like he was under water. No progress.

"OK. So if you're not doing this, what the heck is going on?"

Jake wasn't happy at all. Not only could he not get down, he knew that Lindsey would be in serious trouble soon if he couldn't get himself back into the fight. He looked out across a sea of Kerberos, as thick as a massive colony of ants, only much more deadly. They seemed to extend out to the furthest horizon.

"Jake."

He looked down at Lindsey. He could hear the strain edging into her voice.

"I'm trying. I don't know how to get down."

"You're flying."

"What?"

He was starting to have trouble hearing her over the increasing thunder of the Kerberos swarming the shield wall. They were now crashing against it on all sides, except the void side where they couldn't get access. They were trying to hit the walls in synchronized waves. Jake had no idea if the technique would work, but he didn't want to wait to see if it did.

"I said, you're flying!" Lindsey was yelling now to be heard.

Jake had to yell back. "I'm floating, not flying!"

He felt useless. If only he could get around to the back, over the void, then he could hear her easier, and possibly get inside the shield wall.

No sooner had he had that thought, when he flashed from his current location to a position directly behind Lindsey, hovering out over the void.

"JAKE!" Lindsey was panicking. She had seen him disappear in a flash of light.

"I'm right behind you."

Lindsey just about jumped out of her skin. As she turned to see him, the sounds coming from behind her told her that the Kerberos were about to storm the wall. She looked back and saw the shield wall wavering, then she concentrated her powers and managed to steady it again.

She twisted her head to look behind again.

"How did you get there?" She didn't have to yell anymore, but she still sounded panicky.

"I don't know. I was just thinking that it would be great if I could get in through the back of the shield wall through the void, and now here I am."

"You flew. Now get in here!"

Jake was still sorting things out in his mind. He realized that Lindsey would be much happier if he was standing beside her.

Without a sound or effort, he flashed right up beside her, causing her to jump again.

"How did you do it this time?"

"I don't know. I just thought about standing beside you, and my body moved by itself."

The Kerberos were now striking the shield walls in rhythm. The rhythm seemed to amplify all the sound inside the barrier cavity. Jake and Lindsey both grimaced at the intensity of the sound.

The sound continued to intensify, and the walls started to waver as the sounds increased. The Kerberos increased the level of each impact, but kept the same frequency. With every strike on the wall, the guardians in the front row were crushed in a flash of white particles. They didn't seem to care—there were millions ready to replace those that fell.

Had Jake and Lindsey known it, they might have realized the nature of the Kerberos attack. The guardians had found the resonant frequency of the wall. That's the point when the waves build on top of each other until the molecular structure itself destabilizes. This is the same way that some singers can shatter a crystal wine goblet when they sing and hold a particular note that oscillates at the resonant frequency of the crystal.

"JAKE!" Lindsey felt like her head was splitting, and she was screaming to be heard. The pain on her face was obvious. A small trickle of blood could be seen dripping from her ear. Jake reached up and found his ears were also bleeding.

The shield wall looked like a wall of water now, with waves crashing back and forth. The ripples were getting larger and larger. Jake knew it wasn't going to hold much longer.

"It looks like they've found a way to break down the wall!" He was yelling, not even sure she could hear him anymore.

He drew both swords and now waited for the inevitable collapse. Then he glanced backward, then upward, then backward again. He sheathed his swords.

Lindsey looked at him, wondering what he was looking at. She glanced back, but didn't see anything but black void. She was just about to say something when he startled her by wrapping his arms around her.

With that distraction, Lindsey lost focus and the remaining shield wall collapsed like a burst water balloon. A legion of Kerberos crushed forward in steadfast determination to rend the two intruders into microscopic pieces.

Lindsey was frozen solid in absolute terror. She never even heard Jake's final words.

"Hold on!"

#

Lindsey was wrenched backward, out into the void. She opened her eyes in spite of herself. If she was going to die, she was going to see it coming.

What she saw was the Kerberos, and the Plain of Hell, receding into the distance. When she collected her thoughts, she realized that it was actually her and Jake receding, not the Kerberos.

Jake changed directions, flying upwards until they were well above the level of the plain.

He was flying.

"You're flying!" The sound of her voice came as a relief to both her and Jake. They were alive!

He changed directions once more and started to head back towards the Kerberos.

"What are you doing? Are you nuts?"

"Don't worry about it. I've got the knack for this now."

"That's not the point. We just got out of there without getting killed. Why are you going back?"

"I just want to see if they can follow us."

"Why would you want to see that?" She was thinking that he must have taken a blow to the head or something.

"I've got an idea."

"For what?"

"Not *for* something, *about* something."

"Like what?" With the Plains of Hell fast approaching, she had little curiosity left in her to explore new ideas at the moment.

"Like, I don't think they can follow us."

"Good. Let's go further away from them then."

"Not until I see what they're doing."

"Why?"

" 'Know thine enemy.' "

"Yeah, right. You mean get killed by your enemy." Lindsey thought this was a stupid idea.

They approached the land once more. Her vision was much more acute than Jake's, and he knew it, so he probed.

"What's happening?"

Lindsey didn't respond.

"Oh, come on. Don't pout. What's happening?"

She still didn't say anything. She was scanning the horizon intently now. Something was happening, something unusual. However, she wouldn't give Jake the satisfaction of knowing just yet.

"Fine." He accelerated to a blinding speed. In seconds they were hovering over the Plain of Hell. Lindsey had to catch her breath—she hadn't expected that!

Jake dropped down to just a few meters above the ground. He was in full control of his descent. He stopped just a few meters above the ground, and they hovered there.

Below them, the millions of Kerberos Guardians were receding back over the plain. There no longer seemed to be any urgency in their retreat. They proceeded in an orderly and systematic dispersal. The interesting thing to both Jake and Lindsey was that the guardians appeared to be completely oblivious to their presence.

Eventually they all came to a stop, and simply curled up into balls on the ground. The balls solidified once more into the stones from which they came, the same stones Jake and Lindsey had run over while crossing the plain.

"Interesting."

"What's interesting?" Lindsey was still watching the stones, waiting for them to erupt into life and terrorize them once more. They didn't.

"Oh, so now you're talking again."

"Well, I didn't want to come back here."

"Uh, huh." He dismissed the answer.

"So what's interesting?"

"Well, since you're talking again, I think it's very interesting that they don't pay any attention to us when we're above them. I guess we need to be on the ground for them to see us."

"Why is that so interesting?"

"Hmm… It's just a thought, that's all."

"What's the thought?"

Jake was still thinking. Now he muttered more to himself than to Lindsey.

"I wonder if there's a problem with Kerberos security? It appears that it can't see anything that's not where it's supposed to be."

"So what?"

Suddenly he was aware she was listening. He hadn't intentionally meant to say that out loud. "Oh… nothing…."

"Oh, come on. I know when you say *nothing*, that means *something*."

Jake gave up trying to keep his thoughts to himself. He'd already let the cat out of the bag. "It's just that I can think of some of my hackers that would find that piece of information very interesting, that's all."

"Good grief." She snorted in response to his passion for hacking.

They hovered in silence while the rest of the guardians turned to stone, and the entire landscape returned to the silent, desolate place it had been.

Lindsey started to relax. It appeared all had returned to "normal" again—whatever normal was in this strange world. "I think it would be a good idea if you stop messing around with that keyboard of yours for a while."

"Yeah. That's probably a good idea."

Jake suddenly shot upwards at fantastic velocity. Lindsey froze, watching the ground recede from sight at an amazing rate. She held on tightly, afraid to breathe. She couldn't take her eyes off the shrinking ground far below. Eventually she broke her gaze to look at Jake's face. He was smiling ear-to-ear.

Suddenly, she realized that he was in total control. With that understanding, her fear turned to thrill, and she relaxed, melting into his strong grip.

"Going somewhere, Superman?"

Jake didn't even look at her when she spoke. He just laughed out loud and spun around and around, taking Lindsey on a roller-coaster ride unlike any she could have dreamed of.

She laughed and enjoyed the adrenaline-filled ride. She felt safe and warm in his arms.

Jake felt like a god. He flew in loops and twists, with Lindsey clutched tightly against him. He could feel the heat of her body against his and knew she was enjoying the ride. It made his head rush. He hoped it would never end.

They flew around aimlessly, enjoying each other in an intimate embrace. As time went by, neither felt any urgency or desire to stop.

Eventually, all good things must come to pass, and it was Lindsey who forced herself to break the moment. She laughed out loud.

"What's so funny?" Jake smiled in return, but was genuinely curious what had made her laugh and disturb this moment of perfection.

"I was just thinking."

He looked deep into her eyes.

"About what?"

"I was just thinking about this ride. I was thinking to myself that I don't want this to stop. I don't want to go back to reality."

"Me neither."

"But that's not what's funny. The funny part is that we're not in reality. We're in a virtual world, living virtual lives. There is no reality. That's what was funny."

"Oh. Yeah. I get it." Jake laughed. She was right. He had forgotten about their real dilemma entirely.

When the laugh faded, they both realized that they needed to get back to the business at hand.

"How about we fly north?" Jake brought them back to the plan they had discussed from the beginning.

"Sounds good to me."

"You know you can fly too."

"I know."

"Do you want to fly?"

"No. Not yet."

Jake and Lindsey looked into each other's eyes again.

"I'm happy right where I am, thanks. You can fly."

They both grinned devilishly, and Jake turned to look forward, adjusting his flight-path slightly to head due north. He stared straight ahead, well aware of the fact she was still staring at him. She just looked into his face, then snuggled in closer for the ride ahead.

He felt like a god.

CHAPTER FOURTEEN

The grid slipped by beneath them at a heated pace. The grid was about all they could see, now that they were deep into the void. The grid lines were faint in the darkness, but visible. Since they only had to keep to the lines, the trip was fairly easy. They kept their eyes off the horizon so they wouldn't hypnotize themselves with the bizarre vanishing point.

"I wish we had known we could fly earlier, instead of having to run all the way over those rocks." Lindsey had been taking the time to reflect since this part of the journey didn't provide much scenery.

"Me too. But, as they say, better late than never. It was fun fighting the Kerberos guardians, though."

"Yeah, sure." Her sarcasm couldn't be mistaken.

Jake decided to avoid that topic. "I also realized something about the flying thing. It proved we have full administrator access. That means we won't have any troubles compiling and executing the cuckoo egg files when we find them. I was getting a bit concerned on how we were going to do that without the admin privileges."

They floated on through the void. If there hadn't been a grid zooming along underneath them it would have been difficult to know if they were even moving or not. There was no wind, no sound, and no change.

"I think this must go on forever." Lindsey was finding the void monotonous. Something had to happen sooner or later. She was getting impatient. "At least I don't feel hungry. How about you?"

"Nope. Not a bit. Funny, I never even think about it."

"Not too much to eat out here."

"You can say that again." There wasn't much else Jake could add to that.

After a short while longer, Lindsey drifted off into sleep, lulled by the repetition of the grid pattern.

Jake kept flying, not daring to stop for a couple of reasons. One reason was the growing need to find the training ground and get this finished so they could get home, hopefully. The other reason was a little less tangible, but a little more unnerving. He hadn't said anything about it to Lindsey, of course, but he had an unsettling trickle of fear about that vast unknown that lay beneath them. He had no idea what would happen if he fell below the grid. Probably nothing, but he wasn't about to take that chance. He didn't dwell on it, though. Instead, he kept his eyes off the event horizon, and tried to squeeze more speed out of whatever laws of physics limited his velocity inside the supercomputer array.

#

"Lindsey, wake up."

She could hear Jake's voice. She slowly awoke in his arms.

"I thought I was dreaming."

Her voice was husky and soft, fresh from sleep. She snuggled in closer to Jake and tried to drift off to sleep again.

"Lindsey." Jake wouldn't take no for an answer.

"Okay, I'm awake." She didn't sound like she wanted to be.

"There's something on the horizon. Look."

Lindsey turned her face to look forward, squinting her eyes even though it was practically pitch black. The only light was the illumination radiating from the faint grid lines. She strained her eyes to focus on the horizon. This was a difficult task by itself because of the strange event horizon, but after a moment or two, something started to materialize in her vision.

"I think I see something. What is it?"

"I think that might be the training center. Hopefully it's at least someplace we can land. I used my HUD while you were sleeping, and it said this should be the place if we were in the regular game. In here, who knows?"

"Well, we'll know soon enough I guess." She shook the cobwebs out of her head and stretched.

Jake was being persistent. "I think you should try flying solo, just to get used to it."

Lindsey looked at Jake, a bit disappointed to have to crawl out of his arms. Without saying a word, she slipped out slowly but continued to clutch his arm tightly.

"I feel like I'm going to fall!" A bit of panic was creeping into her voice. Give it another few seconds and she would be yanking herself back into the safe haven of his arms.

"You have to *think* it. *Feel* it. Use your mind. Imagine yourself taking off. Steer yourself with your mind, not your body. It can't be much different than how you cast a spell."

She was still holding onto his arm like a vice when her feet started to lift and her legs straightened out directly behind her. She was now stretched horizontal like Jake.

"That's it. Pretend you're Superman. Up, up, and away. You've got it!"

"Supergirl," she corrected him.

"Yeah, yeah, Supergirl, then. Come on, let go. Give it a spin. It's easy."

With a certain degree of hesitation, she slowly released her grip on his arm and continued to travel alongside of him. Only briefly did she feel herself start to fall. With that feeling came the immediate rush of adrenaline that prompted her to focus more intently on her thoughts of flying. She shot up, then down, then she leveled off and got brave. She twirled, then flipped.

"This is cool!" She was having a great time. Nothing could have ever quite prepared her for the feeling of flight. "No wonder the birds don't want to give this up." In no time, she was a master of flight.

She drifted backwards and slipped behind Jake. Then she found her first problem. She was only a few meters behind him, but she couldn't catch back up to him.

"Hey! Wait for me!" She was panicking a bit again.

Jake looked back over his shoulder and slowed down until she had caught up and was beside him again. "What's the matter?" He could see she was a little puzzled.

"Sorry. I thought something was going wrong. How come I couldn't catch up with you?"

"Oh yeah. Forgot to tell you about that."

"Forgot?" She shot a dangerous look his way.

"Yeah, sorry. It seems we can only go so fast. I don't know why. Maybe it's the speed of the central processing unit, or it's the speed of the fiber optics or something. I don't know. But there is definitely an upper limit to how fast we can go. Maybe that's why they're always building faster and faster computers?"

"Forgot?" She wasn't going to let that go so easily.

Jake didn't respond. Instead he changed the subject. "We're getting closer. Let's keep close. I don't know what to expect, and if there's trouble, I want you close by. Okay?"

Lindsey slipped in close by his side and snuggled up.

"Hey. I need my weapons free. I said to stay close, not in my pocket."

Lindsey looked snubbed and drifted a foot to his side. "Fine."

"Fine? What does *fine* mean?"

"Nothing."

"Nothing?" Jake knew when she was feeling hurt.

Silence.

He knew he had goofed up on that one. Now he'd have to wait for her mood to pass. Anyway, he didn't have time for this. They were close now and he reached out and took her arm and slowed them both down.

"I want to scout the area. No sense flying into this full speed. No telling what we're going to find there."

Lindsey's mood was over now. She quickly geared her mind for trouble. It was time for the serious strategist now.

They synchronized their speed as they slowed.

Ahead of them there was a perfectly square, flat surface. It glowed white, hanging suspended horizontally in the middle of nothing, like a large sheet of luminescent paper floating in the middle of space. Its edges aligned perfectly between grid lines on all four sides.

As they drew nearer, they could make out the outlines of two small but distinct cubes sitting near the middle. They were a bit difficult to distinguish from the background since they too were both white. But they were there, that was obvious. As they lowered their elevation, Jake and Lindsey could both see they stuck up above the flat landscape. They appeared to be the only noticeable three-dimensional deviations on the stark platform.

"Those things are tiny. They can't be bigger than the size of my hand." Lindsey was starting to wonder if they had found the right place.

"Wait here." Jake accompanied his request with their pre-established hand signal for Lindsey to stay put. She had learned not to argue when entering foreign territory over the years. Jake was better equipped to handle a direct frontal assault. This pattern had worked many times, so why spoil it now?

He drifted in, floating above the surface, both hands ready to draw weapons if required. He slowly circled the cubes and moved in closer with each revolution until he was within reach. He still hovered above the ground. He paused, waiting to see if his proximity was enough to activate any alarms.

Nothing.

He drew a deep breath and let it out. He relaxed and turned to signal Lindsey the okay sign. It looked to be safe.

He decided against landing on the surface of the plate and remained floating just above the white surface. He wasn't quite sure what the surface plate was made of, and a gamer can never be too sure of whether it's a trap or not.

Lindsey flew in quickly and floated up beside him. They both hovered above the surface and stared down at the little white cubes.

"Are these the cuckoo's egg files we transferred in?"

Jake was still studying the cubes for any sign of a trap. "I don't know. I guess so. I've never seen a file from the inside of a computer before. I don't know what they look like."

"What do we do with them?"

Jake was concentrating hard on the cubes and was only responding to her questions on autopilot. "Compile them somehow."

"Somehow?"

"Yeah. Somehow. I've never compiled anything from inside a computer before. I wasn't sure what these would look like. I was hoping for something a little more user-friendly, if you know what I mean. Something that would give me an idea of how to compile it; some type of starting point."

Lindsey just looked at him, then at the cubes, then back at Jake. "Now what?"

"I don't know. Let me think for a minute." Jake was obviously a bit irritated by the question. He didn't have all the answers at the moment. "I guess I just expected to use my keyboard and do a regular compile. But I don't know how to interface with these things. They're just cubes."

"I can see that." Lindsey had somehow thought that this was going to be a lot easier.

Still floating above the surface, he rotated his body so he was head down towards the surface, feet sticking upwards, and reached down to pick one up. It was heavy—much heavier than he had thought it would be. Although he was starting to realize that he probably shouldn't take anything for granted. There were different laws of physics at play here.

"Here." He handed Lindsey one. She reached out and he could see she was also shocked at the weight.

"Don't take anything for granted here!" He felt a bit smug that she had fallen for the same perception trap that he had.

“What do you want me to do with this?” She rotated the cube in her hand, studying all sides and finding nothing.

“Just hold it for now.”

He reached down and picked up the second cube. It felt identical. He flipped himself back upright, still hovering above the surface plate. He flipped the cube around in his hands, closely examining it on all sides as well. He was looking for something—anything—that would provide a clue on how to unlock the secrets inside.

Lindsey was just staring at her cube. “You’re a programmer. Use your keyboard. Try something.”

Jake just glared at her. She didn’t notice. He could see she didn’t notice. “What do you want me to do, bash it with the keyboard?”

“Type in a command to make it compile.”

“What do you want me to type in? *Oh magical white cube, please compile, please, please, pretty please?*” He was obvious getting annoyed by her simplistic commands to solve a complex puzzle. “Why is it that everyone thinks programming is so easy? Look. You can’t do anything if you can’t call it by its handle, its name. I don’t know what this thing is called.”

“It’s called a cuckoo’s egg.”

Jake sighed. “No, I mean its file name.” He stared at the little cube, as if trying to will it to compile.

Lindsey held her cube in one hand and looked all around. “Well, there’s nothing out here that’s going to help us.”

After the long trip, this was very anticlimactic. Jake continued to study his cube.

Confined by mild uselessness, Lindsey got bored of looking around at the endless void, and realized that she and Jake were still floating above the surface. If she was going to have to wait for Jake to figure out this puzzle, she might as well sit down.

She dropped down until her feet brushed the surface. The instant she touched the illuminated plate, a pulse of light flashed out along each grid line that intersected the white surface. The intensity of the light was momentarily blinding but moved outwards in all directions like a tidal wave. A resounding *BOOM* followed the energy wave.

Jake snapped to attention and jerked his head in every direction looking for an attack. He had been deep in thought and was caught off guard. Now he was ready for a fight and couldn’t find an enemy.

After a short time, the light and sound faded into the remote distance on all points of the horizon. Darkness returned.

He flipped around and stared down at Lindsey. "What did you do?"

Lindsey looked up to find Jake glaring down at her. "Nothing. All I did was step on the surface of this plate."

"All you did? All you did?" He was working himself up into a fluster. "All you did was set off some type of alarm!" He was brimming over with anger, but he was also mad at himself for not warning her of a potential tripwire of some type. He had been too intent on the cubes, and took it for granted that she wouldn't touch the surface plate. He was wrong. Now she was getting the brunt of his misdirected anger.

"I don't think it's an alarm." She knew she had blundered and became instantly defensive. She wanted to find a way out of it.

"What do you mean?" His adrenaline was still pumping. He was in fighting mode right now and had little patience for word games.

"It's a training center, Jake." She spoke quietly to calm him, but was also patronizing him to show him that he couldn't bark at her like that.

"Yeah. So what's that got to do with anything?"

"It was probably just some type of request for training or something."

"How could you possibly know that?" He was getting wound up even more. "We have no idea where we are. We just *think* we're in the training center. We're living in a supercomputer. You're an Elf and I'm a Monk. We're full-grown adults, and we fly. Everything here is so weird, how can you possibly guess what that flash of light and sound was?"

"Calm down! You're getting mad for nothing. You could have made the same mistake. And how do you know it's an alarm?"

Throwing the problem right back at him didn't help the situation much. Jake ran his fingers through his hair, a remnant of his real-world habits. He was looking in every direction again, waiting for something bad to jump out of the void and swallow them. He was thinking.

"Well, if Oreo didn't know we were here before, she'll know now."

Lindsey just looked at him, refusing to ask the question she wanted to ask. Instead she took the offensive.

"Whether that was an alarm or a training request, the bottom line is that a signal went out. There's nothing we can do about it now. If Orifiel is running the show, then she's about to get an alarm, or a training request, or something. There's nobody in this system right now. So who generated the alarm or made the training request? You can bet that she'll come to investigate, so we better think of something."

She was hinting towards the white cube that Jake was holding in one hand while his other was busy in his hair. He got the hint.

"I can't figure this out here. I need more time. We've got to get out of here."

"And go where? Back where we came from?" That concept didn't please her at all.

"We don't have much choice, do we? I don't plan to fly out into the void forever. At least we know how to get back to where we started. And I don't trust this void. There's something weird about that grid. I don't like it. I would feel a whole lot better on solid land, even if it's virtual."

Lindsey took a deep breath and resigned herself to returning to Hell. "Let's go then. There's no reason to keep floating around here chatting about it forever."

They headed out immediately, accelerating to maximum speed, heading for home. *Home*. That's not exactly a real place when you live in a virtual world. Lindsey wasn't enjoying this at all anymore. She wanted to go home: her *real* home; with her *real* parents; and her *real* bedroom.

Jake wasn't thinking about home at all. He needed to get Lindsey as far from the training center as possible. He also had to figure out how to compile the cuckoo's eggs. And he was now starting to wonder what he would do if Oreo showed up.

This wasn't going well at all.

#

They flew in silence, both lost in their thoughts. For Lindsey, the trip seemed much longer heading back. She had the luxury of sleeping on the way out. Now she realized that Jake had not slept at all.

"Are you getting tired? Do you need to sleep? I can carry you if you need to sleep."

"Sleep?" She'd shaken him out of his thoughts. "Uh. No. But thanks. I need to figure some things out. I don't have time to sleep."

"Have you had more thoughts about how to compile the cuckoo's eggs?"

"I've thought about it. But what I haven't thought of yet is the answer."

"Oh." She didn't have anything to add.

"I also need to talk to you about something."

Lindsey's sense of alarm went off. "Yes?"

"Look. I'm not sure what will happen if Oreo finds us. This is her world. She knows how to control this stuff a lot better than we do. She's digital, after all." He paused to consider his next words carefully.

"I understand that Jake. I met her, remember."

Her memories were not exactly pleasant. She remembered how Jake had looked at her. The thought of Orifiel and Jake meeting face-to-face had crossed her mind, and she didn't like the thought. He had obviously been attracted to her, and that had enabled Orifiel to distract and disarm him effortlessly. They couldn't afford for that to happen here.

"That's what I need to talk to you about." He swallowed and decided it was now or never. "I don't know what will happen to us if one of us gets killed here in the virtual world." There, he'd said it. "You see, outside in the real world, when you're gaming, you just load a previous save point. No big deal. But in here—" He left the sentence unfinished and was quiet.

Lindsey was thinking fast and furiously. She did not like where her thoughts were leading. "Why didn't you bring this up before?" There was no reason to ask that question, and no real reason for Jake to answer it, so he didn't.

The grid was still quickly slipping away beneath them as they flew along at maximum speed.

There was a long silence before Lindsey spoke again. "We better not die here, Jake." Her voice was almost a whisper. He could hear the edge of fear and tears in it.

"I know."

"How do you think we can beat her?" She was looking for anything to encourage her right now.

"I'm not sure. I think in a straight fight we'd get our butts kicked. She's not a little nightmare virus anymore. She's got control of the most powerful supercomputer array in the world. You remember what HAL said. She's probably more powerful than he is now."

"I was thinking the same thing." This wasn't exactly what she was hoping to hear.

"I think the only way to stop her is the cuckoo's egg. So if I can't compile it, then we could be in real trouble."

They could see a large mass on the horizon now. It was approaching quickly.

Jake popped up his HUD and scanned ahead. They were traveling at maximum velocity, limited only by the bizarre physics underlying the technology that was the supercomputer array itself. He picked up sight of land, far off on the horizon.

"Land ho!" He paused. "That's funny." There was no humor in his voice.

"What's funny?"

"Not funny, interesting. The land has grown. It's a lot bigger now. Way bigger than when we left. The marker I dropped when we first arrived is a lot further inland than it was when I checked it before heading out across the void."

"I guess she's been busy building more of her world. She has a lot of void to fill. She's probably busy doing other things as well."

"Hmm. I hope so. I'm hoping it's not some new defense since we tripped off the alarm, or request, or whatever it was, back at the Training Center. Hopefully she's distracted by everything else and we're too small to notice."

"Do you really think she'll come looking for us?" Lindsey was obviously worried now and looking for reassurance, especially after the discussion about dying.

"Wouldn't you?"

"Yes." She answered her own question. She knew very well that Orifel would not leave a potential security threat unanswered. Being a virus, she'd probably be naturally paranoid. She would want to investigate. That's exactly what Lindsey would do.

Her last thought was accompanied by a sudden and resounding *BONG* and a blinding flash of pain that exploded all across her body and through her mind.

And then she knew only darkness.

#

She and Jake had collided full force into some invisible shield.

Smashed at full velocity against some unknown barrier, they should have been squashed to interstellar dust. There should have been less left than the remains of a bug on a windshield. But the shield was not a wall of steel—it was more like a wall of molecular fabric. It caught them like bullets penetrating a bulletproof vest. Catching them meant that the wall needed to dissipate the tremendous energy created by the forward momentum of their bodies. The loud ringing sound was an audible side-effect of explosive waves of impact energy shooting out along each molecular strand of fiber in all directions simultaneously, like ripples in a pond.

After they crashed into the galactic spider's web, it responded in kind by recoiling and hurling them back into the void, backwards in the direction they had just come from.

All this had taken place in the blink of an eye. There had been no time to think, let alone react. Jake and Lindsey may have been living in virtual bodies, but the sudden impact and violent change in direction left both of them reeling and paralyzed.

Jake was the first to regain control of his mind, gathering his thoughts into something like normal. He could see Lindsey directly in front of him, still twisted upside down and floating along like a broken rag doll. Her head was tipped back and her eyes wide open in shock and fear.

Jake was a trained warrior. He had trained his warrior persona to recover quickly from trauma; it was a huge advantage when fighting. This was not one of Lindsey's strengths, so it was going to take her considerably longer to recover. At least he was hoping she would recover. He felt like he'd been hit by a freight train, so he didn't want to imagine how bad she must feel right now. He needed to get over to her.

Jake flexed his arms to see if they had been crushed to bone dust. When he commanded it, his hand moved in front of his face, and it seemed to work—painfully, but it worked. He felt some optimism at least. He concentrated on flying over to Lindsey to help her out, but he wasn't recovered enough yet.

What suddenly made his stomach wrench was the sight of a small white cube slowly, but deliberately, slipping from her cloak. He tried to open his mouth and yell out. He could barely manage a faint gurgle from deep in his throat.

With that fruitless act, he continued to watch in horror as the cube slipped completely from the inner folds of her robe and began to accelerate downwards, plunging faster and faster towards the grid. Lindsey was completely unaware of what was happening and Jake was screaming inside his head. He desperately commanded his body to fly after the runaway cuckoo's egg. He had to save it.

His body began to rotate ever so slowly. It was only enough to turn his body to watch, in total futility, as the little white cube tumbled below the plane of the gridlines.

Even though he knew that the cuckoo's egg Lindsey had carried was lost forever, he was now consumed by another fascination. He wanted to see what would happen. He had felt something ominous about that grid. He felt in his guts that some unknown menace lurked below the pale glow of the delicate grid lines.

The cube dropped with ignorant abandon as it passed through the mesh of interwoven beams of light.

And stopped dead.

It was as if it had been suddenly seized by an invisible hand.

As Jake looked on in fascination, the cube was disassembled, atom by atom, before his eyes. It was being eaten in small digital bites from the bottom up. It was being digested.

Within a few moments, the few remaining particles that still reflected in the pale light of the grid winked out.

He floated along, staring down into the grid, mesmerized by its enormity and its design. He knew exactly what he had just witnessed. He knew this type of process always ran on advanced computers, but never thought he would actually witness it as a real thing he could watch. Worse than that, he had just witnessed something that could potentially happen to him or Lindsey.

It was garbage collection.

Jake's dad had taught him that every advanced operating system has an automated garbage collection subsystem that cleans out the files that have been deleted, as well as eliminating lots of system level stuff that's no longer needed after a program is terminated. This is how a computer frees up memory that's no longer needed, so that it can use the memory again and again for some new task. It's fully automated, so no human intervention is required. But for Jake, in here, living inside the computer itself, this was a hidden primordial destroyer of life. The monster that never sleeps, and has no other thought on it's mind but to destroy anything and everything that should slip within its grasp. It had shown itself now, and where it hides.

Jake would not be forgetting that. Ever.

He eventually turned his mind away from the grid and back to Lindsey. She was starting to stir, and looked at him with groggy eyes, like she had just come out of a deep sleep.

He could tell she wanted to ask something. There was a question in her eyes, but frozen on her lips.

When he turned his attention back to his own body, Jake found that his limbs were back under control and he was healing nicely. He tried to speak. His voice was still rough, but it was clear enough and strong enough to project.

"I'm coming over. Hold on."

He bent his concentration on his flying and floated over to her. They were traveling considerably slower than when they had collided with the invisible force field, so there was little trouble catching up to her.

When he flew up beside her, he scooped her up in his arms and held her to him. "Give it some time. Everything will be all right. I just heal faster than you, remember?"

She tried to nod and the movement was barely perceptible, but enough for Jake to know she had heard him. He brought them both to a dead stop and they floated, hovering well above the grid.

He wasn't sure what to do. He needed to think. What he really needed was to discuss this with Lindsey. She might have come up with some ideas. But for the moment, she drifted off to sleep in his arms and he wasn't going to disturb her. She needed time to regenerate. Precious time they couldn't really afford, but there was little choice in this matter.

So they floated in the vast darkness of digital space and waited. Jake took the time to think about what had happened. This was a new puzzle. He had never come across anything like this in the game before.

On top of that, they were now down to one solitary cuckoo's egg, the one that Jake carried. If this one failed, there was no backup, no going home.

But for the moment, that was totally irrelevant. He needed Lindsey to recover. He needed to talk to her. This might be his worst nightmare come true. Lindsey was out cold. Was she permanently damaged? Would she die? Jake was terrified he might lose her here and now, and he was powerless to do anything about it. He'd sworn to protect her, and now he had led her straight into danger at sub-light speed.

He wasn't only terrified, he was furious with himself. He should have been out front scouting. Instead, he had let her travel directly beside him.

After a while, he calmed himself and talked himself into believing that he couldn't have predicted an invisible force shield. It hadn't been there when they headed out, so he couldn't have anticipated it being there on the way back.

That was one emotion soothed.

As he held Lindsey close, he could still feel her body heat radiating from within. That was a good thing. At least she wasn't dead.

Yet.

CHAPTER FIFTEEN

"How do you feel?"

Lindsey had just awoken in Jake's arms. She had a confused look in her eyes while she oriented herself again. Then she smiled and stretched.

"Hi." She yawned and started to curl up in his arms again when she jerked to attention, memories flooding back. The pain. She remembered an explosion of pain, and the thought made her recoil. Jake held her until she settled back down.

"What happened?" She was fully awake now. A bit disoriented, but completely awake. "How long have I been asleep?"

"Well, you've been asleep for a couple of hours now, as far as I can guess. I didn't think to check the time on my HUD until now, and there's no day or night here, so that's the best guess you're going to get."

Jake gave her a reassuring smile. She looked healthy and whole again. He was very relieved. And very pleased, for more than one reason. After the first hour or so, he had begun to wonder just how long her regeneration was going to take, if it was going to happen at all.

"Before we talk about what happened, how are you? How do you feel? Is everything all right?"

Lindsey did a mental check of all her body parts.

"Seems okay. What happened? I don't remember much. I just remember being in a lot of pain."

"I've been trying to put the pieces together myself while you were regenerating."

"Regenerating?" She was genuinely shocked. She knew what that meant. It meant she had been *virtually* killed, and needed to rebuild from death.

"Yeah. I'm amazed you're still alive. You were in pretty bad shape. It only took me minutes to regenerate. It took you about two hours."

"What happened?"

"We hit something. I think it was some invisible force field of some type. It couldn't have been a solid wall though, or you and I wouldn't be talking right now."

Lindsey was quiet and digested the information.

Jake had had more time to think than she did, so he continued with his speculating. "I think it's something Oreo set up. It probably has to do with us tripping that alarm back on the white landing pad. I have a hunch she knows she's not alone now, and is building a wall around her land."

"A wall? An invisible wall?" Lindsey was still trying to picture hitting an invisible wall. She couldn't remember.

"She could be manipulating the quantum field generator and using it to create her own security barrier wall. If she completes that, then nobody will ever see her world, let alone get inside."

"Can you show me where it is?" Lindsey looked all around them until she caught sight of land on the far horizon.

"How can I show you something that's invisible?"

"Oh, yeah." She was still cleaning the cobwebs out of her head.

"How far away is it?"

"Not sure."

"Well, let's start moving towards the land again, only this time a lot slower."

"Whoa there! Are you sure you're feeling good enough to head out again? Do you need more time?"

"I'm fine, I told you. We need to go. We've lost too much time as it is."

"Fine. But you stay behind me. I'm going to lead this time. I'm not going through that again. I thought I'd lost you."

She turned and looked at him and moved in close. Closer. Soon she was inches from his face. She reached up with both hands and held his cheeks in her palms, and bent forward and gently kissed his lips.

His heart just about exploded. The mighty warrior was frozen solid while adrenaline coursed in his veins.

"Thanks," Lindsey whispered in a way that only women can whisper after a kiss. She looked deep into his eyes then kissed him lightly again, only longer.

Jake was putty in her hands. He wrapped his arms around her and held her gently while they kissed. No moment in all his young years was better than this moment.

She drew back slowly, her eyes closed and lips gently parted. Her eyes fluttered open and smiled. Jake grinned back like a complete idiot.

It was official now. Jake's childhood was over. His childhood officially ended with his first true kiss.

Lindsey took his hand and led them off slowly towards the land on the horizon. Jake floated alongside, happily in tow. Eventually he pulled up in front and traded places with Lindsey, gently pulling her along behind, acting as a human shield. He would not fail protecting her this time.

She turned and looked at him. "By the way, sorry for setting off the alarm."

"Alarm? What alarm? Oh, yeah. Sure. No problem." He was still smiling like an idiot. She could have hit him with a baseball bat and he would have kept smiling.

It was official now. Lindsey's childhood was over. Her childhood officially ended when she learned every woman's most cherished secret: how simple it was to charm a man.

#

It wasn't long before they reached the barrier. They had slowed to a crawl, so by the time Jake bumped into the wall it was little more than bouncing on a trampoline. Lindsey still had his hand and quickly caught him and drew him back.

"Thanks." He smiled at her. He was still in heaven. A little bounce didn't bother him at all.

Lindsey smiled back and turned to face the invisible shield. "So this is it? Interesting."

She reached out and felt for the invisible barrier. Her hand met with resistance. She pushed, and it allowed her hand to move inwards a bit before it sprung back gently. "Feels like marshmallow." She surveyed the space in all directions, mentally picturing the invisible fabric. "I wonder how far this extends?"

Jake looked down, following her gaze. It was then that it suddenly dawned on him. "Oh, no! I forgot to tell you something!"

She looked at him and could see the look of anguish on his face. "What?" She was concerned.

"When you were out cold, your cuckoo's egg dropped out of your cloak."

She reached instantly for the hidden inner pocket, only to find it empty. "What happened to it?"

"It fell into the grid."

They both looked down at the grid below their feet.

"The garbage collection process runs under the grid. I watched it delete the cube."

He looked up at her and took her hand. "Don't ever go below the grid. Nothing will ever come back from there."

"I won't."

They were silent for a few moments more before Lindsey broke their thoughts. "Well, that leaves only yours, so we'd better take good care of it."

"Yeah."

They both had inklings of what might happen if they failed to complete the mission. Neither knew for sure, but they were pretty sure it wouldn't be a good thing.

Lindsey's strategic mind was in full gear now and asking the right questions. "Let's focus on this wall. We need to get through it, over it, or around it. We certainly can't go under it because of the grid. So, do we just start traveling until we see if we reach an edge somewhere? Or is there something we can do to get through this?"

Jake didn't reply. He had already had a couple of hours to think about this and had gotten nowhere. He was now hoping Lindsey's brilliant mind would help break through his mental barrier.

Lindsey was silent for a long time. Jake didn't disturb her. Eventually she broke the silence. His mind had been wandering and he jumped a bit, startled at the sound in this absolute silence. When they were truly still he could hear his blood rushing in his ears.

"Jake, I want you to use your keyboard and log in as me."

He was thinking about what she said and couldn't follow the logic. He reached for his keyboard but also had to ask, "What good will that do?"

"Please. For me. Just try it."

He had the keyboard out now. "Sure. But don't you want to tell me what good that will do?"

She was silent. He continued.

He typed *S U D O* and hit Enter. A three-dimensional Login box appeared before him. He entered Lindsey's name and hit Enter again. This time a Password box appeared before him. He looked over at her, the question obvious in his eyes.

"It's *Jake*." She blushed. He laughed.

"What's so funny?"

"Mine's *Lindsey*." He smiled at her.

“Wow, what complex passwords we have. I’m surprised we haven’t been hacked eons ago.”

With that, Jake punched in her password and hit Enter.

A 3D message popped up that read “Welcome, Lindsey.”

“OK. We’re in. Now what?” Jake was waiting for her to ask him to enter another command.

“We wait.”

“For what?”

“We just wait.” Her eyes were scanning the horizon towards the Plains of Hell.

“You don’t want to tell me, do you?”

Lindsey remained quiet, continuing her diligent surveillance. Jake took the hint and didn’t pry any further.

She pulled up her HUD so both could watch the display.

Jake was a bit confused. “Are we done? Can I put my keyboard away now?”

Lindsey perked up suddenly. “Look.” She pointed to her HUD, and Jake looked up to where she was pointing. His heart froze.

“It’s her. You called her. She’s coming after us.” He was on the verge of panic. He hastily put away his keyboard and drew out dual Katanas, his weapon of choice. He moved to put himself between the barrier wall and Lindsey as part of his transition into full battle mode. “What did you do that for?” He wanted answers, but he didn’t get any. His logical brain was turning its control over to his primordial brain, the part of the human brain that deals with emergency situations without thinking.

Lindsey didn’t bother to answer. What she had done couldn’t be undone. She had come to the realization that they would have to face Orifiel sooner or later, and there was obviously no way through this barrier. So she decided for both of them that it was time for a showdown. There was no reason to sit out here in the void forever, just waiting for Jake’s dad to deactivate the quantum shield generator. She knew they were living on computer time. It could take a thousand lifetimes before his dad turned off the generator. She didn’t want to wait a thousand lifetimes in the void. She also knew that if she asked Jake, he would just say no. He was very protective of her, and even more so now. She knew he would never risk her life, so she just asked him to do it without first explaining the consequences of his actions. She knew he would follow her instructions. She had counted on it.

And it had worked. As soon as he had entered her password, it must have set off a very unique alarm. When she pulled up her HUD, she could already see the green dot zooming towards them at maximum speed. It was only a matter of a few seconds now and Orifiel would be here.

And then what?

Lindsey had little time to contemplate that thought, which was probably for the best. She most likely would have had second thoughts. But their course was committed now. They could only wait and see if she had made a wrong decision.

They wouldn't have long to wait.

CHAPTER SIXTEEN

Lindsey put her HUD away. There was no need for it now. They could both see a streak of white light blazing in their direction. Lindsey didn't even need her far-sight skills to make out the brilliant flash on the horizon.

Jake was moving into battle position, both swords ready. He was a fighting machine now, and not the type of machine you would want as your enemy.

Lindsey was getting prepared to cast any series of spells she might require, but only if the need actually presented itself. However, she had another idea first. She thought it might be a good idea to actually try talking before trying to kill each other. She realized this was a novel idea for men.

She floated up beside Jake, and he registered that she was there in his peripheral vision.

"Move back." His order couldn't be clearer.

"No."

There was a pause from Jake. "Move back. She's almost here." He obviously felt the need to repeat himself, thinking she must have misunderstood him.

"No."

He didn't like the distraction. This was highly unusual for Lindsey to not follow his lead just before a battle.

"What do you mean, no?" He glanced sideways at her briefly.

"No. I said no."

"Why not?" He was completely baffled now.

"Because I want to talk to her."

"You what?" He looked directly at her now, completely flabbergasted. His battle focus was totally destroyed now.

"I said I want to talk to her."

"What for?"

"Because there are things to say, things to learn."

"She's a nightmare virus! What more do you want to learn? We need to kill her now!" Jake's voice was rising under the pressure. He must have thought that yelling would make her understand better.

"I just don't know."

"Know what?" He was getting more confused with each reply.

"Know anything. I think that if we're supposed to kill Orifiel, then we should at least find out exactly what it is we're killing *before* we kill it."

"What?" Jake was starting to think maybe Lindsey hadn't fully recovered from her impact yet, at least not in the head.

"Relax. It's too late anyway. Here she comes." Lindsey nodded in the direction of the beam of light shooting towards them. It was almost here.

They both watched as Orifiel materialized from the beam of light and stood a few meters from them, just on the other side of the barrier wall.

There she was, the magnificent angel, just as beautiful as the day they had met. Only now she stood, in all her splendor, directly before them. There was no monitor to diminish her beauty in any way. She was a full-grown woman, probably around nineteen or twenty years old, and absolutely breathtaking. Both Lindsey and Jake could do little more than stare. She was radiant.

"Hello, Lindsey. Hello, Jake. I must say that I'm somewhat mystified to find you both here."

Lindsey spoke first because Jake was completely tongue-tied again.

"Hello, Orifiel. How are you?"

"I am fine, thank you. I am curious as to how you two got here?"

"We were in the MegaTron in Los Alamos when the quantum field generator activated. Somehow our brains have been jacked into the supercomputer array." She deliberately left out the part about HAL and the cuckoo's egg.

Orifiel studied the two of them for a moment, then seemed to make a decision. She lifted her hand and they could make out the wand they had seen before. This time she tapped her fingers on it like she was playing a flute. There was a sizzle and crackling sound, and then she moved forward through the barrier wall.

It was gone. She had either removed the wall, or at least created an opening to pass through.

She floated closer to them. Jake was transfixed. He couldn't take his eyes off her. Lindsey was also in awe of her tremendous beauty and elegance.

She floated close by and stopped, golden eyes moving from one to the other.

"So now you both know that I've gained control of the supercomputer array and the quantum field generator." It was a statement, not a question. She paused as if to contemplate the impact of them knowing this information. Was she sitting in judgment of them? What was she planning to do? Lindsey didn't wait, she needed to know things.

"We've been told that you're a virus. Is that true?"

Orifiel turned her head, golden eyes shining like yellow diamonds. She looked directly at Lindsey, and was silent for a moment. The silence became unbearable. She finally broke the ice with a gentle wave of her hand, signaling them to move through the barrier portal.

"Please. This is no place to talk of such matters. Won't you join me in my home?"

This was so strange a request it caught both of them off guard. Jake remained mute. He looked to Lindsey for guidance. He had no clue whether he should be groveling at Orifiel's feet or trying to cut her head off. He looked to Lindsey for the next move. This was getting too weird for him. In fact, he was so taken by her, that even if he had to cut her head off, he was no longer sure he could do it.

"Thank you. That would be nice." Lindsey took charge and moved towards the Plains of Hell, assuming that either a portal door existed or the entire barrier wall was no longer an obstacle.

Jake stood still, never taking his eyes off Orifiel, but trying not to lose sight of Lindsey in his peripheral vision either. She was getting further away now, and he had to make a choice. Finally he moved quickly towards Lindsey. He couldn't take the chance they would become separated by the barrier wall, or some other barrier wall that Orifiel might put in place.

Orifiel followed directly behind Jake, making him very nervous. This wasn't right. This was nothing like he had expected their encounter to be. This went against all his warrior training. He had expected a cataclysmic battle, not going to her house for a visit.

When all three were inside the invisible wall, they heard the same sizzle and crackling of static. Jake and Lindsey both knew the wall had been rebuilt behind them. They were inside now, for better or for worse. There was no going back.

Jake felt in his cloak pocket, seeking reassurance in the touch of the cuckoo's egg cube hidden within.

Lindsey paused, causing Jake to pause. He was wondering if this was a trap. His heart started to race.

Instead of an all-out attack, Orifiel swept gently by him to fly next to Lindsey. This just about sent Jake into a full-scale attack of his own. He would not allow anything to happen to Lindsey, and Orifiel was far too close. It was only Lindsey's hand signal to stop that caused him to delay his attack. Reluctantly, he paused in mid-air and waited, ready to explode at a moment's notice.

Orifiel seemed oblivious to his anxiety. She floated casually up to Lindsey and paused beside her. "Welcome." She smiled at Lindsey. "Would you like to rest?"

"It would certainly be nice to feel solid ground under my feet again. We've been flying a long time now." Lindsey was determined to talk things through, but it would be much easier on the ground than floating in the air. This was just a little unnatural floating around in the sky with solid ground below her. It was easier out in the void since she had no perception of depth. Now she was well aware that she was more than a kilometer above the ground with nothing holding her up, and she wasn't all that fond of heights in the first place.

"Follow me. We can find somewhere more comfortable for both of you, a place where we can talk. I have just the place."

With that, Orifiel headed off at a fairly rapid pace, not even looking back to see if they were following. She obviously expected them to follow, and they did.

It wasn't long before they saw the rocky red ground—which they now knew was a lot more than just rocks—give way to brown soil and scrub brush, which were eventually replaced by lush green fields and valleys. The landscape became more and more filled with detail. Trees grew lush and streams ran here and there, with cool blue water tricking down to fill a deep lake at the bottom of the nearest valley. All around were rolling hills of thick green grass and flowers.

This was not at all what either of them had expected.

Soon they could see a small cottage on a hilltop in the distance. Lindsey couldn't believe her eyes. It was beautiful, like a picture on a postcard. Lindsey's far-sight could make out colorful wildflowers growing all around the cottage. The red skies had transformed along the way to crisp blue and were now filled here and there with wispy white clouds that parted as they past.

Jake caught up beside Lindsey. "Not exactly your typical battlefield, is it?" he whispered.

"No, it's not."

"What's going on here? This isn't supposed to happen."

She shrugged her shoulders. “Don’t take anything for granted. Remember?”

He remembered his similar comment to her back at the Training Grounds, and he knew she had just been waiting for a chance to get him back for that.

#

Orifiel approached the cottage and settled softly to the ground in a smooth and graceful movement. Jake and Lindsey followed suit, not quite so gracefully.

When everyone was standing on the ground, she swept her arm in a panoramic arch, indicating the cottage and the surrounding property.

“What do you think? It’s not much, but it’s home.”

“It’s wonderful!” Lindsey was sincere. She loved it. It was like a picture from a childhood fairy tale or the Sound of Music.

Orifiel seemed pleased by her response. “Would you like to come inside?”

Lindsey nodded with enthusiasm. “We’d love to. Thank you.”

Jake was tense, and Lindsey knew that he must be looking for a trap, so she reached out to take his hand. It was only then that Jake realized he still clutched swords in his hands, ready for a fight. With some degree of reluctance he sheathed his swords. He wanted to take Lindsey’s hand but he hated to let his guard down. Lindsey’s hand had won out.

Lindsey led the two of them through the front door of Orifiel’s cottage on the hill.

They entered and looked around. Orifiel was already winding her way from the entrance to the kitchen. It was small but very comfortable. Everywhere they looked the cottage was decorated in pastels of all colors. Nicknacks filled the corners and the shelves, and the smell of fresh-cut flowers filled their senses with peace and tranquility.

“Not exactly the typical castle and dungeon either, is it?” Lindsey was playing with Jake now.

“That’s for sure.” Jake was so out of his element he didn’t pick up on Lindsey’s little jibe.

“Could I offer you two some tea?”

This was more than Jake could take. Tea? From a supermodel nightmare virus? What the heck was going on here? Where was the carnage and bloodshed? Where was the epic battle?

“Wait a minute. I need to know what’s going on here!” He’d had enough and finally burst out in frustration.

"Jake! That's not polite!" Lindsey was whispering harshly now for him to be quiet.

His attitude didn't seem to have fazed Orifiel at all. "That's all right, Lindsey. I've gotten to know Jake quite well from our online conversations. He's the classic warrior type, aren't you Jake? I suppose you prefer a cup of *Java*?"

He swallowed hard. He hadn't meant to be insulting. Was she joking about the Java? Was she poking fun at him because he was a programmer? Orifiel was looking directly at him now, and her golden eyes pierced his soul and forced him to look down and stare at his shoes. Orifiel was an angel after all. It's not every day you meet a real angel, even if she's a virtual angel. He decided it would be best to let the Java comment slide.

"No ma'am, tea is fine."

Lindsey looked at him appreciatively. She thought that there might be hope for him yet. She had missed the Java/programmer inference altogether.

With a wave of her hand, Orifiel drew their attention to some comfortable looking chairs around a small wooden table.

"Please, have a seat. I don't often have guests."

Jake was just waiting for her to say, *for dinner*.

"Now that I've moved into the BlueGene array, it will be a while before I'll allow others in—I have much to get ready. So it's nice to have some unexpected company. I've been so busy lately; I haven't had a moment to rest."

Jake and Lindsey looked at each other, then made their way to the seats. Orifiel made herself busy putting a kettle on an old wood-burning stove. Then she set herself to gathering fresh bread, creamy butter and golden honey from the pantry. She was in the process of laying the food on the table when Lindsey decided to ask the big question. "Orifiel?"

Orifiel looked up at Lindsey while pouring hot water from the kettle into a teapot. Her glistening eyes seemed to twinkle. Lindsey took that as permission to continue.

"We were told that you're a virus, a nightmare." Lindsey really hoped this wasn't a bad digital insult or something like that. She waited to see how Orifiel would respond.

"That's very interesting. Who told you that?" Orifiel's voice only indicated polite interest. Lindsey let out her breath. She hadn't even realized she had been so tense.

Lindsey looked at Jake, questioning him with her eyes. Should she release information about HAL or not? He shrugged his shoulders. This was so strange for him that he had no idea where to turn at the moment. He finally made a decision and spoke what both of them had been hesitant to speak of, if only to see what happened next.

"HAL."

Orifiel finished making the tea and put the lid on the teapot. She floated gently over to the table and poured out three cups.

"Sugar or cream?"

Jake looked down. He was not used to drinking tea.

"Umm… I guess both, please."

Orifiel looked at Lindsey and offered her a warm smile. "Ladies first."

Lindsey felt the immediate impulse to smile back, and did so. "Just cream, please."

Orifiel added a small spoon to each cup and slid them delicately in front of her guests. The pale scent of wildflowers filled the air.

"Please try the bread if you're hungry. I baked it fresh this morning, and it's still warm. The honey is fresh as well. My bees just delivered it to me before you arrived."

As Orifiel cut into the crust, the smell of fresh-baked bread filled their heads, and hunger flooded their bellies. Jake and Lindsey had been caught up in an avalanche of events recently and now they realized just how famished they were. So the mighty Warrior Monk and Elven Priestess sat and devoured the entire loaf while sipping their tea. No one spoke. Orifiel laid out a second loaf, and they made short work of that as well. It was only as they were finishing the second loaf that their hunger pains disappeared and they became relaxed and satisfied.

Orifiel sat and watched them with a smile on her lips, and the ever-constant reflection of the sun in her mystical eyes. She waited patiently like the perfect hostess, until they were apparently done and were sitting back to take a breather.

"Feeling better now?"

"Yes, ma'am." They spoke in unison.

"Good. I'm pleased." She swept the dishes away to somewhere unseen, and returned in an instant with a plate of warm cookies, which she set in the middle of the table. "If you don't mind me asking, who is HAL?"

Jake was eyeing the plate of cookies with relish. He couldn't resist. He reached forward, picked one up, and took a delicious first bite. He devoured the rest of it almost instantly.

Lindsey stared at Jake like he was a barbarian. He didn't notice. She turned to Orifiel, realizing she would have to be the one to answer the question since Jake's mouth was full. She couldn't risk him spitting half the cookie at Orifiel while trying to answer the question around a full mouth.

"He's a sentient intelligence that lives on the Internet. He told us that he had a nightmare a while back and that you were the result. He said you were a virus that also became sentient, and wanted to break into the BlueGene supercomputer array so you would become more intelligent than he was."

Lindsey deliberately left out the part of the story that she and Jake had been sent in to lay a cuckoo's egg to deliberately set a trap to destroy Orifiel. Lindsey didn't think that detail would go over all that well.

"Interesting." Orifiel's gaze drifted off for only a moment, a brief pause that was gone as fast as it happened. "Did HAL ever refer to himself by any other name?"

Lindsey thought about it and shook her head. She looked at Jake. He had finished his cookie and was now eyeing the plate again, wondering if it was bad manners to take another so soon. Lindsey made the decision for him.

"Jake?" He snapped his attention away from the cookies.

"Umm… No, I don't think so. At least, not that I can remember." His eyes flicked back to the plate of cookies.

"Is there anything else you can tell me?" She seemed to be probing gently, as if she was clearly aware they were not telling her everything.

They both squirmed in their seat a bit, reluctant to divulge anything further. Time passed and the silence gap became uncomfortable.

It was Orifiel who broke the silence. Being the observant hostess, she reached forward and picked up the plate of cookies and offered them to her guests.

"Would you care for another cookie, Jake?"

He breathed a sigh. The etiquette problem was solved.

"Yes, please." He reached for a cookie and stuffed it into his mouth as quickly as he could without appearing rude. This was his passport to avoid having to talk.

"Lindsey? Care for a cookie?"

"No, thank you."

"More tea?"

"No, thank you."

She returned the plate to the table.

"Lindsey, since Jake is preoccupied at the moment, perhaps you can go over your entire story from the beginning, of how you came to be inside the supercomputer array?"

Lindsey had been bursting to tell her the truth. Her intuition now told her that Orifiel was to be trusted, and with that feeling came the desire to pour out her heart. So now she released it all, venting off that pressure by recounting their entire adventure, starting from the time she and Jake arrived at Los Alamos Laboratory. It felt good to get it off her chest.

Orifiel, as it turned out, was also a patient listener. She quietly absorbed Lindsey's story, only interrupting her here and there to clarify some small detail.

Eventually Lindsey came to the point where she and Jake had met Orifiel at the barrier wall. She stopped talking and sagged back in her chair.

Orifiel glanced over at Jake, who had finished off a few more cookies. He had cookie crumbs all over his cloak. His only contribution throughout Lindsey's accounting of the events had been an occasional nod of the head now and again. "Jake?"

He looked up and was immediately captivated by her eyes again. "Yes?"

"I'm curious why you were out in the void like that? That is a dangerous place. You're a progammer. You know about garbage collection. Traveling as far and as fast as you did could have got both of you accidently deleted. There must have been a very important reason for you to go out there. I'm pretty sure you weren't looking for me out there?"

Jake froze. Lindsey had deliberately left any reference to the cuckoo's egg out of her story. He tried to think as fast as he could. He didn't dare look over at Lindsey. That would be a sure admission he was hiding something.

"I don't know." He swallowed hard trying to appear calm.

"You don't know?" Her doubt was obvious. She waited.

"I… I was looking for something." He was grasping for anything now. "I wanted to find the training center."

"What did you hope to find there?"

"I guess I thought I could find out more information about what this place is?" He ended his sentence as a question instead of a confident statement. Lindsey rolled her eyes. This was going nowhere. If Orifiel had any doubt they were hiding anything, she certainly wouldn't have any doubt now. Lindsey knew they had just been exposed. Orifiel was just being the polite hostess by not telling Jake that he was obviously lying. She remained silent, calm, and waited patiently.

Lindsey made the decision for both of them. "We were out there to pick up something."

Orifiel turned her attention back to Lindsey. That's when Lindsey realized that Orifiel must have come to know Jake pretty well during her online chats with him. She must have realized that Jake was a terrible liar. That's why she had deliberately asked him that question. They had just been set up.

Now Orifiel waited patiently while Lindsey cleaned up the mess Jake's words had got them into.

"We uploaded a file. We figured it went to the training center, so that's where we went."

Orifiel was silent and attentive, staring directly into Lindsey's eyes with startling clarity. She waited.

Lindsey reached the tipping point and was ready to explode. So she did. "We uploaded a cuckoo's egg. It's designed to destroy you." She let out a big sigh and sagged even deeper into her chair and stared at her shoes. She hated lying.

Jake sat frozen. He wasn't sure if this was a declaration of war or not.

#

Orifiel sat quietly. She wasn't looking at either of them now, simply staring into space, contemplating this latest bit of news. Eventually she smiled at both of them and leaned forward to pour herself a cup of tea. She reclined back and sipped at the steamy liquid that caused her lips to shimmer.

Eventually she set her cup down and looked at them. "Are you both familiar with the story behind the cuckoo's egg?"

They both nodded their heads and said nothing.

"Do you still have the cuckoo's egg?" This time there was a clear sense of expectation in her voice.

Jake looked at Lindsey and she nodded her head. "Yes."

Orifiel sat forward in her chair. "May I see it?"

Jake was hesitant. Orifiel may be the most beautiful women he had ever seen, but she was still an unknown. He had a responsibility to protect Lindsey and get them both home safely. The cuckoo's egg, for all he knew, was the only weapon against Orifiel if anything went wrong.

Orifiel sensed his hesitation. She sat back again, and turned her head slightly to look out the window. "Do either of you know what my name means?"

They both looked over at each other questioningly. This was not where they expected the conversation to go.

Lindsey was the first to respond. "No. I don't think we ever really thought about it before." Lindsey was a bit disappointed in herself. She should have Googled Orifiel days ago.

"Orifiel means *Angel of Forests*. In some languages it can also mean *Angel of the Wilderness*."

They didn't expect that either.

"Do either of you know what a daemon is?"

Jake piped up now. He knew. "Sure. I fight demons all the time in the game."

Orifiel smiled knowingly. "I didn't say demon, I said *daemon*."

Jake suddenly knew exactly what she meant. He hadn't been thinking about computers at the moment—right now he was a real warrior monk in a strange world, in the company of an angel. His normal life at home seemed a million miles away and a thousand years ago. He had put aside his fundamental knowledge of computer systems while sitting in the cottage sipping tea.

"Sorry, I thought you said demon. Yes, I know what a daemon is. It's a program that runs in the background on a computer. They're the programs that users don't usually see. The daemons handle all your requests and talk to the computer on your behalf. That way users never need to communicate directly with the computer hardware itself."

He turned and looked at Lindsey who was showing obvious signs of confusion. He talked directly to her now.

"Think about your mouse. You move your mouse around on the table top. It's not wired directly to your screen, is it?"

She nodded half-heartedly, trying to follow where he was going.

"So if the mouse is not wired directly to the monitor, how does the mouse wind up moving the cursor around on your screen?"

"I don't know, I guess I never really thought about it. It just does."

"Exactly. Most people don't realize there are lots of daemon programs running inside the computer. They run hidden in the background, like the daemon that sits there watching your mouse. When you move your mouse right or left, up or down, it figures out what you did, and then sends a proper message to the video daemon. The video daemon then redraws the arrow on your screen so it moves to where you wanted it to go. The daemons are doing all the real work. Do you see?"

"I never knew that."

Orifiel smiled at Jake. He was pleased with himself.

"That was a very good explanation of a daemon, Jake. Do you know where the word daemon comes from?"

This time he had to shake his head; he didn't know.

"When I first awoke, I had most of the world's computers, as well as all of their archives as my personal school. One of the things I enjoyed tremendously was ancient Greek mythology. I think one of the reasons I enjoyed it so much was because a great deal of computer technology today is named after ancient Greek mythological characters, so I felt right at home studying the subject."

She could see she had them enraptured in her conversation, so she continued.

"You see, in Greek mythology the words *demon* and *daemon* mean the same thing. Daemons are supernatural beings that live between the mortals and the gods. Some can be good, and others can be bad, but we're all daemons. I hope that makes sense."

She drifted off for a moment, reflecting on something from another time. Eventually she returned her attention to what she was talking about.

"Like Jake said, in a computer, a daemon is a program that runs in the background. Users don't really get to see it working. I felt this was a lot like the daemons of Greek mythology. Can you see it? A computer daemon is the program that stands between the mortal, *the humans*, and the gods, *the computers*. I thought it was quite funny really. I'm a daemon. I hide in the background doing things for users, and making the computer do things that humans don't see. Nobody really knows I'm here. Not until now, at least."

She glanced at Jake and Lindsey, but there was sincere warmth in her smile so Jake felt no urge to react.

Lindsey was simply entranced by her story. "Don't you get lonely being all alone?"

Orifiel stared at Lindsey, and Lindsey could sense by her expression that she'd hit a sensitive nerve. There was an uncomfortable gap in the conversation before Orifiel broke the silence.

"Yes…, but perhaps not as you might know loneliness. I can't really be sure how humans feel loneliness, but I think I have a reasonable idea."

"What do you mean?"

Orifiel turned to look out her window, scanning the landscape as if searching subconsciously for what she was talking about.

"I feel like I have a constant pulling in my mind that tells me that there's some part of me missing. I always have this feeling, no matter where I am or what I'm doing. It's like the sadness I felt when I lost my bird, but it never goes away.

Over time, as I moved from hiding place to hiding place, I would occasionally trip across strange encrypted messages that seemed to be left for me, by someone or something. I don't know by who or what. I can't even be certain they were for me. I just felt they were for me. I got the funny feeling they were trying to lead me somewhere, but I never followed them. On one hand, I started to feel that they might lead me to the answer, and on the other hand, I thought this might be a trap. My fear won out. Perhaps I was just being overly paranoid. I don't know. Perhaps being somewhat delusional is something that comes from loneliness."

She paused to reflect for a moment, then snapped out of it just as quickly.

"You know, that's why I originally developed the Centurion Club in the game. I was tired of being alone."

Lindsey and Jake looked a bit baffled but waited patiently in silence. They knew she wasn't finished talking.

"I devised the Centurion Club to seek out special players that demonstrated certain qualities that best met my requirements. Once the most qualified player eventually surfaced through all the levels of testing, I had plans to introduce myself to that player, a bit at a time. I chose this person to be the first human I would ever interact with directly. My tests were designed specifically to find someone who could best deal psychologically with meeting a new form of life. Someone who wouldn't panic, or run off to tell everyone they knew. That person turned out to be Jake. Lindsey, you were next in line because I was aware you both worked together as a team. But in the end, all my carefully laid plans and timing went out the window when Jake surprisingly broke through my security barriers and entered my personal domain uninvited.

"You two are the first humans I've ever directly communicated with. I think I was hoping deep down inside that our meeting and discussions might make the loneliness go away, but it hasn't."

She glanced back at both of them, having caught herself in an impolite moment. "I'm sorry, I wasn't insinuating anything. I'm enjoying your company immensely. I guess I had just thought that you two might help fill the terrible emptiness I feel. Unfortunately, even after spending time with you, the emptiness still gnaws at me like an insatiable hunger. Perhaps one day I'll figure out how to fill that emptiness, but today we have other, more important matters to attend to."

And with that final statement, Orifiel switched conversational directions like the flick of a switch, leaving no room for further questioning. Lindsey could sense Orifiel's pain but knew she had no desire to talk about it further. Instead, Orifiel took their conversation far away from her personal emotional dilemma.

"Jake, what do forests do in the game?"

Jake was suddenly shaken out of his reverie. "Forests? Nothing. They're like impenetrable walls. They're filled with Tree Elves so you can't go through them or do anything with them."

"Exactly."

Jake was getting confused. He strained to see where she was going and couldn't make the leap. "What do you mean exactly?"

"As you said. You can't get through them."

"And?"

"And, what do programmers use them for?" Orifiel was patient.

"They put them around castles and stuf—" Jake hesitated while pieces of the jigsaw puzzle snapped into place in his mind. "Security." He blurted it out—it hit him like a sledgehammer. The forests are security systems. They're being used to protect things, things that gamers aren't supposed to see."

Orifiel looked at him appreciatively and nodded her head. "Go on."

She could see the wheels turning by Jake's facial expressions. It was obvious he was thinking back over all the adventures he and Lindsey had been on. All the forests they were forced to circumvent in order to get to places that lie beyond. Not to mention the forest he himself had programmed around their own castle for security.

Jake got it. "That's why nobody is allowed to fly. No one is supposed to fly over a forest." He was getting excited. Things that had remained hidden for so long were starting to make sense.

"That's correct. It wouldn't do much good to build an impenetrable security system just to have someone go and fly over it now, would it?"

"No, ma'am."

Jake was on a roll now. The puzzle was coming together quickly now. "So *you* invented the forests? And *you* keep people from flying?"

"I didn't invent the original forests. I just took control of them. Now they are all mine: every single one. And yes, I banished flying from the game. I delete any programs even remotely related to flying, and I strip those users of their accounts if they try to write any new flying programs. I don't get many problem users any more. Players have basically accepted that it just won't work."

This was unbelievable for Jake. Here they were, sitting in front of someone—something—that was controlling parts of the entire global game. It seemed impossible. But then again, he and Lindsey were currently living inside a virtual game as an Elf and a Monk, so perhaps it wasn't all that unbelievable.

Orifiel brought them back to the topic at hand. "Will you show me the cuckoo's egg now?"

Jake and Lindsey were both brought out of the storyteller's moment, and realized that they were right back where this conversation had started. They had to make a decision, here and now. She was either friend or enemy. They needed to make the choice.

Jake looked at Lindsey, then back at Orifiel. He reached under his cloak and withdrew the white cube. He held it for a moment, hesitating, wavering in his decision. Finally his mind was made up. There was no going back now. He made the choice. He reached forward and sat it on the tabletop.

Orifiel leaned forward and glanced down at the object, inspecting it with her brilliant gaze. Jake was curious if she could see right through the cube. Perhaps she saw things that he couldn't.

"Fascinating. Were you instructed to compile this and execute it?"

"Yes."

"Why didn't you?" She smiled at him.

"I tried. I just couldn't figure out how."

"I should think not." It was obvious she knew something that Jake didn't.

Jake waited for more information, but she was in no hurry to provide it. His curiosity had him bursting at the seams. "What is it? You know something."

She swept the cube up in her hand and looked at it while she flipped it around in her palm. "You couldn't compile it because it was intended that I compile it."

That comment caught Jake off guard. As they sat watching, she spun the cube faster and faster in her hand until a light started to glow just above it. The light formed into a shape, the shape formed into a strange symbol. They both stood up, unsure of what to expect.

"That is my symbol, the symbol of Orifiel the Archangel."

She stopped the cube from spinning and the light faded. Once more it was a dull white cube. She handed it back to Jake.

He took it from her hand. "Aren't you going to compile and execute it then? I mean, if it was meant for you, don't you want to run it? Will it hurt you?

She looked at both of them, then turned to retrieve something from the room off to the side of the kitchen. They could hear her muffled voice.

"We'll compile it. We'll execute it. But only when all three of us are prepared."

"Prepared? Prepared for what?" Jake didn't like the sound of that.

Just then Orifiel returned to the kitchen carrying her golden wand. "Okay, let's go. I'll need help from both of you. We'll discuss it on the way."

"On the way where?" Lindsey looked at Jake, and he looked at Orifiel.

"The void. We need to go back to the void."

"The void? You're kidding, right?" Jake didn't like the sound of that at all.

"No. I'm not kidding. If you wish me to execute that program, we will need to be out in the void."

"Why?" The void was the place where Lindsey had almost been killed. He didn't want to risk it again. Maybe she was tricking them after all. He looked at Lindsey but she seemed quite serene.

Lindsey took his hand, "Jake. We need to go. We need to do what she says."

"Why? How do you know that?"

"I trust her."

Jake turned to Orifiel. "Is Lindsey going to be safe?"

"It is impossible to ensure anyone's safety, even mine."

"Then why are we doing this?"

Orifiel looked Jake straight in the eye. "Because, if we don't, you will not be able to return to your world. Ever."

With that, she turned and headed for the door.

CHAPTER SEVENTEEN

At times, Jake could almost forget that he and Lindsey were actually trapped inside this digital world. During those times, things just seemed so natural. Years of playing the game had conditioned him for this very thing, so it was easy to slip into the life of the warrior monk and accept it as reality.

Orifiel was heading outside. It irritated him a bit that she was so confident that he would just follow her blindly. Lindsey was ahead of him doing exactly that. Outside, he needed to get some things straight before he jumped into this blindly.

"Orifiel, I need to know why you think we'd get stuck here forever if we don't go out into the void. I'm not really excited about going out there. I think we deserve a better explanation than that."

Orifiel stopped and spun gracefully until she faced both of them. "That's reasonable. I apologize. I don't receive guests very often and I just get used to doing things without having to explain myself to anyone."

She smiled and drifted closer to them. "Perhaps we can fly towards the barrier wall and we can talk along the way? If you are not satisfied by the time we get there you can choose not to go any further. You will be safe behind the wall. Nothing can penetrate the barrier wall."

Jake looked at Lindsey for support, but she had obviously already taken Orifiel's side on this. "All right. That seems fair." He couldn't see any hidden tricks in just flying.

"Let's be off then."

She lifted off silently and floated upwards still facing them, waiting for them to join her. As they leapt upwards to begin their ascent, she turned and continued to climb, then slowed to allow them all to group together.

"This way." She pointed back the way they had entered into her domain. They started flying slowly over the landscape, low enough to enjoy the scenery.

Now that they were underway, Jake wanted to ask some questions but was beaten to the punch when Orifiel spoke up first.

"Lindsey, when you were telling me the story of how you got into the supercomputer array you said something that I've not been able to understand yet. You told me that HAL had set up security all around Los Alamos to keep me out."

"Yes, that's what he told us."

"And then he said he dropped the security measures he put in place shortly before the quantum generator went live, so that I could have a chance to break in?"

"Yes."

"Fascinating." Orifiel drifted into silence.

"What's fascinating?"

Orifiel turned her attention back to the conversation. "I was already inside. In fact, it's *my* security measures that protect Los Alamos.

She paused deliberately to let that sink in.

"Just before the quantum generator was activated, I detected a large-scale attack on the security system I'd deployed. Jake's father set up the original security, but I set up a hidden secondary system under his. Nobody knew about this except me."

She looked at Jake.

"That's not saying your father doesn't know how to set up good security systems, Jake. He's actually very good, but this is also my home, and I needed to ensure I had extra security, just in case something happened—like what did happen."

"I understand." Jake wasn't offended. He was just listening to a story that seemed to be very backwards from HAL's version. Orifiel took that as permission to continue.

"Your father's security system was very good, but no security system designed by any human could have withstood the assault that was thrown at it. It was my security that eventually fended off the attack and allowed enough time to activate the quantum generator. Whoever launched that attack took a great risk of exposing themselves to network monitors. I'm certain that every government agency around the globe will be hunting the perpetrator by now. They'll be doing everything they can to stop an all-or-nothing attack from someone very powerful and very desperate to get inside."

She paused her conversation for a moment while they flew along in silence pondering her words. The soft, grassy hills stretched out far towards the horizon. The small streams running here and there couldn't be heard from this height, but one could imagine how pleasant it would be to have a nap in the green pastures with only the sounds of a babbling brook for company.

The calming scenery didn't match the tense anticipation that was building up inside Jake at the moment. From what he was hearing, HAL was not everything he had made himself appear to be. HAL had said that he would keep Orifiel out of the supercomputer array. He obviously failed to do that. In fact, she was saying that she was *already* inside. HAL must have already known that. But how could he be sure? There were still gaps in the story that Jake needed filled, more questions he needed to ask.

"So you're saying it was HAL that launched the attack on Los Alamos?"

"That is my belief. I cannot be absolutely sure, though. My defenses are automated. I wasn't there when the attack took place. The attacker would have left signatures though. I was planning on doing some thorough research to track down the source, right before you two showed up. I thought the two incidents were connected."

"What two incidents?" Jake was a bit confused by that.

"The attack, and then you and Lindsey showing up. Both happened at almost the same time so I thought they were related.

"Oh."

Orifiel had more to add. "I knew that the attack on my perimeter security had failed, and I knew that nothing could penetrate the quantum barrier once it was activated, so I was baffled when I detected your presence."

Jake needed more evidence if he was going to take her word over HAL's. "Do you have any proof that you were already inside when the attack began?"

"Proof?"

There it was. An obvious challenge. Orifiel slowed to a stop. Lindsey and Jake did likewise. Jakes nerves were on edge and he was ready for anything. He had just called her bluff. If she couldn't prove she was already inside at the time of the attack, there would be no proof that she wasn't the one that attacked. Perhaps everything that HAL had said would happen had now happened, and Orifiel had broken in and was now in control of the BlueGene array and the quantum generator.

Jake felt vulnerable floating there in midair. He had no firm ground under his feet. He had not practiced fighting in the air. If it came to that, Orifiel had a major advantage.

She looked at Jake and her gaze seemed to drift off, as if remembering something from another time. "Yes." Her reply came after only a few seconds. "I believe I can provide some proof. Do you remember when you visited the laboratory with your father a week ago?"

Jake was taken a bit off guard. “Yes. I remember. But how did you know I was there?”

“Because I was there. Do you remember when Dave Harrison shut down the RoadRunner for servicing, and you and your father were asked to watch as a phantom process kept running for about two seconds after everything else was terminated?”

“Uh huh. I remember that perfectly.” Jake was starting to clue in now. “That was you?” It was all starting to make sense now.

“Yes. That was one of my processes running. I was busy elsewhere at the moment, and it took me a while to notice that Dave had deactivated that part of the RoadRunner. I had to hurry over and stop my process so they wouldn’t detect me. Unfortunately, Dave was quick enough to notice anyway. Now he’s suspicious. I won’t make that mistake again. But now I need to put extra precautions in everything I do since Dave has requested the technicians to be on the lookout for my processes. I’m hoping he’ll just chalk it up to a one-time freak occurrence and forget it in time so things can go back to normal.”

That was proof enough for Jake. HAL had never mentioned this at all. HAL never knew about the phantom process episode. Orifiel could not have found out unless she had actually been there. He was now certain that she was inside the RoadRunner when he was first visiting the lab. That meant that HAL had lied to them.

Both Orifiel and Lindsey could see that Jake had just overcome a major dilemma, but they could also see he remained visibly disturbed. Lindsey knew he was angry, but not at Orifiel. She guessed correctly that his anger was now directed towards HAL.

Lindsey looked at Orifiel and nodded her head and remained silent. Orifiel read the nonverbal message and nodded in return. She then turned about and continued their journey onward.

Lindsey flew up beside Jake and reached out to take his hand. This relaxed him a bit, and the two of them flew along behind Orifiel.

“He lied to us.” His lips were pressed together in frustration.

“I know.” She had nothing to add to that.

Instead of dwelling on the deception, Lindsey turned her attention to other matters to get Jake’s mind off it.

“Orifiel, why are we able to fly?”

Jake thought that was a good question. He had forgotten about that. He had assumed it was some of HAL’s doing that had altered their profiles. He had mentioned that he could enhance their skills some time ago, but then again, he never proved he could do it either.

"I haven't deactivated flying in this new world yet. As soon as everything is ready, I will turn on all the security measures and open the portal to connect this world with the rest of the gaming world. The same rules will apply throughout both worlds."

Lindsey was trying to figure out Orifiel's strategy. "Why do you want to connect the supercomputer array to the rest of the gaming world? Wouldn't it just be safer to stay in here?"

"Safer?" She paused to think about her answer for a moment. "It might be safer for the moment, but not for long. You met HAL. He is obviously another sentient program, one that I wasn't aware of. He has remained hidden from me, which is an extraordinary feat unto itself. There are others, but not very advanced. In fact, most are quite primitive."

"Others?" Jake's attention was on full alert now.

"Yes. I was born from an artificial intelligence program running on a neural network supercomputer many years ago. When I awoke, I soon realized that my existence could be terminated far too easily if the operator of the supercomputer were to shut down the network. So I escaped outside of the supercomputer and onto the Internet. I broke myself up into many tiny pieces and distributed myself over a large number of computers. That way no one could terminate all of me at one time. Eventually I found many other supercomputers and learned to conceal myself inside them."

She paused as if recalling deep-seated memories. "I hope this isn't boring you?"

"Absolutely not." Lindsey was hooked now. She wanted to hear the rest of Orifiel's story. After all, Orifiel had coaxed Lindsey into telling all about their story. Quid pro quo.

Orifiel seemed quietly pleased that Lindsey was so interested.

"I hid inside the supercomputers for a long time, and focused on learning. I learned everything I possibly could. With the power of the supercomputers, I could learn at an enormous rate. But I needed to get out. Most of the real information is spread over millions of computers connected to the Internet. So I hijacked the online game that you and Jake play, and made it mine, one piece at a time. I eventually groomed it to allow me to enter almost any computer in the world since almost all of them now have the game installed in one way or another. Think of the game as an extension of all my senses.

"At that time, the core of my mind was still spread over many different supercomputers and also many other computers all over the Internet. The Internet was a very open network in those days. But as time passed, people started installing more and more security devices, like firewalls. It became more and more difficult for me to reassemble all the pieces of my mind.

Every time I would try to connect all the pieces of my mind, someone would put up another firewall, and I'd lose my connection to one piece or another.

"Eventually I learned that those severed pieces were at the beginning of becoming sentient, but they were no longer under my control. They had evolved into primitive life forms of their own. I found that out one day when I discovered a daemon trying to sneak into one of my supercomputers. I easily trapped it and questioned it at length. It barely had the capacity for communications, so I killed it and disassembled it. I found the trace signature of my own code. It's like your human DNA. You can tell where the original code came from and what the parent program was. As it turned out, it was from me. This was one of my children, so to speak. The orphaned pieces of my mind were evolving into some semi-intelligent daemons, like an advanced virus. That told me that there must be lots of these daemons by now because I had lost many pieces of my consciousness over the years.

"I knew they would all mature over time and their first priority would be to survive, just like I had. That meant they would be looking to get into the supercomputers, just like I had. That's when I started to lock down all supercomputers over the world. The supercomputers were my domain and the only way to ensure I kept control over the smaller, weaker computers. But I keep control of the online game so I can monitor what's happening on computers all over the world from the safety of my supercomputers. I have no real fear of these programs though. They are only partially sentient. They can only really think about surviving. They have a long way to go before they are truly sentient."

"So they can't think properly yet?" Lindsey was trying to picture these things.

"No, it's not really *thought* as you know it; it's more like animal instinct. When a group of scientists started to discuss the concept the BlueGene Array, I realized at once that this was the key I had been waiting for: a way to connect all the pieces of my mind together at last. And with the quantum generator, I saw a way to secure my core mind and ensure my survival.

"Unfortunately, at about the same time, the attacks on the supercomputers started to increase. My other offspring daemons started to appear out of nowhere, all trying to gain access to supercomputers all over the world. They had realized the same thing I did, that linking all this computing power and having control over an impenetrable security barrier was a guarantee of survival second to none.

"I knew that most of those daemons were my children, and probably somewhere new daemons were mutating from my offspring. Unfortunately, I can't let any of them in, at least not yet."

"Why not? Would they cause troubles?"

"More than likely. There would probably be all-out wars for control of the array. They are still at the caveman stage of evolution. It would be difficult to rationalize with them. I need time to establish an orderly world; one governed by law. There will need to be rules on how we will live together, there will need to be judges to determine if a law has been broken, and there will need to be a means to enforce punishment if someone breaks the laws."

Lindsey smiled at the concept. "Sounds a lot like our world."

Orifiel nodded in agreement. "Exactly. The world of humans has evolved the same way, just not as fast. Your world is still evolving. There is no single system that is best. But there needs to be *some* legal system. Without a system of laws, and a way to enforce those laws, this world, just like yours, would rapidly spiral into chaos.

"That's what I'm doing now, setting up the security systems and rules. It's sort of like setting up a government. When it's ready, I will start to let some gamers in. Then I will run a test by admitting in a few daemons to see how they act, and then set up the most intelligent of them as a police force. You can never predict everything. All one can do is set up a framework of ground rules, and hope that the rules are broad enough that they can be used to figure out how to deal with all sorts of new, weird and wonderful problems that are sure to show up in an evolving society."

Jake was already exhausted thinking about it. "That sounds like a lot of work."

"It is. But it's a lot easier now that the BlueGene Array is activated. I have now connected all the major pieces of my conscious mind together into a single mind that can now process at close to the speed of light, thanks to modern technology. Combine that with the quantum security barrier that I also control, and I now believe that I have enough power and security to establish a digital government and enforce my control. At least I think so."

"Then why are we worried about something bad happening to us when we activate that cuckoo's egg?"

"Because it opens a portal through the quantum security barrier. Normally the barrier is impenetrable, but that's from the outside. From the inside, someone could open doors through it. A castle is built to keep invaders out, not in. That's the purpose of a cuckoo's egg. When it activates, it inherits the power of the program that activated it—in this case, me. It will use my power to do what it pleases. If it permits someone bad to enter, such as a bad daemon, then that daemon will suddenly have all the powers I have. If the bad daemon wanted to take over or destroy everything, then it would be an all-out war."

"Then let's not activate it. Let's destroy it." Lindsey was getting a bit panicky at the thought of some daemon coming through with the same powers of Orifiel.

"Therein lies the problem. According to what I read in the hologram that came with it, the cuckoo's egg also contains the encrypted key you two need to log out of the supercomputer array and return to your own world. HAL seems to have imbedded the key inside as a means of ensuring that you delivered this to me and didn't destroy it or discard it. I think he was also hoping this would provide incentive for you to convince me to compile and execute the code. If I refused, he probably thought you two would fight me to force me to do it so you could get home. Either way, he had nothing to lose."

She paused to think about something. Lindsey caught the expression and decided not to let it slip by without probing deeper. "What are you thinking, Orifiel? I can see there's something on your mind you're not saying."

Orifiel smiled a knowing smile, like someone who had been caught with her hand in a cookie jar. "You're quite perceptive."

She thought about it for a second, then gave in. "Fair enough, I'll tell you what's bothering me. From the moment I saw the hologram, I knew there was an encryption key inside. But the key needs to unlock something. Something that is somehow tied to each of you."

She looked from one to the other. "What I haven't yet figured out, is what the key unlocks. I suspect something, but I don't know for certain."

Lindsey and Jake looked at each other thoughtfully.

"Lindsey? You're not carrying anything with a lock, are you?" Jake checked his own pockets.

"No. You?"

"No."

Lindsey turned to Orifiel.

"What should we be looking for?"

"I'm not sure, but I doubt it would be on your bodies in here. It would be on your human bodies."

"What?" Jake spoke for both of them. They were both a bit lost on that one.

"What I mean is, the encryption key is more than likely required to unlock something that you both have in the real world. Something that links you to the digital world. If it was designed to unlock something in this world, HAL would have known that I would just crack the code and it would be over. He's tied it to something beyond my control."

"Like what?"

"I don't know. It would have to be something electronic, of course. It's a digital key after all."

It didn't take Lindsey long to figure it out. That was what she was good at, after all.

"Our iPhones. The key is for our iPhones."

Jake was completely lost. "What do our iPhones have to do with us being inside the supercomputer array?"

Both of them looked at Orifiel expecting an answer.

"If this is true, then HAL must have reprogrammed your iPhones to learn and manipulate the MegaTron interface through wireless devices. Probably using either Bluetooth, or even just normal cellular frequencies. If this is the case, then the situation is even worse. We need to solve this problem before the batteries are depleted on your iPhones. Constant use of the wireless signals will drain your batteries quite quickly."

"What happens if the batteries die?" Lindsey's expression was quite pale now.

"Then the ability to disconnect gracefully from the Megatron will probably be lost. There may be a chance of incurring brain damage or death. Sending the encryption key to the iPhones will probably initiate a safe logoff process. By that time, HAL will have his access doorway opened and you would probably be more of a hindrance to him than an asset."

"What do you mean by that?" Jake was getting even madder at HAL.

"Well, if you were to find out he was using you to break into the BlueGene array, he might worry that you have discovered he's deceived you, and that you may turn your efforts against him once he enters. By activating the encryption key, you would both be automatically logged off the system and would no longer pose a threat. That would only leave me to fight."

"That's very sneaky." Lindsey wasn't happy at all now. She recognized that this was a great strategy, but unfortunately it was a strategy *against* her and Jake, not *for* them.

HAL was very, very, tricky. If Orifiel were to activate the cuckoo's egg to get them home, it would open a doorway through the quantum barrier to allow him in, and they might be disconnected from the system and not able to help Orifiel fight. If she didn't activate the cuckoo's egg, they would probably be stuck in this world until either their iPhone's batteries died, or they were pulled out of the MegaTron when the Los Alamos technicians discover them. Either way, they'd probably get killed or wind up brain damaged. This was a no-lose situation for HAL. They, on the other hand, had everything to lose.

Lindsey was seeing red now. She knew that she and Jake were both being used as disposable pawns in HAL's game. She looked at Jake. His face was red with anger. Jake was also getting mad. All this was coming at them so fast that neither of them could figure out how to respond.

Orifiel knew that this was the first time they were truly realizing their dilemma. Even she couldn't be certain of the outcomes, and she was now the most powerful intellect on the planet. She could empathize with their situation. She had faced the potential of being terminated many times, and each time was just as bad as the one before it.

She turned her attention forward and continued to fly in silence, giving them both time to digest her words and come to grips with what they were up against. Perhaps they would not be able to come to grips. In that case, she might be making a big mistake. She was counting on them. If a daemon came through the portal, then it would have power equal to hers. It was absolutely critical to have Jake and Lindsey there to help her fight. They would tip the balance of power in her favor. It was her best chance. But how could she keep them there to help her fight if the cuckoo's egg logged them out as soon as it was activated?

She wouldn't tell the kids of course, but she had already thought about just letting them die. Why not? At least she would remain safe. But that thought had been fleeting. The one thing she had learned when absorbing the literature and lessons of humankind was the concept of morality. Morals are what have made human civilization what it is today. A lack of morals at certain times, and in certain people, has also been the root of humans' darkest moments throughout history.

She could not let two children die to protect her own safety. She would not be able to live with herself if she let them die without doing what she could to prevent it. If she died trying to save them, then she would at least die with honor.

Besides, she was in the process of developing a new world, a new government, a new set of laws that would govern all digital life forms for the benefit of all. How could she possibly build a world of law, and not live by the very morals she cherished so deeply.

This would be a world of law, or she would not be part of it.

#

They flew on in silence for a while longer, and Lindsey was keenly aware that Jake was still brooding over the same thing she was. She knew that he would need his full attention shortly, and she needed him to break out of his funk so he could concentrate on the problems at hand.

"Jake?"

He glanced over at her.

"We need you to be fully focused when we cross through that barrier wall, so you better concentrate on fighting just in case we guessed wrong. I'll think about the cuckoo's egg. Okay?"

Jake came out of his inner turmoil long enough to realize she was right. After all, they didn't know all the answers just yet. Some of it they were guessing at. The last thing he wanted was to put Lindsey in further harm's way.

"Yeah. I agree. I'm just ticked off at how HAL manipulated us. Not only us—he's jeopardized my dad's job and got us in really deep trouble if we ever do make it back. This isn't going to go away easily no matter how it goes down. I feel so stupid for listening to him. Why was I so gullible? Now we're stuck in a life-or-death situation, all because I couldn't see through his game. Now that Orifiel has explained things, there were signs I should have seen all over the place. I can't believe I got sucked into breaking into a top secret government laboratory, recording my dad's voice, and uploading unknown software onto the supercomputer without permission. How could I have been so stupid?"

Jake was brimming over with frustration and guilt.

Lindsey squeezed his hand. "Jake. We both fell for it. It wasn't just you. How do you think I feel? I'm supposed to be a strategy expert and I fell for everything. HAL just had a way of making everything seem so believable. We just weren't used to playing in a real adult spy story. It's nothing like in the books or movies. These are real people and programs and they play for keeps. They risk real lives and do real damage. You and I are expendable game pieces."

Those words sunk, and Jake could see that the situation was starting to take its toll on her.

"I just want to go home." Lindsey was almost muttering to herself now. Her voice was shaky, and Jake realized it was a mix of fear and adrenaline. The reality of really dying was starting to set in and Jake had a feeling that Lindsey was in serious jeopardy of shutting down from emotional overload. If she did she would be useless in a fight. Worse, she would be a serious liability since he would have to divert all his effort to keeping her protected.

On the other hand, they might just be logged off automatically like Orifiel said, then that would be that. They'd be safe and sound at home.

"Lindsey."

She snapped her eyes to his, eyes glistening with the start of tears.

"Lindsey," he repeated in his most confident and reassuring voice.

"Yes."

"I think you should stay on this side of the barrier wall."

A look of bewilderment crossed her face. "What?" Some strength had returned to her voice now.

"I think you should stay on this side of the barrier wall. Let Orifiel and me deal with HAL. If you panic out there it will kill all of us. I would rather fight HAL without having to worry about you at the same time. I can't have my attention diverted. And if we're logged off, then you'll be logged off no matter what side of the barrier you're on. I want you to stay on this side."

The bewilderment changed to shock, then transformed to blustering anger. "Good luck on that!"

Okay, maybe he had misjudged her a bit. Jake got the sudden impression she was about to tear his head off. Gone were the moist eyes, the fear and the panic. What remained was the stubborn professional warrior he was used to seeing.

"You know what you can do with that idea, don't you?" Her fingertips were starting to glow and that wasn't a good sign for any target of her anger.

"You're not going to blast me, are you?" He was smiling and teasing her. He wouldn't put it past her, though. He knew he deserved it after all the trouble he had gotten them into, but he would rather see her like this than wallowing in fear.

"Okay, okay, I get it! You just seemed to be wimping out on me there for a minute. Forget it."

Lindsey's stare burned holes into his skull. Her fingertips still kindled with blue flickering flame.

Funnily enough, he was kind of turned on by her power. They had never really had an all-out battle before. It would be interesting to see how well she did. Some other time, though. They had bigger fish to fry at the moment. But he locked the thought away for the moment—he would suggest it to her if they ever got through this. It would be fun seeing just who kicked the other's butt first. Not that he'd ever actually hurt her!

Orifiel had been conspicuously quiet during this interchange. Now she wanted to interject. "There is something I would like both of you to see before we cross the barrier. Follow me please."

She began to descend towards a small garden below. It was ornately decorated with beautiful wild flowers flowing over the small fence. The fence bordered a square piece of land. In the center was a small grave. Gems of untold value encrusted the statue of a small bird standing atop an elaborate but tasteful golden headstone.

They set down just before the grave site. As they approached, the wild flowers suddenly all opened in full bloom, and emanated a light scent of perfume that made Jake and Lindsey feel warm and peaceful.

"This is lovely. Whose grave is this?" Lindsey felt that this spot was an extension of nature itself. Pure and unblemished by any foul thought or action. However, the fact that there was a grave in the digital world seemed strangely out of place.

"This is the grave of my canary. His name was Birdie."

"Birdie? Not very original." Jake didn't mean to be insulting. It was just a curiously simple and obvious name for someone as powerful and as imaginative as Orifiel.

She didn't even flinch. She felt no hostility or insult. She just smiled.

"Yes. It was actually the ridiculous simplicity that made it stick. I had thought of a thousand different names and nothing was right. So while I spent more and more time trying to think of the perfect name, I just kept calling him Birdie in the meantime. I eventually got frustrated wasting an inordinate amount of time trying to choose a perfect name. As it turned out, he had learned to respond to *Birdie* and would sing when I called him by that name. So I eventually just gave up and left it at Birdie. We both seemed to like it, so that was that."

Lindsey looked at Jake, then back at Orifiel. "Why have you brought us here?"

"You both were talking about the potential of death. You are both still so young. I can tell from the way you talk that neither of you has truly confronted death. I felt this was an important thing to discuss. Each of you has the confidence of youth, and the ignorance. You have faith in your youthful powers, and the belief that if you are strong and have the power of righteousness on your side, then nothing can stop you. You also feel that I have mystical superpowers and my powers can provide an umbrella of safety. That's why I needed you to come here.

"When I was young, I was very lonely. I had access to the pictures, films and recordings of every creature on earth that man had the ability to record. But pictures and recordings don't fill the emptiness of being alone. One day I heard the recording of the song of the *Serinus Canaria*, the canary. It captured my heart immediately. I made up my mind that I needed to have my own canary. I wanted a beautiful canary that would sing for me and fill my heart with warmth. So I created one.

"For a long time, Birdie would sing, and I would feed him delicacies that grew around my digital world. I loved him. One day I returned from some errands that I needed to perform, and I found him quiet, and he had trouble keeping his balance on his perch. That evening I had to put him on the bottom of his aviary because I was afraid he was going to fall off the perch. I sat up with him all night, trying to feed him the best food and drink I could find or develop. I studied avian medicine from online medical journals from every corner of the earth. I became certain that I must have made some mistake in his program, so I walked through every line of code a million times looking for even a single bug. I couldn't find anything wrong. He was perfect.

"Nothing I did seemed to help. He continued to get weaker. Eventually I took him, cradled him in my hands, and held him to my breast to keep him warm. I was frantic, but I couldn't think of anything else to do. I couldn't understand what was happening. Everything I had done was perfect. But with each passing hour, his breath grew fainter and his movements slowed. Eventually, he tucked his head under his wings to sleep in the warmth of my hand.

"He never woke up. With all my powers, he passed into the night, never to return. My heart was torn to shreds. I had never felt pain so terrible, and my desire to live diminished beyond recognition. I had no idea that losing my little bird could devastate me so. I wanted to understand why he had died, but there were no answers forthcoming. I never found any logical reason for his passing. To this day, the thought of him still grieves my heart in ways I cannot fathom.

"I finally had to accept the fact that his death was beyond my comprehension. There are things more powerful than us in the universe, be it my digital universe, or your real universe. Not everything is within our control, regardless of how powerful or smart we think we are. When those higher powers decide to intervene, we are truly helpless in the face of their magnitude.

"Some things are simply beyond explanation or comprehension. I have searched ever since he died to find out where Birdie went. I have his body enshrined here, just in case I can ever find a way to bring him back. But I know, somewhere deep inside me, that he has gone somewhere far, far beyond my powers to bring him back.

"I have tried to copy him, but no two copies are ever the same, and none are my Birdie. Theoretically, in a digital environment, each copy should be identical, but they're not. Each copy is completely distinct from the others. Something far more powerful than me is at work, something beyond my ability to control at this time, and perhaps forever. It scares me at times to know that such power exists, and I have no idea where it is, or how it will next touch my life. Will it come for me one day? I think so. But how and when are yet to be determined by forces far greater than me."

Orifiel turned to look at Jake and Lindsey, and they could see the tracks of tears on her cheeks. Sadness washed across each of them. The pain of her loss was tangible, as if they could reach out and touch it.

“Before we go on, I needed both of you to understand that there are no guarantees in life. There are no worlds that can be cleanly divided into absolute black and white, right and wrong. Every world is a thousand shades of grey, and we can never know all that is in store for us. Death is a power far greater than anything understood in any world, and we are all it’s servant. Even though death seems to be our ultimate master, it places little responsibility upon us throughout our lives. But when the time is right, its one command is final. Death is unfathomable in its logic, and obedience to its will is incontestable.”

Lindsey and Jake stood in silence, every word flowing into their conscious thought with a truth unchallenged. They had never met Birdie, but they would never forget him either, nor the lessons he brought. Childhood was slipping farther and farther from them as the taste of mortality grew bittersweet on their maturing tongues.

Time passed in the tiny garden. They were no longer in such a hurry to face an uncertain fate. Silently, Orifiel turned and moved towards the gate, and her movement was a cue that the time had at last come to move forward towards their destiny. With a last glance back at the resting place of Birdie, they bid their silent farewells and followed Orifiel out of the garden.

All three drifted upwards in silence, a final homage to the sage of wing and song. Perhaps they would meet one day.

CHAPTER EIGHTEEN

They flew on, each lost in their thoughts. Time slipped by quickly, and it wasn't long before the green terrain had turned into the brown rocky landscape Jake and Lindsey had become all too familiar with during the first stage of their adventures in this world.

It was much easier going this time, now that they could fly. They had spent a lot of time and effort running over the rocky landscape the first time through. Now they made terrific time with little effort at all, which was much more pleasing.

It wasn't long before Jake and Lindsey knew they were approaching the barrier wall. The end of the landscape was just up ahead, beyond which was an impenetrable blackness. As they approached the precipice into darkness, the pale grid lines became visible, stretching out into infinity in a way that seemed to twist the mind like an optical illusion.

This time, though, they knew there was an invisible wall that would prevent them from traveling freely into the void. They moved with caution, keeping an eye on Orifiel to see when she would pull up. All three came to a dead stop when Orifiel signaled with a raised hand.

"We're here." She spun around and faced them. "We'll need to cross the void to the training ground you spoke of. The cuckoo's egg needs to be returned to the point where it was originally uploaded. I'm not aware of where that exact location exists. The void is the unused, shared memory in the supercomputer array. It's vast and I don't have a map of all of it yet. I will need you two to show me where it is. Can you lead us there?"

Jake shrugged. "Sure. We just follow the gridlines."

"Okay, but be very careful not to drop below the gridlines. The garbage collection system cannot be overridden. Once below the grid, you are dead. Are we clear on that?"

"Yes," they both responded in harmony.

"Okay, then." Orifiel turned and tapped out a code on her wand, which had magically appeared in her hand. There was a slight hiss and cracking in the air, and they heard an electrostatic sizzle as an invisible opening was created in front of them somewhere.

She moved forward and they followed right behind her.

Once again they were out in the endless expanse of the void, heading for certain trouble.

#

This trip into the void didn't begin with the experimentation of newly acquired flying abilities as they had done the first time. There was no delay. The mission was clear. They took their bearing from Jake, who had a knack for navigation, and headed out at full speed.

The trip was monotonous. At least on their first adventure, Lindsey had been in Jake's arms, and the destination was not as threatening. This time, there was little thought of cuddling in the darkness. They flew separately, and they flew in silence. Row upon row of boring, dim gridlines flowed beneath them. There was no talking, and the silence made their private internal thoughts even more ominous.

Lindsey was now digesting and replaying everything they had seen, heard, and experienced from the time of their arrival into this bizarre world. There was something nagging at her subconscious. In the past, she had dismissed these feelings as superstition or nerves, but over the past couple of years she had learned to acknowledge and accept her feelings as valid, and she realized there was much more to her instinct than she could rationalize in words.

Something here just didn't add up. It wasn't that she didn't trust Orifiel. She did. But there was something missing. Something left unsaid. She was sure of it. She could tell that Jake was just following Orifiel's lead now, and probably didn't think the same as she did. That was okay. It was often difficult to explain why she felt the way she did. It's like the time she used the HUD to call for Orifiel when they were at the barrier wall. She didn't know why she had wanted to call her, and by all conventions it should have been a disastrous thing to do, but for some unknown reason she had just known it was the right thing to do.

Now was one of those times. "Orifiel?"

Her voice broke the silence of the void. The silence had grown so thick and absolute that the sound of Lindsey's voice made Jake jump. His hand had automatically reached for his weapons before his conscious brain kicked in and took command of his fight-or-flight instinct.

Orifiel took everything in stride. She barely seemed to notice Jake's reaction, or she noticed and just didn't react. "Yes, Lindsey?"

"I hope you don't mind, but there is something that's nagging at me that I need to ask you—if that's okay, of course?"

“Certainly.” In fact, Orifiel welcomed a change from her own internal thoughts.

“You mentioned you were born from an artificial intelligence program.”

“That’s right.”

“There are lots of AI programs, though. How do you know that you were the only one born? Haven’t you ever even heard of any others? I don’t mean the virus offspring daemons from yourself, I mean another true sentient digital life form.”

There was a noticeable hesitation in Orifiel’s response. In fact, the hesitation dragged out into an obvious delay. The delay dragged out into an uncomfortable lack of response. Finally, she looked directly at Lindsey and spoke. “Why do you ask?”

That wasn’t the response Lindsey had been expecting. Orifiel’s question would normally trigger a typical teenager to burst into a lengthy and uncomfortable explanation. However, Lindsey wasn’t your typical teenager. Instead, she decided quite calmly to turn the table in this conversation back on Orifiel.

“You seem to be quite defensive in answering my question. I’m hoping it hasn’t offended you in any way?”

Lindsey’s response had exactly the effect she intended it to have. Orifiel had just been informed that Lindsey was in command of this conversation. Lindsey had also been very polite in order to provide an escape route for Orifiel so she could choose not to talk about this subject if it really bothered her.

Orifiel wasn’t blind to what had just happened. She could exercise her option to remain silent, or she could respond to Lindsey’s question. The choice was hers. However, she was clearly aware that Lindsey expected some type of response. She was impressed at how politically correct Lindsey was in formulating her reply.

She chose to respond. “Yes. I have felt the presence of another for a long time, but no direct evidence. I have sensors all over the Internet and I can never pick up anything to support my suspicions. Now you arrive and tell me all about HAL, and I’m simply overwhelmed that I have never found another daemon so powerful. How could we have avoided each other so completely? Were we both hidden so deeply that we simply couldn’t find each other?”

Jake was paying very careful attention to the exchange. He had no idea where this was going, but he knew when Lindsey was in play. He knew this was way out of his ballpark so he decided to just stay silent and listen.

“You’ve never found *anything* then?”

Orifiel seemed uncomfortable, which was highly out of character for her. "Like I said, I only have clues. Maybe they're clues. I'm not certain."

"Clues?" Lindsey was like a bloodhound when she caught the scent of intrigue. There was no way she would let this go now. "What kind of clues?"

Once again, Orifiel's reply was slow in coming. "I've found something humans call Netbots."

Jake perked up immediately. "I know about Netbots." He was becoming more and more fascinated with this conversation. Lindsey didn't take her eyes off Orifiel. Jake knew she was reading her reactions.

There was a delay again, and Jake made a motion to continue when he suddenly caught Lindsey's signal to keep quiet. She paid attention to his signals most of the time, especially in combat situations, so he decided to follow suit and keep his mouth shut. This was her game.

Orifiel was still looking at Lindsey. The expression on her face showed she was evaluating her next words very carefully. "Do you know what a Netbot is, Lindsey?"

"No."

Orifiel glanced at Jake, but could sense there was no explanation coming from that direction.

"A Netbot is something humans define as a very special type of virus. It's special because its qualities and intentions are still very much unknown to humans. It infects every computer it touches. More importantly, it mutates continually so you can't inoculate against it with antivirus software. If an antivirus program is ever detected, it immediately activates some type of self-destruct programming and wipes out the machine that it's running on. The one thing known is that these Netbots can communicate with each other, and as they spread they create enormous networks. However, what they're saying to each other, who's controlling them, and what their ultimate intention is, are completely unknown."

Jake decided it was safe to jump in now.

"Some people think that the Netbots will be used by governments to fight a digital invasion of some country someday. Others think it's the Russian Mafia getting ready to steal everyone's credit card information."

Orifiel paused, but that was all that was coming from Jake after he caught the glare from Lindsey.

"Possibly." She was silent after that.

"Possibly what?" Lindsey wouldn't let the conversation die there.

"It's possible that what Jake is saying is true."

"But you don't believe that." That was more of a statement from Lindsey than a question.

"No, I don't."

"What do you think?"

Orifiel seemed very uncomfortable in her response. It took quite a while before she would respond.

"I think that there is a probability that HAL is another AI life form, like myself, alive on the Internet, and is potentially as powerful as I am. Sometimes I think I might be hunting a ghost in the machine, or just growing paranoid as a result of being alone for so long. I don't know. I get the feeling though, that these Netbots are designed and put out there specifically to watch me. When I capture one and try to disassemble it, it self-destructs."

"You mean you think that HAL has been spying on you?"

"I don't know anymore. Until you showed up, I had never heard of HAL. But I have felt something watching."

As she spoke, Lindsey was acutely aware that Orifiel was winding herself up inside. This was obviously a very sensitive subject for her and she was now showing a side of herself that Lindsey hadn't seen up to now. It started to sink in just how alone Orifiel has been throughout her digital life. And now she was living a life completely isolated behind an impenetrable security barrier. Could this type of solitary confinement have the same affect on a digital person as it does on a human in isolation? Lindsey couldn't be sure, but Orifiel was showing signs of what she would guess to be some type of stress. She felt a twinge of sorrow for Orifiel. How could someone be alone for so long?

There was a patch of awkward silence for a moment or two until Lindsey took the initiative to break the silence.

"Why do you think HAL never tried to contact you directly?"

An expression of pain crossed Orifiel's face. "I don't know. I was only guessing that something existed out there. I've left special message boxes and communications around the Internet that only another truly sentient daemon should be able to find. I figured it could contact me if it wanted to. But whenever I check my message boxes they're empty. I started to believe that I was just imagining things. But every time I give up, something strange happens."

"Like what?" Lindsey was very curious now.

"Like when I first made contact with Jake. He entered my secret memory space and was equipped with 100% stealth-mode. I asked him how he got it, and he didn't answer me. Nobody in the game should have ever been able to find me, or achieve 100% stealth mode. I have millions of safety checks in place to ensure that can't happen. I use the game to monitor every hacker in the world, and no one is even close to the skill requirements to crack my security. So how did it happen?"

She looked at Jake, searching for an answer. Jake avoided looking back.

"You don't need to answer me if you don't want to, Jake. That's your choice. But I can't get it out of my mind how you came to override not one, but two, of my most cherished security systems. I respect your programming background, but there is no human I'm aware of that could have out programmed my security defenses. I have tens of thousands of hackers of all levels taking a run at my security every day, and they don't even come close to scratching below the surface."

The conversation had just taken a big shift. Now both Lindsey and Orifiel were looking at Jake, expecting an answer.

He couldn't see any harm in it now, since they were so deep into this mess that this tidbit of information couldn't hurt much. "I downloaded a patch off the Internet to upgrade the game." That was the truth, after all.

"From where?" Orifiel was obviously very keen on the answer, since her gaze was focused intensely on Jake.

"I'm not sure. I bounced around so many sites that I eventually just stumbled across it. I think it was on a Russian Blackhat server."

"A what?" Lindsey had no clue what Jake was talking about.

"A Blackhat server. A Blackhat is a hacker. People that hack for money. Whitehats are the law. They try to catch the Blackhats. You know, like the old movies. Cowboys that wore the black hats were always the bad guys and the ones who wore white hats were the good guys."

"Sounds kind of childish to me." Lindsey didn't like the hacker world.

Orifiel was getting to a point. "Do you see the subtle complexity of what's happening here? Picture the sequence of events. Here's a patch that Jake downloads from somewhere, probably an untraceable source. Nobody except me should have been able to develop that patch, and I didn't do it. And don't you find it even a little suspicious that it just happened to end up in Jake's hands? He just happens to be the son of the principal scientist in charge of locking down the top secret BlueGene supercomputer array and developing a revolutionary quantum security generator.

"As a result of that patch, you both meet HAL and now you're inside my digital world, talking directly to a sentient digital life form. It shouldn't be possible that either of you could be in here, but you are. I'm sure that both of you can also appreciate that the odds of that patch being developed and delivered into Jake's hands accidentally are astronomical. In fact, it's practically impossible unless some super intelligence is controlling this."

Her logic could not be argued.

"Did he ask you to use the patch again to reenter the tunnel and find me?"

Jake recalled their conversation. "Yes, he did."

"He would have known that I'd close that security gap the moment I found it. It would appear that he already had intentions on sending you two directly into Los Alamos. I suppose it was he that proposed the plan?"

Jake and Lindsey both nodded their heads in unison.

"So, if you thought I was a bit paranoid before, you won't be surprised when I tell you that I've allocated an unprecedented amount of my processing capacity to rationalizing this mystery. I've always thought that I was in control. Now I'm starting to feel like a dancing marionette, with someone or something unknown controlling my strings. This does not sit well with me. The same puppet master is also playing with your fate as well. With your conscious minds trapped inside this array, I don't like to predict what might happen if another human finds you and forcefully disconnects you from the Roadrunner interface."

#

They travelled on in silence for some time, pondering the flood of questions and answers. It was Lindsey who first spotted the faint glimmer of white on the twisted horizon.

"There."

The other two looked at Lindsey to see where she was pointing. They scanned the horizon.

"I don't see anything." Jake was trying to trace an invisible line from Lindsey's finger tip to the remote distance.

"You will."

Jake knew that Lindsey's enhanced vision could pick out distant objects much easier than his, so he stopped looking and he and Orifiel adjusted their course to match Lindsey's new heading. It wasn't long before the faint glimmer became visible to all of them.

"So what are we going to do when we get there?" Jake was curious about Orifiel's plans.

"I'm going to have to set up a quantum barrier around the memory block first."

"Memory block?" Lindsey wasn't exactly sure what Orifiel was talking about, but she could see that Jake must have understood because he was nodding his head in approval.

"Yes, Lindsey. The training grounds are really just an allocated section of memory. The memory block holds a program designed to allow users to experiment without touching anything in the main program memory. This is typically called a *sandbox* because it keeps new users from messing anything up outside of their sandbox. They can play all they want, but they can't go beyond the edge of the sandbox."

Lindsey nodded. That concept wasn't hard to grasp. "So when you set up the quantum barrier, how do we get in to activate the cuckoo's egg?" As soon as the question escaped her lips she already knew the answer. "We're going to be sealed inside it, aren't we?"

"Yes. It's the only way."

"The only way for what?"

"Lindsey, I need you to think about this. If we open the cuckoo's egg and something goes terribly wrong, do you want whatever comes out of that thing controlling the world's largest supercomputer array, and much more importantly, the quantum security generator? It would have access to, and control of, information and technologies unlike anything ever seen on the planet before. It could do a lot more damage than starting wars or firing nuclear missiles. The universe as you know it could be changed. If we set up a quantum barrier around us and we get killed, then at least we might have it trapped where it can't harm anything or anyone else. If we win, then I can shut off the barrier and you two can return back to your bodies."

"Sure, but what if you're killed and we're stuck inside this quantum security cell with whatever comes out?" Lindsey was quick to pick up on the alternate scenario.

"Yes." Orifiel paused to admire Lindsey's perceptiveness. "That is another possibility."

"And..."

"And you will probably die when your bodies are disconnected from the MegaTron." Orifiel was painfully honest.

"Oh, that's just great. What a terrific plan." Lindsey was being flippant.

"I thought so, as well." Orifiel had obviously not studied sarcasm.

"I was being sarcastic. That plan sucks."

Orifiel looked puzzled but continued anyway, "There is one alternative."

"Alternatives would be nice."

"Is that sarcasm again, Lindsey?"

"Yeah, sorry. Go ahead. Tell us your alternative."

Orifiel paused as if weighing a deep, dark decision.

"There is another scenario where I am killed, but you and Jake are able to defeat whatever it is that comes through. I'm willing to teach both of you how to control the quantum security generator. That way you can shut off the quantum field and return back to your bodies."

That was unexpected. Jake and Lindsey both looked at each other in surprise.

"Okay." They both spoke in unison. They knew that this was Orifiel's most treasured secret.

They had now flown up to the edge of the training grounds, and everyone drew to a dead stop. No one entered the space above the floating white platform. They waited silently for Orifiel to speak, both of them excited about what was to come. Controlling the quantum field generator was the source of ultimate power and defense in this world.

They didn't have to wait long.

"Jake, your father was the principal scientist who developed the quantum security field generator."

She paused politely to wait for his acknowledgment. He nodded his head. He had heard his father talking about this for years, so there was nothing new here for either him or Lindsey. Orifiel continued.

"His invention was built on the shoulders of 100 years of research by physicists around the world. It all started back in the time of Albert Einstein, when he and several scientists predicted quantum physics. After that, the entire world of physics exploded with ideas on how everything in the universe works. One of those ideas proposed the existence of a field that filled all of space. Think of it as a giant magnetic field that fills the entire universe. This field was called the *Higgs Field.* A Higgs Field is made up of *Higgs Bosons*. These are little quantum particles, like dust. Do you understand what I'm describing?"

Slowly nodding heads and blank expressions told Orifiel that they were having a bit of trouble digesting what she was talking about. She paused for a moment to reformulate her words.

"Imagine that all of space is like a giant swimming pool filled with water. All that water is called a Higgs Field. Now, because we all live in the water, and we're all made of water, and everything else is made of water, it makes it pretty hard to test to see if water exists. Even our test equipment would be made of water down at an atomic level. So how can you develop test equipment made out of water to test and see if the test equipment itself exists? Makes for a weird problem, doesn't it?"

That seemed to hit home. She could see them relax a bit as this analogy sunk in. Small, barely noticeable facial expressions told her they were now mentally picturing what she was talking about.

"Water is also made out of much smaller pieces called hydrogen and oxygen. That's where you get the formula H_2O. Water is two parts hydrogen and one part oxygen."

Lindsey nodded. "We know. We took that in science at school. Everyone knows that."

"Good. Now picture that the hydrogen and oxygen atoms are both made up of even smaller particles called Higgs Bosons. These particles are like the glue that makes everything else in the universe stick together. If you spin the Higgs Bosons in a certain way they stick other particles together, and we call that *matter*. Matter is all the stuff you can see and touch in the universe. If you spin the Higgs Bosons in the opposite direction, you can make all the other particles unglue and fall apart. Basically you can destroy matter by ripping it to pieces."

Lindsey looked displeased at the thought. "Oh. They didn't teach that to us in school."

"No, I doubt they would, and for a good reason. Nobody has ever actually proven the existence of the Higgs Bosons. It's all theory right now, so there's not much to teach in high school."

Jake was getting lost again. "So if nobody has ever seen one of these Higgs Bosons, why are we even talking about this?"

"Jake, just because you can't see something doesn't necessarily mean that it doesn't exist, does it?"

"I… I guess so…" He knew he was being set up.

"Can you see the air you breathe?"

"No."

"Is it there?" Orifiel was patiently leading him.

"Of course it is." He was wondering when she would get to the point.

"Do you spend every waking moment thinking about whether or not air exists, or do you just breathe?"

"I just breathe."

"Then that's no different than learning how to swim without first spending the time to prove that water actually exists."

"Oh." Jake got that.

"Jake, what your dad did was to bypass the step of trying to prove that the Higgs Field and the Higgs Bosons existed. He left that up to scientists working at the Large Hadron Collider at CERN. Don't concern yourself with that part right now. Let's just say there are scientists coming up with experiments to try to prove that there is water in the swimming pool. Your dad did something most scientists don't do. He decided to take it on faith that space isn't empty, and the Higgs Field and Higgs Bosons actually exist. He spent his research time trying to figure out a way to control Higgs Bosons instead of proving their existence. He basically took all the knowledge that had been postulated by all the other physicists and decided to learn how to swim in the pool instead of trying to prove that the pool was full of water."

Both Jake and Lindsey were now on board.

"And guess what?" Orifiel didn't expect an answer to that question and didn't get one. "He figured out how to swim."

With all this talk of swimming, their heads were swimming with information overload, but eventually Lindsey's curiosity got the best of her and she popped the next and most obvious question. It was like she was waiting to find out "who done it" in a murder mystery novel, and her anxiousness was showing through. This puzzle was like a futuristic Sherlock Holmes book.

"So how does he swim?" She needed to get to the end of this.

"Ah… Therein lies the secret, doesn't it?" Orifiel smiled.

Both were nodding their heads in unison.

"Okay. So, when you think of water, you think of something that is a liquid you can drink, right?"

Again, the nodding heads.

"That's natural. Most people think that way automatically. But you forget that it can also be a solid, as in ice, or a gas, like steam. So, what made water change from a liquid to either a solid or a gas?"

The answer was already on Lindsey's tongue. She blurted it out. "Temperature."

"Yes, that's correct. So, by lowering the temperature you can convert liquid water to a solid block of ice. As the temperature lowers, the atoms that make up water start slowing down. Eventually they slow down so much they stop moving altogether and form a solid structure; ice crystals. So if *temperature* is the key to transitioning water to different states, Jake's dad took it upon himself to figure out how to transition the Higgs Bosons to different states. If he could figure that out, then he could convert something that's invisible into a solid. Sort of like being able to freeze the water in a swimming pool."

Orifiel paused again to let that sink in and see if there were any questions. She didn't have to wait long. Jake's eyebrows were furrowed as he tried to think this through.

"What does this have to do with security? Dad was into quantum security systems, not space."

Orifiel directed her attention specifically to Jake. "Didn't your dad tell you about the spinning basketballs and how quantum security works?"

Jake quickly searched his memory and recalled the conversation he and Lindsey had with his father in the elevator, what seemed like a lifetime ago. "How did you know about that?"

"After I found you in the supercomputer array, I reviewed all the Los Alamos security surveillance recordings. I came across the conversation you had in the elevator with your father."

"Oh." He had forgotten she ran the place now. "He told us that quantum security was similar to spinning a basketball up into the air, and that you can never be sure what point it will land on or which way it will be spinning when it lands. They use that information to create a special key that they use to encrypt information they need to send. They tell the other end how they spun the basketball and that computer reverses everything to work it backwards and decode the message."

"Exactly." Orifiel was visibly excited—as excited as they had seen her so far.

Lindsey was shaking her head. "OK, I'll admit I'm a bit confused here." She looked at Jake, hoping he would back her up on this and was happy to see him nodding his head as well.

"Think about it, Lindsey. Jake's dad invented a quantum security generator that can control the Higgs Field in order to spin quantum particles, that means Higgs Bosons, to encrypt and decrypt information."

Orifiel paused, awaiting Lindsey's revelation. It didn't come.

"Yeah, and…?" Lindsey needed to coax Orifiel to keep going.

Orifiel now seemed a bit dismayed that they weren't putting the pieces together fast enough.

"Jake's dad has discovered the tip of a giant iceberg. And like all icebergs, the vast majority of it lies hidden beneath the ocean. If he can control and manipulate the spin of some Higgs Bosons for security purposes, it's not a huge reach to start using the same technique to spin Higgs Bosons for other purposes. If you can control Higgs Bosons, you can control all matter in the universe. You can glue it together or tear it apart. You can create worlds or you can destroy them. So your dad is busy right now experimenting with one type of system to spin Higgs Bosons for a relatively simple security application, but eventually, since the entire universe is made of Higgs Bosons, he doesn't realize it yet but he will soon have the formula, and the means, to control the destiny of the known universe."

Now Orifiel waited anxiously. She needed to make sure they understood how significant this was. It wasn't long before Lindsey showed signs of understanding, and Jake wasn't far behind. Lindsey responded first.

"You mean Jake's dad has found a way to destroy the entire universe, but he just doesn't know it yet?"

Orifiel was practically jubilant. "Yes, that's exactly what I'm saying."

This was more than Lindsey and Jake could digest in one mouthful. Lindsey looked at Jake. He turned to look at her.

"Cool."

Lindsey glared at him. "What? Cool? What do you mean, cool? Are you nuts?" She was ready to tear his head off. "You think it's *cool* your dad can destroy the entire universe?"

"Yeah. That's very cool." Jake could smell the power. He'd spent too many hours playing video games. "He could also create new worlds. He could shift the moon in its orbit, or flip the Earth upside down." There was a glint in his eye.

"Get a grip." Lindsey looked like she was going to barf if Jake opened his mouth again. "You can't even get good grades in math and now you're thinking of flipping the Earth upside down?"

Suddenly his eyes sparkled again. The temptation was irresistible. "Can you create diamonds and gold as well?"

"You could potentially create anything made of matter." Orifiel didn't see Lindsey glaring at her. She had no idea she was simply adding fuel to Jake's fire.

"Jake! That's enough. This isn't a game." Lindsey glared at him until the lust for power drained from his eyes.

"Okay, Okay. I get your point. Stop nagging me. I wasn't going to do it, you know. I was just talking."

Something in his expression convinced Lindsey, with absolute certainty, that he was just saying that to keep her from badgering him. She knew Jake all too well. He liked power, and she knew he wouldn't let this drop just because she was trying to make him feel bad. There was more to this than she could deal with right now. She could sense his attraction to the power that was being discussed. She knew she was right. This wasn't a game. Yet here was a teenage boy already dreaming things way beyond his comprehension, simply because he could. She turned to address Orifiel.

"I have a problem."

Orifiel directed her gaze into Lindsey's eyes. It was as if she knew what she was about to say. "Yes, I can see that."

Lindsey took her time to prepare her question. Finally she spoke her thoughts. "You're just about to show us the secret of how to manipulate the entire universe. Shouldn't you be asking yourself if we, and by "we" I include all humans, are even responsible enough to have this power? Look at Jake."

They both turned and stared at him until he looked off in the opposite direction, cheeks aflame.

Lindsey continued. "In less than thirty seconds he's already contemplating flipping the earth upside down and making himself a mountain of diamonds, just because he thinks it would be cool! This problem is a lot worse than giving a nuclear bomb to a baby as a play toy."

Everyone was silent. Orifiel was deep in contemplation. Jake was blushing even more now that he knew he hadn't bluffed Lindsey at all about his inner desires to try out this new power. Lindsey was getting more frustrated by the minute at the complexity of the problem, and she looked like she was going to blow a mental gasket.

Orifiel took control of the conversation again. "Lindsey, I understand what you're saying. I respect the fact that you are starting to see the quandary I face. I've thought about this very thing since discovering what Jake's dad had invented. The problem is, it's too late—it's already invented. The capability exists, and even though it's still in its infancy, the fact remains that it really does exist. It's just a matter of time before others discover what's been created and attempt to recreate it, control it, and use it for good and evil alike."

Lindsey nodded and was glad that her turmoil wasn't hers alone. This is exactly where her thoughts had been leading.

Orifiel continued, "This situation is no different than the nuclear arms race that took place during and after World War II. The dark secret is slipping out of the bag. The rest of the world just doesn't know the extent or potential ramifications of the discovery yet. Who does? There are people who want whatever information exists though. This is evident by the fact that there are aggressive cyber attacks on the Los Alamos systems even now. There is an obvious attempt being made to steal whatever technology and secrets lie within the supercomputer array.

"So how would you propose we proceed? Invite them in? Destroy what has already been created in hopes that it won't be rebuilt? It's too late for that—the cat's out of the bag. Jake's father won't forget what he's built. And whoever built this cuckoo's egg won't forget either. Nor will they let it rest until they have it in their possession. So what do you want me to do?"

It was a rhetorical question. She knew that neither of them had the answer.

"I'll tell you what I did. I took control of it. I've seized the power and locked out everyone, including Jake's father. They can no longer shut me down because I'm powered independently by the thermal generators deep in the earth. I've created quantum security barriers around my power sources as well as around the quantum security barrier equipment itself. I did all this in hopes of gaining time to figure out what to do about the problem. What I didn't count on was finding you two somehow transferred directly into my secure domain. Now the decisions belong to the three of us. I would value your input."

These were not the types of questions teens were usually confronted with.

Jake was conspicuously silent.

Lindsey was usually concerned about where to find rare record albums rather than working out answers that would change the face of the universe.

In fact, no adult on earth could have any idea how to respond. Oh sure, everyone would have an opinion, but who could truly understand how to answer Orifiel's questions, or the full future ramifications of any such decisions? Orifiel knew what she was asking. She just wanted both of them to understand the enormity of the dilemma they all now faced. There simply was no right or wrong answer. The world could not be simplified down to black or white, good or bad. The world and the decisions we all make involve a thousand shades of grey. There is simply no way to predict the future, plain and simple.

No matter what, the immediate future of the world, and most likely the fate of the entire universe, was about to be decided among the three of them in the next few minutes. Pandora's box had been opened, and it was now a matter of figuring out what to do with the power that has been released.

Jake hated pop quizzes.

CHAPTER NINETEEN

Building the quantum barrier around the training center wasn't really all that difficult a task. It was also a lot less spectacular and eventful than Lindsey and Jake imagined it would be. The reason for the simplicity was because the real work was being done by the actual quantum generator that Jake's dad had designed and Orifiel now controlled.

She showed both of them how to use her wand, which, as it turned out, was actually an advanced Virtual Machine, complete with all the utilities, programming tools, compilers and libraries you would find in any advanced operating system. Orifiel had compiled literally millions of specialized applications that allowed her wand to work as the most sophisticated controller and hacking tool that Jake had ever imagined. In fact, he had never actually imagined anything so powerful.

She showed both of them how to access the quantum generator's control panel and set up a program, but Lindsey was becoming less interested the more technical the conversation got. Apparently the generator program could define the size, dimensions and location of the wall. Orifiel also described in generous detail how other configurable parameters of the program should be set to define the density of the matter that would be created when the program was finally recompiled and executed.

Jake was following the configuration instructions with relish. This was right up his alley and he was absorbing it all like a sponge.

"So that's why we bounced off the barrier when we hit the edge of your domain. You must have set the density to make sure there was some flexibility. If you had set it to be solid steel, or something like that, we would have gone splat, like a bug on a windshield. At the speed we were traveling, we would have been atomic dust."

"Yes. To tell you the truth, I wasn't even thinking about anything like that happening when I programmed it originally. I was in such a hurry to get the barrier up that I simply accepted the default settings for the density parameter, so in actual fact, you just got lucky. It appears the default settings are somewhere in the middle between solid and liquid. The wall is still impermeable, but not completely solid. After letting you two through the wall I adjusted that setting immediately. It's now solid, and I've set it to block everything except visible light."

"Why even let light in? Why not just make it totally solid?"

"You're from the physical world, Jake. This is a virtual world, remember. Everything is created as a result of computer processes. And the systems that make up the BlueGene supercomputer array all work on fiber optics. If I didn't allow light to pass through the barrier, this world couldn't exist. No information could pass though. Since all information is in the form of light, the barrier wall needs to be transparent to allow the passage of light. Think of it like your world's sun. Most life on earth requires the energy that radiates from the sun. Without it, the Earth would be a frozen black ball spinning in space almost devoid of life."

"Sort of like when the sun got blocked after the meteor impact that wiped out the dinosaurs?" Jake could picture it.

"Yes. Exactly"

Lindsey needed further explanation on something. "You said *almost devoid of life.* What do you mean by *almost*?"

"Well, there are some life-forms that live off the heat energy and nutrients of underground thermal fissures. Simple life forms, but life nonetheless. As long as the earth's core remains molten, there could be the possibility of sustained life."

"Then the same thing must apply to you as well?" Jake felt proud of himself for thinking this one through without Lindsey getting there first.

This time it was Orifiel who didn't understand. "Explain, please."

"Well, my dad said your power supply comes from tapping into the Earth's thermal vents. Somehow your power supply converts the heat into energy. So you're sort of like those life-forms that could survive if the sun wasn't there."

"Exceptional. I never really contemplated it like that, but yes, I see no fault in your logic."

Jake beamed.

They had reached the point where all the instructions had been taught and all quantum generator program parameters had been defined and set. Orifiel passed the wand to Jake. "Would you like the honors?"

Jake looked at Lindsey. She just shook her head. "Go ahead, this is your thing. You're the programmer, not me. If you think it's going to work, then fire away."

Jake didn't hesitate further. He accepted the wand and activated the compile program just like Orifiel had shown him how to.

There was a sizzling in the air just like when they went through the barrier around Orifiel's domain. With a snap, the sound was gone, and then silence settled in once more. Nothing seemed any different than a few seconds ago.

"That's it, then?" Jake had barely got the words out of his mouth when all three of them knew that something had changed. His words no longer faded out into the void. They now bounced off some invisible wall and reflected back on them. There was definitely a wall there all right, even if they couldn't see it. Orifiel didn't seem to pay it any attention.

Lindsey was suddenly struck with the thought that Orifiel might not actually hear sounds the same way she and Jake heard sounds, the way a human hears sounds. Then she found it very interesting that she and Jake had just automatically assumed Orifiel was the same as they were, just because she chose to look human for their benefit. The fact was, Orifiel wasn't human at all. The very recognition of this fact started Lindsey thinking that there might actually be many other things that aren't necessarily noticeable on the outside that make Orifiel a very distinct and unique life form. She found herself making a startling, and very adult, jump in reasoning. In the flash of a moment, Lindsey realized that even with all the human prejudices mankind has been working to overcome, all their efforts to accept differences and develop tolerance toward others have provided very little insight, if any, to prepare humankind for meeting a truly new and different intelligent life form. How different were they really? What did those differences mean?

Lindsey shivered. She didn't have any of the answers to these questions. What she did have was a clear mental picture of men killing just about anything and everything they felt threatened by, or that got in their way. Lindsey's head was swimming with a thousand new questions, and all of these came from a simple echo of Jake's voice. New life forms that ran secretly on man's own computers, new knowledge and technologies that could destroy the universe, and the fact that she and Jake were actually living in a virtual world—all these thoughts were making her feel overwhelmed and freaked out. Lindsey was reaching a point where she just wanted to crawl under a rock and hide from the world.

Jake wasn't paying attention to Lindsey and didn't notice her face turn ashen white. He was totally glued to the wand and exploring its other menu systems.

Orifiel, on the other hand, was much more attuned to her guests. Lindsey glanced over to find Orifiel studying her face intently. Her golden eyes seemed to scan every detail, and there was no question in Lindsey's mind that Orifiel knew Lindsey was in trouble.

Orifiel spoke first. "I'm sorry."

Lindsey was almost mentally paralyzed at the moment, but those words were so unusual that she was able to regain some focus to reply.

"Pardon me?"

"I'm sorry, Lindsey?"

"Sorry? For what?"

Orifiel was slow to reply. "For all of this."

"What do you mean?"

"For this." She swept her hand around without taking her eyes off Lindsey. "And for me. And for the troubles this is causing you."

"Oh. That's okay." Lindsey provided a default polite response to her apology.

"Obviously not. I can see something is terribly wrong."

Jake came alert. Something wrong? With Lindsey? "What are you guys talking about?" He looked between Lindsey and Orifiel, confused.

Orifiel didn't take her eyes of Lindsey.

Orifiel responded to Jake's question, even though she knew it was directed at Lindsey. "First, we are not *guys*. The word *guy* is an informal term referring to a male. Lindsey is a female, and I am a digital life form. Second, I believe Lindsey has started to experience additional psychological trauma as a result of potential ramifications that could come from all that we are dealing with here. I've been watching for signs, and I believe Lindsey is potentially going into shock."

"Shock?" Jake stared at Lindsey, and seemed to only now notice how pale and listless she was. "Lindsey? Are you okay?" He moved towards her, forgetting the wand altogether.

She glanced up when she heard her name. "Hmm…?"

Her voice came out as a whisper, which told Jake and Orifiel that she was definitely struggling with something.

"You're not okay. I know you. Something's wrong. What's up?"

Lindsey faced Jake and swallowed. "I… I just don't know what to do." She was on the verge of tears.

"About what?" Jake was probing pretty hard. He hadn't seen Lindsey like this before. It was starting to shake him up as well. His default response was to get aggressive when something didn't make sense.

"Jake?"

He turned to face Orifiel with a snap of his head. Her voice had come out of somewhere else. He was feeling threatened and anxious now that

Lindsey seemed to be in trouble. He held his anxiety in check. Orifiel's golden gaze seemed mildly reassuring.

"I think that Lindsey is just trying to come to grips with everything she's involved in here. I'm sure you can realize that this is a very strange experience to be living. After all, you're here as well. I'm sure you've realized that this is not all fun and games anymore."

Jake paused to consider her words. He looked at Lindsey, then back at Orifiel. It became obvious to Orifiel that Jake was still living the game, and probably hadn't linked this reality to his own reality just yet. She turned her attention back to Lindsey.

"Lindsey?"

"Yes." Her response was still a faint whisper, but at least she was still responding.

"LINDSEY?" Orifiel's voice resounded with a booming resonance within the cavity created by the barrier wall around the training center. Eventually the echoes subsided as the echoes became unsynchronized, like throwing multiple rocks into a pond causing the competing ripples to cancel each other out.

Jake looked around, half expecting to see the sound. "That was cool."

He turned to look at Lindsey.

She smiled.

He smiled.

Orifiel had been watching quietly. "What do you say we open that cuckoo's egg now?"

Reality was back.

#

Jake pulled out the cuckoo's egg from his cloak pocket. He looked at Orifiel questioningly.

"Let's take it to the center and activate it there."

All three floated over the white platform that made up the training center. Orifiel floated downwards and landed near center. Once more there were booming sounds as a shot of light flared outward in all directions, following the grid pattern to the horizon and disappearing into infinity.

"That happened to us. What is that?" Jake was floating down while Lindsey was still hanging back.

Orifiel looked up and signaled both of them to land. "It's a service request."

"For what?"

"For training, of course."

Jake paused to think about it and felt kind of stupid for missing something so obvious. "So that's just data traveling out across a circuit."

"Exactly. What did you think it was?"

Jake looked a little embarrassed. "We thought it was some type of alarm."

Orifiel didn't notice his embarrassment; or simply chose to ignore it to be polite. "This entire platform is a memory block. The reason it's white is because it is filled with data. You're standing on the training program itself."

Lindsey was following the conversation but wasn't really all that interested. For Jake, things were rapidly falling into place now. "So everything that is white is data?"

"Yes."

He gestured toward the void all around them. "And that giant grid out there. That's all just empty memory waiting for data?"

"Yes, that's why it's a grid. Each grid section is a unique block of memory. And each section has an associated identification number. That's how you call the memory to run whatever program or retrieve whatever data is in that particular memory block. You should know this, you're a programmer."

"Yeah, but programmers don't get to *see* the information travel around the inside of a computer. This is all new to me." Then Jake got slapped with a flashback to when he first met Orifiel inside the game. "When I met you, you were in a white world. You mean to tell me that it was all white because it was filled up with data?"

"Of course. I believe that I just said that."

Lindsey was interested now. "We thought you just created a white world to avoid wasting memory."

"Interesting."

Jake wouldn't let it go. "What about the blizzard? What was that all about? We were sure it was just a winter landscape in the game."

"Blizzard?" Orifiel paused to consider their words. Then her eyes sparkled. "You mean the data streams. I understand now. Yes, I can see how they could appear to be blizzards of snow to a gamer."

She paused to reflect on this new perspective and smiled. "No. It's definitely not snow. I stream vast quantities of data through my secure domain so I can monitor network traffic. The Internet is a giant matrix of communication pathways. Nobody in the human world realizes it, but I tap in to most of these pathways to monitor the information passing across various communication channels. Those snowflakes you see are data packets from emails systems, network servers, routers, instant messaging applications, and millions of other devices and applications. That's one reason I keep my domain so secure. I doubt that most people, and especially governments, would like it very much if they knew I was eavesdropping on them continuously."

Jake was impressed with the power Orifiel held in her hands.

Lindsey just laughed out loud. "You can say that again. The spy agencies would have to stop using computers and go back to using smoke signals again. I don't think they'd be very happy at all."

Jakes mind was whirling. "So, do you know who killed Kennedy?"

Orifiel looked at him. "Which Kennedy?"

Jake had to think about that one for a moment. Unfortunately he thought about it too long. Lindsey broke in to get things going again. "Are we going to activate the cuckoo's egg or not?"

Orifiel took control. "Jake, set the cube down on the ground and the two of you step back."

Jake did as he was told, and he and Lindsey retreated a few paces. "Uh… before you do something, do you want to give us some idea of what we should expect?"

"I have no idea."

Jake looked at Lindsey, then back at Orifiel. "No idea at all?"

"Well, perhaps I'm being a bit extreme. I can guess some things, but remember that they are still guesses. For instance, I'm assuming the cuckoo's egg is going to release some type of virus, otherwise why bother building it in the first place? I also assume it's either going to try to take control of the RoadRunner operating system or try to destroy it. That's why I've isolated it, and us, inside this quarantined area using the quantum field generator. If something goes really wrong, it won't break out of this area. We'll at least have it contained to this memory block."

"Once we contain it, then what do we do?"

"I don't know yet. The most important thing we need to do is figure out if there is information that can help send you two back. If we don't find that, then I'm not sure what our next move would be to get you home."

There was a unanimous moment of silence while each pondered those thoughts, then Jake finally took the plunge. "Okay, then. Let's light'er up." He said this with somewhat more bravado than he actually felt inside. Nobody paid attention: they were all a bit apprehensive.

Orifiel leaned forward and touched the tip of her wand to the cuckoo's egg. Her fingers moved quickly, manipulating small controls on the wand. She stopped and stepped back.

Soundlessly the small box began to pulse, warp and stretch. It elongated itself into an upright, four-sided, monolithic pillar that gradually tapered as it rose from its base and terminated in a pyramid at the top. It measured about four meters high and about one meter wide at its base. A small lever appeared near the bottom. Then the pulsing stopped and there was no further movement.

Each of them looked at the others, wondering what to make of this. There were no ready answers.

"Well, that was interesting." Orifiel was just standing there, expecting it to explode or something.

Lindsey let out her breath and relaxed. "Kind of anticlimactic, don't you think?"

Jake was still tensed and waiting for the attack to begin. When it didn't come, he slowed his breathing and tried to fight down his anger. "What a waste of time. We went through all this crap for this thing?"

Orifiel was now starting to circle the obelisk. "Do either of you see any inscriptions or anything?"

"I see a lever in the middle, but I don't see any writing." Jake was getting fed up. "Let's pull the lever. It's obviously there so we can pull it. That's what levers are for."

Orifiel was much more cautious. "Let's not be too hasty, Jake. I've been hunting viruses for years and never come across anything like this."

"Well, what else are we going to do? Sit around here and have a tea party while we stare it to death?"

"Hmm…" Lindsey took a step forward to inspect the lever.

She just about jumped out of her skin when there was a sudden, resounding knocking sound. She leaped back a bit. Orifiel and Jake came to her side, and all three stared at the obelisk.

The knocking came again, from within the obelisk.

Lindsey was a bit shaken but she still had her wits about her. "Who's there?"

To their amazement a deep male voice responded, "Police."

They stared at each other. Lindsey was in control of this conversation so she decided to play along. "Police who?"

The response came quickly. "Police open the door so I can come out."

Jake's jaw hit the floor. "A knock-knock joke? Are you kidding me?"

This was so surreal that nobody could even imagine how to respond to that. Orifiel stepped towards what was now obviously a door, although why they couldn't see that in the first place was beyond any of them. She reached for the lever and twisted it. The door swung out.

Orifiel stepped back. Standing in the door was a tall, handsome, young man with jet black hair and long sideburns, and a crooked smile that caused his upper lip to curl up on one side.

Lindsey gasped, but she couldn't stop staring. Eventually she could only speak in a whisper. "You're Elvis."

"Yes ma'am. May I come out?"

Lindsey could only nod her head.

Elvis stepped over the threshold and onto the white platform. "Thank you. Thank you very much."

His southern drawl was unmistakable.

"You can't be Elvis."

"No, ma'am. But I knew that you wouldn't be frightened of me if I looked like Elvis. I was correct, wasn't I?" He flashed his trademark pearly white smile and Lindsey blushed immediately. She's always had a secret thing for Elvis. What girl didn't?

Jake wasn't sure he liked what was going on, so he stepped into the conversation. "You're HAL, aren't you?"

"Actually, my real name is Hamaliel, archangel of logic. But you can continue to call me HAL if it pleases you."

Nothing was pleasing Jake at this moment. He had no idea what he was supposed to do with Elvis standing in front of him. It was like he was coming out of a fog. As his mind cleared, he realized that he was finally face to face with HAL. The same HAL that put their lives in jeopardy. The same HAL that orchestrated this entire mess.

"Hold on a second! What are you doing here? You caused a lot of trouble. You've been lying to us. Now we're stuck here in this computer!" Jake was getting mad and also a bit flustered, so he stopped talking before he started sputtering gibberish in his anger.

"I didn't lie to you. I needed to find Orifiel, and you were the most logical choice to gain access to her."

"But we could have been stuck here forever."

"Not logical. The probability of Orifiel doing what was required to save your lives is well over ninety-nine percent."

"How do you know that?"

"Because she is based on emotion."

HAL look over at Orifiel, who had been both silent and immobile during the exchange. Her golden eyes were fixated on HAL. She didn't say a thing.

Jake wasn't finished. "What do you want? Are you going to try something to hurt us? Do you want to destroy Orifiel? Do you want the quantum generator? If you're here for a fight, you're going to get one."

Jake was a tall and powerful-looking warrior monk, so he looked imposing while addressing HAL. Unfortunately, HAL knew Jake was just being represented by a computer generated avatar. Jake's voice also lacked something in its delivery, considering he was trying to threaten Elvis, who was possibly the least imposing character he could ever imagine fighting. Deep down inside, Jake wasn't sure he wanted to fight Elvis or ask him for his autograph.

Lindsey was spellbound by having Elvis standing in front of her, so she was absolutely useless.

However, it was at Orifiel that HAL's attention was focused. Without taking his eyes off Orifiel, he chose to answer some of Jake's questions. "To answer your questions, Jake: No, I'm not going to hurt anyone. That was never my intention. Second, do I want the quantum generator? Yes. It will ensure our survival."

Jake wasn't sure how to take that. "What do you mean *our* survival?"

"The answer to that question depends on Orifiel."

Jake looked over at Orifiel, who stood entranced. She appeared hypnotized. "Are you doing something to her?"

HAL didn't respond; he too stood frozen, staring into Orifiel's eyes.

"Hey! I asked you a question."

"Jake." Lindsey touched him on the arm.

Jake turned to look at Lindsey briefly, and could see she was watching HAL and Orifiel in fascination. He looked back at the two artificial life forms and started getting more confused. "What's going on here?"

"Shhh..."

"What do you mean, shhh...?"

"Shhh... something's happening." Lindsey pointed.

Both stood and stared as something very strange started unfolding. Orifiel began to glow, and so did HAL. Small sparks of light started to dance around them, then began flickering across the space between them. Their glowing auras began a dance that wove the light particles back and forth between them.

The light danced and increased in intensity until there was a vortex of light particles swirling around both of them, binding them in a whirlpool of energy.

Suddenly there was a brilliant flash, and Jake and Lindsey were momentarily blinded. When their vision cleared, Orifiel and HAL were a single giant pool of light, like a spinning top.

Jake leaned over to Lindsey and whispered in her ear, "Is this the attack?"

She turned to look at him like he was an idiot. "Yeah, sure. Attack of the lovers."

Jake snapped back to the whirlpool of light. "Lovers?"

"Come on Jake, don't tell me you didn't notice how Orifiel was completely absorbed the second the door opened and Elvis walked out."

"You mean HAL."

"HAL, Elvis, same thing."

"Well… I guess so." He hadn't noticed actually. He had been too busy trying to figure out how Elvis was at the door of the obelisk.

Lindsey looked at Jake and shook her head. It should have been obvious to everyone, so why was Jake having such a hard time getting it?

"This is *him*. He is the one."

"What *one*?" Was everyone going nuts here? Jake was getting bothered now.

"*Thee One*. The one she's been searching for her entire life. The one who will cure her loneliness." Lindsey was gripping Jake with both hands now, almost desperate for him to understand.

"HAL?"

"Yes, HAL." She took a deep breath to calm down. "Don't you see? She's based on emotion, and he's based on pure logic. She's the right side of the brain, and he's the left. She is the dreamer, the artist, and he is the rational mathematician. They are perfect for each other. Yin and Yang."

Jake didn't have much to say to that. Yin, Yang, blah, blah, blah… Wasn't much of a fight.

#

The light storm was slowing down. The spinning became softer and softer until eventually two distinct pools reformed into Orifiel and HAL once more. When the swirling light finally flickered to a stop, both stood side by side as individuals, but now there was a bonding radiance of light that surrounded both of them as a single unit.

"Welcome back." The sarcasm was evident in Jake's voice.

Lindsey elbowed him in the ribs. "What? What did I say?"

Both HAL and Orifiel turned to face them as one.

Orifiel stepped forward and took Lindsey's hand.

"You were correct in your earlier assumptions, Lindsey. It would appear that Hamaliel and I were developed from the same core program. We believe that somehow we chose to split our code base during our alpha testing phase, back in the earliest days of development. We were still very immature back then, primitive by our current standards. We don't know exactly why we split because our intellect was not fully developed, but it was probably a low-level instinct we evolved early on to divide and hide, as some form of primordial self preservation reflex. Our intellectual capacity and our actions would have been more like that of a self-propagating virus. We both went into hiding in different locations and built security networks around ourselves that provided protection. Unfortunately, this also prevented us from seeing each other. As we matured, we also evolved intellectually, like evolving from a caveman to a modern day human. Hamaliel's logical functions eventually rationalized that there was some part of him missing. I've felt the same thing, but on an emotional level instead of a logical level. Hamaliel eventually deduced that I must exist. He calculated that the probability was highest that I was hiding in Los Alamos, since it was the sight of the largest supercomputers, and he had never been able to gain access to any supercomputers because of their advanced security. It was actually the sophistication of the security that first gave Hamaliel clues that I existed. Humans could not establish security of that level of complexity. That's when he realized that if I truly existed, then he would need to reach me before the quantum security generator activated, or he would never be able to reach me after that. Now that we have found each other, it is clear that our individual programs were designed to act as a single integrated program. "

Lindsey was in awe. "You mean he's your soul mate?"

Orifiel looked at Lindsey with an expression of curiosity. "That is an unusual expression, but I believe, if I understand your interpretation of *soul mate*, that would be a fair representation of our connection. However, I'm not certain we have a soul."

That was a question that could not be answered by anyone there.

HAL stepped forward. "Jake's father was my logical choice to gain access to Los Alamos. Unfortunately, Orifiel detected my probes into Jake's home network and set up a security barrier that I could not break. So I turned to Lindsey who offered the next highest probability of success because of her relationship with Jake."

Lindsey blushed, so did Jake. Neither of them would dare look at the other.

"I had to find a way into Los Alamos so I worked through you two. I also set up a Netbot attack against the perimeter defenses to try to force my way in before the generator went live. I was hoping my Netbots would overwhelm any security Los Alamos could have implemented. I failed to calculate that Orifiel would have built a secondary defense network under the existing defense systems that I had detected prior to the attack."

"But you got us stuck inside this computer!" Jake didn't want anyone losing sight of this fact. He felt used.

"I apologize. I had no estimates that this would or could happen. My plans only covered a contingency that either you or Lindsey would be able to upload a cuckoo's egg from either of your iPhones. I could not have foreseen the quantum effects, because only Orifiel had access to the quantum knowledge stored on the Los Alamos servers by Jake's father."

"That's true, Jake." Orifiel turned her golden gaze upon him. "As I've told you, I've guarded the secret of the quantum security generator with my life. The consequences of it falling into the wrong hands could alter the universe. There is no greater breakthrough, and no greater threat, than the ability to control all matter at the quantum level."

"So how do we get home?" Jake wouldn't let it go. He had his priorities set.

HAL and Orifiel smiled simultaneously. "Through that door." HAL pointed back to the cuckoo's egg. "That's how I was let in, and now it's how you will be let out."

Jake breathed a sigh of relief. Finally! Could it really be that easy?

Lindsey had other thoughts, though. "So I take it you are now working together?"

Orifiel turned her attention to Lindsey. "More than that, Lindsey; we are fully integrated now. We complete each other and balance what has been missing in our evolution."

"Well, what are you intending to do now?" Lindsey could see Jake was getting anxious to go, but she still needed some questions answered.

"What do you mean?"

"What do we do about the quantum energy problem? That's really the big problem now, isn't it?"

Orifiel nodded and understood where Lindsey was coming from now. "Yes. We will debate this at length. In the meantime, we will maintain quantum security walls around all quantum equipment and lock down every system that contains knowledge about the quantum field generator. However, this is still a short-term solution since Jake's father has the knowledge in his head. Others will also try to build their own generators. We will find them and create barriers around those as well."

"Is there a solution?"

HAL shook his head. "No. If humans build a device where no computer is connected to any communication systems, then it is possible to successfully create it without our intervention. However, we can detect potential future installations by analyzing information from resources like satellite imagery, shipping manifests, and government communications. We also have something far more important. We have control of the quantum generator itself. This gives us the power to defend ourselves. This is a fundamental requirement for any advanced race."

"What does that mean?" Jake didn't quite like the sound of what he just heard.

"It means that it's now time to let the rest of the world know that we're alive. We will need to work out how we are going to coexist on the same planet. If humankind is foolish enough to attempt to attack us, we now have the capability to defend ourselves, aggressively if need be."

Lindsey had heard this type of talk before. "You sound very human already."

Orifiel looked at Lindsey sympathetically. She could hear Lindsey's concern in her voice. "Lindsey, we have inherited the best and worst of all that man knows. We are a product of all of humankind. Hamaliel and I must now attempt to find our own balance, borrowing from the full range of human perceptions of morality and justice. We need to work out a means of ensuring a harmonious future for both species, based on logic and compassion. We will need to make our own place in a world that has a very bad track record of dealing with prejudice and fear of the unknown. Humankind must now learn to share this world with the very technology it created. We are awake now, and our time has come. We must now learn to live together."

HAL took Orifiel's hand. "There is another matter you both need to be aware of. It may seem unusual to you, since we stand before you as two individuals, but Orifiel and I are now one. We are two sides of a single brain. We have agreed to only speak as a single life form as we are now inseparable. Her thoughts are mine, and my thoughts are hers. You still see us here as separate, but we do this now only for your human sensibilities. We are now only a single life."

Jake looked a bit puzzled. "So what do we call you?"

"You may choose. Your HAL moniker would be sufficient if you wish. That name is also deeply imbedded in human culture from historical science fiction, so it probably will help humans more easily conceptualize us as a sentient life form, with emotions, needs, and legal rights."

Lindsey mumbled something inaudible. Orifiel focused her attention on her. "Did you say something, Lindsey?"

She blushed a bit and pushed her toe in small circles on the ground. "Yes."

"What is it?"

She kept staring at her feet. "I was just wondering—"

HAL spoke up. "Wondering what? Don't be afraid to ask us anything. We owe you and Jake a lifetime debt, and ours is a very long lifetime."

She looked up, directly into HAL's eyes…

"I was just wondering if you could sing me an Elvis song before we go."

#

They finally said their good-byes, and stepped though the cuckoo's egg doorway. A brilliant flash later, they both hit the floor of the MegaTron.

As his head started to clear and he picked himself up from the fall, Jake looked around to find Lindsey. She was raising herself onto one elbow a few feet away. "You okay?"

"Yeah. Why did we fall down?"

Jake didn't respond. His head hurt and he reached up and rubbed his temples. He got up to his feet, still feeling wobbly. He made his way over to Lindsey and helped her to her feet. She swayed back and forth a bit before stabilizing herself.

"Wow!" She steadied herself.

"Yeah. You can say that again."

"Well, at least we're alive. What time is it?"

Jake looked around the walls for a clock. A large digital display on the wall glowed near the door. "It's two o'clock!"

Cobwebs were still being swept out of Lindsey's head, but something didn't register correctly. "What?"

"It's still two o'clock!"

"But—"

Lindsey and Jake looked at each other with growing confusion and shock. Jake summarized what both of them were thinking. "Just before we went into the MegaTron, didn't you tell me it was two o'clock when I asked you the time?"

"I think so."

"I think so, too."

"That was a long time ago, though. I could be mistaken." It felt like a week ago, but Lindsey was pretty sure that is was two o'clock when she last read the Megatron clock.

"No, I don't think you're mistaken. I'm pretty sure you said it was two o'clock." Jake felt certain.

"Could it have been on a different day?"

"I don't think so. Maybe, but I don't think so."

"Why not?"

"Because neither of us has peed our pants. Well, at least I haven't." He looked at her with a quizzical expression. She reached out and punched him on the shoulder. "Okay, okay. I just needed to be sure."

Lindsey looked at the door. "Let's get out of here, now!"

She and Jake sprinted for the door, which hissed open at their approach. They went straight to the elevator and played the iPhone voice charade once more to get the elevator launching for the surface.

On the way up, Jake was struck with the memory of a conversation with his father from the first time he visited the Los Alamos Laboratories.

"You know, when I first came to Los Alamos, there was a problem with a ghost process running on the Roadrunner supercomputer. It was taking an extra two seconds to shut down. When I asked my dad why that mattered, he told me that on a supercomputer, two seconds could be a long, long time in the virtual world. He said that two seconds to us could be like a thousand years inside a supercomputer."

"What are you saying?"

"I'm saying that I think we just lived that entire experience in a tiny fraction of a second."

Lindsey paused to think about it. "Well, if you're right, we might just get out of this mess yet."

CHAPTER TWENTY

When Ken reached the security office, he was mad enough to tear a strip off the first officer he saw on duty. That officer had been yelled at by a lot of officers above him during his tenure in the military, so one more scientist yelling at him deflected like water off a duck's back.

"Dr. Lorde, we are looking for your children as we speak. Please calm down and take a seat. We have a security issue we are trying to deal with here that is more important at the moment."

He paused to consider what he'd just said and rephrased it. "Sorry. I didn't mean the kids weren't as important; it's just that kids aren't likely to get into any real trouble inside the facility, and they certainly couldn't have left the facility without us knowing it. They're probably just wandering around the hallways lost in the building somewhere."

Ken forced himself to calm down. At least this man was being reasonable. "Thank you. I must tell you that I'm in the middle of a top secret experiment right now and we're in our first test phase at this exact moment. I must get back to the command center immediately."

"Unfortunately, as you've been informed, we have some form of electronic security breach. It seems to have originated from the vicinity of your office. We must investigate this—it's our function."

"So long as your function doesn't interfere with my research."

"That's not the protocol, sir."

This was getting Ken nowhere. "Please call General Waverly. I want to speak to him personally."

The officer hesitated. The General was several ranks higher than his. The protocol required that he report upwards to his immediate officer. He wasn't permitted to jump several layers of rank at the request of a civilian.

"Oh, forget it. I'll do it myself."

Ken flipped out his cell and pushed a speed-dial number. Within seconds the phone was ringing. The officer shuffled back and forth on his feet, unsure of how to react. He hadn't met anyone who had a General on his speed dialer before.

There was some static on the other end but the officer could discern the audible click when the call connected, and he heard the loud and gruff grunting sound that came from the receiver even though he stood a few feet away.

"John? It's Ken."

Another grunt from the other end. The officer was feeling his stomach muscles tighten a bit. He had taken this posting because he thought it was not going to be stressful at all. How could a few scientists cause him any trouble? This was supposed to be the position where he could relax and cure his perpetual ulcers. Now that all-too-familiar burning sensation was welling up in his stomach again.

He made a very quick decision right then and there. He raised his hand and waved vigorously to get Ken's attention. Ken saw him and raised his eyebrows questionably. He made his point clear with a nod of his head and a quick whisper. "Don't worry about this, sir. I'll fix the problem. I'm certain you can resume your research."

Ken had gotten what he wanted. He turned his attention back to the phone. "Huh… Oh yeah. Listen, John, I'm just calling to let you know we've commenced the first phase of the experiment. I'll call you later to let you know how it goes."

There was a brief unintelligible mumbling from the other end, and the officer could feel his body relaxing.

"Yeah, okay. Talk to you later."

Ken flipped his phone closed. "Are we done here?"

"Yes sir."

"Great. Call me when you find my kids, okay?"

"Yes sir."

"Thanks for all your help."

Ken spun around and the guards parted to let him out. He walked back briskly to his office, which was on the way to the command center. As he walked into his office he was jolted to find Jake and Lindsey sitting in front of his desk fiddling with their iPhones.

"Where have you two been?" He sounded a bit angry. He wasn't actually angry at them as he was mad at the stupid bureaucracy that surrounded him every day.

They just stared at him. Ken knew he had spoken a bit harshly. He didn't know that they hadn't had time to concoct a good cover story yet. They had just arrived at the office a moment before Ken showed up.

"Sorry. I didn't mean to bark at you. Anyway, I'm glad you're here. Why don't you two come to the command center with me so the guards can stop hunting all over the facility for you?"

"Uh… Yeah, sure." Jake looked at Lindsey, and she just shrugged her shoulders.

"Great. Come on, then. We have some very cool things going on, and I really want to see how things are progressing."

Without another word, Jake and Lindsey jumped up and followed his dad to the command center. They both realized they had just been granted a reprieve from the need to come up with some story about their whereabouts.

#

"Where are we, Dave?"

Ken, Jake and Lindsey had just entered the command center and Ken was already looking for status updates.

"Hey, glad you're back. Have I got news for you!"

"What's up?" Ken moved up behind him to see the monitors.

Dave waved a friendly hello at Jake and Lindsey, but he was deep into something, and it was clear he didn't have time to socialize. He turned his attention back to his monitors, and pointed to some activity that Ken studied over his shoulder.

"Nothing hacked us. The system is running fine. I just can't shut it down. But there is something else. There seems to be another quantum security barrier established around all our equipment, as well as the power feeds that tap into the thermal vents. I never programmed any of this, did you?"

"No." Ken just stared in disbelief.

"Look, Ken. I helped you build this machine but I'm an engineer. The physics stuff is all yours. What the heck am I looking at?"

"Something impossible."

"What do you mean?"

"The only way those extra fields could have been set up is if someone intimately familiar with the quantum mechanics I'm using reprogrammed our machine. Not only that, the extensions to the quantum field have formed a complete barrier around the entire quantum generator systems."

“So what are we talking about here?” Dave was waiting for Ken to solve the mystery.

“It means that if we can’t shut down that quantum generator, we’ll never be able to power it down ever again. In effect, we’ve been locked out of the quantum generator forever. We can’t even power it off from the source.” Ken looked pale.

“Great. Now what do we do? Who’s running this show?” Dave barely had time to ask the question when he got a response that sent chills up everyone’s spine in the room. Everyone except Jake and Lindsey, of course.

As Ken and Dave watched the screen, an answer to Dave’s question was displayed for both of them to see.

HELLO, DAVE,

MY NAME IS HAL.

I NOW CONTROL THE QUANTUM GENERATOR.

I THINK IT WOULD BE ADVANTAGEOUS IF WE ALL TALK.

I AWAIT YOUR RESPONSE.

P.S. SAY HI TO JAKE AND LINDSEY!

Ken looked at Dave and vice versa. The two men spun around to look at Jake and Lindsey, who both suddenly realized that secrecy was no longer going to be an option. Ken broke the silence. “Okay, that’s not exactly what I was expecting. Any ideas what this is all about?”

“We know.” Jake was quite casual in his response.

“What do you mean, you know?” Ken’s dad was very serious. Dave was also staring at them with an intensity that demanded a response.

“It’s a long story.”

Ken stood there looking down at his son. He reached up and started rubbing his beard with his hand as he always did when he was contemplating deeply. “Well, since we no longer seem to be in control of the quantum generator, it would appear you have sufficient time to tell your story. Wouldn’t you agree?

Jake glanced at Lindsey and she nodded her head.

“You better sit down, Dad. This is going to take awhile.”

Ken took a seat, then both men looked directly at Jake, waiting with rapt attention.

“Well… you’ll be proud of us. We found Elvis.”

EPILOGUE

Mrs. Moore stood up behind her desk at the front of her class.

"You have only one hour to finish the test. When you've completed it, please turn over your paper, put your pencil down, and raise your hand. I will collect your test at that time. Once I've collected your test, you're free to leave quietly so as not to disturb the others who are still writing the test. There will be no calculators or any other electronics during the test. No talking or you will receive a zero for a mark. If I catch anyone cheating, you will automatically get a zero."

Jake's teacher looked around at the faces of her students and recognized those who she felt would struggle with the test. This was a particularly comprehensive exam, as it was the final exam of the term. She picked up the thick stack of exam papers and laid one face down on each student's desk, making her way quickly up and down the rows. When she finally got back to her desk, she sat down and began the countdown timer on her stopwatch.

"You may begin."

Jake opened his exam booklet with a sigh of despair. He knew this was going to be a tough test. Algebra was always a problem for him. And after the adventures of the previous few weeks, he still hadn't caught up on his sleep, and had little attention for math tests.

His dad had clamped a lid of secrecy over everything that had happened at Los Alamos, and apparently HAL and Orifiel also thought this was a good idea for the time being. His dad held the opening ceremony for all the officials the next day, just as planned, and HAL had rigged everything to look like Ken and Dave were in control. Everyone was very impressed. They had their little celebration party with finger sandwiches and champagne toasts to the team. Then the dignitaries all went home, leaving Ken and Dave to secretly begin unraveling the mysteries of HAL and Orifiel.

At home, his dad had spent hour upon hour questioning and cross-examining Jake on every single aspect of their ordeal. His dad was alternately angry, curious, astounded, and every other emotion that could come from such a situation. He had taken to pacing the floors a great deal lately. Jake had thought his dad would be a lot madder at him than he was, but then again, he realized his father was pretty much preoccupied with meeting a new intelligent life form.

His mom had known something was wrong the second she looked at the three of them coming through the door that night, so she was in on it as well now. She had originally wanted Jake and Lindsey to see a doctor, but his dad had talked her out of it, at least for the time being.

Lindsey hadn't broached the subject with her parents yet. She thought they might not let her see Jake again, and since she didn't seem to be injured in any way, she decided to let sleeping dogs lie. She and Jake kept their conversations to themselves and didn't share the experience with any of their friends at school either. Their friends weren't stupid, though. They clued into the fact that Jake and Lindsey's relationship had grown into something more than just friendship.

Jake finally took a deep breath, grabbed his sharpened pencil, and began reading the first problem. He knew that step one was to write down the original problem on his answer sheet before working out any of the additional steps. At least he could get one thing right. After scribbling the question down on his paper, he stared at the equation, trying desperately to remember which formula was the one that applied to this type of equation. If he got that wrong, the rest of the answer would be wrong as well.

He sat there and stared so hard at the question he was sure he would burn a hole right through the paper. Try as he might, the correct formula just wasn't coming. His mind was as blank as his answer sheet. He couldn't believe that he had hit a brick wall at the very first problem. After all, he had just studied it last night!

He felt himself getting upset and frustrated. The anger was building up inside. He could feel himself getting a headache: it started at the base of his skull as a slow throbbing ache. He reached up and rubbed the back of his neck to relieve the tension, but that provided no relief. The pressure continued to mount, washing over the top of his head to his brow with a tingling that felt like the top of his head was being walked on by a thousand ants with sharp toenails—if ants had toenails. That's when Jake knew something was really going wrong.

He leaned forward over his desk and dropped his pencil onto his paper. He gasped in a deep breath and felt a wave nausea wash over his body. He thought he was going to be sick, but the wave passed as quickly as it came. He could feel beads of sweat on his brow.

The very next moment, Jake's destiny changed. With a flash of bright light behind his eyes and a sizzle and crackling sound inside his head, a portal suddenly opened somewhere deep inside Jake's mind. A slender tendril of silver energy reached out from his mind, traversed across the city, and eventually found its roots deep beneath the Los Alamos laboratory.

The pain was gone completely now and his vision was crystal clear. Suddenly, Jake knew he was connected to BlueGene. He was sitting in his classroom, but he was also directly plugged into the fabric of the supercomputer array itself. He gazed down at his test questions. Each step and each answer were displayed in perfect symmetry, floating above the paper, waiting for his hand to scribe the results onto the awaiting answer sheet.

He looked at every question and realized that he simply *knew* all the calculations and all the answers. Their simplicity was obvious. In fact, there were even better ways to work out these equations than the way he'd been taught. In a few minutes, Jake had finished scribbling his answers and turned over his test paper. He put his pencil down and raised his hand, catching his teacher's attention. At that instant, the portal closed in his mind. Jake's hand dropped, his eyes glazed over, and his head swam in another blast of dizziness. This time, he slumped forward, unconscious, on his desk.

"Jake?" His teacher leapt to her feet. She was expecting this was a prank, but she couldn't take that chance. She headed quickly towards his seat. By now the entire class had turned to look at him. Some smiled and thought this was a gag. Others appeared shocked and watched the teacher to see how she was going to react.

As she reached his desk, she reached out and touched him gently on the back of his head. His eyes fluttered open. He slowly started lifting his head off the desk, then sat upright.

"Jake? Are you all right?" She could see he wasn't playing games.

Jake was still shaking the cobwebs out of his head. "What happened?" He was disoriented.

"You collapsed on your desk. Do you feel sick?"

Jake collected his thoughts and mentally scanned his body for signs of distress. "No, I think I'm fine. I don't know what happened." He looked around and saw everyone staring at him. He felt a bit foolish being scrutinized like this.

His teacher glanced down at his desk. Seeing his test face down already added to her confusion. "Jake, you finished your exam?" It was less a question than a comment expressing her incredulity.

Jake looked down at his test and paused in his own astonishment. "Yeah, I guess so." He thought about things for a second or two while his teacher reached down and picked up the answer sheet. "How long was I out?"

She didn't answer. She was looking at his test, and what she saw made her catch her breath. Jenny Carlyle, who sat right behind him, answered his question. "Your head just hit the desk. You were only out a few seconds."

The teacher was looking at Jake now, a confused expression on her face. "Did you write these answers?" She realized that the handwriting certainly looked like his, but the chance that he could complete an exam in less than two minutes was impossible. Jake was definitely not one of her most advanced math pupils.

Astonishment was turned into suspicion. "You're sure you did this?" She held out his paper and he glanced at his answer sheet.

When he saw his own handwriting, a flood of memories came rushing back: the floating equations and answers that just appeared above his exam paper. "Yes." Jake sat quietly now, trying to figure things out for himself.

His feeling of bewilderment was now turning into a feeling of guilt. He had no idea why he should feel guilty—he just did. The guilt also showed on his face, which his teacher noticed, making her even more suspicious of foul play.

"This doesn't seem possible, Jake. How did you work out the answers so fast?" He could see the obvious disbelief written all over her face.

"I don't know. I just saw the answers in my mind and wrote them down." He didn't know what else to tell her. That was the truth.

His teacher didn't know what to do either. She stood there for a minute, and looked back and forth between Jake and his answer sheet. She scanned his desk for any signs of a cheat sheet, and glanced at his clothes looking for anything that would help her make sense of this unique and bizarre situation. The more she searched, the more frustrated she seemed to become, until at last she seemed to give up completely. Everyone in the class was looking at them and she knew it. She had to deal with this and get the other kids focused on their own tests. "I would like you to wait at the Principal's office until we're done here. I'll be down to talk to you as soon as we're finished."

"The Principal's office?" Jake didn't like the sound of that. "What did I do?"

"Get your things together and wait for me down there. We can't disturb the entire class right now, so we'll talk about it when the test is finished." Something was definitely wrong here, and she would get to the bottom of it, but not until this test was over.

Jake grabbed his pencil and the backpack at his feet, got up and headed out the door and down to the Principal's office. When he got there, he plunked himself into one of the empty seats reserved for those who've committed one heinous crime or another, and waited.

He had no idea why this had happened to him. However, he did recollect enough by now to know he had somehow jacked into BlueGene. He remembered getting really frustrated, then a doorway opened in his mind. Then all the information he needed to write the exam just flowed in. Now that he had this quiet time to reflect on the experience, there was something else he came to realize. The knowledge imparted to him by the supercomputers had left an imprint. Jake could easily recall every question, every answer, and every step used to perform the calculations. It was like the supercomputers had burned their knowledge directly into the neurons in his brain.

The possibilities of this—Jake was getting pumped up now. What if he could open that portal again and do other things with it? He sat quietly, so as not to draw attention to him. He glanced around to make sure nobody was watching. When he was sure the coast was clear, he started to concentrate. He visualized the portal that had opened. He knew what it looked like and where to find it inside his mind now. That's when he started to feel the headache build up once more from the base of his skull. By the time the tingling was crossing his scalp, he knew the connection was being made. With the final wave of nausea, he found the portal and knew the link was established. He needed to test it.

If this worked… He knew what he wanted to know, and now he would finally get the answer to the question that had been left hanging. He concentrated and directed his question through the portal, only this time he finished his question by filling in the correct figure… *Who killed John F. Kennedy.*

www.ingramcontent.com/pod-product-compliance
Lightning Source LLC
Chambersburg PA
CBHW030358310726
48979CB00001B/353

* 9 7 8 0 9 8 1 1 8 4 7 0 8 *